THOMAS F. MONTELEONE

NIGHT OF BROKEN SOULS

ASPECT®

WARNER BOOKS

A Time Warner Company

Aspect® name and logo are registered trademarks of Warner Books, Inc.

Warner Books, Inc., 1271 Avenue of the Americas, New York, NY 10020

 A Time Warner Company

Printed in the United States of America

First Printing: March 1997

10 9 8 7 6 5 4 3 2 1

Library of Congress Cataloging-in-Publication Data

Monteleone, Thomas F.
    Night of broken souls / Thomas F. Monteleone.
      p. cm.
    ISBN 0-446-52048-9
    I. Title.
  PS3563.O542N54 1997
  813'.54—dc20   96-31682
                                              CIP

Book design and composition by L&G McRee

This one is for
a special night in a Fells Point restaurant
—the night man discovered fire—
and for the woman who gave it to him.
Te quiero, Elizabeth.

ACKNOWLEDGMENTS

Writing this book was only part of the process that gets it into print and into your hands. Other people had jobs to do, and I'd like to thank them for performing them so well. And so: heartfelt thanks to Matt Bialer at the William Morris Agency for believing in me; and grateful appreciation to Wayne Chang and Betsy Mitchell at Warner Books for all the suggestions along the way that made this story be as good as it could be.

The conviction that life has a purpose
is rooted in every fibre of man,
it is a property of the human substance.

—PRIMO LEVI, *Survival in Auschwitz*

PART ONE

FALSE DAWN
Spring 1999

ONE

RODNEY McGUIRE
Pittsburgh, Pennsylvania

W*here am I?*

The question ghosted through Rodney's mind, gradually bringing him back to self-awareness and *scaring* him deeply.

His sense of balance was precarious as he stood in the darkness. It was as though he'd been yanked from a deep sleep. A cold wind tried to slip past the pulled-up collar of his jacket; a distant street-lamp cast everything in pale yellows. Looking from side to side, he saw that he was standing on someone's snow-covered property, alongside a split-level suburban home. Directly in front of him was a window with its shade only half-drawn and through which Rodney could see a family of white people seated at the dinner table.

Oh Lord, what am I *doin'* here?

Dad, a man in his late thirties, sat at one end, flanked by two preadolescent boys and a teenaged girl. Mom swept in from the kitchen carrying a serving tray of roast beef. The tableau was so achingly typical, he could have been watching a generic commercial for any number of household products. As he continued standing there, growing ever colder, he watched the family bow their heads for the briefest of prayers before beginning to eat. There was absolutely nothing remarkable about the scene.

And yet, an incredible compulsion gripped him.

Rodney *knew* he should be watching this family intently, observing every nuance of their expressions, gestures, habits. As though he were trying to absorb the total experience of this unnamed family, as though some force had chained him like a slave to this spot.

Suddenly a wave of emotion shocked through him. Like a blast of radiation, he felt a horrible sadness penetrate him: all the feelings of loss and incompleteness, of bitter despondency at things never dreamed, never to be accomplished. It was such an overwhelming flood of emotion, as though he'd opened an unknown hatch, releasing a torrent of grief and pain that would surely carry him away in its terrible tidal grip.

A soft kiss of new snow began to fall, and he blinked the flakes from his eyelashes. Tears replaced the crystals, sending warm streaks down his face. He began to sob, but did not know why.

And that scared him, too.

Because Rodney never let himself cry about *anything*.

Time passed without notice as the family's dinner progressed. Rodney felt like a third party to the event, watching his other, voyeur-self, and knowing there was something terribly wrong with what was happening, but having no control over himself. He knew he should get his black ass out of there, but he couldn't do it. Something was holding him to this place. Something about this family he was supposed to see. It was a totally bizarre scene, and one that became truly . . . *frightening* the longer he thought about it.

Was he going nuts?

Was there some part of his mind that was somehow taking over the rest of him? What the hell was he doing here, spying on these people? Was he getting ready to hurt them? Rob them? Acting like some zombie in a bad movie? The idea of doing those things sent a shudder up his spine, and he felt suddenly disgusted for even thinking of such a thing.

He was a hard-working man who'd never done anything wrong to anybody.

But that fact didn't make things any better.

Another scary thing was the neighborhood—because Rodney didn't recognize it. And him being a cab driver for twenty-seven years, he figured he knew just about every street in every borough of New York. Unless he'd somehow ended up way out on Long Island somewhere. Nassau County. Or even Suffolk . . .

But how could that be? He had *no memory* of driving to this place, no memory of arriving.

That was impossible, wasn't it?

The only explanation gave him no comfort—that he was in the middle of a dream so real, so perfectly grounded in detail and sensation that he couldn't tell the difference from his real life. He'd been in dreams like that before, and the way it always worked was that once he realized he was just dreaming he could pull himself out of it, wake himself up, or even "switch channels" and start dreaming about something else.

But he couldn't do it now.

Something was very different here. Very weird.

Because *this* was no dream. He was really standing in the snow, feeling very sad and lonely and increasingly scared. That he couldn't remember getting there disturbed him, and he—

"Okay, pal, why don't you just hold it right there . . . !"

The masculine voice was soft, almost whispered, but the words were delivered with force and confidence. In the sound-absorbing baffle of the falling snow, the voice seemed much louder than it probably was. It startled Rodney, and he turned quickly to his right, looking down the driveway that led from the house to the street.

Twenty feet away stood a uniformed policeman, holding his service revolver with both hands, arms outstretched, legs spread, and training the barrel at a point in the center of Rodney's chest. Behind the officer, his partner, gun also drawn, was running toward him with the wide, wary eyes that came with the job.

Slowly raising his hands and turning to face the cops, Rodney did not expect such rough treatment as when the partner grabbed him and muscled him quickly into the snow, slapping handcuffs on him. Like a grim litany, he grumbled the Miranda phrase into Rodney's left ear, then yanked him up to his knees. "Now what the fuck you doing up at this window, nigger?"

Rodney looked up to answer him. The cop was himself a black man and so the slur took on an entirely different shade of meaning.

"I . . . I don't know. I was—"

"He on somethin'?" the first cop said, drawing close, leaning down to look at Rodney more closely.

"Who knows . . . " The black cop pulled him up to his feet. "Get up, my man. We takin' a ride down to Shady Side."

As Rodney was led down the driveway to the waiting cruiser, the other officer knocked on the side door to the house. Rodney felt terribly embarrassed as the man from the dinner table appeared at the door. It was a weird feeling, as if the man should know him and would be shocked to see Rodney playing Peeping Tom. The notion lingered until the cop had hustled him down to the curb, where the patrol car awaited them. Its lights were off, but the streetlight and the reflective snow threw enough illumination across the door panel for Rodney to see something that didn't make any sense at all.

If he'd already been confused and even scared that he'd somehow blacked out and couldn't remember a chunk of his life, *now* he figured he might be just plain stone-crazy.

The red-and-blue trimmed emblem on the door of the car read CITY OF PITTSBURGH POLICE DEPARTMENT.

Pittsburgh? What the fuck was he doing in *Pittsburgh?*

The cop opened the car's rear door, pushed down on Rodney's head to bend him low, and shoved him inside. "In you go, brother," he said.

"Wait a second," said Rodney. "I need to ask you somethin' . . ."

The cop looked at him with an expression of supremely weary tolerance. "What's that?"

"Is this *really* Pittsburgh?"

The black cop laughed. "Let me ask *you* somethin', Home—is this *really* the planet Earth?"

"No, you don't underst—"

Roughly, the cop pushed him into the car. "Get the fuck in that car, you goofy bastard!"

Slamming the door, the cop moved around to the driver's side and slid behind the wheel. Rodney was going to say something, but the officer grabbed his radio mike and rattled off the status of their call—that they'd apprehended a suspect and were planning to bring him in. Rodney only half-listened to the smear of police buzzwords and code numbers; he was still trying to sort out the chaos that swirled around him like old newspapers in a midnight wind.

The last thing he remembered was . . . *what?*

—was sitting in his cab on Fifty-sixth Street at Sixth Avenue. Right. He'd just dropped off a couple of tourists going to the Harley-Davidson. Yeah, just sitting there, writing down the fare in his log. And then . . .

And then that was *it.*

Rodney couldn't remember a damned thing after that. It had been what, maybe, two in the afternoon. And here it was sometime after dark in another freakin' city hundreds of miles away. Ain't no way he drove a fare all the way out here and couldn't remember it. This was downright spooky. It made him think back to his twenties, when he was a big malt liquor and cheap rye man. He used to like to get so lathered up, he had a hard time crawling into his cab at the end of a night of hard drinking and looking for pussy. But no matter how drunk he'd get, he never had what the real professionals used to call "blackouts." In fact, he couldn't imagine being so drunk you didn't remember what you did for hours on end, and had always figured that anybody telling you that kind of stuff was dishin' the bullshit.

But something like that must have happened here, right?

Only thing was, Rodney McGuire wasn't a drinker anymore. No way. Not after they cut off a piece of his liver at Mount Sinai fifteen years ago and told him if he kept straining that cheap-assed rye through what was left of it, there wouldn't be any liver left for the next operation. And that would be time for the old Lights Out.

So what was happening here? No drinking and no lumps on his head. Ain't nobody whacked him and threw him in a truck heading west on the Pennsylvania Turnpike.

So how come—?

The second cop interrupted his thought when he opened the shotgun door and jumped in. "Everything's cool with the guy in the house," he said. "How's it going with our friend back there?"

The black cop chuckled. "A real space cadet . . ."

"Junkie?" The second cop looked back at Rodney.

"Nah, I think we got ourselves a funny farmer," said the driver, slipping the cruiser into gear and hitting the accelerator. "But, hey, let them worry about *that* down at Central. All we gotta do is collect the garbage—not dispose of it, right, partner?"

Both cops laughed as the cruiser hurtled down a snowy residential street called Beacon Avenue. Rodney noticed the name on the sign at the first intersection they crossed. Force of habit. Part of the job. All that jazz. The cops started bantering about a basketball game between Pitt and Seton Hall, leaving Rodney to face the grim facts. He wanted to tell them it was thoroughly impossible for him to be in Pittsburgh, that he had no idea how he'd gotten here. He wanted them to realize how scared as hell he was, but he knew there was no talking to these lunks.

Pittsburgh.

The idea refused to take hold in him; he *had* to be dreaming. And yet the cold steel of the handcuffs around his wrists was as real as any illusion could ever wish to be. Rodney watched the neighborhoods drift past him all covered in a white shroud, equal parts snow and moonlight. For a moment, he was transported to his childhood in Raleigh, North Carolina, when his Uncle Shorty would come by his mama's house every Christmastime in his farm truck. He would take all the kids for a ride through the neighborhoods where all the white people lived, so they could see all the fancy houses all trimmed with pretty lights.

Man, that seemed like *so* long ago. . . .

Rodney rocked back and forth as the driver whipped the car around corners and through back lanes until it emerged on Elmer Street. The car turned left, and Rodney saw the precinct house looming off to the right. When they pulled into a space on the back lot, the white guy finished filling out a report on a clipboard while he whistled "Ruby Tuesday." Then they took him through the back doors, down some steps, to a bullpen of desks and phones and old Selectric typewriters. Everything was painted in dull dark greens and browns. After breaking off his cuffs, they sat him down in front of a young guy in a crisp white shirt and a fashionably colorful tie with matching suspenders. He looked more like a Wall Street trainee than a detective.

"This guy's a peeper," said the black cop. "Picked him up in Squirrel Hill."

Officer Shirt-and-Tie nodded.

The white cop dropped his report next to the typewriter. "Here's the skinny, okay, Sarge?"

Another nod. "Okay. See you, John . . ." Then he looked at Rodney. "I'm Sergeant Nimitz. I'm going to need some information, okay?"

"Listen," said Rodney, "this isn't what you think."

"It never is." Nimitz smiled wearily, placed his hands on the keys of the old IBM. "Name and address . . . ?"

"Rodney McGuire, Sixty-eight East Twenty-eighth Street, Brooklyn, New York."

Sergeant Nimitz looked up. "What're you doing in Pittsburgh?"

Rodney wanted to scream out that he had no fucking idea what he was doing here, but he exhaled slowly, forcing himself to speak in a soft, controlled voice. "Listen, Sergeant, that's just it—I *don't know* what I'm doing here!"

Before the cop could say anything, Rodney launched into a quick summation of his plight. He spoke rapidly, but clearly. He tried to use vocabulary that would distinguish him as smart guy rather than some jive asshole. He tried to capture the weirdness and spookiness of the sensation as quickly as he could.

". . . and I'm tellin' you, that's the truth," he said in summation. "It was like—I'm sittin' in the cab, then I blink my eyes and *bang* I'm standin' outside this dude's window watchin' everybody get ready to eat supper."

Nimitz ran a hand through his carefully trimmed hair and grinned. "I have to give you a lot of style points, Mr. McGuire. I don't hear that story every day."

"Look, man," said Rodney as he pulled out his wallet, threw his Medallion card and driver ID on the desk.

"You see that card? I've been a cabby for almost thirty goddamn years! I ain't no B&E man, and I sure as hell ain't no Peepin' Tom!"

"Then what were you doing at the Goldbergs' house? Says here you were looking in their window."

"That's right, I *was*, but I don't know why! Aren't you listenin' to me?"

"You ever had any . . . you know, psychological problems? Ever been hospitalized?"

Rodney tried to smile, to act as normal as possible. "Look, Sergeant, I understand you askin' me a question like that. I *know* I sound like a nut, but believe me—I. Ain't. No Nut. Everything happened just like I told you. You can check my record, man. I ain't never even been jaywalkin'. You got to be*lieve* me!"

The sergeant stopped typing and paused to look at Rodney a little more closely. The cop was obviously young and educated. He spoke well and he had manners. "If Mr. Goldberg—that's the man you were looking at through his window—if he doesn't want to press charges, I don't *have* to believe you."

"What do you mean?"

"It means I can just let you go."

Something relaxed in Rodney's gut. "When you gonna hear from Mr. Goldberg?"

Sergeant Nimitz shrugged. "You want me to call him?"

"I would really appreciate it." Rodney leaned back in his chair and began rocking ever so slightly to release some nervous energy.

Nimitz keyed in a number, identified himself when Goldberg picked up. He explained the man's options to him, then added the following: "I've been talking to the suspect, Mr. Goldberg, and I think there's been some mistake. The man's a driver from New York City who was sent to pick up a client on Beacon. He got the houses mixed up in the snow."

Pause.

Then: "Yessir. Mr. Goldberg, I think that's a good idea. Thank you, sir. Yes, it's my feeling, too."

Nimitz exchanged good-byes, hung up the phone. He looked at Rodney for a moment before speaking. "No charges."

Rodney leaned forward. "You just lied for me, Sergeant. *Why?*"

Nimitz tilted his head. "Because for some goofy reason I believe you. At least I believe you believe *yourself*. I get a . . . shall we say . . . *variety* of human types coming through here, and it doesn't take long to figure out who the real people are."

"Thanks, man," said Rodney, a genuine smile breaking on his face. "I don't know how to—"

Nimitz had his hand up. "Wait a second. You're not out of the woods yet. I have to make sure what you say about your record is true. If you have a clean sheet, I'll sign off on this thing. But I want you to do me favor."

"Name it." Rodney moved to the edge of his seat, gathered up his belongings from the desktop.

"I want you to just tell your story to our shrink, Doctor Hanover."

"Man, I told you, I ain't no nut—"

Nimitz held up his hand again, like a traffic cop. "Hey, give me a break here. I didn't say you were. I just want her to refer you to someone in New York—just in case you, ah, have any more problems, and you want to talk to somebody about it."

Easing back into his chair, Rodney nodded slowly. Yeah, that made sense. And it wasn't anything threatening. Nothing anybody would ever know about. "Okay, I can dig it. Sorry, Sergeant . . ."

"That's all right," he said, getting up. "You can wait here. I'm going upstairs and see if your sheet came in off the network. Also see if Doctor Hanover's still here."

"Kinda late, ain't it?"

"Hey," said Nimitz with a smile, "this is a big city—we pay a lot of overtime."

Rodney nodded and watched the cop leave the big room. Everything looked like it was going to be cool. For a while there he was thinking he'd have to call his oldest daughter, Dahlia, and tell her to scare up some bail money. She was an assistant professor of music at Howard University in Washington, D.C., and he was very proud of her. But he winced when he imagined what she would think when she found out he'd been arrested for looking in white people's windows.

Nothing like this had ever happened to him and he wasn't at all comfortable with the whole police scene. He was lucky he'd caught a sympathetic guy like this Sergeant Nimitz here, instead of some racist numb-head. Rodney felt better, but that didn't explain the basic reason he was here in the first place.

Pittsburgh, Pennsylvania.

How in God's name had he gotten here without knowing how he did it?

And why did he go look in that family's window?

Maybe he *did* need to talk to a witch doctor? Maybe he was running into some early sign of Alzheimer's. That would be just fine, wouldn't it?

Or maybe—

"Okay, Mr. McGuire . . ." said Sergeant Nimitz, walking back to his desk with a curled-up sheet from an old fax machine. "Your record is just like you said it would be. If everybody was like you, I'd be out of a job."

Rodney grinned and shook his head. "You don't have to order my harp and wings just yet."

"Doctor Hanover's still here, by the way," said the sergeant. "She said you can come up to her office whenever you're ready."

The forensic psychiatrist assigned to the Shady Side Precinct was a woman in her mid-thirties with ash-blond hair and a long, horsey face. She reminded Rodney of the people in the British royal family—the same basic facial features. Not exactly homely, but certainly *not* what he'd call an "attractive" woman. The clothes she wore didn't help much, either. Ugly brown suit with a black, mock-turtle blouse made her look real drab. But Rodney had been around long enough to know that some women just *wanted* to look unattractive to men.

"I've read the officers' report and some notes from Sergeant Nimitz," she said in a pleasant voice in stark contrast to her appearance. "Would you like to tell me about the experience in your own words?"

Rodney nodded, repeated his story, slowly and clearly. He tried to choose words that would make him sound as intelligent as possible. He hoped that by going over everything, it would make it more real, less scary, more explainable.

Dr. Hanover nodded as he wrapped up his tale. She sat behind a beat-up desk, triangled into the corner of the small room. There were no pictures on the walls; the room was featureless other than a single window opposite the door. It was a grim little place, and he would have hated to have to work in such a cramped space all the time. Then she asked him the required questions about drugs and alcohol, history of seizures, blackouts, mental illness, etc., and he said *no* to all of them.

"What about dreams?" she said. "Are you having any strange dreams?"

Rodney paused to think about exactly what he *did* dream about and had a hard time recalling any details about any of them. He told her that.

She nodded. "As we grow older, and our lives become more complex, many of us remember very little of our dreams. That's very normal."

"Glad to hear that," said Rodney. "But I was hopin' you could give me some idea what happened to me."

She shrugged. "There's a semitrance state of mind called *hypnogogia*," said Dr. Hanover. "But usually it occurs with the subject lying on his or her back and for short periods of time."

The word made Rodney think of something else. "What about bein' hypnotized? Could that last guy in my cab have . . . you know, put me in a trance?"

She smiled primly, as though following a stage direction. "It's possible, I suppose, but we must ask the question: *why*?"

She had him on that one. He sighed. "It just doesn't make sense."

The doctor looked at her watch, nodded, scribbled down a few lines on a memo pad, then handed the top page to Rodney.

"Here's the name of a colleague of mine. He's a very respected therapist in Manhattan. I met him at a conference where he was presenting a chapter from his latest book . . ."

"Thanks," he said, holding it delicately.

"I'll tell him about you. What happened here tonight, and that you might call him if you have any more . . . trouble. Any more experiences you can't explain."

"So you don't think I'm crazy, do you, Doc?" The question leaped from his mouth. He'd been dying to ask it, and when she didn't act like she was going to volunteer the information, he just knew he had to let it out.

She smiled another of her controlled little smiles. "No, Mr. McGuire, of course you're not. Your record indicates you've been a very stable, productive person all your life. There's no reason to believe things are any different now."

"That's good to know," he said evenly.

"Don't lose that paper," she said. "Just call my friend if you feel a need to talk to someone like me, or if anything like this ever happens again."

Rodney nodded, put the sheet in his shirt pocket.

Standing up, he paused awkwardly for a moment, then reached out to shake her hand. He felt silly doing it, but she responded as though it were just fine.

They looked at each for a moment, then he said something else that had been on his mind. "I guess I have to start figurin' out how to get back home. How far is the airport from here?"

"It's not too far. I'll see if Sergeant Nimitz can get you a ride." She walked to the door and ushered him out of the shabby office.

Rodney thanked her again, followed her downstairs to the lobby that led to the bullpen area. He waited patiently for someone to tell him about the airport and absently pulled out the piece of paper she'd given him.

An impulse was telling him to throw it in the trash, but another part of him was screaming to hang on to it. He looked at it closely for the first time, hoping he'd never have to talk to this guy.

Printed in very neat, block letters was the name, address, and phone number of *J. MICHAEL KEATING, M.D.*

TWO

MARTHA PASEK
Baltimore, Maryland

The rain had just about let up when Martha got off the bus at the corner of Park Heights Avenue and Fords Lane. It had been such a *cold* rain all day, she couldn't figure out how it hadn't turned to sleet or maybe snow. Didn't matter because she'd thought to bring her umbrella and wear the "duck" boots her son, John, had gotten her from that L. L. Bean store catalog last Christmas. She was plenty dry, and besides, it wasn't but a few blocks' walk to her little duplex—the house she'd lived in since the day she'd been married twenty-seven years ago. Her son kept bugging her to move out of the old neighborhood that was becoming disfigured with graffiti, litter, and the spreading stain of crime. But it was the only home she'd ever had, and Martha knew that leaving it was going to take a lot of effort, especially if she had to find new homes for all her little kitties. Right now, she didn't want to face that kind of sadness.

Every day, since Gus had died and she'd taken the cleaning job at the *Baltimore Sun* building downtown, she'd been taking the Number 15 bus to and from work. The job had been the best thing in the world for her, yessiree. Her schedule allowed her to get home by four in the afternoon—just the right time—after the kids got out of school and before the rush hour traffic.

She walked along with an easy stride, feeling good despite the dreary weather because it was Friday, and that meant a weekend of cable TV and bingo games at the volunteer fire hall. As she walked along the sidewalk on Fords Lane, she noticed the first few groups of orthodox Jews leaving their modest homes and apartments to walk to evening services at their synagogues.

Hard to not notice them. They weren't tough to pick out because all the men wore the same black coats and hats, and many of them sported beards and long, curly sideburns. The women wore muted colors, long dresses, and their hair long and unstyled under scarves and hats.

To Martha, the Jews were a familiar and welcome sight. They had been a large part of the neighborhood for more than a hundred years, and they showed every intention of remaining, even though the area had been changing for the worse. Drug dealers, teenage gangs—both black and white—and homeless drifters were becoming more frequent elements on the corners of the side streets, and it worried her more and more. Maybe John was right: maybe she *would* have to move out one of these days.

It bothered her, but not the orthodox Jews. They just went about their business like the quiet, respectful people they'd always been. They had a solid, earnest way of living their lives and they bothered absolutely no one.

But people did like to bother them. . . .

All her life, Martha had heard her friends and neighbors talk about the "kikes" and the "dirty Jews," or the "Jew bastards," but she could never understand why they were despised by so many people. No Jew had personally ever done anything bad to her. Sure, they kept to themselves, ate funny foods, and they certainly went out of their way to look *different* from everybody else, but none of that was so awful, was it?

She especially couldn't fault people for what they looked like. Just the other day, she passed a big plate glass window and caught a glimpse of herself walking down the sidewalk—what a *shock*! She looked like a dumpy, dough-faced bag lady, aging far more rapidly than her fifty-one years should have allowed. How could she go for days and weeks at a time and not take the time to really get a good look at herself? She pondered that for a moment, then struggled to get her thoughts back on track.

What was it she'd been thinking about? Oh, yes—those Jewish people.

Martha had never figured it out. What was so terrible about the Jews? And if truth be known, she'd always found their ways to be kind of . . . well, fascinating to her. And she'd had a longtime curiosity about what the insides of their churches (only they called them "shools" or synagogues) looked like, and things like that. Often, growing up, she'd wondered what it would have been like to go out with one of those Jewish boys with their little skullcaps on the back of their heads.

Smiling at the memory from her youth, she was surprised to hear the crying of a child from somewhere up ahead. It sounded like it was coming from the alley behind a row of apartments at the next corner.

Leave it alone.

The thought lighted through her in bright neon-red.

Just keep walking.

The crying grew louder, although she could now hear that it was punctuated by rough laughter.

"Don't hurt him!" said a small voice, a little girl's.

Suddenly, Martha was running as fast her fifty-one-year-old legs would allow. She didn't recall ever making a conscious decision; she'd just started running to the corner and down the alleyway.

The figures at the far end of the narrow lane must have been startled by the sight of her fireplug body filling the alley, racing toward them, because they stopped their business and stared blankly at her with expressions mixed of surprise and stupidity. There were two of them, both tall and gangly. All arms and legs it seemed. Wearing baggy, army surplus fatigue jackets and black sweatpants and identically shaved heads, they looked like members of a gang.

Cowered in front of them were two children: a boy of perhaps twelve wearing an oversized black fedora and a black topcoat, and a girl with long brown hair and a long, baggy dress, who could not be more than eight years old. The boy's face hung slack, spattered with blood from the blows he'd already taken, and his eyes were rolled back into his skull. One of the punks was holding him up by the collar of his topcoat like a battered marionette while the other one had been pounding him. The little girl continued to scream.

Martha snapshotted this entire scene in an instant as she ran toward them. The two thugs stared at her with fascination and humor, as though they welcomed the distraction of a bowlegged bag lady wading into their midst.

"Hey, dig the old hag!" said one of them.

They snickered and spit viciously.

"C'mon, Momma. Let's see what you got!"

The taller of the two squared his shoulders and faced Martha head-on; the other one dropped the little orthodox Jewish boy into a heap, ready to meet the unlikely challenge of a crazy, old woman.

The little girl continued to scream for help even as she noticed the old woman rushing toward her.

Smoothly, as though she'd practiced it hundreds of times, Martha reached up to close her umbrella as she ran. In perfect syncopation with her running stride, its folds collapsed to form a steel-tipped weapon. She held in it both hands like a short pike and ran harder.

What was she *doing*?

The thought whispered through her, not in warning, but more like the question of an outside observer. She'd never done anything like this in her life. It was as if some other person or force directed her, pushed her on. Although she was only vaguely aware of it, the sensation was immensely exciting, almost pleasurable—as though something had suddenly sparked into life in her, and now it burned with a raw, powerful flame. Now, everything moved with such ease, such smoothness, Martha felt so . . . so *alive*!

The closest of the two punks hunched over as he faced her and held out his arms as though he would catch her in a wide bear hug. He threw back his bald head and started to laugh at her as she homed in on him.

What happened next was so quick it passed in an eyeblink, yet Martha would never forget it. Every detail would play in her memory under the slow, careful eye of a slow-motion camera. She screamed at her target, so loudly that the sound almost scared her as well, and lunged forward so hard she left her feet. The sudden sound and motion shocked the punk; he remained immobile, his mouth still open. Still airborne, Martha collided against the youth's chest, but not before she had thrust the point of her umbrella upward violently, as hard as she could. The punk's arms surrounded her, but fell limply away as they both hurtled backward into the alley. For an instant, her enemy's body convulsed beneath her, his motorcycle boots tapping out an arrhythmic beat upon the gravel and asphalt.

Half-stunned by the impact, Martha pushed away from him before he could grab her. But as she tried to get up, still holding her umbrella, she found it hard to move . . .

. . . because its point was jammed through the roof of the punk's mouth, up into the mush that functioned as his brain. His eyes bulged open, as though they'd tried to escape the force that had intruded into his skull space. Surprisingly, little blood leaked from his mouth, but Martha was familiar with the slack, empty slate of his ugly face. She'd seen it when Gus fell out of his La-Z-Boy while watching the Orioles and his heart had seized up like an old truck engine. The skinhead was dead.

And Martha Pasek had killed him.

Turning toward his friend, she smiled. "You're next, sonny," she said.

"Man, *fuck* you, lady!" said the remaining punk.

Without thinking, Martha rose up out of her crouch and lunged for him. She loosed another Valkyrie scream that so unnerved her prey, he started running. With a savage thrust, he pushed past the Jewish boy and his sister and cleared the length of the alley in long, shaky strides. As the enemy left them, Martha could feel the rage draining out of her. She felt exhausted, beaten up. The two children both stood there, taking in everything with a kind of solemn acceptance, a grim understanding of terrible Old Testament vengeance revisited.

"All you all right?" asked Martha as she bent down to regard the little girl, whose face was still stained with drying tears. Martha offered her a hug, but did not push the issue.

"Yes," said the little girl, collapsing into Martha's arms.

"Who are you?" said the boy, wiping the blood from his face on the dark sleeve of his coat. "How did you do that?"

"I'm . . . I'm not sure," said Martha, trying to collect herself. Her whole body was trembling and her thoughts were getting jumbled as she began to realize what had happened, what she had done. There was no way she could have done such a thing, but she *knew* she had.

What was going on?

"I want to go home," said the little girl. "Will you take us?"

"Of course I will, sweetie," said Martha, feeling a wave of nausea pass through her. Her knees felt weak, but she knew she must be strong for these children.

Walking slowly with the girl and her brother, they exited the alley and made their way to a little row home on the next block. Their mother greeted them silently, as though she already understood the evil they had endured. Martha tried to explain, but the woman stopped her.

"It would be better if you speak to my husband," she said. "He's gone to the evening service. He will be back—"

Martha nodded, held up her hand. "That's okay, ma'am, but in the meantime, I think I'd better call the police. Can I use your phone?"

The woman looked at her oddly. "It's almost sundown," she said.

Martha didn't get what she was talking about. "So?"

"You are not Jewish?" asked the woman.

Martha shook her head. "No, I'm a Methodist."

"I am sorry," said the woman, pointing to the phone on the wall. "Please, it is there. I am sorry I was being so presumptuous."

Martha nodded, reached for the phone.

Several hours later she was still at the city precinct station south of Rogers Avenue. The officer who'd arrived at the scene was a young black man named Jimson. He'd been very nice, very careful to be mannerly and speak softly. When the ambulance finally left the alley with the boy she'd killed, he drove her to the precinct to fill out what he'd called "routine" reports, even though Martha couldn't imagine a fifty-one-year-old lady killing a street punk ever being routine.

They sat at his desk as he finished typing up his report, after which he'd promised to drive her home. Finally he looked up from the page in the roller and nodded.

"Is there anything else you can think of, Mrs. Pasek?" he said softly. "Anything else you want to tell me?"

She was ready to say no, but she paused to take a deep breath, exhale. "I've never acted like that in my life," she said finally. "Never."

"I kinda figured that," said Jimson. "So what made things different tonight?"

She shook her head. She was tired and hungry, and she was

starting to feel confused, frightened. "You're not going to do anything to me, are you?"

Jimson gestured at the sheet in his typewriter. "Says here 'self-
defense,' Mrs. Pasek. You were a victim defending yourself and
those kids. That's the way it's going down. Nobody wants to put
you in jail, ma'am."

She continued to shake her head, wondering what she could say
to make the policeman understand what had happened. "It's like
something came alive inside me," she said finally. "I heard that little
girl screaming, and it was like . . . like I'd heard it before . . . a long
time ago."

Yes, she thought softly, listening to what she was saying as
though someone else was doing the talking. *That's exactly what it
was like. . . .*

"Only *this time* I wouldn't just try to ignore it!" Her voice had
attained an urgency and a sharp edge. "This time I knew I had to do
something about it."

Jimson picked up a paper clip, started rotating it through his fingers as he leaned closer, listened a little more intently. "What do you
mean—'this time'? You seen these creeps beating on the kids before?"

"No, not at all. That's not what I meant. . . ." Martha shook her
head, chuckled to herself. "I'm sorry, but I'm not sure *what* I mean.
It's like, like I have this memory in my head that somebody was
doing something terrible to a little girl, and I . . . I didn't do anything to stop them."

"When did this happen, Mrs. Pasek?"

Tears suddenly escaped her eyes. Hot, salty. Big, heavy tears. "I
don't *know*!" she said, trying to hold back the sobs. "God help me,
I don't know! But I feel terrible! I feel so . . . so *guilty*!"

"You didn't do anything wrong, ma'am," said the policeman.
"You're a hero. You saved those children from God knows what."

"No, I mean *before*! From when . . . when I can't remember . . .
Oh, God, if I could just *remember* what this is all about, I'd be okay."

The officer produced a box of Kleenex from an adjoining desk,
offered her one. "Here, take it easy," he said softly.

"Do you understand what I mean?" she said. "Do you see why it's
important to me?"

"It'll come to you," said Officer Jimson. "Sometimes we work
things out in our dreams."

memory allowed him to review hundreds, even thousands, of psychiatric cases in his mind. Whenever he listened to the anguished confessions of a new patient, he was automatically sifting through the case histories for appropriate responses and treatment.

Sadly, the whole experience had started to feel like a drill—a memorized routine he could perform, regardless of the tune called by the patient.

Michael shrugged to himself, leaned back in his chair, and looked at a glass-and-teak case where he'd arranged a variety of artifacts he'd found on archeological digs all over Manhattan. Michael had joined the Amsterdam Museum Archeological Society about ten years ago and was firmly hooked on the buried mysteries beneath New York. He helped uncover Dutch catacombs, Indian burial chambers, and even lost sections of the subway system.

If he could leave the psychiatric profession, he would have more time for the museum work, and more time to pursue great literature. Maybe it was time to plan an early retirement, he thought as he reached for his copy of Italo Calvino's *As a Man Grows Older*. The Mondadori paperback was in the original Italian, a gift from an appreciative patient, and he was reading it slowly, enjoying the story in its original form, so that he might savor every nuance, every poetic rhythm of the author's style. One of the major Romance languages, Italian was grounded in Latin, which he'd been forced to study in his four years at a Jesuit prep school. Back then, he'd hated it, but as he passed through college and professional school, he realized what a treasure he'd been given. Latin had been been the key that unlocked all the other knowledge. It had turned Michael into a lover of language and had forged one of his favorite pastimes: reading great writers in their original words. He smiled as he thumbed for his place in the thick book; Calvino was such a powerful writer, he made Michael envious and wish that he could be such a fine stylist.

And even though he admitted it to no one, he secretly wished he had been able to make writing a profession. It seemed like everybody wanted to be a writer, and thought they had the right stuff to pull it off.

At least Michael had enough objectivity to know he would have to be satisfied doing it vicariously.

He smiled as as he hunched over his desk, favorite fountain pen in hand, to begin a new page in Calvino's book. But he did not get very far.

His intercom buzzed, and the voice of Pamela Robbins, his receptionist, whispered professionally to him. "Excuse me, Doctor Keating, but we have a . . . patient . . . out here who would like to see you."

Michael was surprised by the intrusion. "What're you talking about? We don't have anybody scheduled, do we? What's going on?"

"Ah . . . Doctor, I'm sorry, but . . . could I see you for a moment?"

Michael detected a conflux of emotions in Pamela's voice. He knew it was not like her to *ever* interrupt his private hour. Something must be very wrong.

"Yes, of course," he said quickly into the intercom. "Please, come in."

The door opened and closed quickly as Pamela entered the room. Wearing a beige wool suit, she looked crisply tailored and very professional. Her dark hair was cut in a medium length, styled in the latest fashion. Removing her glasses, she looked at Michael with an expression of concern. "I'm sorry, Doctor, but I don't know what to do. . . ."

"What's going on? What's the matter with you?"

"A woman just came into the office," said Pamela. "Saying she *had* to talk to someone, or she was going to—"

"Go crazy?" Michael grinned and shook his head. "Yeah, I've heard that one before. . . ."

Pamela gave him a look born of ten years' familiarity and a friendship that transcended her station as employee. It was a look women give men who have acted like jackasses. She was obviously unhappy by his not-so-clever interruption. Michael gestured for her to continue.

". . . before she did something regrettable," said Pamela. "Like killing herself."

"Come on, Pamela," he said, smiling. "We've heard this stuff before. They never mean it. They're just looking for attention, and we give it to them."

"She *means* it," said Pamela, unconsciously straightening the lapels of her suit.

"Really? How do *you* know?"

"Because she's sitting out there with a gun in her mouth."

Her words slapped him with an icy sting. "Jesus Christ," he said in a whisper.

"What're we going to do?" said Pamela. "Should I call the police?"

Michael felt his stomach begin to sink. He *loathed* the idea of guns, of violence, and although they terrified him, he knew he

couldn't let the fear control him. All his life, he'd been proud to
know that he'd always controlled his fate.

Fear never lets you do that. Fear was indeed the mind-killer.

"No, no police. Not yet."

"Doctor . . ."

He moved around to the front of his desk, ran a hand through his
still-dark, wavy hair. He straightened the knot of his Brioni tie, and
drew a deep breath.

"You tell me there's a woman out in my waiting room," he said.
"And she's so very upset she wants to kill herself. She told you she
wants *my* help, Pamela, not the police. If she wanted the police, she
would be sitting in *their* waiting room with a gun in her mouth."

"So what should I do?" Pamela looked at him in a way he had
never seen before. Fear defined her expression, but there was more:
a suggestion she was willing to do whatever he wanted.

"Stay here in my office," he said. "I'll leave the intercom on. If
you think things are getting out of control, you can call the police
from my phone. Fair enough?"

Pamela nodded, tried to swallow, and did a bad job of it.

He rolled his shoulders, adjusting his suit jacket and shooting
his cuffs. Best to look presentable, professional.

Without another word, he walked to the door, opened it slowly
to reveal a woman sitting on one of the mauve ottomans. For far too
long, Michael stood mute and rigid in the doorway, staring at her.
At her gun, actually. Heavy and so black it looked blue, it looked
too big in her small, pale hands. Its thick barrel rested on her lower
lip, giving her a grim, not at all seductive pout.

"Hello," he said softly. "My name is Doctor Keating. I understand you wanted to talk to me. . . ."

Slowly, the gun eased away from her mouth as she rested it across
her lap. Michael did not feel very secure, but as long as the weapon
pointed away from him and her, he would be able to carry on the
semblance of normality.

"I'm sorry to act like this, but—"

"You're feeling very alone, very desperate," said Michael, as he
chanced taking another step into the room, then slowly closing the
door to his office behind him.

"Yes," she said. "That's right! How could you know?"

He shrugged, tried to smile as disarmingly as possible. "It's my
job to understand how my patients are feeling."

"Is that what I am—your *patient?*"

"Only if you want to be." Michael moved slowly to Pamela's desk, leaned against the edge casually. His outstretched hand rested next to the intercom, where he easily touched its On button. "How did you know to come here?"

"You mean did I get a referral?" She chuckled darkly.

Michael shrugged.

"No, my dentist is in this building, that's all. I've seen your name on the directory downstairs." She looked at him sadly.

"All right," he said, waiting for her to proceed at her own pace.

"I need help. . . ." said the woman, attempting to hold back tears.

"It's perfectly all right to need help. Everyone does at some point in their lives."

"Really?"

Michael nodded as he studied her, tried to get a handle on what kind of a person she might be.

She appeared to be in her mid-thirties, wearing a Mets baseball jacket over jeans and a white sweatshirt that read *Carpe Diem.* Her hair hung from her head in thick clumps, unwashed for many days. Hers eyes had sunken into her skull, accentuated by dark circles of fatigue. Obviously lacking sleep and nutrition, the woman looked far older than whatever her true age might be. Her shoes were trendy purple-and-white athletic shoes, expensive, but poorly made, and the choice of the masses easily duped by TV advertising. It was difficult to assess her intelligence or socioeconomic situation because she presented him with mixed signals. A former girlfriend had once advised Michael that he could always tell the status of a person by checking out their shoes—and to his surprise, he'd discovered over the years she'd been correct. But the woman sitting before him was an enigma. The shoes said one thing, but the sweatshirt with the Latin aphorism spoke of a different person.

"Can you help me?"

"Of course, but we have to get a few things out of the way, first," he said.

"Like what?"

"Like telling me your name, and that . . . gun."

She looked at him with an expression of equal parts relief and embarrassment. "I feel so stupid! I'm so sorry. . . . My name is Allison. Allison Enders."

Michael nodded. "It is very good to meet you, Allison. Now, what about our friend, Mr. Gun . . . ?"

Gingerly, carefully, she lifted the weapon off her lap and placed it on the adjoining ottoman. Michael felt all the muscles in his back and neck suddenly unclench. A throbbing ache pierced him through the shoulder blades, but it was a welcome pain, signaling his body's gradual retreat from on-the-edge tension.

"That's fine, Allison. Very good," he said.

For an instant, Michael felt everything locking up in his mind. No thoughts would come.

Nothing.

Empty.

The woman was looking at him expectantly, the first twinges of hope illuminating her eyes. "Yes . . . ?" she said.

"Why don't we come into my office," he said, and the words slipped free of him like bubbles from a child's toy. Finally, automatically. "And . . . and if you'd like to tell me anything, you can do it there."

Allison Enders nodded and slowly stood up, smoothing out her jacket, touching her hair, as though aware of her clothes and general appearance for the first time. "Yes," she said softly, breathing deeply and trying to gain some composure. "That would be just fine."

Michael opened the door to his office, held it for her as would any gentleman. She took several steps toward him, then stopped, as confusion ghosted across her features.

"Is something wrong?" he said.

"What about *that*?" said Allison, pointing to the revolver on the ottoman.

Michael forced himself to smile as he glanced at the polished, black thing of death. "Let's just leave it there for now, all right?"

The woman nodded quickly, walked past him and into his office where Pamela Robbins sat in a chair next to Michael's large and very modern slate-topped desk. She stood up instantly, but said nothing as she awaited instruction.

"Everything is just fine, Ms. Robbins," he said softly. "I'm going to spend a little time with Allison."

Pamela moved to the door, but paused at the threshold. "Shall I contact your last two appointments?" she said.

Michael forced another smile. "Yes, that'll be great. Thank you,

Ms. Robbins. Tell them we'll have to reschedule due to . . . an emergency."

Pamela flashed him an expression of concern, silently mouthed the words *Be careful*, and closed the door.

After directing Allison Enders to the client's chair, Michael sat behind his desk, where the Italo Calvino novel still awaited him. He wondered when he would ever have the peace of mind to return to its lyric passages, then turned his attention to his newest patient.

Carefully, he negotiated the minefield of her emotions and fears, easing into the session with a series of nonthreatening questions. Slowly, a mosaic of information and a detailed portrait emerged.

Ms. Allison Enders was thirty-five years old and employed as an audio technician on the daytime soaps at the ABC-TV studios west of Central Park. She had no children and no other relatives living in the city. She lived alone on the Lower West Side, currently separated from her husband, who owned and operated a café in the Village. She'd been trying to make it on her own for almost eighteen months, but things had been getting progressively worse for her—psychologically rather than economically.

Michael found himself mildly intrigued with her desperation. What had driven her to think about using that gun? (The weapon her estranged husband had insisted she keep for protection in her small, vulnerable apartment.)

Was there a mistress driving her crazy? Unlikely. Her husband's overt care for her welfare indicated he still had feelings for her.

The pressures of urban living?

A reluctance to start a family?

No, something obviously more intense. Whatever it was, Michael would probe a bit deeper, asking the most subtle of questions until enough layers fell away to reveal the burning core.

"Do you still love your husband?"

"Very much. I need him so much right now, but that's part of the problem. I can't go to him like this. He's had enough of my craziness. He can't handle it."

Michael nodded. "Do you believe he loves you?"

Allison began playing with strands of her hair and nodded without hesitation. "Yes, I know he does. He wants to be with me, but I've pushed him away. I made our life together too crazy for *anybody* to put up with it. But he did, for about a year after they started."

Leaning forward, Michael steepled his hands on his desk blotter. "After *what* started, Ms. Enders?"

She refocused on him, as though suddenly aware he was in the room and listening to her. "Oh . . . the *dreams*. Didn't I tell you about the dreams?"

Michael shook his head ever so slightly, gently. "No, but you can tell me now, if you'd like."

The idea of doing this instantly changed her demeanor. Where she had begun to grow relatively calm and in control, she began to become more animated, as though uncomfortable with her clothes, her seat, her hair.

"I . . . want to tell you," she said after a pause. "I know I *have* to tell you. That's why I came here. I *know* that. . . ."

Michael said nothing. Allison Enders was obviously a fairly intelligent and capable person. For her to have been driven to the edge of the abyss suggested that larger forces were at work, forces beyond her control or understanding. She was intriguing him; there was something as yet indefinable about her case history that raised warning flags. With an intuitive power, honed from experience, he sensed something special about her, something that warranted cancellation of previous appointments and staring down the barrel of a Colt revolver.

"The dreams, Allison . . ." he said softly. "It's okay. You may tell me whatever you like. Take as long as you like."

She drew a deep breath, exhaled, and tried to remain unmoving as she prepared to speak. "It's hard to know how to start . . ."

"That's okay. Take your time. Relax."

"All right, let's see . . . a little more than three years ago—I remember because the O. J. Simpson case was on TV all the time— is when I started having these dreams. On a kind of regular basis. Actually, they started three or four years before then, but not very often. Once in six months, maybe. And it's the same dream. Well, not really, but . . . it's like this one huge dream, and I keep dropping in and out of it. Like a movie that's always running. . . ."

Michael nodded, leaned back in his chair as Allison Enders continued.

"The first time was very weird. . . . I'm a little girl, seated at a table with lots of people who are probably my family. Things don't look very modern. Old World. Someplace in Europe. The furniture is old and heavy looking. There is lace and doilies. It appears to be sundown, and the windows are open. Outside we can hear the sound of crowds and sirens, even cracking and popping sounds that I know are guns going off. I try to get up from the table to look out, to see what is going on, and the man at the end of the table—who I just *know* is my father—puts out his hand and says 'No, Sarah, get away from there. Sit down.' He is speaking to me in a foreign language, but I understand what he is saying perfectly. . . .

"And then I am eating from a bowl of soup with a piece of black bread in my hand. The noises from outside our window are getting louder, and it sounds like whatever all the people are doing, they are doing it right downstairs, right on the street below. The noises are bad. Even though I am a little girl, I know the sounds are bad. Down the table from me sits an old woman, my grandmother, and next to her a little boy I know is my brother, and he starts to cry. He is very small as he sits in a high chair made of wood. I feel tears on my own cheeks. They are so hot it surprises me. My father tells me not to cry, that everything will be all right, and that's when there is a horrible pounding at the front door. So loud, so hard, I am afraid the whole door will fall in. I watch my father as he carefully lays his linen napkin on the table, stands, and adjusts his tie and collar. He walks to the door and opens it and suddenly there is more noise and people are screaming, moving quickly all around me. . . ."

Allison paused, rubbed her mouth with the back of her hand. She had been speaking in a faraway voice, so eerie in its gentle power to conjure up images of such stunning clarity. Until she trailed off, Michael had been totally and utterly placed with the little dream-girl and her family. Allison looked at him blankly, compelling him to speak.

"Is that it?" he said in a whisper. "Does it end there?"

"No, I'm sorry, I was just trying to stop thinking about it, to put it away. But I can't," she said. "And no, it doesn't. It doesn't end there. That's just the first dream, the first time I entered this whole . . . this whole *world*."

"These people," he said. "They're not your real family, correct?"

"Oh, no, of course not. But from the very first, I felt like I knew them maybe even better than my own parents, my sister."

"And you have this dream often?"

"Yes, it always starts here, always the same. And every night for the next few years, I would get farther into the . . . story that was being told. It's gotten so I know every detail of so much of it. . . ."

"You dream this every night?"

"No, maybe once or a couple of times a week."

"Do you want to keep going?" he said, adding a small hand gesture of invitation.

Allison almost smiled. "No, but I *have* to. The dream goes on and on. Each night a little more. Up to where it is now. When I dreamed a couple nights ago . . ."

He glanced at his watch, surprised at how quickly the time was passing, and wondered how Pamela was regrouping from the earlier tension. No doubt, this session would run past her quitting time and she would be wanting to know what to do. Better to take care of it now, at this natural break, than to interrupt later at what might be some kind of crucial point.

"Excuse, Ms. Enders," he said, standing up. "I just remembered something . . . I have to take care of it right away, okay? Please, remain comfortable. You're doing just fine."

Her eyes widened, brightened. "Am I? God, I hope so. . . ."

"Oh, yes—beautifully. I'll be right back, okay?"

Michael exited the room, closed the door.

"How's it going?" said Pamela, looking up from her monitor. "I've been so tempted to listen in."

Michael looked at the ottoman, noticing the gun had disappeared.

"It's in here," said Pamela, pointing to her upper right desk drawer.

"How could you even *touch* that thing?" he said.

Pamela shrugged. "My women's volleyball team. We have a self-defense class we all took last summer. They taught us how to handle guns."

Michael pointed to his watch. "It's late. You can leave if you want."

"What about *you*? Are you going to be all right? I can wait here for awhile. Read my book."

There was something about the way she asked that question that made him wonder if she cared about him maybe a little too much. He'd never given her any indication they enjoyed anything more than a professional relationship, but lately Pamela had been letting small gestures and phrases slip, as though intended to send him subtle messages.

"No, I'll be all right."

She smiled, touched his arm. "You sure?"

"Fine. I'll be fine."

"All right, but don't forget, you have to be at the Manhattan Library Association dinner tonight—eight o'clock."

"Oh, Christ! I almost forgot. Maybe we should cancel . . . ?"

Pamela shook her head as though she were his mother. "You *did* forget, and you *can't* cancel—you're one of the speakers."

"All right, then, let me get back to this poor woman," he said. "I'll see you on Monday."

"Call me if you need anything. And, please, Doctor, be careful."

Returning to his place behind the desk, he was pleased to see Allison patiently awaiting him. She appeared to be far more relaxed, more willing to jettison the terrible freight carried for so long. When he gestured for her to continue, she slipped back into the narrative with much less effort this time.

"The door to our apartment explodes inward just as my father begins to turn the knob—like he's released a great pressure from a dam or a dike. But no water comes crashing into our home. Only soldiers. Germans. Nazis. Like they would never stop. One after the other, they flood into the small room, surrounding my father until he disappears, until we can see nothing but their gray-and-black uniforms. The soldiers are yelling out orders and looking very mean. I wonder why they are angry at me. For an instant, everyone stares in shock, in silence. Then a soldier moves quickly to our table where we are all still sitting. He grabs the lace tablecloth and yanks it roughly away from us. Dishes, serving trays, and glassware all goes crashing to the floor and we are screaming in terror. The soldiers order us to get our things. They tell us we are leaving the apartment, being taken from the building. I feel myself being carried aloft by my mother, and she is crying, calling out for my father, whose name is Stefan. She calls out his name over and over. I see him being dragged from the room, out into the hallway of the building by a soldier. As my father sees me, he cries out and tries to reach for me and my mother, but the soldier strikes my father with the back of his hand. When he falls to the floor, the other soldiers kick him with their heavy black boots . . ."

Allison paused, looking for a Kleenex, which Michael knew from experience to always keep nearby his patients' chair. She dabbed at her eyes, fought back a choking sob. "God, I feel so silly," she said. "It's just a *dream*. Why do I *get* like this?"

"It's all right, Allison. Do not feel embarrassed. We don't have to continue if you don't want to. You can come back and see me another time. . . ."

That seemed to surprise her a bit, judging from her expression, but she nodded silently, exhaled.

"No, it's okay. I can go on," she said.

Michael nodded and she continued.

"Then everyone is moving and I can't see what happens next to my father. Soldiers are yelling and pushing us around as we try to gather up some things into baskets and valises. There is more yelling and crying out in the hall and I can hear children wailing. We are swept along roughly out of the wreckage that had been our home, down a hallway filled with more soldiers barking out orders: 'Schnell! Schnell!' and other people, neighbors. We are all pushed down narrow stairs to the street below. It is cold and a wet wind reaches for us. When we get there, I see my father curled up on the street where other soldiers are laughing at him as they kick him in the stomach and back. My mother cries out, tries to break away from the line we are in, and gets slapped across the face by a soldier. My grandmother sags to her knees and begins to wail. Another soldier tries to drag her to her feet, but she has gone completely limp. I watch as the soldier looks to one of his leaders, who nods his head. So fast, right in front of me, I watch him take out a pistol and place it roughly against my grandmother's head. I hear a sharp smack as part of the old woman's head flies apart, covering the street with a red mist. Everyone is so stunned, so scared, we do not make a sound. Even my father. He struggles to his knees and retches violently, then tries to stand up, to join us. We watch as they drag my grandmother's body away from us and down the nearest alley.

"Then we are riding, riding. Endless riding. First in open army trucks, packed in with so many other people we can hardly move. An icy rain stings my face. Later we are at a train yard, where more soldiers take our bags and baskets and push us into train cars. My mother holds me the whole time and I watch to see that my father, who is now holding my baby brother, stays with us. His face is so sad. I know I have never seen him so sad and it scares me. I know that it scares me far more than the soldiers. The other people in the cars are crying and calling out for help, for mercy, but there is no one to help. And the soldiers, they have pushed so many of the people into our car that we cannot move our legs or arms. Older people can't breathe, and even though it is cold outside, the train cars get so hot with all the bodies pushed in there. People are peeing themselves, or worse. The smells and the heat make others either throw up or faint. It is so scary for me. Even though I am held high above the crush, I can feel my mother getting weak, swaying, even though there is no place she could fall. There seems to be a long time where there is just a burning hunger that chews at me from the inside out, and being so thirsty I can feel cracks in my lips. The whole world is just a tiny opening in the corner of the cattle car where the sky tries to seal us in with a piece of its gray slate.

"Days and nights go by as we stay like bundles of sticks all standing on end. Some of the people have died, but they still stand like the rest us, slack jaws and hollow, open eyes. There is no place for them to even fall down. I keep thinking of the old woman, my grandmother, and how she died so quickly and how nobody seemed to care. I don't know if I feel like I really knew her—I'm not sure I really know anybody in this dream. But I just *seem* to know things about them. . . .

"Finally the train stops. It is late in the day. The sky and the land are all kind of gray like an old black-and-white movie. When the soldiers throw open the doors, and the cold damp air washes over everyone, it is like a summer day at the beach. People try to walk, but they are so stiff from not moving that everybody starts falling all over each other. The soldiers are angry about this, yelling for everyone to keep moving. I see a sign on the roof of one of the platforms where the boxcars are unloading, and even though I cannot really read it, I know that it says *Oswiecim*. Soldiers are everywhere, and as I am carried by my mother, she stumbles but keeps her footing. The air is filled with noise: crying, screaming, shouting, the rumble of gasoline engines, and gunshots. I look up and down the train platforms and see nothing but thousands of people pouring from the trains. Some are pushed and driven into trucks and vans, while others are directed to walk along a road which follows the tracks.

"My mother is pushed into a group of women. They are all holding babies or small children in their arms or by their sides. I hear the panic in my mother's voice as she realizes we are being separated from my father and little baby brother. She sees him and begins yelling, '*Stefan! Stefan!*' but he can do nothing. I watch as he tries to signal to us as the group of men begins to march up the road to waiting trucks. When he raises his hand, a soldier takes notice of him and runs up to him angrily. My baby brother is yanked from my father's arm by the soldier, who holds the little boy up by his ankle in one hand while he pulls out his Luger with the other and shoots the baby through the chest. Tossing my brother's body into the mud, the soldier uses his pistol to crush my father's jaw, sending him reeling into the crowd of prisoners. He is swallowed up by the crowd as it moves along, and my mother and I never see him again.

"My mother is crying, sobbing, but trying to keep from wailing openly. We are in another truck now. Filled with women and children. The trucks take us along winding roads through the forest, away from the town, until we get to a place that looks like a fortress of barbed wire fences and towers. We pass under a large set of doors, and above them is a strange sign: *Arbeit Macht Frei*. I know that this means "work gives freedom," but I am confused and terrified by it.

"We are taken to long rows of low-roofed barracks, where a man wearing a white coat stands outside the doors waiting for us. Standing with him is a man wearing the stripes of a prisoner, but who is strutting among us and smiling. He has a single gold tooth that marks his smile as something odd and somehow frightening.

"Behind the barracks there are brick buildings like warehouses and bunkers and factories with smokestacks that are pouring out black smoke. There are more soldiers, forcing us out of the trucks where we stand in a huge crowd. There is barbed wire everywhere and we are like farm animals in pens. They yell for us to take off our clothes and many of the women begin crying. Some of them will not undress and the soldiers either crush their heads with rifle butts, or they just shoot them with their little pistols. I can hear the soldiers laughing at us, and it is a sound that is suddenly terrifying. Twilight covers us as we finally stand naked and shivering, feeling the cold leering stares of the soldiers as well as the bite of a gathering wind.

"Coldly, the officers turn from us and look in the direction of the man in the white coat and the smiling prisoner who is carrying a notebook and seems to be his assistant. According to the gestures of the man in white, some of the crowd is pulled off to a smaller line that winds off to the barracks.

"The rest of us receive less attention from the man I begin thinking of as a doctor, but his smiling prisoner-friend never stops his leering attention and seems to delight in our debased nakedness.

He tells us he is going to be 'our little angel' and I assume he will be watching over us, taking care of us. I am wrong.

"I watch as the women and children are herded into long lines that snake down into two buildings with double doors. There are smokestacks behind the buildings filling the air with thick, greasy soot. It falls over us like a foul-smelling, black snow.

"My mother hugs me and I feel her naked breasts against me. She is warm and soft and she is so beautiful to me. 'I love you, Sarah,' she says. 'And believe it or not, God loves you, too.' I hold her so tightly it hurts my arms. As we get closer to the big double doors, I hear some of the women screaming as they try to run the other way. One woman pushes her little girl away from her and starts yelling at the soldiers that she has no kids, that she doesn't belong here. The soldiers think this is funny. They are all laughing and smiling as one of them picks the little girl whose mother is trying to get away from her. The soldier tells her to hold her, that everything will be just fine, and the woman begins to cry, pulling the girl to her. I watch as the soldier shoots both of them with one bullet—it goes right through the little girl and into her mother.

"The big doors open and my mother carries me into a room that is big and dim and empty. There are pipes running along the ceiling, no windows, no furniture. I hear the metal doors clang shut and the muffled prayers of so many weeping women. 'I will never be away from you, my angel,' says my mother. I try to say something to her, but the darkness seems to get heavier and the air gets very hot. My tongue begins to swell up and my nose stings and my eyes burn so badly they begin to bulge. My spit turns into paste and my throat and lungs feel like they are catching fire. It feels like my chest has been split open with an ax and fire pours in. Sparks of light sparkle in front of my eyes as red foam bubbles from my mother's mouth. She collapses and falls on me as the darkness and endless fire lace through me with a thousand points of pain. My mother begins to shake, and I feel her whole body writhe and convulse over me. It is a violent, terrible dance of death. All around me, I hear the bubbling screams of the dying and then there is nothing left but darkness and pain stretching to the edge of forever. . . ."

Michael only now realized he'd closed his eyes as he suddenly blinked them open to stare at the suddenly silent woman seated before him. He'd seen the look on her face before—that of a patient who had finally expelled all the poison, so totally *emptied* they could speak no more, could barely see or hear. There was nothing to do until Allison Enders recovered from the session. Gradually, slowly, she was pulling herself out of the void, the place where *nothing* remained but the empty husks of her dreams, the loosed cages of her fears. Her breathing had become more stable and she had rubbed her eyes. Checking his watch, he could see he would be late for his benefit dinner. But did he really care? They would have no choice but to wait for him, or do without his words.

He used the time to reflect upon Allison's session, and his first impression was the high degree of detail contained in her descriptions. Detail which added a layer of not only reality but a hard-edged loathing, a palpable horror that lingered at the edges of his thoughts. Hers was no ordinary nightmare. He was also impressed with her command of the language and wondered if she normally possessed such a range of vocabulary and lyrical expression.

Somehow, he doubted it. The average person in America employed a vocabulary of fewer than 400 words, while being familiar with the meaning of no more than 900.

Michael shook his head and smiled ironically as he was reminded of the ancient Greeks with 4000 words at their disposal. . . . *And we Americans think we're so civilized!*

There was something about her descriptions of the Nazis that touched him as had no other accounts. Allison spoke with such an exact knowledge of the events, but also with a naïveté that was curious. She did not seem to know the soldiers' identity, their collective name. Or at least the character in her dream did not know.

The case of Allison Enders excited him. She represented a real, professional challenge. Instinctively, he knew this was no prosaic case of parental fumbling and the resultant, familiar path of resentments, fears, and rejections. No. There was something substantive and dynamic at work. Maybe he was looking at a real case of multiple personality? Not necessarily the sensationalism of the well-known Bridey Murphy case, but maybe the chance to create a thoroughly detailed case study like *The Three Faces of Eve*. As strange as it might seem, Allison Enders might make him famous in his field.

Appropriate to the drama of her entrance into his office, Allison's story had *invaded* him, and Michael could feel himself responding automatically.

She was looking at him now, apparently relaxed enough to refocus her attention on the attendant reality of their session. He'd been letting his thoughts run freely, but now he knew he had to rein them in, take control of the encounter. Looking at her, he smiled gently. No teeth, just a friendly grin, but without the connotations of impishness.

"How do you feel, Allison?"

She raked her fingers through her hair, nodded. "Better, thank you. I feel a lot better. . . ."

"Can you explain what you mean by 'better'?"

"I . . . I don't think I'm afraid to go to sleep. Afraid to dream like I was."

"Is that why you came here in the first place?"

"Yeah. I couldn't go back to sleep and go through that anymore."

"The end of the dream?"

"The end, yes," she said. "It's only the last month or so that it's taken me that far. To the end. Where I . . ."

"Where you *die*," he said. There was no sense avoiding the core of the experience.

"Yes, where I . . . die." Allison rubbed her mouth nervously, tried to get more comfortable in the chair.

"Go on," he said.

"I can't! It's too real," she said in a sudden outburst. "I couldn't keep going through that! Over and over. Night after night."

"And you thought killing yourself was the only answer, but you didn't have the courage to go through with it."

She nodded. "But I wanted to. I *really* wanted to."

Michael nodded, waited for her to go on.

"What's wrong with me?" she said, sounding anxious. "Am I crazy?"

"No," he said. "Not at all."

"Can you help me?"

"Yes, I think so. But you're going to find you'll be able to help yourself as well."

"I hope you're right. I can't keep going through this." She chuckled ironically. "I drove Kevin nuts with it. He got so sick of holding me in the middle of the night, getting pulled out of a deep sleep by my screams, hearing the same story over and over."

"I need to ask you a few more questions," said Michael. "Is that all right?"

"Sure. Anything."

"You said it's the same dream, each night?"

Allison nodded. "Every time it would come to me, yes. And every time, it would go a little farther. Until now. And now it's at the end."

"The end, yes. And you feel that you . . . experience death every time the dream comes?"

She nodded vigorously. "It's horrible. You can't imagine it."

"Do you recognize what it is you are describing to me?"

"Of course. It's the concentration camps, the Jews getting killed. You know—they call it the Holocaust." She answered him with a hint of anger.

"Does my question upset you?"

"No, not really. It's just that I might have done a stupid thing—coming in here with that gun. But I'm not a stupid person. I read a lot. I like The Learning Channel and the Discovery Channel."

Michael nodded. "Perhaps I should have worded my question differently. The person you are in the dream, the little girl, she doesn't seem to know the historical facts, and so—"

"How *could* she?!" Allison said in a rush. "Sarah's just a little girl. They killed me when I was just a little girl!

"I understand," he said. "Let's go on, shall we?"

Allison looked contrite. "I'm sorry. Yes."

"Are you Jewish?"

"No. My parents were Lutheran. I don't know *what* I am—agnostic, I guess."

"Any Jewish relatives or close friends?"

She shrugged. "No relatives. Quite a few of the people I work with are Jewish. In television. Why?"

"Do you think you have any special interest in the Jewish faith or their culture?"

"I'm not very religious," she said. "And as far as the rest of it, about the culture, no. I grew up in a small town in Ohio. There were hardly any Jews in the whole town. I never even *heard* of kosher or Yiddish till I came to New York."

Michael paused, watched her as she settled back into her chair. She was being truthful; it was revealed in her body language and her tone of voice. "Why do you think this is happening to you?"

She shrugged. "I don't know."

"Have you ever had elaborate dreams like this before? Dreams that repeat like this one? A history of nightmares?"

"No, *never*. Just this one."

"Do you think this is just a dream, or do you think it could be something else?"

Allison looked at him sharply, and something flared behind her dark eyes. He knew he had probed into a sensitive area. "It's not just a dream," she said in a very flat voice.

"What do you mean? How do you know."

"I think it's *real*. I think there really *was* a girl named Sarah and she died, just like in this dream."

Michael nodded. "I see. And have you tried to check any of the details? The facts?"

"What do you mean?"

Michael shrugged. "Was there any detail in your dream that would tell us what city your little girl lived in? The year?"

"I don't remember offhand."

Michael tapped his pencil on the desk blotter. "There's always hypnosis," he said as much to himself as to his patient.

"You can do that?"

"Yes, Ms. Enders. I use the technique frequently. Do you have any objections to being hypnotized?"

She shook her head. "Not if it'll help."

"It may. We can schedule that for your next session. We'll try to get some more information so we can check the historical record—if there is one."

"Is that possible?" Allison looked for an instant like the little girl that lurked in her dreams.

"There are databases and organizations we can check, yes, I think so. It's a good place to start." Absently he glanced at the office window. Twilight had receded, lapping the shores of total nightfall. It was getting very late.

"Do you have any idea what all this means? Or *why*? Why it's happening to me?"

"I have some initial thoughts, but we're not far enough along for me to offer them to you." Michael tried to smile gently again. "We're going to have to try to gather more data, more information. It wouldn't be very smart to try to guess at what might be going on."

"What about my dreams?"

He looked at her, confused. "What about them?"

"Will they still come?"

That was a good question, and he had no idea what to tell her.

The very act of unloading the entire story, the "secret," as it were, might have been enough to quell the maddening repetition. Or it may have only been the beginning of a new set of problems. . . .

"It's too early to tell," said Michael. "We'll have to wait and see."

"I think I can do it."

"Good," he said. "That's good to hear you say that."

Allison stood up and tried to smile. "It's so late. I should go," she said. "I know I've kept you."

"It's no big deal," he said, standing in respect and also to stretch his own legs.

"How can I pay you for what you've done?" She reached for her purse. "And I know I messed up your schedule."

"Ms. Enders, please . . ."

She suddenly burst into tears. "I'm so sorry. It's just hitting me—what a terrible person I was to just break in here. God, I'm sorry for what I've done to you. . . ."

Michael walked around the desk, put his arms around her. How he hated dealing with women who wouldn't stop with their weeping! It was the single most difficult part of his job, and a task he'd never seemed to learn how to do well. No matter what he said, it was never the correct response and always seemed to launch women into a new round of tears. "Allison, listen to me, honestly— you haven't done anything wrong."

"I just want you to know how sorry I am. . . ."

"Just relax now," he said, stepping back from her. He took her hands in his. "I want you to call my assistant, Ms. Robbins. Call her Monday and make another appointment. I'll see you as often as you'd like, until we get to the bottom of your problem, okay?"

"But I'm not sure I can afford this sort of thing. I was just so . . . so lost."

"Don't worry about the cost," he said. "I have plenty of patients who can afford to pay me. Your case interests me. Enough for me to want to work with you at no charge."

Allison looked at him with naked surprise. "You're not kidding, are you?"

"Not at all. I'm usually a very serious man."

"Oh, thank you, Doctor Keating . . . Thank you."

"You're welcome," he said, smiling.

"Thank you," she said again as she retreated toward the door.

"Promise to call me if you have trouble tonight."

"I promise."

"Good night, Ms. Enders. I look forward to our next session."

She nodded and left the room. Slowly he followed her to the threshold of his office, watched her exit the reception room, the door click-locking behind her. It was only then that he realized she'd left that damned gun in Pamela's desk.

Fine. A problem for his receptionist to deal with, not him.

A glance at the wall clock confirmed the hunger gnawing at him. It was late, and he'd now be a tardy arrival to the benefit dinner. But he realized he didn't care. Today had been a good day. The tragic and strange Ms. Allison Enders had forced her way into his life and made him realize why he'd originally found psychiatry so intriguing, so much of a challenge to the human spirit and imagination.

Walking to his private washroom, Michael looked at himself in the mirror and grinned his trademark grin. His face remained uncreased despite the stress of his profession, the laws of gravity, and time. His complexion was clear and gave him a healthy, vibrant aspect. His hair was still mostly dark, matching his eyes, and women still found him attractive. Surprisingly, he'd discovered that the older he became, the *more* women seemed to be intrigued with him. And he wasn't stupid enough to discount his financial stability as well as his associations with people of true power and influence. All these things were of interest and import to women of substance.

But after one disastrous marriage, he'd been in no hurry to find another woman for supposedly the rest of his life. As long as he had his books and music, and pastimes like baseball and the archeology group, he'd convinced himself he was a happy man.

As he locked up the office and walked to the elevators, he kept replaying Allison Enders' dream—a running tableau of hard-edged images that detailed the terrible death of a little girl more than half a century past.

Michael's instincts were often uncannily correct, and he had a very definite feeling about this afternoon's entire encounter. There was more to the experience than was first apparent—this he knew in his gut. As he left his building and watched for an available cab on Riverside, he decided he would pursue the source of Allison Enders' night terrors.

FOUR

MORRIS LITTLEJOHN
Bath, England

Morry knew it was going to be a bad day from the moment he woke up.

For starters, he'd had one bugger of a bad dream. And even though he could *never* remember his dreams, he knew he'd been sweating up his bedclothes for a reason.

Must have been one hell of a bloody nightmare . . .

Good, then, that he'd never remember the sod.

Then, half asleep, he shambled to the loo and jammed his big toe on the threshold. He wanted to shriek out his pain, but bent low, clamped one hand over his mouth and the other over his throbbing digit. It would just make things worse to wake up Maggie. Jaw muscles gradually relaxing, he stood at the window, waiting for the pain to dull down. Outside, the streets of his quiet neighborhood of Larkhall were still awash in the dun colors of night. A man wearing a cap stood just beyond the pool of light from a streetlamp, and Morry could just barely see his shape edging out of the shadows. The man seemed to be just standing there, looking up at the square of light that defined his bathroom window.

Now what would anybody be doing out there at this hour?

thought Morry as he reached for some tooth powder and his brush. When he looked back out the window, the figure near the street-light had vanished. He rubbed his eyes, massaged his temples and looked at his ruddy face in the mirror.

Thank bloody Christ he wasn't waking up with one of those par-alyzing migraines again. . . .

Sometimes, when he knew he'd been having a bad dream, he'd come up from the dead, dark nothingness of sleep with a headache that felt like somebody'd left a hatchet half-buried in his skull. Talk about starting off the day on a bad patch. . . .

He washed up and shaved mechanically as he'd done every morning for the last nineteen years, working all that time with Bigston Reilly Van Lines. As he buttoned up his company coveralls, he reflected on the one, real job he'd had as an adult—something he found himself doing more and more as he grew ever older.

Almost forty years old and he was nothing more than a moving man. He told people he was a "driver" because that could cover any number of sins, but driving the company's lorry was only a small part of the job. The majority of his days were consumed with lug-ging and lifting, grunting and huffing, easing and muscling. Furniture and office fixtures. His company specialized in the "diffi-cult" jobs, so that meant lots of pianos and safes and custom-made conference tables, as well all the usual rubbish people can't bring themselves to toss when they move from one wretched, little warren to another.

Forty years old, and Morris Littlejohn wondered what the rest of his life was going to be like. At more than six feet and two hundred twenty pounds, he had strapping good size and strength. But for how much longer? How long could he continue to put his body under all that stress and punishing bull-work? What had he been thinking when he'd seen older men on his truck being told they no longer had a job because they were no longer strong enough, no longer young enough?

And when would it happen to him? How many good years left?

He shook his head as he left his little terraced house and eased his bulk behind the wheel of his little Escort. One of these days he was going to need another car, and then what? With Maggie losing her job at W. H. Smith, things would be tight until she could find something to put a few extra quid in the till. The old Escort was going to have to hang on for a little while longer. His mind on the pressing facts of working-class life, he hit the A4 and followed it through the center of Bath. Morry had driven this route so many times, he could probably do it in his bloody sleep.

He suddenly came to full attention in the middle of the city, just about at the point where the A4 changed its name from the London Road to the Lower Bristol Road. How had he driven so far without even realizing it? Scary stuff, that. . . .

As he drove west past the British Rail station, he continued to think about his future. He and Maggie'd never had the money for kids, and she was complaining that soon she'd be too old to have 'em without asking for problems.

Kids.

Just what he needed to keep him awake at night and put new pressure on a budget that was already buckling under. . . .

And what about when they were ten or fifteen years old? And he was on the wrong side of fifty and Bigston Reilly was fixing to tell him to hang up his overalls? What then? Oh, he'd be in a fine mess, he would. Nothing like looking forward to going on the dole at a time when some people were planning to retire to a quiet cottage in the Cotswolds.

Fine mess he'd be in, for sure. . . .

He stopped at a transport café off Castor Road for some tea and a couple of bangers and rolls. The waitress was a skinny, young girl with an earring in her nose and very bad teeth. She smiled at him for the morning-regular he was and prepared a plate of his usual order. Smiling, he slid her several pounds, scooped up his change, and walked slowly to a booth by the window overlooking the main road. Bath was half as much a tourist town as anything, and in the winter months, there just weren't that many people out and about. Traffic was light, other than the occasional early-rising working stiffs like himself.

Back when he was right out of secondary school, his father had wanted him to learn a trade. The Littlejohns had been a long, proud line of tradesmen (Morris' grandfather had been his town's last cooper, making barrels for the local brewery; his father had labored as a first-class machinist for Wessex Tool and Die), and it had been expected that Morris would select a trade and begin his apprentice-ship.

But he'd buggered them up, hadn't he? Morry had it in his muddled head that he wanted to be a rock star. Guitars and drugs and plenty of birds. The next David Bowie or Elton John at least, although he'd really wanted to be the one to take the throne from King Mick. And so he took a succession of dreary jobs while he wrote his music and his tunes and played in Gramps' garage with his mates. Like so many thousands before him, his band never got beyond the wedding and club circuit. Never got the look or the nod from the right record scout.

Eight bleeding years he toughed it out before finally listening to what everybody was telling him. And by then he'd already been driving for Bigston Reilly a few years, and he met himself the girl he was going to marry and, well, it was time to start earning a living, right?

The bangers slid down his throat without giving up the slightest whit of taste. He'd been eating the same breakfast at the same place for so long, his taste buds had long ago given up being on the alert. He knew his life was heading for a collision with a brick wall, and if it wasn't already too late, he was going to have to find something important and meaningful to do with the rest of his days. Maybe he would take a weekend and—

His thoughts locked up on him like an engine losing its oil pan as he saw the man come into the café.

Tall, with an angular face, and the cap he'd seen on the figure near the streetlamp. The man's broad shoulders filled his black leather jacket, muscular thighs swelled his jeans. He moved with a stealthy, confident grace as he approached the counter. Morry couldn't stop looking at this stranger, this intruder upon the humdrum of his life.

The man didn't even glance in Morry's direction as he walked to a table with his tray of tea and sausage rolls. The man sat down and pulled from his pocket a paperback book by James Herbert. Nobody else seemed to notice the newcomer, but Morry found himself growing outright uncomfortable, even a touch frightened by the other man's presence.

But why?

What was going on here? Morry had no reason to feel this way. No reason to *fear* this man. Odds on him being the same character who'd been lurking across the street from his house were practically nil, weren't they?

Just your bleedin' imagination getting away from you, it was.

Regardless, Morry felt an overwhelming urge to dash down the rest of his hot tea and get off to the warehouse early. And so, a couple of anxious swallows later, he was out the door and stuffing himself into the Escort's ill-designed driver's seat. Keying the ignition, he chanced a look toward the window of the shop. The engine caught and his foot slipped off the clutch, making the car hitch up in reverse and die. Morry hadn't been paying attention because there, through the window, dark eyes burning through the glass, the stranger was staring at him.

Christ! he thought as he struggled to get the car moving. *Just get out of here! Don't let the bastard see you freaking out.* Good plan, that. But the Escort wasn't in the mood. Once stalled, it just sat there while he almost twisted off the key in its slot. The starter continued to grind and the car wouldn't budge. Morry had looked away from the window, trying to appear disinterested, casual even, but the stalled car seemed to be screaming for attention. Everyone had to be watching him by now.

Just a peek, he thought.

Just a quick cut of his eyes toward the angular man in the cap. He had to know.

Then suddenly, the little car's engine kicked in, belching and farting white smoke. As Morry slipped it back into gear and clutched into reverse, he scanned the café with a quick glance to the side.

The man's gaze had him targeted like a turkey in a gunsight.

Get. The. Bloody. Hell. Out. Of. Here!

The thought hammered out its urgent message, and the car lurched forward, bucking and hitching its way back onto Manvers Road. What an embarrassment . . . ! How *daft* he must've looked to everyone back there, especially the stranger.

The newcomer.

The shadow man.

The image would not leave him as he pushed down on the accelerator and the Escort finally smoothed out as it picked up speed along the still dark, tree-lined roadway. His headlights burned a path for him, and automatically he negotiated the turns along the Lower Bristol Road that led to the van lines' central warehouse near the banks of the Avon. His thoughts, meanwhile, centered on the weird encounters of his morning so far.

Coincidence. That's all it was. There was nothing to any of it. The man in black leather was watching him because his motorcar was acting like a stubborn mule in the carpark. To make anything more of it was to make Morry sound like some crazy paranoid the likes of which were calling in to Radio Four all the time to talk about crop circles and witch's covens in their villages.

Load of rubbish is all. . . .

He kept going over these basic concepts until he reached the warehouse and went into the foreman's shack to get his papers for the day.

"Mornin', Mor'," said Ollie McGill, his foreman. McGill had been with the company forty years and looked it: fat, bald, and red gin blotches on his face fighting for space with all the liver spots.

"How's it, Ollie?" said Morry, reaching for his clipboard hanging from a nail on the wall over McGill's filthy desk.

"Can't complain. In early, eh?"

"A little, I suppose. . . ." Only four sets of invoices were pinioned to his board, and that usually meant long pulls between pickups and drop-offs. The first stop was in Trowbridge and then a drop-off in Millcourt, a village just north of Salisbury. After that it was a long haul north to Swindon, then back to the south for a small job in Chippenham. As he'd imagined, it would be a long day, certain to pick up a few extra bob in overtime.

"Yer crew's not in yet," said Ollie, chewing on the stub of cigar he rarely lit. Last year his doc told him he was getting those white nodules on the inside of his lower lip that can turn into tumors. Since then, Ollie just kind of chewed and moistened his cigars, then sucked the juice out of 'em a little at a time. It wasn't pretty to look at, and it didn't *sound* any better, either.

"Who's running with me today?" said Morry, not really caring, but preferring a hollow chat with McGill to thinking about some weirdo watching him through the bathroom window.

"Freddie and the Duke."

Morry nodded, but inwardly he was smiling enthusiastically. All the drivers wanted the Duke on their lorry—he was a big West Indian who didn't talk much and had the strength of any two other men. Maybe it wasn't going to be such a bad day after all.

Grabbing up the morning *Express*, Morry went down to the dock and climbed up into his cab, reading the doings of the world until his crew arrived . . . and trying to keep his mind off the guy in the leather jacket.

"Christ, that was a tussle, wasn't it?" said Freddie as he bounced along in the lorry's passenger seat. He gestured with his thumb back toward the enclosed van, where the Duke sat in stony silence. "Good thing we had the big cricket player with us, eh?"

"You always say that," said Morry, watching the oncoming traffic squeeze them as he hauled their full load along the winding A-road.

"Guess I do," said Freddie, a young man still in his twenties who didn't seem to have a dream or an ambition in his head—other than to pick up his pay and spend the weekend in the clubs looking for some skirt. He was gazing absently out his window to the north. "Going right by old Stonehenge, are we?"

"I suspect . . ." said Morry, idly watching the road ahead. He was not much interested in the rolling countryside of the Salisbury Plain.

"Getting hungry," said Freddie as he tapped Morris' elbow. "Let's stop at the next village and find a pub. I could go for a pint of Newcastle."

Morry checked his watch. "You want to eat before we pitch this stuff?"

"Why not?" Freddie shrugged.

Why not, indeed, thought Morry. It was close enough to lunch to knock off for a spell. The pickup at Trowbridge had taken most of the morning, as he'd figured, so it was about time for a break. He swung the lorry and their heavy load into the next village, a little burg called Hedgeton, parking the big brown and orange van on the central street.

"Did you see a pub round here?" asked Freddie as he walked to the back of the van to spring the latch and set free the Duke.

But Morry wasn't hearing any of it. He'd just dropped down to the paving when he noticed a low-slung sedan behind them glide up the central street, then turn left onto a side street. The driver was only visible for an instant, but that was all Morry had needed.

The man in the cap.

Black Leather Jacket. The Café Man. Whatever he wanted to call him. The bastard was following him. Stalking him. What the hell was going on here?

"You gonna let that big monkey out of his cage or what?" said Freddie with a silly grin on his long, pale face.

"What's that?" said Morry as a knot of anxiety twisted up in his bowels.

"Christ, mate . . . what gives? You look like some bugger knocked the wind out of your sails! You okay?"

"I . . ." Morry struggled to get his thoughts together. *It was him. What's he doing here?*

"I said you gonna let the Duke out or what?"

"Oh . . . right . . . of course I am," said Morry, knocking back the latch and throwing up the van's sliding panel. The big West Indian man was crouched at the edge, surrounded by stacked-up office furniture. He gave them one of his usual, big-as-piano-keys smiles.

"What is it we're doin', mahn?" he said as he jumped down to the street.

Morry must have been still staring blankly at the now empty side street behind them, because suddenly Freddie tapped his shoulder and he wheeled quickly on him, uttering a startled *"Huh!"*

"Hey, mate, what's with you all of a sudden?"

"You look like you seen a jimmie-jahm, mahn!" The Duke chuckled at his own little joke.

"I . . . I don't know what I seen," said Morry. They were both looking at him queerlike, and he figured it best to try to push it off. No sense getting them into it. Besides, they'd probably think he was slipping his tether.

"Somebody was a-walkin' on yore grave, Mistah Mawrris," said the Duke. "Happens sometimes."

"Fook it," said Freddie. "Let's get us a pint."

With that, he led them down the road less than a block to a corner pub called the Russet Quiver. They entered the cool darkness of the place, and Morry instantly smelled the hoppy aroma of spilled spirits on the wood floor. If a pub didn't have that odor, it was either too new or too clean—and in any case, not authentic.

They docked at the bar and Freddie hailed the landlord for three pints of Newcastle plus some fish and chips. They took their glasses to a booth by the street window, and Morry found himself scanning the street for another glimpse of Mr. Leather Jacket. His mates' conversation had drifted to the football scores and how Tottenham was looking stronger than ever, but he was only half listening as he gulped from his pint.

Settle down. Get sensible. The brown ale calmed him a bit, and he started telling himself he'd been mistaken, that he'd just seen some lad who only *looked* like the one in the transport café. What was the chance, really? And for *what*?

Why would anybody want to stalk him? He didn't have a pile socked away somewhere, and he wasn't famous, and if the Café Man was a bit of an arse bandit, Morry certainly wasn't what you would call "cute."

Quaffing down the last of his Newcastle, Morry chanced a little grin. Sure, that was it. Coincidence and then a little mistaken identity.

A waitress brought them their food in hot baskets lined with paper serviettes and they all dug in like hungry sailors. They had shared their assessments of several women walking past the window and a few laughs, and suddenly Morry was feeling much better. The mealtime passed without sight or another thought of any trouble.

Half an hour later, and the three of them were sustained and fueled for the rest of the day's labors. Morry led them back down the street to their truck, first sealing the Duke in the rear compartment, then climbing into the cab. Freddie climbed in the passenger's side, and Morry turned the key. He listened to the engine backfire and grind into action, and—

What?

—the left side of his face was suddenly stinging. Something spattered his cheek like a wet slap. Something heavy and warm. And his shoulder erupted into fiery pain.

The sensation was so sudden and unpleasant he was shocked, and the thought lightninged through him that Freddie had upchucked his lunch all over him or maybe emptied a spitoon in his face.

But Freddie had done something far worse.

He'd gotten his head in the way of a hollow-point slug, and it had erupted like a melon under a mallet. The pulp and mist of his brains had smacked Morry's left side in a shiny, gray-and-pink patina. Fragments of the slug had also tagged his shoulder and bicep, both bleeding freely. Freddie's almost headless corpse lurched to the right to reveal the Café Man and his canonlike handgun filling the passenger door window.

"Christ!" screamed Morry as he lurched against the closed

driver's door. His foot slipped the clutch and the lorry surged forward before stalling out. The movement was just enough to foul the man's aim. The silenced bullet singed Morry's nosehairs as it passed.

Automatically, he'd yanked the door handle and was suddenly tumbling free of the cab. Another shot whispered from the gun and the slug exploded his shoulder, pieces of himself rocketing away from the impact like holiday fireworks.

Running wildly away from the truck, up the narrow village street, Morry was barely aware of the pain from his ravaged shoulder. Blood rivered down his overalls, clinging to his flesh warm and sticky. His left arm hung useless at his side as he ran, stumbling and staggering. At one point he brushed the brick of a building and the pain radiated through his left side like a road flare going off.

Keep moving.

Run.

Any second he expected another bullet to exit his chest or splatter his skull like a piece of overripe fruit. But he pushed himself forward, trying to run, trying to gain the corner of the building, the perpendicular side street.

Don't let the bastard get you.

His feet seemed suddenly huge, like clown feet, slapping the cobblestones, threatening to trip him in a deadly, final fall. He staggered, reeled, felt himself slowing down. Things were beginning to look hazy, as if a veil had fallen over his eyes.

What was happening?

Your blood. Losing way too much.

If he let himself, he could slouch down, slide off the wall of the building and just pass out. An almost *overwhelming* urge to close his eyes and sleep reached for him like spent waves at beach's edge.

Finally, he reached the end of the block, and as though moving through quicksand, he turned the corner.

Twin rows of buildings seemed to lean in toward one another.

The street seemed impossibly long. Narrow. Deserted.

The gunman.

Where . . . ?

And other people in the village—didn't they see what was going on? Where *was* everybody? Why didn't somebody come out to give him a hand?

Lurching along the sidewalk like some bad actor in a B movie, Morry looked for a doorway, a gate, anywhere he could slip in and hide. His overalls were stained almost black with blood now, and he knew he might look a fright, but *somebody* had to help him, somebody had—

"That will be the last of it," said the voice.

From behind him, the man spoke in even tones, an accent foreign but not placeable. He had a pleasant voice, resonant and full like a BBC announcer.

Slumping against a closed door, Morry slowly turned to face his predator. The man in the leather jacket loomed over him like a piece of polished sculpture. His face was angular, with an unfinished look, as if his creator had been using a dull chisel. He held the large-bore gun up close to Morry's temple, but slowly retracted it, nestling it deep within his jacket.

"What . . . do . . . you . . . want . . . ?" Morry's own voice sounded so *thin* to him, so weak, like a tin whistle with a hole in it.

"You would not understand," said the man. "I am not certain that even I do."

Morry coughed and pain pitchforked through his shoulder and upper chest. He felt dizzy, almost giddy. "Why don't you give it a go, mate? Try me."

The man sighed as he flicked his wrist and a swivel-jointed razorknife unfolded instantly. "I only know I must kill you."

"But *why*? I don't even know you!!"

The man reached out and grabbed Morry by his thinning hair, pushing his head back against the door, exposing and stretching the pale tube of his neck. There was the sound of a *snick!* and a flood of something hot and coppery-wet.

The man smiled and spoke softly.

"You *do* know me . . . in your *dreams*."

The last three words Morris Littlejohn ever heard jolted through him as no bullets ever could. The final seconds of his life stretched out, like warm toffy. And the frantic, idiot buzz of his last thoughts gyred around a single dream-image: a tall, bald man, smiling, his gold front tooth shining in the gray light of the camp dawn.

FIVE

J. MICHAEL KEATING, M.D.
Manhattan, New York

Several days passed, and Michael became increasingly obsessed with the Allison Enders case. On Monday, after Pamela disposed of the woman's handgun (he didn't want to know any of the details), he realized he wasn't in the proper mindset to deal with his regular patients. After two morning sessions, in which he'd sat there daydreaming, he blinked his eyes to suddenly discover his thoughts had drifted great distances from the concerns of his patients.

And this disturbed him a lot—because he prided himself on being an honest man, a man of principles, who could be trusted and depended upon to perform as people expected him to. His father had lectured him through all of his childhood that the most important virtue was to be a responsible person—to yourself and to those around you. One's level of responsibility was an accurate barometer of one's character. Michael believed this implicitly, and it was the single most important character trait he looked for in everyone he met. If they were intelligent, creative, industrious, or whatever else, it was all for nothing if they weren't responsible people.

And here he sat, taking up his patients' time and their money, and he would suddenly realize that *he hadn't even been listening; he had no idea what they were talking about.* Very disconcerting, to be sure, but even more embarrassing to himself, even though no one else would ever know.

Try as he might, he couldn't get the session with Allison Enders from his mind. Meeting this woman marked a pivotal moment in his life. He couldn't shake that belief and desperately didn't want to call it *intuition*—because his logical, empirical side had always refused to admit such nonsense existed.

At last, his appointments for the day wrapped up. His 4:00 P.M. patient had departed, and he'd reached the hour in the day when he'd usually unwind by translating a few pages of one of his books. But not today. Touching the hot button on his intercom, he spoke firmly: "Pamela, could you come in here for a moment?"

Only a second passed before his assistant opened the door and leaned into the office. Wearing one of her trademark tailored suits, Pamela Robbins looked at him. Her auburn hair accented her full features, the most prominent her large, expressively dark eyes. "Yes, Doctor?"

"Sit down for a minute, Pamela," he said softly. "I need to talk."

She glided into the office, taking the chair opposite his desk. She had a smooth, efficient way of moving, which contributed to her appearance of a woman completely in charge of her life and surroundings. "Well, now, that *is* a switch, isn't it?" She smiled, making him wonder if she was just being friendly or . . . something else.

"I'm going to need to take a break. A week or so, I think." He had the urge to get up and pace the room, to not look her in the eye, but he fought the mild panic he was feeling as he knew he was about to reveal some of his inner feelings. "Can you reschedule all the appointments?"

"Sure," she said, looking at him with genuine compassion. "Are you okay? Still upset about Ms. Enders?"

"I don't know if 'upset' is the right word. More like . . . concerned . . . but I don't need for it to become . . . obsessive."

"If you're worried about that gun, I've already—"

Michael waved her off with a waggle of his hand. "That gun's the least of my concerns." He gave her a brief summary of his session with Allison Enders, the dreams, the details, the feeling that the woman might be an exceptional case of multiple personality, that she might be the makings of a noteworthy case study. Afterward, Pamela sat silently.

"I need more time with this patient," he said.

"To the exclusion of all your others? Is that fair?"

Michael grinned ironically. "Fair? Nothing in this line of work is very 'fair.' Most of the time I just have to use my judgment to decide what's most urgent, what my own priorities must be. Listen, Pamela, there's something really fascinating about this Enders case. I've got to pursue it, don't you see what I mean?"

"I . . . think I do," she said in almost a whisper.

"Okay, good. Please contact Ms. Enders and see if she can see me tomorrow at her convenience."

Pamela nodded and looked at him.

"There's more to this whole thing than we might think," he said, finally giving in to the urge to do a little pacing. He got free of his chair and stood behind it like an actor preparing for a monologue. "I can't explain it, but I know I have to pursue it."

"I understand, Michael."

He found himself getting hung up on her last word. It was the first time she'd ever called him by his first name, and it had sounded so natural, so . . . appropriate that she do that. It suggested an intimacy not really present between them, a "comfortableness" at least, that he obviously required right now. Having lived alone for so many years, he'd almost forgotten the times when a man can't be stolid and solitary, when he needs the quiet comfort of a woman's confidence. She must have sensed this and offered it to him. No promises. No strings attached.

Slowly, he began pacing behind the desk, pausing every now and again to look absently out his window. "It's almost the year two thousand," he said. "In less than a year . . ."

Pamela looked at him, nodded, but offered no comment. He took it as a signal to continue his ramblings. ". . . and it's supposed to be a time of great changes, of all kinds of apocalyptic babble. Remember that lecture I gave about the millennium? It's already been bringing out the crazies and the weirdos. The end-of-the-worlders. Remember that cult that occupied the Grand Canyon a couple of months back? The End-Time Coalition, or whatever they called themselves. It's a crazy time, don't you think?"

"Is that what you think this is about? Ms. Enders . . . ?" Pamela didn't conceal her confusion.

"Not really," said Michael, smiling gently. "I don't know. I'm just free-associating, as they say. Letting my thoughts slip their leashes. I mean, you seem to pay a lot of attention to world socio-economic politics . . ."

"Sure," she said. "The world's in flux right now. Look at the banking systems in places like Switzerland, Japan, and Germany and you can see we're in trouble. If they collapse, Europe's going to be devastated economically. The Third World industrialists in Malaysia and Vietnam, and of course China, have been *burying* us with superior products and cheap labor."

Michael smiled thinly. He'd pushed one of Pamela's hot buttons: her notions of strategic economics.

"If it weren't for much of the Third World still being in the hands of fundamentalists, the West might already have been crushed. Lots of people in Europe and North America aren't accustomed to hardship anymore."

"Meaning?"

"Meaning hard times often look to hard solutions—like abdication of personal freedoms. I'm a Libertarian," said Pamela. "And that kind of thinking bothers me."

Michael nodded. "Jung saw the wheels of history grinding like the clockwork of a great machine, and he suggested maybe there *is* a cycle, a loop that must be traveled. Many economic thinkers see a horrible depression taking shape. Not just here but almost throughout the world."

"You mean maybe there *is* something to this Apocalypse stuff?" said Pamela.

Michael shrugged. "I'm only a parrot on stuff like that. I can talk back to you what I've heard the other guys saying. I don't know how valid it might be, but I'm just trying to order things in my mind, you see. Because *everything's* connected, Pamela. No event ever really takes place independently of all others, and it *will* have an effect on everything else. The world society is changing, being shaped by many different forces: our money, our technology, our beliefs, our fears, and so many other factors. We've got be careful to not get swept away."

Again, she didn't comment, perhaps sensing that he'd needed to simply vent some anxiety and random thoughts of trouble that everyone must feel from time to time. And he appreciated that. He wasn't, by nature, a subscriber to every doom-and-gloom philosophy that achieved currency, but there was much in the wind these days that should seem troubling to anyone who cared to analyze it. Michael often joked to his friends and colleagues that he wasn't one of those people who saw the glass as either half-full or half-empty—he was more concerned with whether or not we were using the correct glass . . .

In the case of Allison Enders, Michael had no idea why he'd attached significance to her frightful dreams. Or why he'd even suggested they had a place in the larger scheme of world events . . . but he *had* tried, even if so feebly, to explain his feelings to Pamela Robbins. There was clearly much going on in his unconscious that would need time to ferment and develop. His mind kept racing ahead of his thoughts, seeking safe passage through the rough channels of anxiety, looking for beacons of understanding and a rationale. And it was his belief in himself, his own abilities to perceive and interpret reality, that would see him through this . . .

 . . . *crisis?*

The word came to him, but he didn't really think it was accurate. The feverish dreams of a stressed-out young woman would hardly qualify as the stuff to move mountains and warp the path of history, but Michael couldn't ignore the compulsion to give in to fears he suspected were atavistic and dripping with Jungian symbolism.

Granted, he'd found Ms. Enders dream-tale disturbing in a way he was never affected by the grimmest of accounts from any of his other patients. And also granted, he had no trouble confessing to an endless fascination with the Nazi horror that so laced the dream with the pervasiveness of a poisonous gas that inexorably drew him into the mystery of it all.

How the hell did it ever happen?

Isn't that the question we've all asked ourselves at one point or another? Generations of scholars, historians, theologians, and philosophers had devoted their entire careers attempting to explain the stark and inarguable *reality* of Hitler's dark empire. It was like trying to "explain" the random movements of dust motes against a sun-drenched windowpane. You couldn't do it.

How to understand even the *possibility* of the Nazis, was inconceivable. That they actually existed at all was an enigma no one might ever "explain."

Michael looked up suddenly, realizing he'd been daydreaming . . . far, far away from the sleek comforts of his office and the now curious gaze of his assistant. For a moment, he'd lost all sense of time. How long had he been drifting, musing, turning over his thoughts for casual inspection from all sides and angles?

Pamela must have sensed his unease and, professional as ever, moved to assist. "Is that it for now, Doctor?"

He nodded, as though embarrassed, but he forced himself to speak. "Thanks, yes. Be sure to call Ms. Enders and see what kind of schedule you can arrange for me."

"I will," said Pamela. She stood there, looking at him, expecting something else, but he was at a loss to read her correctly.

"Is there something I forgot?" he said.

"Are you planning to stay here for awhile?"

Michael sighed. It was a good question. He didn't know what he wanted to do. The idea of retreating into his evening routine of a solitary dinner at one of his usual restaurants, then a cab ride back to his co-op for several hours of reading, was somehow unattractive to him. She seemed to be aware of his state of mild agitation and confusion, and was offering . . . what? He decided to find out.

"To be honest," he said, "I don't know what I want to do."

"Then why don't you do it with me?"

"What?"

Pamela smiled. It was a pretty smile, one that she obviously did not allow everyone to see. Warm, radiant, inviting. "Have dinner with me. Talk if you want to. Or don't talk. It's up to you."

"That's quite an invitation," he said, genuinely surprised by it.

She shrugged. "It seemed like maybe you didn't want to be alone right now. I was just trying to tell you: you don't have to be . . ."

Michael admired her frankness. "Thanks," he said. "Let me get my coat."

SIX

ANNA SMITHSON
Chicago, Illinois

She'd forgotten to take her asthma medicine before leaving the house, but it was such a clear, clean day, Anna hoped it wouldn't matter. It was more of a bother than anything else, but sometimes she had the feeling that her asthma would cause her more trouble than anything else in her life.

But not today.

Asthma or not, it certainly was a pleasure to go into the city on a shopping spree, thought Anna as she parked her Riviera on the fourth floor of the parking garage off Dearborn. She locked her car and walked slowly to the elevators, being careful to adjust the blouse of her Donna Karan ensemble and accessorizing scarf so that everything fell just so. At forty-seven, she knew she still looked damned good, and still got whistles from passing cars and trucks when she was out jogging or walking. Watching her nutrition, exercising, and keeping abreast of the latest fashions had all contributed to her youthful body and face—her entire *look*.

She had paid an equal amount of attention to her mind and considered herself not only well read and widely cultured, but extremely interesting as well. Anna believed in herself, and it paid dividends every day. When the kids left the nest for college and their own lives, she started her own small mail-order catalog for one-of-a-kind art and sculpture, and the business had grown into a substantial little company.

Good thing, too.

When they found Stephen facedown on the blotter of his executive desk, his brain and his life short-circuited by a stroke at age fifty, she discovered his terrible secret. He'd been borrowing against his life insurance policies to play games with penny stocks on the Vancouver Stock Exchange. Other than some Social Security benefits, he left her with nothing but a lot of debt. It had shocked her at first, actually angered her—that he would do something like that. He hadn't planned on the stroke, figuring he'd have plenty of time to funnel his "play money" back into the proper assets.

But time had just . . . run out. Nothing to take personally, although it was hard to not feel cheated at the time. And gradually Anna accepted it for what it was—Stephen had simply miscalculated. She loved him, missed him, and often spoke of him as any respectful widow should. It had been several years now since she'd been on her own, and other than the occasional nightmare or migraine, she seemed to have survived all the stress and trauma associated with losing your husband and your security and your home all at the same time.

The migraines.

As she reached the street and began to idly search out the small shops and boutiques that featured not only the headline designer pieces, but also the works of the up-and-comers, she found herself dwelling on those terrible, blinding headaches.

Sometimes Anna could not stop thinking about them, fearing them, and the way they would just burn into her head from out of nowhere.

And the nightmares.

Yes, go on and toss them in as well. Dark, grim, full of death images. The doctors had told her the nightmares were a natural outgrowth of her situation. Undefined fears and anxiety about being alone, about taking care of herself, all that sort of thing.

Maybe . . . she thought. Maybe that's what it was, but sometimes she felt convinced it had to be something else.

The notion began to nag at her as she turned a corner, but

quickly left her as she found a place specializing in one-of-a-kind bolts of hand-painted or hand-dyed exotic fabrics. Oh, she thought, the gowns she could create from some of these would be matchless! One-of-a-kind specialties.

She spent the next several hours roaming around, searching for places that were off the familiar beat, where she could find items no one else had even considered. After lunch in an authentic kosher deli, she drifted into the frontiers of an older neighborhood known for its ethnic traditions. People on the street were dressed in subdued clothing, nothing fashionable as much as supremely functional. Everyone looked clean and neat, but certainly . . . different . . . and most assuredly not the type of people who would be her customers.

But Anna continued her stroll through their territory, following an instinct that she believed was telling her she would find exactly what she needed for her business. The afternoon grew as long as the shadows filling the narrow streets full of storefronts advertising basic services and trades that were becoming lost arts: hand laundries, shoemakers, woodcarvers, tilecutters, appliance repairs.

Then, as she slipped around another street corner, she was engulfed by the penumbral presence of a large building made of red stone with a slate-shingled roof. The architecture was austere, hard, functional, almost ugly. There was absolutely *nothing* to attract her interest or her sense of aesthetics, but she found herself staring at the edifice, unable to break her trancelike gaze. And then she was moving, lugging both handfuls of shopping bags up a low case of wide stone steps.

Halting for a moment in front of the building's double doors of thick, weather-worn oak, Anna blinked and almost stopped herself from acting so impulsively. What was she doing here? What was this place?

The thoughts passed through her quickly like invisible radiation and she reacted to them not at all. As though someone else was guiding her hand, she pushed open the door to the strange building and slipped within its cool, dim embrace.

For a moment, Anna could see nothing, but her eyes adjusted to the lack of light quickly and she could see stained glass in the vaulted distance. Was she in a church? Her gaze shifting from place to random place, she caught glimpses of familiar images blending together to form a particular motif. Images of multistemmed candelabras and six-pointed stars.

She *was* in a church, but not like any she'd ever seen before. This was a Jewish church.

A synagogue, thought Anna as she stepped more deeply into the place of worship. With each step, a feeling of déjà vu grew more intense within her, and as though she were walking ever inward to the center of a walk-in freezer, she began to shiver from the sensation that she'd been here before, that she'd walked down the aisle toward the altar where the holy Torah resided.

Where the *what?*

How did she know that? Her everyday, conscious mind was trying to push through the filmy skin that seemed to be encapsulating her, to make sense of her thoughts, her actions.

What was happening to her? Why was she here . . . and what did this mean?

The questions buzzed around her like insects, but they were less than an annoyance. They didn't matter. Something else was going on here, and Anna could feel it, in the core of her soul, something trolling down into that dark well of being, probing, grasping. It was an unsettling feeling, at once frightening and exciting, as if she were having sex with a total stranger. There came a subtle resonance in her head as though she had leaned close to a just struck tuning fork. It grew in power until it became like the sound of the sea in a shell, then louder still to be an actual susurration, a gentle but persistent *roaring* in her inner ear. The sound evolved and changed so that it was now becoming a kind of chorus of human voices, all twined together in a kind of an atonal harmony.

But there was no suggestion of real harmony in the sound. It was more—a rising statement of pain, of anger, the confusion of prayers never answered.

Anna felt her legs growing weak, her breath shortening.

Got to sit down, she thought. *Just for a minute. I've got to just relax.*

But as she eased into the closest seat, the sensation of disequilibrium intensified, and the roaring in her ears grew louder, crowding out even the steady rhythm of her innermost thoughts. Leaning back, she looked up at the images in the stained glass where the indistinct figure of a man seemed to dominate the fractured mosaic. A total paralysis gripped her, as though she were having a seizure, and she could feel the muscles in her body straightening, lengthening, locking up. Anna's eyes began to flutter as she collapsed stiffly across the hard lines of the bench. She—

—blinked her eyes and looked out the doorway of the barracks. There was very little color in the world she surveyed. Grays and blacks and pale flesh. A sky like chiseled stone and a breeze edged with coming winter. Her breath danced and roiled in front of her as she held out her arm to see what she was wearing: a coarse pajama top of gray-and-black stripes, and a badge made of two sewn triangles, one yellow and one white, one over the other and opposed to form a Star of David.

She was looking out upon row after row of sooty, colorless barracks, where open windows and doors gaped like hideous wounds. Within them, stacked like cordwood, lay the workers of the camp. Anna knew this as she stood looking out at the grim tableau of her daily life. But her name was not Anna. Some disconnected part of her had used the name, but she knew it was a fantasy. Just like the rule that had come down in Germany, when she was living with her family in Munchen, that all the Juden females would have the name Sara added to their passports. She knew that her real name was Ruth.

She and her sister, Hilda, had arrived at Dachau along with so many others from the villages around the city, and now they worked in road crews and teams for a factory that made the treads for Panzers and tires for the troop carriers. Each day they worked sixteen hours, living on one meal of soup and bread. The soup was usually half-boiled water with a piece of chicken bone, the bread like a chunk of quarry stone. But it had kept them alive for more than a year when she had seen so many others die. Children were the weakest and died the fastest, but Anna/Ruth had seen others die in the fields working, along the roadways, and even on the factory floor, when they either collapsed, or were shot by the crisp-uniformed guards.

But today was something different, she somehow knew this.

Anna/Ruth stood at the threshold because the rumor mill had been grinding about a strange visitor coming to the camp. Someone from Poland, from a camp there. And now, as if on cue, following the stage directions of an unseen God, she saw the gates to the barracks yard swing back to reveal several camp guards and an armored car. The vehicle moved within the gates, its machine guns bristling like insect antennae, and rolled to a stop at the first of many long, low-slung buildings full of prisoners. Behind the armored car lumbered a troop truck, like a dog following its master. It stopped by the barracks, disgorging a handful of black uniforms, the

Schutzstaffel, *better known as the SS, who waited until their superiors emerged from the armored car. The SS were very mean, and everyone hated them. They were like vicious wolves.*

An officer appeared, then a driver and a tall, gaunt man wearing a long black coat. He looked to be totally bald, with great sunken eye sockets. Even from the considerable distance of her vantage point, Anna/Ruth could tell the man looked frightful, ghoulish. There was something about this scene that held her attention. Her intuition screamed: this visit by the SS would be the most important event in her teenaged life. Time eddied around her in a gray whorl as she continued to watch the officer, his soldiers, and the one she began to think of as "the golem," after a folk monster from her childhood. Several times the soldiers emerged from the endless rows of barracks with pairs of prisoners, who were roughly tossed into the back of the troop carrier. It was when the soldiers exited the barracks only three down the line from her own that she realized what was going on, that she knew her instincts had been correct, and that she should fear these men.

There was something about the prisoners being removed and thrown into the truck that made them special, somehow . . . desirable by this group of Nazis.

And Anna/Ruth suddenly recognized it, then turned away from the threshold, racing down the narrow aisle of bunks, calling out the name of her twin sister, Hilda.

The sound of jackboots tapping out their terrible rhythm on the floorboards followed her. All the prisoners curled into their bunks like hermit crabs retreating into their shells. The golem, the thin, bald man led a single file of SS troops down the long aisle. His long black coat gave him the appearance of a weasel walking on its hind legs. His skullish head and face enhanced by an inappropriate smile, which he displayed almost constantly as he scanned the barracks, obviously looking for something.

"Ruth!" said a whispered voice.

As she reached the far end of the building near the door to the outdoor latrine, Anna/Ruth stopped, looked for who called among the shadows.

"Here, silly . . . !" said Hilda, who had slipped into an empty bunk.

"What's the matter with you?" Anna/Ruth chided. "Didn't you hear me calling you?"

Hilda looked at her and smiled. Head shaved, arms like twigs protruding from her ill-sized camp shirt, Hilda's inner beauty could not be hidden. She was such an ebullient, happy person, had always been Papa's favorite, had always been able to find the best in any situation. Even the grim betrayal of the concentration camp, the filth, the disease, and death had not been enough to dampen her spirit. That she could still smile, still remain playful . . . was truly a gift from God.

"Yes, of course I heard you," said Hilda. "That's why I was hiding . . . !"

Crouching down, Anna/Ruth whispered. "Hilda, you must run! Get out of here! Make like you are going to the latrine, then run down to Barrack Five—they've already been there!"

"Rutha-la, what are you talking about?"

Anna/Ruth grabbed her. "Those men," she said in a voice perhaps too loud. "They are looking for people like us! Go! Hurry! Do as I say."

The look in Hilda's eyes revealed her sudden understanding. She slipped from the wooden pallet, then down to crouch along the floor. "Oh God! I'm so stupid, Ruth!"

"Hilda, please . . . !"

As she began to *actually* push the young girl through the back door, a high-pitched, keening voice pierced her like a spear. "Stoj! *Stop them!*"

Before she could react, Anna/Ruth felt large gloved fingers sink into the bony cavities of her shoulders and collarbones. Like the talons of eagles, they gripped her, yanked her back and off her feet with great strength. One of the SS men slammed past her and grabbed Hilda by her slender white throat, throttling her like a swan.

The golem with the skull face looked at Hilda, then at Anna/Ruth. "Excellent," he said, turning to the soldiers. "You may take them for my master."

Without a word the SS troopers carried them off to the nearest door. There was no attempt made to gather any of their few belongings—all they wanted was their bodies.

They were dragged across the cold dirt to the truck where two more soldiers pushed them up roughly into the back. Already there were fourteen other people—seven sets of twins.

What did this mean? Anna/Ruth knew that she and Hilda had been culled from the herd for a reason, and having already learned the basic nature of the blackshirts, she was convinced their selection did not bode well. As she sat in the back of the truck, no one spoke, not even Hilda. It was as if all of them were in some kind of mental contact with the rest, as if everyone shared the same thoughts of utter and complete dread.

The truck crept along past each barracks building, men's and women's, waiting at each one for the bald, smiling man to make his selections. Finally, when the back of the vehicle was packed with more than forty people, mostly teenaged prisoners, they were faced by their captor.

"You will be taking a trip with me on the 'special trains,'" the bald golem said. *"We will be traveling east into Poland where living will be better for you."*

He smiled and looked at the SS officer who stood by him with a leather riding crop in his right hand. Anna/Ruth noticed that the bald man had a large gold tooth in place of his left incisor. It was so distinctive, so somehow . . . odd, disturbing. She knew, in the deepest part of her soul, that it was not good to have this man smile at you.

As the bald man turned to head back to the armored car, his long black coat flapped in the wind, and for an instant, Anna/Ruth caught a glimpse of his clothing beneath—black-and-gray stripes! He was one of them. This man with seemingly so much power, even the respect of the SS, was a prisoner! Even the most privileged sonderkommando did not enjoy such station within the Nazi ranks.

What was this about? How could this be?

She could not contain her curiosity, her utter amazement at what she had witnessed. The SS were now clambering into the back of the troop carrier, pushing prisoners out of their way, taking up positions in the corners with their semiautomatic rifles trained on the ranks of twins. Almost all of the prisoners were young—in their teens or early twenties. That they would try anything against the armed guards seemed silly to even imagine. Anna/Ruth was not intimidated by the guns. The selection of the twins meant they were wanted for something special. It was unlikely the Nazis would want them harmed . . . at least not yet.

Buoyed by this logic, Anna/Ruth was not scared to speak to her guards.

"Excuse me," she said softly to the nearest SS trooper, a young man with bright blue eyes who could not be more than twenty-two. If there was no war and she saw this boy in a restaurant or a café, she would have considered flirting with him, or at least talking to him. He was very clean looking, well fed, and what any schoolgirl would call cute.

He looked at her and scowled as she imagined he had been drilled to do, as though a surly expression would cow her into silence.

"Excuse me . . ." she said again, speaking quickly. *"Could you tell me who that person is?"*

The trooper's expression reflected his shock, his utter amazement that she would insist on speaking to him. For an instant he seemed so stunned he had no idea how to respond. Then his arm raised to strike her and suddenly held itself in check—a higher order could not be violated.

"Be quiet!" he said harshly.

"I'm sorry," whispered Anna, sensing her safety and leaning close to him. "Just tell me! Tell me and I will be silent."

The young man's face relaxed, belying his exasperation, and perhaps his humanity. He, too, whispered as he deigned to speak to Anna/Ruth: "You are looking at 'Der Klein Engel.'"

The Little Angel.

There was something odd in the way he spoke the words. As though making reference to someone of such note, such renown, that his real name was not necessary to evoke recognition.

"I don't understand," she said.

The young SS man smiled, but it was more of a leering, knowing grin. "You will," he said. "And on that day you will wish he'd never found you."

As Anna/Ruth watched the golem climb into the armored car with his officer, she wondered why they called him The Little Angel. For there was certainly nothing heavenly about him.

She was opening her mouth to speak again just as one of the other SS troopers lashed out with his gloved hand and clubbed her across the side of her head. So fiercely did he impact her skull that her head broke one of the wooden support slats on the wall of the truck. There was a loud, sickening crack! *and a burst of blood streamed hotly down the side of her face. Her eyes watered and she became so dizzy, she knew she would pass out from the ringing pain that filled her head. She tried to scream, but the sound died in her throat like a baby bird being crushed in a man's fist. Falling forward, she—*

—smacked her forehead against the back of the seat in front of her. The edge of the age-hardened wood split her cool skin as though slicing through a sheet of paper. Shocking her with its thick warmth, blood streamed down into her eyes, and she tried to cry out for help before surrendering to the darkness.

SEVEN

EGON BRUNNEL
London, England

The drive along the M-road from Bath was uneventful for Interpol Inspector Brunnel. His driver handled the traffic and the sometimes confusing motorist signs, giving Egon the freedom to consider the facts of his case. Having been a policeman for more than twenty years, he began ticking off a checklist that had been as steady as a mathematical constant in his thoughts for many years now, as natural and invisible as the process of breathing.

He'd made the necessary calls to MI5 and MI6, plus the local authorities at Hedgeton Village, Bath, and Scotland Yard, and once they had arrived, there had been no need for him to get in their way. Better to file his reports and confer with them later tonight. He would also want to coordinate his findings with his FBI contact in Washington. If this case revealed some kind of involvement from any other American agencies such as NSA, CIA (or even one of the super-coverts, such as PSOG, that were always changing their names to keep from assuming any public identity), then the FBI would make the connection and inform Egon he was mucking around in some kind of high-level interdiction.

And that would be the end of the case. Which would make his life less complicated.

Not a big problem if that were so. He had walked into the middle of the Big Boys' games before and had made himself vanish from the proceedings just as easily.

Without conscious thought, Egon retrieved his tobacco pouch from the side pocket of his corduroy jacket and began dipping the bowl of his favorite pipe. It was a hand-carved Freben Holm he'd picked up in Copehagen—a city that, despite its overwhelming socialist tendencies, could still appreciate a fine smoke. His driver, knowing his boss' need for ventilation, cranked down his window, despite the damp, cool air of the impending British spring. Egon tamped down a wad of his own special blend of Turkish and Virginia leaves and fired it up with a wooden match. The smooth rush of billowy smoke pleased him as he cracked his passenger-side window to vent off the excess. Nicotine was his major vice, and he doubted he could ever quit his pipe smoking. Egon enjoyed the tinker-value of pipes and their associated tools. There was an entire ritual he used to help him think that began with the thunking out of cold plug, then the scraping and gouging, the thumb-refilling, tamping, puffing, lighting, and relighting. It was an endless series of little jobs that kept his hands occupied, and it had become so much a part of him, he could not imagine *not* doing it.

But enough of that. The case at hand had him by the nubs, and he had to admit it bothered him quite a bit.

Having just wrapped an interview with a banking officer in nearby Millington, Egon had been asked to check out the scene at the small English hamlet of Hedgeton Village. He was the closest authority with more jurisdiction than the village constable, an old chap near retirement who understandably wanted nothing to do with what had taken place in his town. Whether or not this case was actually Interpol business would have to be determined. But truth to tell, Egon had a gut feeling the killings were the work of professionals.

The two corpses had been IDed and their closest kin were being notified. They had been dispatched so "cleanly," so boldly, that Egon wanted to dismiss the usual robbery and hijacking motives gone awry. He would of course discuss his feelings with the MI5 and Scotland Yard lads, and his superiors, but there was something about this case that nagged at him, something familiar that made him feel there was a larger implication.

About three months ago, he'd been investigating a black-market memory chip operation originating in Korea and using Athens as a conduit to a lucrative underground market in New York City. While in that ancient Greek city, a fishmonger at an outdoor market was murdered in a coolly efficient and very professional manner. The killer had boldly sifted his way through a crowd of early morning customers, walked right up to the merchant, and put a 9mm hollow-point in the center of his forehead. In the midst of the resultant panic and chaos, the assassin slipped from the agora like water through a colander.

Thinking of the perpetrator as an *assassin* had been a purposeful label for Egon. He had been convinced from the beginning that the fish merchant had been the victim of a professional, government-style termination. Despite the thick crowd in the market, eyewitnesses had been nonexistent, other than a twelve-year-old boy who said he saw a man in a safari jacket and an Arab scarf across his face move past the merchant's wagon, right up to the victim, and place a handgun almost directly against his forehead.

So bold, thought Egon. So ridiculously bold and crazy. Only the real pros liked to do it like that. . . .

Egon remembered an instance almost twenty years ago—back when he stumbled into an operation involving the SSV (the College of Cardinals' *very* secret service) and an Israeli Special Unit without an official name (which therefore did not officially exist). The two groups had been closing the net on an anarchist from one of the German "international hippie" gangs, having trapped him on a ferry leaving Le Hague. A much younger Egon had almost scotched the job because of his overzealous attention to his duties as a policeman. He'd tried to arrest one of the Israeli agents for carrying a concealed weapon, thereby blowing his cover. The German fugitive did not want to make a swim for it, choosing to go down in a fusillade of bullets. It was only by the grace of a merciful God that no innocent people had been killed. Afterward, on a train from Zurich to Rome, he had a chance to talk shop with one of the SSV ops—a lean, angular-faced man named Targeno. The man had surprised him with the ease in which he discussed the art of assassination.

Egon learned more from that very frightening man in one afternoon than he had in *years* of academy classes. Targeno knew so many ways to kill, he'd honestly lost count. And some of the more innovative and effective could be carried out with items found in any desk drawer or medicine cabinet. Egon recalled one particularly frightening technique involving a paper clip and a pocket comb. . . .

But the most interesting lesson learned from the conversation had been the level of ennui in the real professionals. Egon had never forgotten it. The whole termination trick had become so easy for them, the pros required more of a challenge, more risk. The surgical, long-distance kills had bored the most efficient and insulted the best of them. It was something that went beyond pride, beyond skill. To be a hired killer, Egon knew, required a special kind of maniac—a person who was totally in control of his emotions and his thoughts, but also capable of total detachment from the things that make us human.

And that was the kind of job this killing in the village was looking like. Hard to figure it any other way. Egon sighed, looked at his driver. "How long till we reach London?"

The man shrugged. "Maybe an hour or so. Depends on what the traffic is like when we get close."

"Time enough to sleep on this one a bit," said Egon, pulling on the little latch that lowered his seat to a reclining position. "Wake me when we're in the garage."

Several hours later, he was in his small but comfortable office just off Leicester Square. Outside his window he could see crowds queuing up to get into a jazz club as the nightlife of the city slipped into a higher gear. To see such sights in times such as these always surprised him. Despite England and most of Europe's other social-welfare states undergoing the worst economies of the past fifty years, there remained a segment of the population that demanded diversion and entertainment.

No matter how bleak things seemed to be getting, the escapist industries continued to thrive.

He thought about that last notion and wondered just *how* bleak it actually was in the world. It was a bad time to be a white European, that was for sure. The rest of the planet—the parts they used to call the "Third World"—had begun to flex its muscles with cheap labor and overwhelming religious fervor to keep their underclasses happy. The old European (and even American) protocols were fading like a poor memory, and it had become fashionable in the world markets to bash and sack basic Western industries such as textiles, electronics, automobiles, and even agriculture.

It seemed as though Europe and America had conceded, allowing the wholesale assaults on traditional ways of conducting commerce and politics. The only places where Egon sensed any resistance were from what could only be called dangerous elements. Ten years earlier, the neo-Nazi movements in Germany, the United States, and oddly enough in some of the then newly liberated Eastern European countries had been small, laughable blips on the socioecomomic radar screens of the world.

But now, the movements had consolidated, gathering steam from such far-flung "allies" as the Skinheads, David Duke in America, and the legacy of French absurdist Jean-Marie Le Pen—demagogic leader of the neo-Nazi mouthpiece group, the Nationalist Front Party. Egon himself had experienced a run-in with Istvan Porubsky, the racist hood of Hungary, who tried to close down the Budapest airport with a demonstration of "Euro-Christian Solidarity."

All throughout the Western world, Egon could see a hideous backlash festering, growing more virulent. Several years ago, he watched in amazement as Benito's *granddaughter*, Alessandra Mussolini, and her Italian Social Movement achieved official recognition, and had watched as each year more dissatisfied and terrified people were drawn to its self-proclaimed "solutions." And how could anyone ignore the hideous *Pamyat* in Russia, or Klas Lund, the twenty-three-year-old convicted Nazi killer and leader of Sweden's underground White Aryan Resistance (also known as *VAM*). These were organizations that had succeeded in creating ever more dangerous splinter groups always willing to commit an atrocity in the name of their cause for a restoration of world power into the hands of the Old Guard.

And right here in England, one of the first places in the world to feel the stinging failure of democratic socialism, growing support surged up from the slime for an outfit called the Nazi Blood and Honour Brigade. In *England*, of all places!

Playing on the international gameboard, Egon encountered a wealth of political factioning, and the list of groups and movements bursting into angry life was staggering and seemingly endless. Despite a healthy economy in the late nineties, even Argentina had begun to listen to old Peronista lies of Alejandro Biondini and his overtly anti-Semitic Argentinean Nationalist Workers Party.

Ever since the reunion of the two Germanys, groups pining for the old ways had begun to appear. Gerhard Frey's neo-Nazi Deutsche Volks Union had foundered for years before suddenly swelling its rosters with new recruits. Something similar was happening in Austria with followers of the notorious Nazi and historical revisionist Walter Ochsenberger.

And these harbingers of tumult did not even take into account another loathsome band of hatemongers such as Arnold Rassenault and his *Journal of Progressive History*, who fostered the hideous lie that the Holocaust had never taken place.

Yes, the world had changed radically in a very short amount of time. Egon wondered if this time of great flux and turmoil were merely a coincidence, happening at the fulcrum of the millennium, or was there some additional significance more mystical—

—or more terrifying . . . ?

Egon settled back in his leather, high-backed chair and fired up one of his "office pipes." There was one aspect of his investigation in Athens that had actually scared him and still bothered him every time he thought about it. He knew he'd feel better if he withdrew from that particular path of thinking. Too many dragons along the way; madness, too. His present case, and its attendant implications, were depressing enough. He took a few puffs before keying in the communications link to the FBI in the States.

"Stevenson," said the voice on the other end of the satellite/fiber optic connection. It was so clear and perfect, utterly impressive. It reminded him of how damned competent the Americans still could be when they put their minds to it. For anyone who'd tried to make phone calls in other parts of the world, they had to appreciate what a pleasure it was to use the Yanks' technology.

"Brad, this is Egon Brunnel, Interpol."

"Hey, how're things in Belgium these days?" Stevenson said brightly. He'd been one of the section chiefs of the bureau's International Division for more than ten years and had established a good relationship with Egon during that time.

"Actually, they've transferred me to England for the time being. I'm calling from London."

"Promotions are always good." said Brad Stevenson. Then: "So what can we do for you?"

"I'm going to be sending you some files and photos on the NetMail as soon as I've coordinated with Scotland Yard and the Intelligence Services. We've got a problem here, and I was wondering if you've had any similar occurrences over there, anything that would indicate a pattern."

"You want to fill me in?"

Egon briefly summarized the two killings at Hedgeton and asked if there was any American operation going on that he should know about.

"Nothing I can think of off the top of my head," said the agent. "I'll have my people run it through the computers and see what they come up with. But it's probably a waste of time. If anything's going down, MI6 would know about it."

"Perhaps," said Egon with a sigh. "But sometimes they do not see fit to include me in their little games. That's why I cultivated your friendship, Brad, did you not suspect that?"

Stevenson chuckled. "Gee, and all this time I thought it was because I'm just a nice guy."

"At any rate," said Egon, "time will tell." He did not tell the FBI agent about the possible connection with the fish merchant's murder in Athens. Without any physical evidence to suggest it, there was no reason to do so.

Once he convened with the London authorities, received the coroner's reports and the official field investigation files, Egon promised to contact the bureau right away, even though he could detect that Agent Stevenson seemed only mildly interested.

". . . I just wanted to let you know in advance," said Egon, "that I'll be back in touch very soon."

"You know, you sound a little weird about this one," said Stevenson. "What's going on?"

Egon puffed on his old pipe, filling his office with rolling blue clouds of aromatic pollution. "I am not certain. You know how every now and then, you get a feeling? And you cannot explain it? Where it came from, or why?"

"Sure," said the FBI agent. "It's called experience."

"Most likely. Well, whatever it is, there is something nagging me. I did not think to check it out until after I had vacated the scene."

"What is it?"

"Probably nothing," said Egon. "It concerns additional marks on the bodies that I did not think to look for."

"You gotta wait for the examiner's report," said Stevenson.

"Precisely. How long before you get your computer report?"

"Just came through . . ." said the agent. "Hang on and I'll take a look."

Egon seized the moment to relight his pipe, then waited.

". . . No," said Stevenson as he returned to the phone. "Nothing even remotely close to you. It's not us, pal."

Egon exhaled slowly. "I suppose that is good news, but we need to get more hard facts."

"Glad to be some help," said the agent. "I'll be waiting to get your follow-up."

"Watch your NetMail," said Egon.

"And the skies . . ." said Stevenson. "Keep watching the skies!"

Egon smiled and signed off. That was another of those things he admired about the Americans—the way they retained a sense of humor, no matter what kind of adversity they were facing.

Yawning, he stretched out his arms and back. It had been a long day, and he had reams of reports to file and duplicate. Turning to the keyboard and terminal on his desk, he punched up the proper screens and began typing.

The insistent ringing chirp of his desk phone startled him into wakefulness.

He had slipped off into a fitful doze, leaning back in his desk chair, his pipe still cradled warmly in his left hand on his lap. The ashes were cold, but he realized how silly he had been, and how falling dead asleep with a lit pipe was such a wonderful way to set your clothes on fire. Checking his watch, he was shocked to see how many hours had passed since he'd finished his work and had begun his wait for a call from the Yard.

Which this should be, he thought as he reached out and picked up the receiver. "Brunnel here . . ."

"Inspector, this is Eddings, Scotland Yard."

"Good evening, sir. I was wondering if I would hear from you tonight."

"Oh yes, oh yes! Sorry about the hour and all that, but we never close here. I'm calling about the Hedgeton murders."

"Did you find anything else?"

"A few oddities," said Eddings. His voice trailed off.

"Care to explain what you mean by that term?" Egon puffed automatically.

"I'd rather you just had a look for yourself," said Eddings. "If you would like, I can send a car for you."

"Yes, I appreciate the courtesy," said Egon. "Just to set my mind at ease. I have a few questions that did not occur to me at the scene."

"Very good, Inspector. Sit tight and I will have a driver on the way. Be there in a spot."

Egon thanked him and rang off. As the minutes dragged by and he sat in the cramped space of his office, he kept wondering why he didn't just pack up and go home. There was no way he should be involved in the resolution of the Hedgeton killings. It was a British affair, even if there was some international agency involvement. No place for Interpol. No need—unless it was part of an international operation that involved the Athens murder. . . .

Standing up, he tapped out his bowl, retired the ashtray to its place and his pipe to its capacious rack, then grabbed up his attaché. Egon turned off the solitary desk lamp and locked the door behind him. Better to wait outside in the growing dampness of the London evening, catch a few clear breaths, and maybe a few clear thoughts as well.

He fought the urge to fire up one of his tobacco incinerators, took in a deep draft of the London night, opened his mind . . .

Deep down, near the dark pool of his most secret thoughts, he *knew* why he was going over to the Yard, why he was bothering to see the autopsy results: because he sensed something very *wrong* about this case.

It was the same feeling he had experienced in Greece as he hunched down over the corpse of the fish market vendor. He could still remember that moment when he saw the . . . the *marks* appear on the victim's arm. There had been no explanation for it. None.

Had he witnessed what the devout call a "miracle"?

Hard to say.

Clearly, he had seen something unexplainable. Irrational. Something he had never discussed with any of his cohorts of superiors. To see something like the stigmata simply *happen* right before your eyes is something you never forget, especially if you are not a religious man. And Egon would certainly classify himself as an agnostic at best, always on the lookout for any sign that atheism was a bad idea.

But what he witnessed had moved him, scared him, and had forced him to lie awake for weeks afterward, praying that he never encounter anything so frightening again. As Egon put some time between himself and the event, it achieved an aspect of perspective that allowed him to, if not dismiss it, at least keep it at a safe distance.

But now, he had a bad feeling about the Hedgeton killings. And he *knew* why he had "forgotten" to check the bodies of the victims more thoroughly than he did at the scene.

He had not wanted to find something he would regret knowing.

In fact, it was probably better if—

The car materialized out of the gathering fog like a ship in search of harbor: slowly, with great bulk and almost complete silence. The driver tapped his horn once, before seeing Egon standing against the stone facing of the steps to his building.

"Inspector Brunnel?" said the driver after winding down his window and giving him a curt little salute.

"I'm ready . . ."

After being led down a poorly illuminated hallway, past offices, Egon was taken downstairs to the morgue, a place he'd visited only on several occasions. The cold tile and pale paint always gave the place the feeling of being antiseptically clean, almost *too* clean, and yet old and *used*. Fighting feelings of distinct unease, he continued into a pathology lab where Eddings and a physician in a white coat stood waiting. He didn't know Eddings all that well and the doctor not at all.

"Good evening, Inspector Brunnel," said Eddings, a tall, very thin man with a goatee badly in need of a trim. "This is Doctor Rajpapol; he examined the bodies."

Egon shook hands with both of them, looked off behind them to the shapes under the sheets on the examining tables. "Anything unusual? You spoke of oddities."

"The younger man, Frederick Cassington, took a 9mm Starfire bullet at close range," said Eddings. "Never felt a thing, I suspect. The other one, Morris Littlejohn—he caught some of the first victim's slug fragments, but the wounds were not lethal. He died after his throat had been cut by a serrated blade."

Egon nodded. "Any clue on the type or make?"

The pathologist, Rajpapol, shrugged. "Hard to say. There are any number of commando knives with the pattern I found. German and Israeli models are the most popular."

"So you suspect a professional hit?"

"Most definitely," said Eddings. "But unless one of these two blokes was the biggest mole of all time, it looks like it was a mistake."

"They're clean, yes?"

Eddings smirked, stroked his goatee. "Completely sanitary."

Egon shook his head. "Does it make sense that the assassin would mistake the identity of *two* of them? And what about the moving van? Wouldn't that be a significant factor in identifying a target? How could that happen? Did you check out the rest of the personnel at the trucking company? Maybe the hitter was looking for somebody else? Maybe the wrong man was on the truck that day?"

Eddings smiled, shook his head. "I appreciate your effort, Inspector, but this *is* Scotland Yard, sir. I can assure you we've thought of all that sort of thing. The rest of the chaps at Bigston Reilly are really rather a bunch of regular types. No possible targets. No connections with *anything* interesting. In fact, they're quite a boring lot, if you ask me."

Egon nodded. "What else?"

"Littlejohn," said Rajpapol, turning around to face the nearest shrouded examining table. He pulled back the sheet to reveal the pitifully pale, going-to-flab body of the truck driver. The man's ravaged throat gaped open like the mouth of a shark, a hideous parody. Egon's gaze avoided it as much as he sought out the marks on the victim's inner forearm, and—

—his heart slipped its tracks for an instant as he saw the black row of numbers on the paper-white flesh of the dead man.

Christ save us . . .

"We found *this*," said the pathologist as he pointed to the inner wrist of the corpse.

"Damned strange," said Eddings. "Looks like the numbers from the Nazi camps, doesn't it?"

"Yes . . ." said Egon. He fought to keep his mind from racing off in a panic. There was an overwhelming fear waiting to sweep him away like a tidal wave, and he knew he must summon all his reserves of calm and rational will to keep it from happening. His knees had gone limp on him, and he desperately wanted to sit down somewhere. *God help me, what's going on here?*

"Inspector Brunnel, are you all right?" Eddings leaned in toward him, a hint of suspicion kindling behind his eyes.

"Oh yes, I was just thinking . . ." said Egon, trying to smile, realizing instantly it was inappropriate. "The mark, yes . . . It certainly does."

"The damnedest thing is," said Eddings. "It's no tattoo. It's not . . . anything we can figure out."

"What do you mean?"

Dr. Rajpapol cleared his throat. "As near as we can determine, the marks are natural skin discolorations—aspects of melanin and nothing more."

"But the odds of the marks being accidentally numbers are astronomical of course," said Eddings. "Out of the question."

"Which makes the marks' existence impossible."

". . . but there they are," said Egon.

"Never seen anything like it," said Eddings.

But that was precisely the problem. Inspector Egon Brunnel *had* seen it before. In fact, he'd not only *seen* the camp tattoo marks on the arm of the fish market vendor . . . far worse, Egon had watched in horror and fascination as the numbers *appeared* on the victim's arm.

As if an invisible hand, wielding an invisible pen, had engraved the line of numbers on the victim's hand at the moment of death.

And the thought that stalked Egon since that day was a complex and terrifying question: *whose* hand had written the number, and why?

EIGHT

J. MICHAEL KEATING, M.D.
Manhattan, New York

Arriving at his office very early, Michael did so with a distinct purpose.

He didn't want to face Pamela Robbins at her desk the very first thing in the morning. Their unplanned evening of dinner, conversation, and perhaps more Pinot Grigio than anticipated had been far better than he would have expected. Spontaneous dates had a way of working out that way.

Maybe too well, he was thinking as he replayed the night under the clear light of day and masculine logic. By the time he escorted Pamela to her apartment on East Seventy-eighth Street, they were speaking in very informal terms, and she even invited him in for a cup of coffee. He'd declined—not because he found the idea unpleasant, but rather quite the opposite. She had smiled and gave him a look that said *Okay, but definitely next time.*

And Michael feared she might be correct. In spite of what he knew *should* be a slight to professional ethics, he found himself growing interested in Ms. Robbins as . . . as what?

As some kind of companion.

Yeah. That was a good way to look at her for now, he thought. It was as close to any suggestion of intimacy or attraction as he wanted to consider for the time being.

The date had made him wonder why he'd never considered her as sexual/emotional partner material before . . . even though he knew intimate entanglements rarely evolved from a rational design. Better if he stopped thinking about it so much and just let it run its own course.

And yet he *had* thought enough about it to arrive early and get himself socked away in his office before Pamela walked in. It was not so much a maneuver to avoid her as an attempt to begin the day from a position of authority by already being there when she came to work.

Women had a way of making men feel powerless, subservient; it was so natural that few of them were ever aware of the ability. But Michael had noticed it last night. When they had removed their masks of Boss and Employee, and slipped through the evening as man and woman, there had been no doubt in his mind *who* had been in control.

And so, for this morning at least, he knew he'd better at least appear to be in charge. He smiled as he realized how valuable it was to understand ritual and body language. All part of the learning process. Never let it stop and you were a hell of a lot better off. Many times he found himself grateful to his father, who'd lectured him daily about getting a good education. Without his years of study and observation, Michael knew how easily people were overwhelmed by the complexities of the modern age—one of its most formidable being the modern woman.

For the next hour, Michael translated a few pages of Calvino. Challenging and totally absorbing, the work kept him happy and oblivious to anything else. When Pamela arrived, she entered his office with a smile that was so . . . knowing, so full of understanding, he almost felt embarrassed. It was as if she'd recognized his ploy but chose to acknowledge it with nothing more than a simple smile. As though it didn't matter and she was saying: *That's okay, Doctor, we know who's really in charge, don't we?*

"Ms. Enders will be here soon," she said, as if he needed reminding.

"Okay, send her in right away."

The early part of their evening had been spent talking "shop," and he had underscored to Pamela his interest and his anxieties regarding the Enders case. It had been difficult to admit to himself that he'd been unable to concentrate on his other patients. Sharing that with Pamela Robbins showed him how much he trusted her.

And while that surprised him, it also afforded him a degree of comfort because Allison Enders' dream had disturbed him deeply. As irrational as that might sound, Michael was glad to confide in Pamela; he knew she'd be there in a pinch if need be.

Sitting back in his chair, his translation abandoned, he drifted with his thoughts until his patient arrived.

"I can't tell you how good I feel, Doctor Keating," said Allison Enders. "I mean, I'm so glad you want to keep seeing me."

"Well, let us just say that I think your case is very . . . special. Very important."

Michael cleared his throat and made a few meaningless scribbles on his notepad. It was a nervous ritual he performed whenever he prepared to begin a new session with a patient. As she looked expectantly at him, he couldn't help but notice how different she appeared today. Her hair had been carefully styled, cosmetics applied to her face, and her ensemble of tailored pants, blouse, and matching vest all contributed to the impression that this woman was comfortable and self-assured.

"Well," she said with a smile, "I just want to thank you ahead of time."

"I understand," he said, holding up his index finger in a gentle gesture of attention. "But we've got to get down to work. First, I want to ask you a few questions."

"Of course. Whatever you want." Allison put a hand to her hair, checking the styling absently. She looked very much the contemporary woman, above average in appearance and a flame of intelligence burning in her eyes. Michael had long ago learned that a bright mind revealed itself by the way it looked out upon the world.

"Okay," he said, "I'm going to assume from your general appearance that you're doing a lot better than at the time of our first meeting . . . ?"

Allison blushed before launching into a long, rambling apology for the way she'd come into the office. The incident obviously embarrassed her and she wanted him to know how badly she felt about it. She didn't want him to think she was really that unstable. He repeatedly assured her all was understood and forgiven, but it was difficult to stem Ms. Enders' tide of "I'm-so-sorrys" and "I'm-really-not-like-thats."

Finally, she paused to get a tissue from her purse, and Michael interjected quickly. "All right, Allison. We have to get started."

"I know. Whatever you say." She pushed a strand of hair from her face, took a deep breath. Michael was impressed with how much better, how much more attractive and composed she now seemed.

"You're sleeping better?" he said.

"Much better. I still . . . worry that I'll have the nightmare again, but . . ."

"But so far, you haven't reexperienced it?" Michael began his notes in earnest now. He was also videorecording the session, but he felt more in control with the fountain pen in his hand.

"That's right," said Allison. "So far, so good. My husband says it's because you finally let me get it out, that it'll never bother me again."

"You're back with your husband?"

"No, not yet. But we're talking again. Kevin says he wants to try to work things out. That's a good sign."

Michael nodded. "That's very good, Allison. But I'm not sure I agree with his prognosis."

"What do you mean?"

"The nightmares might come back and I don't want that to worry you."

This statement seemed to unnerve her a bit, and Michael reacted to the new stress in her face with a calming gesture of his hand. "Listen, Allison. I'm not trying to alarm you, but I'm no miracle worker. I haven't cured you in one session."

"Oh, I realize that," she said softly.

"Then you understand we probably have a lot of work to do."

She nodded, but said nothing.

"Have you ever been hypnotized?"

"No," she said, shifting in her seat.

"Do you have any objections to undergoing hypnosis?" Michael cleared his throat, then continued. "I think it's the only way we can go deep enough . . . to find the answers that are going to ultimately release you from your anxieties."

Allison smiled. It was a fragile gesture, but freighted with courage. "I understand, Doctor. I'll do whatever you think is best."

Nodding, Michael pushed back from his chair and moved around the desk to sit in the chair directly opposite her. "Okay, I'm going to get started. Now, listen to me very carefully, Allison. You're going to feel very relaxed . . . you'll feel very sleepy, but you won't be asleep. You'll be able to hear me . . . and you'll be able to speak to me . . ."

She proved to be a very willing subject and he was able to achieve a deep trance state with relative ease and quickness.

"I'm going to ask you to search the memories of the little girl in your dreams. The girl everyone calls Sarah. Can you do that for me?"

"Yes . . ." Allison's voice was soft, free of tension.

"Look back in her memories, before the beginning of the dream. Can you do that?"

She paused for a moment, her eyes drifting closed. "I think so. . . ."

"Tell me what you see. Do you see your mother?"

"Yes, she is in our house. With my grandmother, and the other children."

"What about your father—the one they call Stefan. Is he there?"

"Oh, yes," she said brightly, with a half-smile. "He is so handsome! And we are not in that dark apartment. We have a house, in a small town."

"Tell me about the house. The town. Do you know the name?"

She paused, eyes still closed, but he could see furious movement beneath her lids. Several minutes passed, and he didn't push her. His instincts told him this would require much patience and care.

"I'm not sure. . . . The house is on the corner of two streets. There is a fence around the front, and a sign on a post by the gate."

"Can you read the sign, Sarah?" Michael spoke so softly, he could barely hear his own voice.

"No, I don't think so. It's written in a different language."

"Are you sure? Look at it closely. Relax. Can you read it?"

"It's . . . it's Polish!" A small smile of recognition flashed on her face for an instant.

Michael paused for a moment, then spoke very softly. "And you can read it?"

"Yes! Yes, I can."

Michael felt a surge of excitement pass through him. He was sharing in the woman's journey backward into time, into a place that was long-ago cold and dead, but somehow still lived within her. After another short pause, he offered a gentle suggestion: "Look at it. Tell me what the sign says. . . ."

"My father's name is there on the sign: Stefan W. Staniciewz."

"Can you spell it for me?"

She did, and Michael's fountain pen recorded the distinctly Eastern European spelling. "Is there anything else on the sign?"

"Yes," she said. "General Practice of Internal Medicine."

"He's a doctor," said Michael, phrasing it as a half-question.

"Yes! Yes, he is! Oh, I *remember*!"

As she finished the sentence, Michael felt a spike of emotion peak in him. He felt odd, as though looking through the lens of some forbidden camera, as though he were violating secrets of a time long past.

"That's very good, Sarah. Can you look around for me? Can you tell me what you see along the street of your home?"

Another pause. Allison's eyes fluttered beneath her closed lids, a perfect parody of REM sleep. Then: "I can see the street. It is long. One way leads to the center of the town; the other down along a river. There are trees along the bank."

"Walk along the street, Sarah. Into the center of the town."

"All right . . ."

"What do you see?"

A pause, shorter this time. Then: "More houses with little front yards. Like mine. Fences. Some dogs. Kids playing. Then lots of shops. Storefronts and stalls where people are selling things. There are lots of people in the street. Some cars, but lots of people walking." Allison's voice quavered. "Oh, my . . . I . . . I *remember* this place."

Michael looked up from his notepad. Even though her eyes remained closed, two thin tracks of tears had leaked from their corners. Her breathing had become a bit uneven.

"Sarah, why are you upset?"

"I don't know. It makes me sad."

"What makes you sad? Seeing your town?"

She nodded. "And everything else. . . . The streets. The children playing. My father's name on that sign. I feel like I've seen it thousands of times . . . and I know I will never see it again."

"I understand," said Michael. "Would you like to stop now?"

"Only if you want me to. . . ."

"You're very brave, Sarah. I'd like to continue—but only if you think we should."

"What do you mean?"

Michael measured his words carefully. "I don't want to cause you any pain, Sarah. I have a feeling you've had enough in your life."

Allison's eyes remained closed as she smiled sardonically. "I am sorry, Doctor, but that is almost funny."

"And why do you say that?"

"Because my life has been a single, unending journey of pain. I can see it—stretching out in front of me like a streaking meteor across the dark vault of night. The pain in me is like a fire that will not burn out."

Her words touched him like the hot iron of a branding tool. Such clarity and poetry in her expression, in the heartfelt *honesty* of the message. He made a note in the margin of his pad: *not Allison here.* Although there was no way to verify it, Michael knew he was not listening to the thoughts or words of Allison Enders. As impossible and unempirical as it might sound, he knew he had somehow tapped into the feelings and memories of *another* person. A person who did not live in Manhattan, New York, in the United States of America, at the end of the twentieth century.

The mere *idea* of it dropped a chill across his shoulders like a cloak. All his life, Michael had prided himself on being a supreme rationalist, a defender of the logical, deductibly reasoned truth. The scientific method made perfect sense to him. He knew that even the most wild-haired theory, if it was valid, lay grounded in previously established *truths*, facts about the universe. There was no place in his life for any of the "kookology" that seemed to preoccupy the thinking of those too lazy to take the next logical step of any inquiry—to ask the next question.

There was always a question.

That notion had been the cornerstone of this thinking, of his life. But as he felt himself twisting in some kind of psychological and physical null space, he toyed with a novel concept: that while life had taught him how to think, *thinking* had never really taught him how to live. . . .

What was happening not only within the heart and mind and soul of Allison Enders, but also within *himself*?

The idea that he wasn't really talking to Allison Enders was absurd! Yet he *believed* it.

And that was the key to the equation that he'd never dared factor into the calculations of his life: belief. Sometimes there was no choice, other than to surrender to the faith of your convictions or the words and promises of others. That Michael had probably never made such an investment had been a hallmark of his life, a factor in the way he lived each day. Ordered. Compartmentalized. Perhaps so prepackaged and devoid of any mystery as to preclude any sense of wonder about the world. . . .

Such thoughts carouseled around him like fireflies as he realized he was losing touch with the session, that he was in danger of spinning off into a far-flung orbit of his own metaphysical wanderings. His patient, whatever her name, her time and place, might be, awaited his next words.

"That is so strangely beautiful, Sarah," he said after what seemed like an embarrassingly long absence. "Not the fact of your suffering, but the way you have described it to me."

A smile ghosted across her face for an instant. "I have always liked writing and books. When I was very small, my father used to read poetry to me. I have always liked it, and I can remember many nights at my desk, writing my own poems."

"And your name is Sarah . . ." He paused to capture the correct pronunciation. ". . . Staniciewz?"

"Yes, that is my name."

"The name of your town—can you remember it?"

"Yes. It is called Chyrnow."

He checked the spelling, which she provided instantly, then he continued. "Where is it?"

Allison paused, her eyes oddly still beneath her lids. Then: "It is north of Warsaw. A farming community, but there is a growing market center where lots of traders gather. A good place for business, my father tells me."

Michael paused, reflecting on what he had so far learned and checked the time of the session. He'd been very careful to keep his questions from becoming oppressive. Experience had taught him that more was usually revealed in situations where there was less pressure. While he'd been pleased with the tenor and pace of the session, he found himself hungry for more information. It seemed that the deeper he probed into this case, the more intensely complex and textured it became.

Almost impossibly so, unless he admitted possibilities he was not yet ready to face squarely.

Carefully assessing his patient's body language, he was satisfied she suffered no apparent physiological stress. He spoke softly as he addressed her. "Sarah, how do you feel?"

"I'm not sure. . . ."

"I'm speaking of . . ." Michael hesitated. How could he phrase what he meant? He wasn't accustomed to struggling with language. "I'm asking about . . . about your 'other' self. . . . Do you understand?"

"Yes, I think so. I think I *do*."

"How do you feel, then? Can we continue?"

"Yes," said Allison, leaning forward, almost opening her eyes in the attempt to emphasize her words. "We *must* continue."

There was something in that last phrase that captured the pain and the urgency of both Allison Enders and the young poetess named Sarah.

"Very well," he said. "But we're going to go forward again. In time. Forward to the . . . the bad time."

"I expected it. I know. I know we must."

Michael appraised the woman seated across from him. She looked suddenly small and fragile, so helpless and trusting. It made him feel guilty that he would be forcing her to a place of such total dread, but there was no place else to go.

"Sarah, let's go to the time when you were separated from your family, except for your mother. Can you do that?"

There was another pause, longer than normal. He watched her carefully and noticed the slightest tremor pass through her, an emotional aftershock almost sixty years later. Finally: "Yes . . ."

"You were in Oswiecim," he said. "It's also called Auschwitz."

"Yes."

"You described a man who has become very well known to the world," he said. "The man in the white coat—he was indeed a doctor. His name was Mengele."

She nodded, but did not speak for an instant. "And the other one. The *sonderkommando* . . ."

"You mean the prisoner?"

"Yes. *Der Klein Engel*. He was worse, maybe. . . ."

"What did you call him? In English."

Allison nodded. "That was what he called himself. 'The Little Angel.' Because he was always with Mengele, I assume."

"I don't see the connection," he said.

"Mengele. The soldiers called him *The Angel of Death*," said Allison, the words venting from her like escaping steam. There was a terrible presence in her words, as though merely mentioning the name could conjure up the demon once again. Fear crouched beneath her voice like a predator waiting to strike. Michael could sense the respectful terror that emanated from the young woman. "And the *sonderkommando* he kept with him—he was *The Little Angel*."

"Okay." Michael nodded, made a note. "I got it."

Allison shuddered, her face twisted with revulsion.

"You don't have to be afraid of him, not anymore," said Michael, grasping for the best thing to say.

"Who?"

"Mengele."

"He was a monster, but the other one was worse. . . ."

"Really? Why?"

Allison's eyes popped open like those of a mechanical baby doll. It was a startling effect, and it frightened him. She was staring at him, but also *through* him. "Because The Little Angel was a Jew!"

"But weren't all the *sonderkommandos* Jewish?" Michael wasn't trying to confuse her. He wasn't sure what she meant, or the true source of her anger. "Weren't they *forced* to work for the Nazis?"

"Yes, but this one was different." Allison's eyes had slipped closed again, but her features were anything but composed.

"Why was he so different?"

"Because I could tell he *liked* his work!" The words issued from her in a vicious stream, her face twisted into a portrait of loathing. "He *enjoyed* the torture and the killing. He kept smiling at us as he led us to the showers."

"What did you call him?" Michael barely whispered the question. "In German?"

"*Der Klein Engel!*" She practically spat out the name. "He was a monster!"

"What happened to him?"

Allison twisted in her seat, her eyes half opening, then slipping shut once again. "I don't know. I only saw him that day when I . . ."

She couldn't finish the sentence, and her hands began to tremble ever so slightly. It reminded Michael of a delicate mechanism, like a tiny clock of hand-carved parts, threatening to hitch up and stop.

"When you *died*," he said softly. The tension in his patient immediately disappeared.

"Yes. Then. I cannot tell you what happened to him."

"We can find out." He said this more for reassurance than from any confidence.

"You can?" There was hope in her voice.

"I think so. Yes." He paused for a moment, then: "Did you know this *sonderkommando's* real name?"

Allison shook her head. "I . . . I am sorry."

"Hey, don't worry about it. You've been doing wonderfully."

Allison seemed to relax a bit, leaning back in her chair. "Are you tired?" said Michael.

"Maybe . . ."

"One more question, perhaps two, all right?"

"Yes."

"To whom am I really speaking—Allison? . . . or Sarah?"

She paused for a moment. "Who is Allison?"

Michael swallowed hard. The idea he had been dancing around was flirting with him dangerously. He knew he had to face it head-on and see where it might lead him—even though he knew it could be to a place he did not want to be.

A place where cold logic and empirical knowledge no longer held sway.

"Allison is the young woman I am looking at," said Michael. "She is sitting in the chair opposite me."

She said nothing in response. He knew he must push further. "Sarah?"

"Yes?"

"Where are you right now?"

"What do you mean?"

"Look around you. Tell me what you see."

She paused, did not open her eyes. "I don't know. It is a vast open space. Dark, but not really. I am floating in some kind of ocean, but it's not water. I don't know if I'm really even *seeing* anything. Maybe I just feel it."

He pushed a little more. "Do you know that you are . . . *dead?*"

Allison's body tensed slightly, then relaxed. After a moment of heavy, sticky silence, she spoke. "Yes . . . I think so. But it's different. I know that I am also *alive.*"

"And you are," he said quickly. "Very much so."

"What does this mean? Who is Allison?"

Michael spoke directly in a normal tone, no whispering. "I think you know. . . ."

She said nothing, and he decided to ease out of the session. Not only was he weighted down with information and implications, but he sensed fatigue in Allison, and if it were possible, anxiety in Sarah. He was surprised that he was beginning to think of them as two distinct entities, but in a major sense they were indeed separate. And yet, another interpretation would say they were the same.

"Please listen closely to me," he began, as he issued the instructions that would end the hypnotic session and leave Allison with a suggestion that she would not remember any of her conversation and that her nightmares would not be recurring.

Michael wasn't certain either posthypnotic instruction would be successful, but he hoped for at least a partial "take." Allison awakened when he snapped his fingers, and he watched her closely as she stretched, blinked, looked at him. It was apparent she suffered no stress or anxiety.

"How do you feel?" he said, as he moved back to his usual place behind his desk.

"I feel great!" she said.

He noticed a different quality in her voice. It was the same voice, but her tone was more relaxed.

"That's very good," he said.

"How did I do?" she asked brightly.

"You don't remember?"

"Not really. I just have this feeling that . . . that it was okay."

Michael smiled. "It was very 'okay.' You're a great subject."

Looking at him expectantly, she assumed he was going to offer more. When he did not, she smiled, tilted her head a bit coquettishly. "Well, aren't you going to tell me what I said?"

"Sure, but not yet. I need to look at my notes and go over the videotape. We can talk about the session the next time I see you."

Her expression revealed her disappointment, but she let it pass. "Okay, that's fine. I didn't know how it works."

Michael nodded. "Well, every session is different, but for your case, I'm going to need more time to fully assess what we have learned."

"Am I going to be okay?"

He smiled. "You're already 'okay.'"

Standing up, she straightened her clothing. "When do you want to see me again?"

"Tomorrow. If that's good for you."

"I think so."

He nodded and escorted her to the door, giving her more reassurances and a reminder to make the appointment with Ms. Robbins.

As the door closed, sealing him into the safety and solitude of his office, he felt a rush of different emotions. Excitement. Caution. Anxiety. Maybe even a tinge of fear itself. He felt challenged, as though he'd been given some special mission. An assignment that only he could see through to its torturous end.

There was so much to do! Research and cross-referencing. It was time to start combing the literature for similar cases and related phenomena. He would also have to decide how much to involve Pamela in the entire process. Last night, he'd spoken excessively about his interest in the case. To not include her in the latest findings would only spark her curiosity even more.

Slowly, he settled into his chair, steepling his hands over his blotter. Time to meditate. To cover all the bases. Retrieving his notebook, he began outlining a series of tasks. He hadn't gotten very far when Pamela buzzed his intercom.

"Yes?" he said, trying to keep the irritation from his tone.

"Sorry to bother you," she said, "but I have a call from a man who said you were referred to him by Doctor Rita Hanover."

For a moment, the name meant nothing to him. Hanover? He wasn't good with people's names unless the person had impressed him in some way. He cast about, trying to connect a face, an event . . . and a dim memory surfaced.

"Is she with the Pittsburgh Police?"

He'd been attending a regional seminar or some such thing about new techniques for forensic specialists, and he'd been invited to speak, reprising a monograph he'd published about hypnosis and crime-solving. Dr. Hanover had approached him to discuss a few points he'd made.

"Yes, that's her."

"What about the referral?"

"He's a middle-aged man. Seems very upset, frightened maybe. He said you can call Doctor Hanover if you want to check him out, but he's afraid he's cracking up, and she told him to see you."

Michael rolled his eyes. Yeah, everyone was afraid of "cracking up." Hardly a reason to interrupt his research and an already declared break in his normal schedule. It wasn't as though Dr. Hanover was a dear friend or even a colleague owed a favor. He remembered her mainly for her uncommonly homely face and drab fashion.

"What's the patient's name?" he said, shaking his head.

"McGuire. Rodney McGuire."

PART TWO

A DARKNESS
AT NOON

NINE

HARFORD NICHOLS
Jaen, Peru

Something was *very* wrong.

Harford was suddenly awake in his hotel room—small and spartanly furnished—with no idea where he was or what he might be doing there. Blinking his eyes, rubbing crusty sleep from them, he sat up on the small sagging mattress and felt every muscle in his still athletic body twist with pain. He was dressed in jeans and a black T-shirt and hiking boots.

Where the fuck am I this time?

The thought shuddered through him like the kind of stomach-turning jolt that yanked you awake from some terror-soaked nightmare. Only problem here was that Harford Nichols was already awake.

And his waking nightmare was getting to be a more constant part of his life.

He'd obviously had another blackout. Which would mean *four* times in the last year. They were getting more frequent and were scaring the shit out of him. And given his line of work, he was not the type to be scared.

Slowly making his way to the tiny bathroom, he shaded his eyes from the harsh daylight crashing through the solitary window. As he relieved himself, he absorbed the details of the scene beyond the hotel window, trying to orient himself. A quick take sketched in the basics: a scurvy little town with all the signs in Spanish, mountains in the background, tropical trees and cacti along a dried-up riverbed, lots of motor-taxis, and a population of short, deeply tanned people.

Harford shook his head. He could be anywhere south of the border . . . all the way down the west coast of South America.

Frantically, he tried to remember where his last assignment had been—and the images of the lush greenery of the Pacific Northwest filled him with good thoughts. After getting back from Brighton, they'd sent him off to do some electronic surveillance and some basic housekeeping on a cadre of Syrian entrepreneurs in, of all places, Portland and Seattle. He loved those kind of gigs because they were typically clean and neat, no interference, and no messes. He was getting a little long in the tooth physically for the wet work, and even psychologically he was wearing out on it. Several sessions with the Company's own shrinks had been inconclusive (or so they told him), but it was suggested that he was reaching what they called the Redline.

Anyway, here he was in some hot, nasty place where the water, the food, and the dirt all shared a very close association, and the last thing he remembered was sitting in a Seattle bar called F. X. McCrory's watching a couple of Arabs in suits trying to act as though they were enjoying a microbrewed porter with two local clients.

Yeah, something was very fucked up here.

A quick search of the room revealed his usual array of accessories: rucksack full of goodies, notebook computer with radio links to the Comsats, and an airline carry-on with a variety of ensembles for every occasion except the James Bond tux that could fit under scuba gear. Yeah, right. . . .

The computer case also contained some document pouches with all his ID sets. The one that caught his eye was a persona he'd used maybe six, seven years back: Victor Connhauer, an American coffee exporter working out of Chicalyo, Peru, who also owned plantations in the Andean slopes that grounded along the Marañon River.

Jesus, what am I doing back in Peru? Or Ecuador, or wherever this steaming little pit might be . . . ?

Harford found his room key on the floor, but it gave no clue to his location. Better to just go down to the lobby and nose around. He should check the e-mail on the notebook computer, but he was afraid of what might be there and for how long. His superiors did not like it when he didn't check in at the proper intervals. They figured something had gone very wrong, and that was bad business for the Company.

Downstairs, he found a surprisingly clean lobby with a truly immense projection-screen TV displaying a live broadcast of a bullfight. Nobody, not even a lone desk clerk, was paying attention. The walls were decorated with cheesy reproductions of American landscapes—always a sign of a tourist hotel, and probably the best accommodations in the village. Nodding to the clerk, he exited to the streets, where he was assailed by the expected splash of unpleasant noises and odors that were even worse: cars with bad mufflers, screaming kids, reeking fried food, urine, and dog-shit vapors. The sidewalks were crowded with everybody trying to get their errands done before siesta closed things down for the middle of the day. The ever-present dusty dirt swirled and settled on everything as he threaded his way among the people, who all seemed to take notice of him because he was so much taller than most of them, and with his dirty-blond hair, so obviously a *norteamericano*.

The heat was oppressive. Wherever he was, he knew he was close to the edge of the jungle. The signs for Inca Kola confirmed his guess that he'd surfaced in Peru, but he hadn't pinned it down. The narrow street looked familiar in a detached sort of way, and as Harford Nichols turned a corner onto a large, central square, he suddenly recognized the place because of the dome-shaped church that dominated the square. He was in Jaen, a large village in northeast Peru several hours from the edge of the trackless Amazon jungle. He'd been here before, back when he'd been posing as a coffee merchant years ago.

But what the hell was he doing here now?

Whatever it was had left him hungry and totally exhausted and grimy-greasy-filthy dirty. Stopping at a *cevicheria*, he ordered up a bowl of plain rice (as plain as it can get when the local custom is to flavor it with a generous chunk of animal lard) and a bottle of Cristal beer. The food didn't agree with him, but he knew he needed some nourishment. Now that he knew his location, his only agenda was to get the fuck out of there.

As he walked backed to his hotel, he began to feel anxious. The blackouts were a serious matter. He was going to have to confide in Marvin Darbesh, his section chief. Even if you were a fifteen-year pro with the CIA, it was no small matter to get yourself from a bar down the street from the Kingdome to a little smear of a village on the fringe of Peru's jungle lowlands. The idea that he could be so mobile, so facile, and *have no memory of it*, sent tremors deep along the fault lines of his soul. It should be impossible, yet he had hard proof he'd done it four freaking times. The thoughts followed him back to the hotel.

When he paid his bill, he discovered he'd only been there since 2:00 A.M. the previous night. The calendar told him he'd been in Seattle Sunday evening, and it was now Wednesday afternoon—which meant traveling all day on Monday just to get to Lima. From there, it was either a flight to Iquito in the middle of the jungle, or Chiclayo on Tuesday morning. Transportation out of Iquito to the west was unreliable and over largely unpaved roads, which meant he'd probably gone to Chiclayo. Not much of a time window to do much of *anything*, especially when you factored in the erratic schedules of Faucett Airlines *and* a six-hour bus ride through the Andes from Jose Quiñones Aeropuerto in Chiclayo to Jaen. That meant Harford had arrived in this village sometime late Tuesday night, did whatever he came here to do, then checked into his room around two in the morning.

He had gone to an awful lot of trouble for something. But *what*?

The blank, stone-cold lack of an answer left him with a sickening fear burrowed beneath his stomach like some hideous larva under a flat rock. It was feeding on him, and he knew that eventually it was going to win out. He was scared, more than he could ever remember, and he'd logged some vicious fucking time in places like Afghanistan, Angola, Rwanda, Sri Lanka, Burma, and a hundred other cesspools. . . .

Returning to his room, he cleared up his gear and checked in through his notebook. The satellite link punched him into Langley within ten seconds, and a fairly clean video image of a young staffer he didn't recognize stared back at him.

"Mr. Nichols!" said the young man. "Mr. Darbesh is waiting to hear from you. Hold please for reconnect." The screen fizzed, then refilled with Darbesh's round, African face.

"Harf! What's going on?! You had a no-show at interval. We've been tracking your communications package all over the place!"

Harford nodded. He knew their equipment had been locked on the super-high frequency beacon his "notebook computer" was always generating. By simple NavSat triangulation, they always had him nailed down. If he'd been at RFK Stadium, they could have told if he was sitting in the end zone or on the fifty-yard line. Of course, they didn't know if he was alive or dead, or if he'd been separated from his equipment.

"That's because I've *been* all over the goddamned place."

"We thought maybe you'd been shanghaied out of Seattle in a crate of salmon headed for the Lima outdoor markets." Marvin Darbesh smiled, but only for an instant.

"And you've got somebody on their way to intercept, right?"

"Let's just say we *did*. Assuming you're okay, I'll call off the dogs as soon as I finish with you."

Harford ran a hand through his unruly, longish hair. "Let's just say I don't need any help."

"That's not good enough." Darbesh's expression had drifted several notches past serious. "Harford, we need to know what's going on. All this activity is unauthorized, and I can't cover it up. I've got to assume you're *not* okay."

Harford shook his head. He felt like a schoolboy who'd been caught raiding the other kids' lunchboxes. "You're going to be in good shape assuming that," he said wearily.

"I think you'd better get in here right away. There're a couple of people who're going to want to talk to you."

Harford chuckled darkly. "No shit? You really think so?"

"Look man, we've known each other a long time," said Darbesh. "I'm not out to get you."

"Any ideas?"

"Meet me when you get in," said the man who was his section chief, but also his friend. "We'll talk about it before you check in officially."

Harford nodded. "Okay. I'll e-mail my itinerary. Where do I meet you?"

"The usual place," said Darbesh.

—Which was far away from Langley and D.C., forty miles up the expressway and into downtown Baltimore's Little Italy. Years ago, Harford Nichols had discovered Da Mimmo, the only place to go if you wanted five-star service and Italian food. It became a favorite place to meet with his oldest and most trusted friend in the Company. Mary Ann and Mimmo knew them as regulars and always gave them treatment reserved for the many celebrities who managed to find time for a visit to the best restaurant in the city.

Harford sipped a Maker's Mark as he listened to Marvin Darbesh wrap up his standard introductory speech about how he was risking his career by being there unauthorized and by possibly aiding and abetting an agent who had slipped his tether, an agent who had possibly started dealing from both ends of the deck. Harford listened for the words that, while unspoken, carried the majority of the conversation's weight—Marvin was trying to tell him that, friend notwithstanding, he could only go so far before his superiors took over and decided what to do with him.

Finally Darbesh paused to knock back the rest of his Absolut gimlet, and Harford took the initiative. "You're not telling me—just how bad is it?"

"Not good. You didn't tell the house shrink about the blackouts, did you?"

Harford felt exposed, vulnerable. "I just couldn't do it. It's too scary to talk about it, Marvin."

"It's going to get a lot scarier if somebody upstairs decides you've turned, Harford!"

"That's fucking ridiculous."

"Sure it is, but you've got major chunks of *time* in your life you can't account for! I believe you're telling the truth when you say that's what's happening, but other people aren't going to be so compassionate."

"That's *exactly* why I haven't said anything to Doctor Jarvis."

"Well, I have to tell you—she's not buying into the standard 'Redline' business with you."

"Meaning?" Harford drained his glass and signaled for another bourbon and rocks.

"Meaning I've read her reports from your two sessions and she's convinced you're covering up something. She's one of the people who can effectively *terminate* you, Harford."

"Anything else?"

Marvin sipped his cocktail and looked around the room more out of habit than true paranoia. "I intercepted a bureau query from an agent named Stevenson. He's got a good rep. Diligent. Real smart. Like a dog with a fresh bone if he thinks he's onto something."

"He was asking about *me*?"

Marvin grimaced, wiped some perspiration off his shining mahogany head, magnificent in its baldness. "Not directly . . ."

Darbesh briefly summarized the Interpol inquiry and the assassination-style killings in the English village. "The FBI wanted to know if we had any projects going on in the area."

Harford nodded. "Same time I was housecleaning in Brighton. . . ."

"Oh, yeah. Exactly." Darbesh looked at him. "Did you have a blackout in England?"

"What if I did?"

"Goddamn it, Harf, you've got to tell us about this kind of shit!"

"What did you tell him—this guy Stevenson?"

Marvin paused and ordered another cocktail when the waiter materialized with a fresh Maker's Mark. "I didn't tell him jackshit. I compromised the interagency accords; I told him we didn't have anything going on in the neighborhood."

"Christ, Marvin, they're going to find out that's a lie."

"I know. But I can cover it. Screwups happen. This is just one of them. But I have to tell you—this is fucking *it*! No more of this business, Harford. You're scaring *me* now."

Harford gulped at his drink, nodded. His friend was right. The missing pieces of time were beginning to smell very bad, like a very old corpse. He needed to face the situation and deal with it.

But he felt so damned helpless. . . .

"I don't know what to tell you, Marvin. You think I'm not *terri-fied* that I might have aced those guys in England? And what about this little junket to Peru? How do you think I would feel if some-body turns up dead along my trail?"

Marvin shrugged. "I don't know—why don't you give it a try?"

The words hit him like mortar fire, each one ripping a deeper hole in his gut. It wasn't *possible*! As he looked across the table at his friend, a wave of emptiness rushed toward him. He could almost see it, like an approaching tsunami, as it effectively washed away all conscious thought, its wake a deep trench of nothingness, devoid of spirit and hope.

What was happening to him?

"Tell me," he said finally.

Marvin exhaled. "Steel worker. Name of Manuel Ortiz. On a bridge over the Chinchipe River, sniper-style. You want details?"

Harford nodded blankly.

"Single slug to the forehead. Just like we always do it. But it was from an old Soviet Army rifle."

Harford shrugged. "Isn't that what the Nacionales still use? Sounds like an inside job."

"Yes, it does," said Marvin. "As long as you don't factor in the dead soldier . . ."

". . . who just happens to be missing his weapon," said Harford, shaking his head. "Christ, Marvin . . . you've got to believe me! I don't—"

"I know, I know. You've told me."

"The steel worker. Who *was* this guy?"

Marvin shook his head. "Just a guy . . . a guy who worked high-steel. Nobody anybody would want to assassinate."

Harford chuckled. "But you think I *did*."

"What would *you* think?"

"No argument from me. But you have to believe me when I tell you I don't know anything! This blackout thing is very serious, very real. If I'm slipping off into some weird killing-fugue, I don't know a goddamned thing about it."

Marvin folded his hands. "Well, if what you say is true—and I believe you—then I have to conclude that you are one extremely dangerous man."

Harford knew he was right. If the deal was reversed, he wondered if he would be handling things as coolly as Marvin Darbesh. "So what're you telling me? Really telling me."

"You've got to check in to Langley and let them crawl all over you. No choice."

"I told you I wanted to come in."

"I don't doubt your sincerity, but we have to be careful. There might be something going on here that *none* of us have any control over. Some agency or some government might have come up with a way to *control* our people—you know, the way the Soviets always wanted to do . . ."

"That psychic business?" He grinned at the memory.

Marvin nodded. ". . . or maybe something else. Something too *weird* or new or experimental. Look, all I can tell you is that there's a good bet laid at the agency that, for whatever the reasons, you're doing some phantom murders, and you're out of control."

Out of control.

Those words described a situation that simply could not be tolerated in a place like the Company. No room for it.

"I . . . I don't know what's going on, Marvin." He listened to the sound of his own voice, hated it for sounding so weak, so ineffectual.

Darbesh continued as if he'd heard nothing. "If you come in, you're going to be okay—they *want* to work with you. If you don't, my orders are to throw you away."

Harford looked at him as he heard the words he'd been expecting all along. No surprises there. It was simply the way things worked on the gameboard where he played. And he didn't need to wonder whether or not his friend could carry out the directive; he could. Any of them could. That's why they were on the team. And he would do the same thing, if necessary.

"Okay, what's the deal?" he said calmly. An unexpected sense of relief cleansed him. He felt suddenly stronger, more willing to face whatever demon had seized him. "Do we have time to have a good dinner, or do you have a chopper waiting down by the waterfront?"

Marvin Darbesh's expression mutated from stony resignation to grim humor. "Actually," he said, "we have both."

Much later that evening, as Harford Nichols lay quietly in a cell euphemized into a "debriefing chamber," he imagined himself a man standing on the edge of the universe itself. In the perfect darkness, the abject, insulation-baffled silence, he found himself truly alone with his thoughts. As though he were some kind of metaexplorer, unleashed upon the continuum, and had reached its end limits, he believed he was very close to understanding what was happening to him. Not that he had even a scintilla of insight or understanding at that very moment—because he didn't. It was something more . . . more mystical, more intuitive.

And there was an odd comfort in that belief, even though another part of him sensed that the unraveling of the enigma could prove to be the ultimate dissolution of the person he'd always known as *I* and *me* and *Harford Nichols*.

And perhaps more strangely, he was not thinking in terms of his own death so much as of some other, far more intriguing transformation. He had been on rather intimate terms with death for a long time now, and the contemplation of his own end had become so second nature it offered him not even the most puerile rush of fear.

No. This new sensation, this subtle . . . *impression* of what might lie in wait for him was more elusive, more truly mysterious.

And there was an odd comfort in it. The thought transported him back along the dark aisle of memory to a time when he was graduating from prep school in a decidedly Waspish little Connecticut village named Upper Westford. His father, a third-generation lawyer and member of long standing in every exclusive club he could find, came up to him after the ceremonies had ended and stiffly shook his hand as though the two of them were complete strangers (which, in large manner, they *were*).

"No time for congratulations, son. Come by my office on Monday. I've blocked out some time so we can plan your next moves."

Harford had looked at him with a wry smile and said: "Sounds like you've got it all worked out. . . ."

His father looked at him with genuine surprise. "Of course I have, son. I'm your father."

"Well what about me?" he'd asked with a youthful and direct sincerity. "Don't I get to say anything about what I want to do with my own life?"

His father had looked around nervously to see if anyone of merit might be witnessing this filial blasphemy, then he spoke curtly, but with an iron edge of firmness. "It's not your life until I decide to give it to you, Harford. I thought you understood that. . . ."

Harford had smiled a crooked little smile that would be his trademark and a mannerism that would endear him to many women during his long bachelorhood. ". . . or until I decide to *take* it," he'd said.

"I don't like the sound of that!" His father's voice notched up several levels as he fought to keep control. Clearly he was not accustomed to anyone not immediately buckling to his will, and he had paid so little attention to his son's ascendancy to adulthood that he had no inkling of the willfulness he'd inherited. "Any more talk like that and you're cut off, young man!"

Harford had said nothing for a moment as he'd unclasped his graduation gown and peeled out of it. Its folds had hidden a full panoply of motorcycle leathers.

"That's exactly the way it has to be, Father," Harford had said. He'd been planning his exit from a world he'd always despised for a long time, ever since the first time he realized he would someday be old enough to do it. Harford had been that rarest of individuals—he could not imagine living his entire life sucking off the beneficent tit of a trust fund and a prepackaged, preplanned life. And if his father would not give him the chance to inject some uncertainty into his life, then he would create his own random pathway.

Square one started with his tuxedoed father standing there with a truly dumbfounded expression. Harford had walked away from him and never looked back.

After several years in the army, he worked his way through the University of Pittsburgh, fortunate enough to be there during the Tony Dorsett years. Then a fling at architectural school, and a stint as a mercenary in various African and Asian theaters before getting recruited into Central Intelligence.

In all those years, he'd never heard from his parents or his robot-siblings, and until this night of darkness, he'd scarcely given them a thought. Harford didn't really know why he'd thought of his father tonight, but if anything, the reprise of his life choices only served to reaffirm his belief that he'd done the only thing his spirit would have allowed him. He'd lived the life intended for him and he was ready for whatever now waited in its shadows.

TEN

J. MICHAEL KEATING, M.D.
Manhattan, New York

Synchronicity.

Once again, the word lit up in his mind like a neon sign. Was it an actual mechanism? Or, were hollow terms such as "luck," "chance," and "coincidence" the only explanations for connected events that were in essence unexplainable?

Making the unknown *known*.

Michael smiled to himself. That used to be called mythology, and now he had colleagues who preferred to call the process fancy names like "synchronistic holotherapy" or "event-centered therapy."

He'd spent his career steering away from trendy pop-solutions to humankind's true ills, and now he felt himself being drawn to conclusions that were beyond his sphere of all that was rational. He shook his head at the bittersweet irony of his situation and considered how different his life would be at that very moment if he had told Pamela to turn away Mr. Rodney McGuire, the Manhattan cab driver.

But something had made Michael ask her what McGuire wanted.

And her answer shook Michael to the center of his being: "I think you're going to want to know about this guy—he's starting to have dreams about dying in a concentration camp."

• • •

Michael huddled within the womblike retreat of his office, trying to regroup his forces: his powers of deduction, intellectualization, and his confidence. It was perhaps that last attribute he needed most right now. Because with each step deeper into the strange world he had encountered, the more he began to doubt the very aspects of his life that had always served him so well.

Especially that elusive entity called *truth*.

Having dedicated his life in search of it, he felt betrayed when his findings did not conform to the model by which he had lived all his years. There was *no* rational explanation for what had happened to Rodney McGuire in Pittsburgh, or the dreams that now plagued him. Michael felt—

"Excuse me, Doctor," said Pamela's voice on the intercom, "but Mr. McGuire is here."

"Good," he said. "Send him in."

Michael stood, walked around the desk to receive a man who could have been in his late forties or early fifties. He was a moderately tall, black man dressed in Reeboks, khaki pants, a cable-knit sweater, and a Charlotte Hornets jacket. He held a floppy baseball cap in his hands and was nervously turning it and flipping and twisting it. A fragile panic lurched behind his eyes, and his mouth was drawn into small whorl of tension.

"Hello, Mr. McGuire," said Michael, extending his hand. "I am Doctor Keating."

"You can just call me Rodney, Doc. Everybody else does." He shook Michael's hand rapidly with a sweaty palm. "I'm really glad you could see me like this, 'cause I gotta tell ya—I'm 'bout to go balls-up crazy, if you know what I mean."

"Well, I think I do, but why don't we just sit and talk for awhile." Michael indicated that Rodney take a seat, then took a position opposite him.

"Thanks," said McGuire, reaching into his jacket pocket to pull out a business card. "Thanks a lot. And by the way, here's that Doc Hanover's card. That lady I talked to in Pittsburgh? She wrote your name on the back—right there, see it?"

Michael accepted the card, glanced at it. "Yes, I'm familiar with your encounter, Rodney."

"You *are*?" Surprise and a hint of suspicion shaped his features.

"I called Doctor Hanover, and she faxed me a copy of your file."

"My file?" McGuire seemed agitated, nervous. "I thought they said I wasn't gonna have any criminal record or anything!"

"No, you don't," said Michael, speaking as softly as he could. "I'm referring to the report from Doctor Hanover—your *medical* record file. All doctors keep files on their patients."

"Oh, sure. I got ya. Sure. . . ." He seemed to relax somewhat, but his gaze darted about intermittently.

"At any rate," said Michael, "I've read what happened to you, and I'm quite certain you're no voyeur."

"You mean a Peepin' Tom, right?"

"You got it," said Michael, who found himself liking this fellow instinctively. There was a forthrightness, a directness that shone through his defensive and anxious posture. Rodney McGuire was most likely an honest enough, hard-working, and very regular guy.

"You got any idea how I ended up in Pittsburgh? I mean—I charged a plane ticket—I found it in my pocket later, but you know what I mean . . ."

"I have a feeling we may uncover some clues, at least." Michael reached for his leather-bound notebook. "Now, can you tell me about the dreams?"

McGuire shuddered ever so slightly. "I guess I have to. . . ."

"You told my assistant that you die in a 'concentration camp'?"

The patient nodded vigorously. "Yeah, that's right."

"What do you mean by 'concentration camp'?"

McGuire looked at him oddly, as if Michael had asked him if he knew what country he lived in. "I mean the camps run by the Germans—the Nazis. You know, those places where they killed all those people."

"You mean you see these places in your dreams and you recognize them."

"That's it."

"And how do you *know* what they are?" Michael paused to see if his patient was assuming a defensive or cooperative posture. His body language communicated the latter. "I guess I'm asking you where you learned about the camps."

"Oh, I see what you mean. Well, you know, from the old newsreels, the stuff that's always on the Discovery Channel, stuff like that." McGuire almost smiled at the television reference. He was speaking more slowly now, more in control. Then he added: "And my uncle."

The last phrase jolted Michael from the rhythm of his routine. "Your *uncle?* Was he Jewish?"

McGuire grinned self-consciously, but quickly resumed his mantle of solemnity. "No, no. Nothin' like that. He was my father's brother; he was in World War Two, the 761st Tank Battalion. Third Army, with Patton. You probably heard of 'em."

Michael looked at the man, confused. Apparently the information should mean something to him. "I am afraid I do not understand. What does your uncle's army unit have to do with your dreams?"

"That was the first bunch of Americans to reach 'em. They liberated Buchenwald."

"Oh, I see. . . ." Michael attempted to remain calm, but inwardly, his mind was aflame with wonder and amazement. The idea that this black American could in some way be *connected* to the death camp phenomenon supported the absurd notion of synchronous events exerting influence upon each other.

"Yeah, he used to tell me and my cousins stories about the war," said McGuire. "Uncle Rupe said they were over there to 'kill the Jerries.'"

Michael cleared his throat. "Yeah, that sums it up pretty well."

"And he told us *lots* of times about the camps. He said the people looked like a bunch of skeletons. He said when they got there, the bodies were piled up higher than rooftops, that the Jerries had been trying to just bulldoze these big piles into the ground, but there was just too many of 'em."

Michael, nodded, doodled some notes and squiggles on his pad. "I've heard such accounts," he said, trying to remain as neutral as possible.

"Unbelievable, but true, you know."

"Yes, I do." Michael leaned forward and looked his patient squarely in the eye. "But I think we have to look at what's happening to you right now. We need to talk about why you feel you are being driven 'crazy,' as you say."

"Oh, okay . . . sure."

"The dreams. When did they begin?"

McGuire considered this for a moment. "Not long after I got back to the city, got myself back to work. Couple of nights later, I guess."

"Do you live by yourself?"

"Yep. Gotta ex-wife. Divorced. A daughter who's grown up." He allowed himself a small smile at the thought of her. "She went off to college. Now she's got herself a nice job."

"How often do you have these dreams of the camps?" Michael made a few notes as he spoke softly.

"Well, at first, not much. A nightmare here and there. Like maybe one night, then nothin' for a couple weeks." He rubbed his chin with the back of his hand. It was a nervous habit that Michael had seen in many people who were heavy drinkers of alcohol.

"Go on. . . ."

"Sure," said Rodney McGuire. "Anyway, it's funny, but I don't usually remember much of my dreams. And at first, I was just wakin' up in a nasty sweat, you know?"

Michael nodded. "But later, you'd begin to remember?"

McGuire's eyes grew momentarily wider. "Yeah, that's for sure. I'd be drivin' my cab, and suddenly a piece of the dream would kinda come to me, you know? Like I could see this long fence made up of posts like telephone poles and just *covered* with bob-wire. All over, you know? Or this soldier in this long black coat, and he's holding a big pistol to this little girl's head. At first, it was just stuff like that, then it got worse. . . ."

"In what way?" Michael leaned forward, but only enough to indicate his interest, in no way to threaten the comfort space of Mr. McGuire.

"Well, it's pretty simple—I started wakin' up and the whole damn thing would be *right there* in my mind." McGuire had been twisting his cap in his hands, but now he was wringing it roughly, as though trying to rip it apart. "And I couldn't get rid of it, no matter what I did. And the dreams were . . . well, *different* from regular dreams."

"In what way?"

"Like they wasn't really dreams at all. Like they was real stuff I'd been rememberin'."

"That's very interesting, Rodney," said Michael, using his first name for the first time. It was a gesture of friendship, an invitation to relax and open up. "Tell me, do *you* think they are memories?"

McGuire looked at him askance. "Well, I *know* they can't be! I wasn't even born yet!"

Michael nodded. "Of course, of course, but that wasn't exactly what I meant."

"Huh?"

"Perhaps they are . . . someone *else's* memories."

"Huh? I don't get it." McGuire gave him an expression that suggested he might be talking to a quack.

Michael smiled disarmingly "I'm not sure I get it either. Not yet. But I think that together we might be able to figure this out. What I meant by *someone else's* has to do with what's called the *perspective* or the *point of view*."

"Okay," said the patient noncommittally.

"Can you tell me—are you watching other people in the camp, like watching a movie? Or are you one of them yourself? Do you follow me?"

"Oh yeah, I gotcha! Sure, I see what you're gettin' at. Yeah, I'm *definitely* one of them! I mean lots of stuff's happening to me, and plus I *know people* in the dream."

"Can you tell me about them?"

"I see my brother there, in the camp."

"Your real bother?"

McGuire shook his head. "Nah. Don't have a real brother. Just a buncha sisters. It was like growin' up in a henhouse. This was different. It's like I see this young boy, and I know his name and I just *know* he's my brother."

"Do you remember his name?"

"Youssef."

"A last name?" Michael looked at him above his reading glasses, which he had nudged down so that he might see his notepad as well as his patient.

The question instantly pulled Rodney McGuire up short. Tension instantly leeched to the surface of his face, and he worked on his baseball cap with renewed energy. "Yeah, he has a last name. I heard the soldiers yell it when they were first calling out names of people to get in these boxcars. You know—at this train station."

Something was wrong, thought Michael. The man was stalling. Either the last name question had disturbed him in some unrelated and irrational way, or McGuire did not want to reveal it, or confront it. Michael knew he had no choice but to pursue what showed to be the only "hot key" so far indicated in the session. "The last name, your dream-brother's last name . . ."

"Goldberg. It was Goldberg."

The name in itself was unremarkable, but it sparked immediate connections for Michael. He had just read that name on a fax. Suddenly, he experienced a reeling sensation, of lapsing into psychological free fall. A descent through howling darkness. His stomach lurched as if the earth beneath him had abruptly heaved away from him. All the wishing against it and a lifetime of training as an empiricist wasn't going to help him here, he knew. He had the feeling of standing on the edge of something massive and daunting. Something outside the hull of his world. Something the mystics would term cosmic or karmic. Just the idea of edging so close to such a thing jolted him with wonder and maybe a little terror as well.

Go on, he thought. *Push this. Wherever it takes you, go for it.*

"Goldberg is the name of the family in Pittsburgh," said Michael. Just saying it somehow made it more real. His mind buzzed. Fear? Excitement? He knew it did not matter.

"Pardon my French," said McGuire, "but, *no shit*, Doc! That's what's got me so freaked!"

"Anything you haven't told me? Anything that might tie these things up?"

McGuire began rocking back and forth slowly, but with a steady motion and rhythm. "It's funny, but on the night that I woke up and remembered that name . . . I couldn't tell you why, but it had me so scared, I couldn't get out of bed. I wasn't sure I could even *breathe*."

"Are you sure that's the right name?"

McGuire nodded vigorously. "Damn straight."

"How can you be so sure?"

The cabbie looked at him with an expression of infinite weariness. "Because no matter what I'm doin' or where I am, I can hear that train with the steam hissin' and the couplers clankin', and I hear that soldier yellin' over the noise, yellin' out that name. I don't know *why* I hear it, but I *do*. And every time I hear it, I feel my back ripple up like chicken skin. *Goldberg.* For some reason, I'm dreamin' that's my goddamned name!"

Rodney McGuire trembled as he almost spat out the last sentence. Michael observed a bitter rush of emotions sluice through him. Fright. Anger. Disgust.

"C'mon, Rodney . . . you've got to take it easy. I can help you. But you've got to let me do it."

"Hey, Doc," he said in a thick, tension-choked voice, "I'm sorry . . . I just don't know what to do, or what any of this stuff means."

"We've got to go deeper," said Michael. They were on a fine edge now, between enlightenment and damnation.

Rodney shook his head. "Can't . . . I can't right now. I don't even know what I remember."

"I can hypnotize you," said Michael. "Do you have any objections to doing that?"

Rather than the expected opposition, McGuire's aspect brightened a bit and he reached out his hands as though in supplication. "You can *do* that?"

"Well, we can do it together."

"And it'll—"

"It'll give us the first step," said Michael quickly. False hope was ultimately destructive. "It's not a miracle or a cure. Just another tool."

Rodney sagged visibly back into his chair. "Oh . . ."

"But we have to decide *now*, Rodney." Michael could not allow him to waffle or fade after going so far into the session. He looked his patient directly in the eyes, demanding an answer.

Rodney exhaled shakily. "Okay," he said. "Let's do it."

Michael leaned back in his chair when he was certain his patient was fully under. McGuire had proved willing and susceptible, requiring very little time to accept standard methods of hypnotic suggestion and follow-through. Gradually, like walking through a minefield, Michael guided him backward through time and the entwined corridors of dream and memory. There was little resistance and Michael had the feeling almost right away that he was no longer talking to Rodney McGuire, but rather someone named Goldberg.

"Now, Rodney, I need you to tell me a few things about your surroundings. Where you are. What you see. Can you do that?"

"Yes . . ." His voice sounded calm, controlled.

"Where are you?"

"I am on a train platform. It is raining. There are thousands of people crowded around us. Everywhere there are soldiers with their rifles pointed at us. We are waiting for the *sonderzüge*—the 'special' trains."

There was something about the cadence of McGuire's words, the rhythm of his speech, that had changed. His grammar. It was subtle at first, almost imperceptible, then quite drastic. Rodney spoke more formally, his diction more carefully constructed.

"Is this what you see in your dream?" said Michael. "Is this part of the nightmare?"

"Yes."

"What's your name?"

"When I am dreaming?" The question posed a subtle distinction, an indication of careful thinking. "Or when I am *in* the dream?"

Michael grasped his meaning. "When you are *in* the dream, that is—when you are the 'other person.' When you are the brother of Youssef Goldberg."

"I *am* Youssef's brother." The voice was strong, confident.

"What is your name?" said Michael.

"My name is Avram. Avram Goldberg." As McGuire spoke, Michael could detect a change in pronunciation. Slight, at first, then more obvious, an accent was beginning to color the words.

"Where is this train platform? Do you have a location, a name?"

McGuire nodded slowly. "Yes, we are in the small city of Leipzig, in *Deutschland*. It is late in the year of 1942."

"Tell me what is happening to you," said Michael.

"I am with my father, who had been a textile importer before the Nazis closed and burned our shop, and my brother, Youssef."

"What's your father's name?"

"Herschel."

"What about your mother?"

"She died several years earlier. After *Kristallnacht*, there were also riots in some of the smaller cities like Leipzig. She was killed by a young brownshirt who struck her in the head with a brick." Rodney McGuire was definitely speaking English with an accent now. German—flavored with hints of Eastern Europe.

"Avram, when you're in the dream, what happens?"

"The soldiers have spent the last three days gathering all of us together. Every Jew in the city. We are being relocated so that we can better work for the Fatherland. We are pushed into boxcars and cattlecars, so many that there is no room to do anything but stand against each other. We are pressed together like fish in a tin. We ride for so many hours, day and night, that people begin to grow faint or sick. The stench of urine and feces is overpowering. I am embarrassed as I pee myself the first time, but it becomes a common occurrence for everyone in the car. After days of this, no one cares anymore. Our friends and neighbors would probably kill us for a sip of pond water or a chair.

"Finally, we arrive at a small town called Buchenwald, where everyone falls from the cars like an endless stream of vermin. The soldiers use their bayoneted rifles to prod us into open-bed trucks. I watch my poor father as he struggles to keep up with the crowd; he suffers from arthritis in both knees. Youssef and I help carry him along, but we are so weak ourselves, we can hardly move. The train ride has sapped our strength, even though we are both young men in our twenties.

"A teenaged boy wearing a long gray scarf refuses to climb into the truck in front of us. He cries out that he will not go anywhere without his grandfather, who has fallen under the gate of the truck and now struggles to regain his footing. The *Schutzstaffel* soldiers on each side of the truck scream at the boy to be silent and move to the front of the truck. But the boy stands defiant and continues to cry out for his grandfather. An SS trooper moves quickly, thrusting his bayonet forward and up, so that it enters the boy's eye socket and exits the back of his skull. The other soldiers laugh and cheer as the boy momentarily dances on the end of the rifle like a hideous marionette, a galvanic response to sudden brain death. Another soldier drags the boy's horrified grandfather to his feet, shoves a Luger into the old man's mouth and pulls the trigger.

"The spray of exploding tissue slaps me and Youssef across the face, we are so close. But I am afraid to wipe away the wet fragments of brain and scalp.

"The soldier drops the old man's body to the roadway and exclaims loudly that the Jew-boy did not want to go anywhere without his grandfather. And now they are together, he says. All the soldiers laugh and applaud their appreciation of the soldier's wit. And the rest of us begin moving more quickly, more efficiently, into the trucks."

Rodney McGuire recited his story with a cold, unimpassioned precision. He was a human tape recorder in playback mode, nothing more. He sat there, opposite Michael, with none of the speech mannerisms or nuances that had marked him earlier as a black, urban cabbie. So unnerving was his performance that it truly *chilled* Michael, convincing him that he was listening to another person. If Rodney McGuire were the most accomplished actor in Manhattan, he couldn't have pulled off a more compelling and charismatic performance: the rhythm of his sentences; the accented English, spoken with exactly the correct amount of residual Teutonic influence; the casual use of German words that did not translate directly.

Michael knew this was no acting job. Although he didn't understand the process, he *knew* he was listening to the story of a young man who was killed by the Nazis more than fifty years ago . . .

. . . and the young man was telling the tale *himself*.

"Avram," he said softly. "Why did you stop?"

"I sensed you wanted me to do so."

"Do you have more to tell me? More of the dream?"

"Yes," said McGuire.

"You were talking about the trucks," said Michael. "Where did they take you?"

"We climb into the backs of the flatbeds very quickly, and we are packed in so tightly, it is a reminder of the boxcars. My brother and I are near the railing, and we watch the landscape scroll past us. We leave the station and pass through the town of Buchenwald, where the people line up to watch us pass, as though watching a parade. Some of them are yelling at us, calling us *Judenschweinhunde*, or even worse deprecations. Some of the villagers hurl more than insults— picking up offal from the streets, rotten garbage, or even stones.

"Finally we arrive at the labor camp. It is a gigantic compound, wrapped in endless layers of barbed-wire fencing, broken up only by the imposing bulk of guard towers. As our truck is admitted inside the first set of gates, into a space between sections of fencing—a no-man's-land—I notice that the towers are bristling with machine guns and helmeted soldiers who are keeping us in their sights.

"A second gate opens and we enter the concentration camp. There are several large buildings in the center, which are well-appointed and house all the troops and the officers. The trucks veer off to the right and bring us to an installation of bleak, low-roofed barracks. As I look at the endless rows of buildings, I see blank, skull-like faces appear in some of the doorways, then quickly disappear. Everything is gray and weathered.

"We are ordered from the trucks and separated into groups of men or women. There are no children with us. They had been culled out of the herd back at the Buchenwald train station. Then the separate groups are filed into separate, empty barracks, and I notice that they have no doors in the thresholds, no glass in the windows. A cold, damp wind races through their interiors like greyhounds on the hunt. Inside, I see nothing but bunked pallets, stacked so tightly one atop the other that a man could barely squeeze into his bed. There is no room for tables, chairs, or any kind of accessory or decoration, and I know that I am looking at my home for what may well be the rest of my life.

"I hear my father whimpering and sobbing as Youssef helps him down the aisle of bunks. They are walking behind me, but I do not dare turn around. Soldiers with rifles seem to be everywhere and their orders rain down upon us from every direction. It is impossible to comply with everything that is being heaped on us, and someone is getting slapped or beaten almost constantly. We are told that we have been brought here to perform labor for the *Wehrmacht*, and that we will die if we do not do our work well.

"We are told to put any belongings we are still carrying in the bunks assigned to us, memorize the number stenciled on the sideboard, then return to a cinder-paved courtyard formed by the quadrangle of four long-sided barracks. When we assemble in the quad, we are ordered to take off all our clothes and stand naked while we are inspected by officers and several doctors in white coats. Several of the men are singled out because of physical imperfections: boils, rashes, deformed hands or limbs, goiters, tumors, and other unnatural growths. Others are removed from our ranks because of advanced age.

"When someone is removed from our ranks, he is moved back to the area of the trucks, forced to kneel down and wait for an SS officer to put a bullet through his skull. The executions are performed without ceremony or the slightest hesitation. The soldiers give no indication that they have even the smallest fleck of emotion or care regarding their acts. The sounds of machinery and shouted orders are underlined by the occasional, random concussions of automatic pistols, and I inwardly cringe and mentally say a prayer for the dead for each life extinguished around us.

"The doctor looks long at my father before nodding and moving along to the next man. I am worried that he may change his mind, decide that the old man is too frail looking, and come back to reassign him to the end of an SS man's Luger.

"But he does not, and finally the demeaning ordeal is finished. We are ordered to stand together while a detail of *sonderkommandos* drag a huge fire hose close by and turn its cold spray upon us. The nozzle-force of the stream is like being hit by a sledgehammer and my skin is turning blue from bruises and the almost-freezing temperature of the water.

"Afterwards, we drag ourselves wet and naked, with cinders sticking to us like baking flour, into the drafty barracks. The only things we are allowed to carry are our shoes and stockings. On our bunks, I am surprised to find that our suitcases have been replaced by sets of clothing that resemble gray-and-black striped pajamas. The material is a coarse fiber like burlap. Heavy, but abrasive. On the back of the shirt are the letters KL, and on the breast pocket, a star of David, formed by a yellow triangle overlaying an opposed white one.

"The SS officer enters our barracks holding a leather riding crop. He announces that we have been detained at this work camp because we have been convicted of 'race violations,' and that we will be given the chance to work off the penalties of the crimes in the camp. He launches into what will become a familiar litany of rules in Buchenwald. Rules that will determine who is going to survive and who is going to die.

"We listen well."

Rodney McGuire paused for a moment, and Michael wondered if it was for dramatic effect. The patient cleared his throat. "I am sorry. I am thirsty."

Moving to his wet bar, Michael poured a glass of mineral water into a tumbler and gave it to McGuire. After sipping it carefully, the taxi driver cradled the glass in his lap and continued.

"For three months, each day is a carbon sheet of the day previous. We are awakened by a klaxon before dawn—a hideous screeching sound— and marched into the quadrangle where other prisoners feed us a piece of hard bread and warm water. It was a time for joy if one of us found a piece of boiled soup bone in his bowl. Then we walk into the quarries, where some of us excavate stone for bridges and bunkers, while the rest perform repetitive tasks of punishment. I watch a group of older men push a huge boulder up a steep hill, only to have the SS send it back down with a few kicks of their boots. Over and over, like wretches out of Greek myth, the men work until they drop. The soldiers are always looking for prisoners to fail in their work so they can use their bayonets or their pistols. Some of us are killed every day. And every Sunday we are assembled to watch someone hanged for a bogus crime.

"My poor father dies after only three months. He worked the latrines, wading through the troughs of excrement hour after hour, keeping them clear, from becoming clogged. Eventually he grew sick from the filth and he died one afternoon in the rain, consumed by delirium and fever.

"My brother, Youssef, is so different. So very strong and proud. The Nazis never break him. He takes everything they throw at him, and he earns the grudging respect of the guards. The officers select him to be reassigned as a *sonderkommando* in a camp in Poland called Lodz. He comes to me the day he will board the special train and says he is going to escape, and when he does, he will kill his captors. He is smiling and he is still strong. Somehow, he has grown bigger and more angry on the diet of bird suet, bread mold, and warm water. I look at him, and I *know* that he is telling me the truth, and I know he will do as he says. I watch him climb into the flatbed truck and stand proudly like a piece of sculpture, and I know I will never see him in this lifetime ever again.

"But I *do* see him, months later.

"In a dream, as I lay twisting on my naked pallet, half-frozen and suffering from dysentery, I see Youssef standing in the doorway. He is wearing a heather-tweed business suit with a vest and a maroon bow tie, and he looks more robust and vital than ever. He tells me that he killed his guards on the train to Lodz, then waited until the train reached the trestle over the Odra River. Leaping into the water, he swam to the northern bank and did not stop running until he reached Miedzyzdroje on the Baltic Sea. After stealing a small fishing boat, he drifted north to the coastal village of Nysted in Denmark and freedom. From there he connected with a resistance group who found him a job in a hydroelectric plant. He remained there until war's end. He told me he could not come back for me, and I told him I understood, that I loved him, and that God had allowed him to escape so he could carry the family name. Youssef nodded and told me his first son would bear the name of Avram.

"I smiled. In that way, I, too, would escape the camp."

Rodney McGuire paused to sip from his water glass. Michael inhaled slowly and glanced at his notes—so many things to cross-check. An excitement burned in him, and he'd never felt so alive, so challenged to justify himself and his existence. His patient's tale was so full of compassion and pain, and told with such control and eloquence, Michael felt moved to tears, but he knew this wasn't the reason he'd been given this message. The time for grieving had long ago passed.

Looking up at his patient, who sat stolidly with eyes closed, Michael spoke to him softly. "Is that how it ends?"

"No," said McGuire. "It ends with my death. As we drag ourselves into the spring of 1943, I hear rumors of new camps being built and others being transformed. They are called *die Vernichtungslagers*— the annihilation camps—and we hear the names on the lips of the guards. Sobibor. Belzec. Birkenau. Majdanek. Treblinka. We hear these names until they become talismans able to instill instant terror in us. They are mythic places of infinite darkness and pain. I know this in my heart.

"Finally the morning comes when I am yanked from my pallet by SS men and taken to the *sonderzüges*. With a group of my comrades, who have become by this time my only family, we are stuffed into a cattlecar. I hear the door slide shut with a fatal thud, and I am rocketed through the night and fog. Days pass in a delirious blur until the doors open at a siding. Beyond the tracks and the platform, I see the stacks of factories rising up like posts to fence in the iron dawn.

"I am led from the train and stripped naked. As my flesh ripples and turns blue from the cold air, I see a handsome man in a white coat approach me and look at me with seeming disinterest. He turns and says something I cannot hear to an SS man on his left, then repeats it to a *sonderkommando* on his right, who is carrying a clipboard and a pencil. The prisoner is doing something I have never seen a prisoner do—he is smiling openly, almost laughing—and I see that he has a gold tooth in his mouth. Sallow-cheeked and with deep-socketed eyes, the man looks like a ghoul, a skull-faced ghoul.

"I have heard of this man. He is a legend among prisoners and carries a legend's name: *Der Klein Engel*—The Little Angel."

Michael's breath caught in his chest.

And for an instant, his entire body seemed to stop like a seized engine.

The Little Angel.

As Michael tried to compose himself, McGuire continued speaking in the voice-not-his voice:

"I look into his face and I see my own. The one beneath my flesh. My real and final face.

"I am moved off to the left and herded into a long line of naked men. Ahead of me, I see double doors of steel swinging open to accept us into a darkened underground chamber. Far above us, the smokestacks billow and there is the smell of burning suet in the air. I am so weak, I am carried along by my brothers in pain.

"When we are prodded into the dark, cold room, I'm only faintly aware of the clang of the doors sealing us in, the serpent-hiss of heavy vapor that settles over us like mist. All around me, people begin to scream and their cries become a unified chorale of agony. There is a furious beating of limbs and gurgling of lungs. The rattles of death dance all around me—*die totentanz*. I open my mouth and my eyes, looking up like a child at the kiss of a spring rain, relieved at last to be free."

ELEVEN

ANNA SMITHSON
Chicago, Illinois

I came as soon as I could," he said, smiling and reaching out to touch her hand.

Anna looked at the man suspiciously. "Thanks, but who *are* you?"

"Rabbi Irwin Klingerman!" He spoke his name as though it were a household word.

An Einsteinian nimbus of silver-white hair, wild eyes bulging from his face like the halves of hard-boiled eggs, a huge beak of a nose, a long Santa Claus beard. And a voice that sounded like a hacksaw blade going through a corrugated tin roof.

She'd heard of people who were supposedly larger than life, but Rabbi Irwin Klingerman was the first one she'd ever met. Everything about him was exaggerated. His hand gestures were wild and very big, as though he were forever directing a jetliner into a parking space. His voice, heavily accented by Yiddish and German, filled any space he occupied with its raspy presence and lilting emphasis at the end of every sentence. She could easily imagine that when he laughed, it would be a head-thrown-back belly-shaker; when he cried, it would be fraught with melodrama and rolling tears. His face flushed scarlet in blood-pressured defiance to obvious obesity, and his clothes sported damp perspiration spots in all the wrong places.

Such was the vision presented to her as he leaned over her hospital bed.

"I'm sorry," she said in her most proper voice. "But should I know you?"

He smiled again. "Sadly, I think not. But! You know me now . . . so it does not matter, does it?"

Anna looked around the room, hoping for a sign of someone from the hospital staff. She did not feel threatened by this man's presence in her room, but she would have felt more comfortable knowing that *someone* knew he was there. Slowly, she disengaged her hand from his, pretended to adjust her hair (which probably looked *awful* anyway).

"How are you feeling now?"

The question refocused her concerns, and she found herself taking a quick assessment of her general well-being. "I . . . I guess I feel better. They must have given me something to sleep."

Klingerman nodded. "They usually do. Tell me, Ms. Smithson, what do you remember of your experience?"

The words transported her; images began to pile up in her memory: a circle of faces surrounding her, paramedics lifting her into an ambulance, the rocking motion of the vehicle, and the siren that announced their quick passage through the city streets, the emergency room staff in their pale green pajamas. She mentioned some of this to him in summary, not certain she wished to get involved with this large, gross man.

"Well, yes, I understand all that, but I was referring to the . . . ah, the *visions* you had. . . ."

"The— Listen, Rabbi . . . I'd like to know what this is all about! What are you doing in my room, asking me these questions anyway? And how do you know I had any 'visions' in the first place?"

Klingerman rubbed his hands together as though anticipating a large meal, then he began waving them about as he spoke excitedly. "Chaplains can go anywhere in here! I told them I was your rabbi of course."

"*I'm* not Jewish!" said Anna, her voice rising. "What are you talking about?"

"Please, Ms. Smithson, do not get too worked up. I am not here to upset you . . ."

"Well, you're doing a pretty good job of it." Anna crossed her arms across her chest and looked for the nurse's call button. "I think you should be getting on your way, Rabbi."

"Ms. Smithson, please! You do not understand . . . I need to talk to you!"

"About *what?*" Anna tried to sound as coldly efficient as possible.

"About what happened to you this afternoon." He gathered in his wild gestures and overdone facial expressions and, for a moment, seemed composed and solemn. The change of posture caught her off guard.

"How do you know about *that* . . . ?" As she spoke, Anna reeled inwardly as a flood of images crested over her: the dreamlike state in which she had become someone else, had been gripped in some kind of seizure full of horrible memories not her own, yet somehow *intensely* personal and painful.

"Because you were in Rabbi Gerstung's synagogue crying out for help. He is a good friend of mine, and he knows of my particular specialty. He called me. I live north of here. In Fond du Lac."

"What 'specialty'?" Anna looked at him with open suspicion.

"You were in some kind of a trance," he said quickly, obviously picking up on her alarm and distrust of him. "You were talking about people and situations that are very familiar to me."

"*Familiar* to you? How?" A strange calmness was settling over her. Anna had a feeling of déjà vu drift through her like a half-felt breeze. For an instant, she felt chilled.

Waving a single, sausage-like finger at her, Klingerman smiled. "Plenty of time for that. You attracted quite a crowd. People tried to move you, but you curled up on the floor and wouldn't let anyone touch you. You were yelling about '*Der Klein Engel,*' do you remember that?"

The words seemed suspended in the gossamer of an old nightmare, their meaning lost or perhaps never known.

". . . I . . . I'm not sure. It sounds familiar. Like I should know. But, it's funny, I feel like it's something I shouldn't *want* to know." She looked at him as he leaned forward in his chair. "Does that make sense to you?"

Klingerman nodded sharply, pursed his thick lips. "If you are talking about what I *suspect* you are, then, yes, it makes perfect sense."

Anna sat up straighter in the bed, looking him directly in his pinched eyes. She did not like him being here, liked looking at him even less, but there was something about his presence and the mostly buried memories of her experience that really disturbed her.

Sensing that this fat rabbi knew something about her—something unknown to *her*—challenged her to find out what was going on. Anna prided herself on not letting anyone intimidate her, especially since her husband had died. She'd learned how to take care of all her affairs in a hurry, and the trait had served her well.

"Rabbi Klingerman," she said in a stern voice, "I have had a *very* bad day, and I would very much like you to get to the point."

"What do you mean, Ms. Smithson? I am here to help you."

"You are *not* my clergyman. I did not send for you," said Anna. "And, to be perfectly frank, I'm not sure I want you in here bothering me."

"I am very sorry you feel that way," he said softly in an effort to not be so animated.

Anna felt immediately sorry for speaking so harshly. He looked like a wounded puppy. "I didn't intend that to sound so bad. But I'm not feeling very well, and I have no patience for dancing around an issue right about now. I hope you can understand that."

"Yes, of course."

"Then simply tell me *why* you are here, please." Anna settled back in her pillows, arms still crossed.

Holding his arms out, palms up, he shrugged and, despite the unruly salt-and-pepper beard, managed to project a boyish grin. "That is a long story."

"Can you summarize?"

"We rabbis are natural-born storytellers. The parable is a great teaching tool, as you may well know." He shrugged again, grinned impishly. "But . . . I will try to be brief."

She again studied him as he drew in a deep breath, expanding his size even more. His clothes, while neat, had a worn look to them: his shirt collar frayed, his tie old and out of fashion, the fabric of his suit jacket faded by time. His synagogue was apparently not the most prosperous in the city. Leaning closer to her, Klingerman tried to speak in what for him served as sotto voce.

"I have been a rabbi for twenty-five years. First in New York City. Queens, actually. But I moved here with my wife, who now reminds God of things he may have forgotten to do each day. Mindel—I loved her very much, and I have not been half the person without her."

"I understand how you feel," said Anna, feeling his pain. She briefly mentioned how her husband had died suddenly. Perhaps this man was not so terrible after all. It always struck her that practically *everyone* was likable and just as fragile as the next person. But we rarely take the time to learn of anyone else's pain or joy. As he began speaking again, she realized her thoughts were drifting and focused upon his words.

". . . and I took the assignment here in Chicago. As time passed, I developed an interest in psychology and eventually took degrees in it. I achieved some success in family counseling in my congregation and became a kind of regional counselor or advisor for other congregations in Chicago.

"Beginning in 1991, and thereafter, I occasionally met a person who was deeply troubled by feelings of terror, of what they believed were horrible acts committed against them and their family. Acts so terrible, they could not articulate them, could not remember them."

"I don't think I understand," said Anna.

"Neither did my patients," said Klingerman. "When I would question them in depth, they could not explain the root of their feelings, other than a shared conviction that *the transgression against them may not have happened in this lifetime.*"

Holding up her hand, Anna made an effort to look serious. "Rabbi, I'm sorry, but that doesn't make any sense."

"You're telling me? I know! I know!" He waved his arms as though flapping them in some pre-takeoff mode. "But wait, let me tell you more."

Anna nodded. Despite her initial apprehension, she found herself interested in the story. Klingerman had not lied; he knew how to spin out a tale. "Go on," she said.

"During my studies, I met a woman, whom we can call Mrs. Jones. She had been a housewife living in a small Maryland town near the Delaware border," said Klingerman. "She had undergone a hypnosis session at her dentist's office—instead of an anesthetic—during a routine drilling and filling. But what happened while she sat in the chair so astounded and shocked her dentist that it changed his life. As well as the woman's."

He paused to take a breath. "Well, what happened?" said Anna.

"Ah-hah! So, I've got you, eh?" The rabbi smiled, then continued. "She sat there rambling on about having lived in Scotland during the eighteenth century. She said her name was Mary McKinley and that she worked as a cook for a squire in a village near Glasgow by the name of Grantham. Named after William Grantham. The woman spewed out enormous amounts of detail about her life on the squire's estate, her children, her husband, the local politics of the village, her family's tartan, genealogy, and even favorite recipes of Squire Grantham."

Anna nodded. "I've heard of stories like that," she said. "Past life regression, right?"

Klingerman brightened and smiled. "That is correct, Ms. Smithson! How could you—"

"Rabbi, anyone who pays attention to what's going on around them can learn a lot about the world." She smiled, then added: "I pay attention."

"So you do, madam," he said as he tipped an imaginary hat in her direction.

Anna nodded. It never ceased to surprise, and even anger her a bit, when men discovered that she had a brain in her head. She decided to press her initiative and advantage. "And in many cases, when the facts or details given by the subjects are checked, they are found to be very accurate, right?"

"Correct again," said Klingerman. "Are you a student of this phenomenon?"

"Not really. But I remember reading about those kinds of stories in books by Frank Edwards and Charles Fort."

Klingerman leaned even closer. "So, you *do* have an interest in the paranormal!"

Anna shrugged. "Like I said—not really. When I was younger, just out of college, actually—so we're talking *much* younger—I spent a few years reading everything I could about the Meaning of Life. . . ."

Klingerman nodded.

"You know how it goes," said Anna. "I read philosophy, comparative religions, astronomy, cosmology, and even the Forteans. I was looking for answers anywhere I might find them."

"It is a common enough pursuit of young people," said Klingerman. "And did you find what you were looking for?"

Anna looked away, past his shoulder, as though trying to catch a glimpse of that young woman who wore the baggy sweaters and the long skirts and always had flowers in her hair, the hippie-chick with the 130+ IQ who scared most men off with her intensity and her bad poetry. "No," she said finally. "No, I don't think I did. . . ."

"We're getting afield of my story," he said, patting her hand as though sympathetic to the flash of nostalgia and requisite pain that had just ghosted through her. "Shall I continue?"

She nodded; he continued.

"The dentist had been fascinated by her story, thought to record it while she was in his chair, and later checked out the details. And it was as you surmised: all the facts checked out, down to details that it would have been practically impossible for Mrs. Jones to have known or discovered. It took professors in English history *months* of intense research to ferret out the details that confirmed her story.

"And, fascinated by the story of what appeared to be solid proof of reincarnation, the dentist devoted his life to the pursuit of additional proofs. He went back to school, took degrees in psychology, and eventually abandoned his dental practice.

"Mrs. Jones was also inspired by the experience and went back to school in search of answers. I met her after she amassed many case histories like her own, and through conversation and friendship, I, too, became interested in the idea that we have all lived before—that reincarnation is most likely *real*."

"Doesn't that conflict with traditional Jewish teachings?" Anna was not at all certain of this, but couldn't remember anything in her readings to support an idea that probably could not be considered orthodox.

Klingerman grinned with only one side of his mouth. Obscured by his beard, and decidedly lopsided, it added to his growing charm. "Well, perhaps. But I have done extensive study in this area and spent many long hours in discussion with some of this country's most respected Talmudic scholars, and there is nothing in the sacred books that specifically denounces or denies the possible existence of the reincarnated soul. In fact, there are references in the Kabbala, an ancient collection of mystical writings, that make veiled suggestions of a transmigration of souls from one body to another. But I will not bore you with the citations."

"Thanks," said Anna. "They wouldn't mean much to me, and I'd end up taking your word for it, anyway."

"Yes, you would. We are talking about something people either *want* to believe in, or they simply *don't*. There is no amount of convincing that can be done."

"I know," she said. "My late husband always thought it was a silly idea—reincarnation. He said that mathematically, the concept doesn't hold up. That there are more people *alive* right now in the world than have ever died. Therefore, they could not all be peopled by souls of the previously dead."

Klingerman nodded. "I am familiar with the argument. Easily refuted by the 'old soul/new soul' interpretation."

"Yes, that's what I used to tell him. Not so much because I believed it or not." Anna grinned as she recalled all those evenings at dinner when she and Stephen would slip into friendly disagreements about just about anything. They had become such a natural part of her life, she had just assumed they would never end. "More because I just enjoyed getting into talks with him where we each had a different point of view."

"Oh my, yes!" said Klingerman. "Women and men are definitely like that, aren't they? Something about husbands and wives bringing out each other's most contentious sides, isn't it?"

Neither one spoke for a moment, and she suspected that the rabbi was indulging himself in a pleasant moment of longing for his dead wife. The experience gave them a common bond, although she began to suspect there was an even stronger element of sharing between them.

"So . . . tell me," she said softly, drawing his attention back to the present. "What does all this have to do with me? Am I a reborn soul? Is that what this is all about?"

Klingerman smiled gently. "You are a very perceptive person, Ms. Smithson."

"That synagogue I was in—I have no idea *why* I went in there, and then, the . . . the attack I had . . . I know it was horrible, but I can't really remember what happened."

"You were unconscious, but you were talking very loudly to the people around you, the people who tried to help you. When Reb Gerstung listened to you, he called the paramedics, but he also called me."

"What was I talking about?" Suddenly she felt an emptiness in her, an absence of knowledge she had become convinced was vital to her. She *needed* to know what she had been saying, what had happened to her in the synagogue.

Klingerman held up his index finger. "I am not certain that merely *telling* you would be the best way to deal with this."

"What do you mean?"

"I mean that by paraphrasing what you said may in some way color or influence what you *really* experienced. I can only relate what my friend heard and then told me, plus the things you said after I arrived. Hearsay, that's what our friends the lawyers call it. Inadmissible!"

Anna felt confused, her frustration lapsing into anger. "You mean you came in here, gained my confidence, raised my curiosity, and now you're not going to *tell* me anything?"

Raising both arms like a cowboy keeping his hands visible and away from his weapons, Klingerman shook his head. "No, no . . . ! Please, Ms. Smithson, that is not the case at all."

"I'm sorry," she said. "Please explain."

He lowered his arms and spoke gently. "I was going to say that it's probably better if you could undergo hypnosis. So that we can more fully recreate your experience. What you were talking about while you were unconscious."

"Well . . ." The thought of being hypnotized intrigued her. She had never done it, had never really been sure it "worked." It was one of those things she'd always wanted to try, but had never found the time, or reason, to actually *do*.

"You see," said Klingerman, "you were not always speaking clearly. You . . . how can I say this delicately? . . . you *rambled* . . ."

Anna had to chuckle. "That's 'delicately'? Rabbi, I don't think there's any way you say that to a woman and have her *like* it."

Klingerman shrugged and gave her one of his boyish grins. She found herself liking this character, even though she didn't want to. "*Nu?* I knew I was walking on quicksand with that one. Twenty-five years with my Mindel and you don't think I know women? Ms. Smithson, I don't know women at all!"

She smiled as he threw back his head and laughed with abandon. Afterward, there followed an awkward silence as they stared at one another, but he broke through the barrier with his usual verve. "So, what do you say?! Would you be willing to try it?"

"Hypnosis? Who would be doing it, you?"

Klingerman grinned. "Me? No! I'm a rank amateur when it comes to that kind of thing. I have a friend who's helped me in past cases. She's a psychiatrist who works for the Hines VA hospital. She's become very interested in my work, and she's even written a few journal papers on it."

"Really, and how exactly would you describe your 'work'?" Anna looked at him coyly.

"I never explained?" he asked with a grin.

"No, I don't think so. Just . . . being a rabbi."

"Well, I am a teacher at the Talmudic Academy in Milwaukee. I have also been an at-large—no pun intended, eh?—family counselor for some of the area congregations. But I also conduct studies in the field of reincarnation."

"Like the dentist," she said.

"The dentist?" For a moment, he had no idea to what she referred, then a light went off behind his eyes. "Oh yes! Of course!

Exactly like the dentist! It was something that I discovered gradually. More and more people I encountered seemed to be involved in
the . . . the same kinds of experiences. It was fascinating."

"Kind of like a hobby?"

"Well, yes, at first. But after my wife died, I began filling my
empty hours with research." He paused, as though reliving the long,
lonely nights with which Anna was so intimately familiar. It was a
particular slant of his eye that communicated all she needed to know.
Suddenly he clasped his hands together, as though breaking a trance,
and continued. "The more I learned, the more important my study
became. The cases and the evidence began piling up, and I came to
believe I had discovered something important."

"And you can't tell me what that is, right?" Anna spoke without
rancor and smiled to emphasize her feelings.

"Well, not right now, no. Nothing personal, of course! But soon
enough you will understand."

"I certainly hope so."

"So . . . !" he said expectantly. "You will agree to a session?"

She hesitated . . .

Why? She'd been so sure just a minute ago, and thought it might
be fun, if nothing else. But as she sat there, a new element slipped
into the equation. Was it apprehension? Fear? Ignorance was, as
they say, bliss. And life was an unending series of new doors to be
opened—just like that stupid prize show on TV—and we were
always being asked to choose.

What's behind Door Number Three?

Her intuition, which was very real to her, and *very* accurate when
she paid attention to it, was blinking like a highway patrol car's
lights. It was telling her to be careful, to not go rushing into this
social contract with this animated and charming man.

Was it him? Did she not trust him? Was he some kind of creep?
Probably not. He was too much of a high profile. People in the hospital obviously knew him. He would be fairly easy to check out.

What congregation did he say he belonged to?

He hadn't said.

Maybe she didn't know all that much about him after all.

And how could she assume the hospital staff even knew him? Ever
since he'd appeared in her room, she'd seen no one else from the floor.
None of the nurses or orderlies. They might not know this guy was even
here. Hell, thought Anna, letting her paranoia completely loose of its
cage, they could all be out there at the station with their throats cut. . . .

Okay, enough. On that path lies madness. Maybe it would be better if—

"Ms. Smithson, is anything wrong?" His voice, gentler again, invaded her thoughts.

Looking at him, he looked like a big teddy bear with a charming accent. She felt ashamed to even have considered him being a dangerous character.

"I'm sorry," said Anna. "I was just thinking everything through. I just don't want to get involved in anything that's going to be trouble."

"I understand . . ."

"My life is complicated enough."

"I'm sure that it is," Klingerman said quickly. "But you have to realize that I wouldn't be here in the first place if I didn't believe what has happened to you was *extremely* important."

"To *you*. But what about me?" She smiled disarmingly. "I'm not trying to be rude, Rabbi, but I am being honest. Try to understand what I'm saying."

"I do, I do! We would say in Yiddish that you have no need for any extra *tssurris* in your life. Perfectly understandable."

"And I must tell you—I am usually a very private person. I have a small business to run, and I am usually *very* busy."

He smiled. "In other words, as they say: this better be good!"

"Yes," she said. "That's right."

He held up his hands in surrender. "Please, Ms. Smithson, do not be short with me. You must trust me when I tell you that my work is very sensitive and very important . . . to *you* as well as me."

"Important like 'change-my-life' important?"

"Very possibly." He spoke the words softly and with a dead seriousness obviously reserved for special moments. His sudden change of tone shook her up a bit, but it also challenged her.

"Rabbi, I believe you. It's just very frustrating and mysterious."

He nodded. "You like a good mystery, do you?"

"Doesn't everybody?" Anna inched up in the hospital bed, sitting straighter.

"I suppose there are people out there with no curiosity about the world around them," he said. "Personally, I cannot imagine such an existence."

She nodded, but said nothing.

"And so, we must make arrangements, yes? An appointment with my doctor friend?"

"All right," she heard herself saying.

Klingerman clasped his hands together solemnly, nodded once as though sealing the deal with a curt gesture. "When do they plan to release you from here?"

"I don't know yet," said Anna. The question refocused her concerns on the immediate situation. Her headache had eased to the point it was hardly noticeable. Klingerman's visit had taken her mind off her discomfort. But she was now wondering how much longer they would want to keep her in this damned bed. If this was as bad as she was going to be feeling, she could be doing it at home, without her insurance payments meter spinning off the wall.

Reaching into his jacket pocket, Klingerman pulled out a beat-up billfold from which he produced a business card and gave it to her. "As soon as you know what your schedule is, you will call me?"

"Yes, I promise," she said, giving the card a quick glance.

He smiled as he stood up, loomed over her, and patted her hand. "Because, if you don't, you know I'll be calling you!"

"Somehow I had a feeling you'd be saying that."

"All right, then, I'm going to go now so you can get some rest," said Klingerman. "I hope you will be feeling excellent, and that my visit has not impaired your recovery."

"That remains to be seen," said Anna wryly.

He chuckled. "You are a very sharp lady, Ms. Smithson."

"Thank you."

"Well, good-bye for now."

"Wait one more second," she said, stopping him in midstride to the door.

"Yes?"

"I forgot to ask you—who is the 'doctor friend' of yours I would be seeing for the . . . uh, the session?"

"Oh, of course!" Klingerman knitted his large fingers in front of his ample belly. "Her name is Mussina. Doctor Isabella Mussina, Veterans Administration."

Anna nodded and waved as he slipped from her room. She was glad she would be seeing a woman. Even though she did not like admitting it, the fact was oddly comforting to her. She knew she could trust a woman more than any man—not out of anything conspiratorial, rather the ability of women to be more *sensitive* to the feelings of other women.

Isabella Mussina.

It was such a pretty name. Like a line of Italian poetry. Anna was certain Dr. Mussina would be good for her.

TWELVE

ISABELLA MUSSINA, PH.D.
Chicago, Illinois

Thank God for Irwin Klingerman.

The thought comforted Isabella as she took the El home from her office at Hines VA Hospital. She had just interviewed and sessioned one of the rabbi's referrals, a Ms. Anna Smithson from the nearby suburb of Riverside, and the material was some of the best she'd accrued in many months. Her monumental case study and federally granted book project had originally concerned the possibly bogus phenomenon of past-life regression.

But things had changed.

They had changed ever since her own recent discovery of several patients who believed they had lived and *died* their previous lives in a Nazi death camp, and the subsequent meeting with Rabbi Klingerman and his own detailed files of people with similar experiences. For two years, she had been working closely with him, comparing their findings and attempting to better understand the phenomenon.

Because it *was* real. She had been since convinced there could be no doubt of the veracity of her patients' stories. The long and harrowing task of verifying facts in their dreams or hypnogogic memories had revealed startling accuracies in the smallest details. When you looked closely at the evidence, it did not fall apart; it became more formidable in its inherent truths.

Ann Smithson's story, still fresh in Isabella's mind, had touched her on several levels. The descriptions of a visit from a man who could be none other than Dr. Mengele were both frightening and challenging. That Ms. Smithson's prior self—"Ruth"—had been a twin also gave credence to the past-life memory. But the most startling and exciting piece of the story had to be the mention of the strange camp prisoner called "The Little Angel." The man with the gold tooth and the disturbing smile.

History, painted with the wide brush it demands, makes no mention of this man, who would be less than an errant fleck on the rolls of the dead millions. Indeed, he would have been nothing more than a scary curiosity to Isabella if she hadn't known that he'd been described in horrifying detail during several *other* patients' hypnotic sessions. This kind of collaboration was groundbreaking, exhilarating, and Kafkaesque. Unlikely in concept, but utterly true in reality.

The pattern she had suspected was beginning to take ever sharper form.

She spent the next several hours writing up her notes, compiling her observations, and composing a carefully worded monograph for her NetFile. From there it could be edited and electronically published almost instantly. Later she would revise and polish her work for a hard-copy publication in one of the journals or magazines, but she had learned how important it was in the Information Age to make her findings available as quickly as possible.

When she shared the findings of the Smithson session with the rabbi, he became so excited, it actually scared her. To Klingerman, the latest mention of *Der Klein Engel* apparently signified dire consequences and held complex meanings. He began spouting off weird quotations from the Kabbala, warning her of the beginning of some kind of unstoppable process. It was more like a recitation than a cogent, intellectual observation or commentary, and it bothered Isabella to listen to him rave on like some fringe-element mystic.

She had been thankful to get him off the phone with the excuse that she had to sign off the ward and officially end her shift at the hospital. Even so, he forced her to make plans to meet with him later that evening, stating that what he had to tell was more important than "anything else known to man."

Overly dramatic?

Isabella certainly hoped so.

She wasn't sure she wanted to be the keeper of such knowledge.

She had not been in the apartment more than ten minutes when the phone chirped.

God, she hated that thing! It never sounded when she wanted it to, when she was waiting for someone to ask her to dinner and a show, or dancing till the after-hours places called it a night. But it *always* shrilled its supercilious alarm at her when she was preoccupied with something else.

It was probably Irwin Klingerman. Impatient. Animated. Kind-of-nutty Rabbi Klingerman. Isabella smiled in spite of her irritation. She and Irwin had been friends as well as colleagues, and her conception of him as slightly unhinged sprang from her fondness for him as a genuinely good person.

But right now, she was shedding her whites and getting naked for a much-anticipated bubble bath. For an instant, she considered answering, but the scented vapor of the bath seduced her enough to ignore the phone until the answering machine picked up.

She was just sinking into the warm depths of the tub when she heard the voice of Jack Hazzard, her equally overworked colleague: "Sorry to bother you, Doctor M. . . . I know you just got off shift, and might not even be home yet, but I just got a call from Glinka at Langley. He says you have to call him *right away*—the usual number . . . sorry about this, so just remember, it's bad PR to kill the messenger . . . *Ciao,* 'Bella!"

The end-of-message beep mocked her as she sank a little lower into the luxuriant water. "Damn!" The word slipped out of her mouth, and it sounded funny to her when there was no one else around to hear it. She wasn't in the habit of talking to herself, but she was feeling very frustrated right about now.

Glinka!

She smiled ironically, thinking how much she would have preferred hearing from Klingerman than that prick, Glinka.

Well, Paul Glinka and his CIA were just going to have to wait.

This water had reached the perfect temperature, and she wasn't going to waste it on a phone call to a government employee.

God, she was so sick of them. . . . Hard to believe, but she often found herself wishing she'd never accepted the terms of the federal grant. Without fully realizing what she'd done until it was *far* too late, Isabella had agreed, in essence, to whore out her psychiatric services to the feds for enough money to conduct her independent study at the University of Chicago. For *six* years she'd had two government vultures picking her bones—the VA hospital three days a week, and the CIA whenever they damn well felt like it.

And the worst part was the way the agency people treated her: exactly like the unpaid, forced-labor drone she was. No respect for time or any other obligations. When they called, you were supposed to drop everything and get down on your knees. And every other sentence out of their mouths was a threat to cut off your funding if you didn't do whatever they wanted. It got to the point where she didn't care about the funding anymore. There was a wall up ahead, beyond which lay whatever was left of her self-respect and time in her life to live based on her own decisions.

And Isabella was getting ready to hit the wall.

She had absolutely no time completely her own. No time for a social life. (When was the last time she'd actually had a *date*? She honestly couldn't remember, and that was *very* scary. . . .) And thank God she had no family—she'd never see them. She was lucky she found time to call her mother in Sarasota once in awhile. The idea of anybody owning her, especially the government, made her want to vomit.

These thoughts swirled around her like the dissipating bubbles of her bath. Just imagining herself rising from the tub and running to grab that telephone made her nauseated, but she knew she'd have to keep doing it, at least until the end of the year. After that, it looked pretty good for obtaining private funding.

Finally.

That would free her of the federal yoke she'd been under for what seemed like forever. And she couldn't dream up anything more pleasurable than telling those government toads to take a hike.

God, she was sick of them!

The minutes slipped away from her and the bathwater gradually cooled. Wrapping a towel around her, she padded to her bedroom, sat down on the edge of her unmade bed, and reached for the phone. No need to look up the northern Virginia number, it was etched in her memory like a cheap engraving. Isabella longed for the day when it would be less than forgotten.

The line picked up on the first ring. "Doctor Mussina," said a flat voice. "I've been waiting. What's going on?"

Paul Glinka, charming as usual. She'd always found it hard to work up enough venom to actually *hate* anybody, but she hated this guy.

"What's going on is that I have a *life*, Mr. Glinka, and I don't spend it sitting by a phone waiting for your calls," said Isabella as evenly and hard-edged as possible. She wanted this creep to know how much she loathed him. "Full time in a sinkhole you call a hospital, and my own research and teaching at a university—just a couple of minor diversions to while away my hours . . ."

"We have a field problem," he said, ignoring her. "Harford Nichols."

"Who is he?"

"An E—Thirty—always been one of our best. He might be OCT, but we want your evaluation first. We're also going to want to know what he's been doing."

"Where is he?" Isabella fell immediately into step as she listened to the cursory details of the case. At least this one sounded intriguing. OCT was their argot for "out-of-control: terminate." It was a condition that rarely came up, but for any agent who cracked under the pressure of being a professional killer, they had a plan— the most expedient and efficient one.

"Currently safe at home. There's a plane to pick you up at Midway. The usual arrangements. Be there by 1930 your time."

"Mr. Glinka, you are calling at a very inopportune time," she said softly, but with unguarded irritation.

The man chuckled. "Tell him to shoot his wad and get out of there."

"You are a vulgar man," she said with open disdain.

"Thank you," said Glinka. "It helps me be a better boss."

"I was referring to my own work. I have a new patient who needs me," she said, already knowing she was wasting her time.

"Tell 'im you'll see 'im when you get back into town."

"And how long am I going to be gone?"

"No way to tell." Glinka chuckled. "If you're worried about what to pack, forget it. Just grab some stuff and get going. We'll send somebody in to bring more things for you—if it looks like it's going to be a long war."

"Oh, would you *really?*" Isabella spoke in a bouncy schoolgirl voice. "Golly, that's sure nice of you, Mr. Glinka!"

The arrogance of this bastard appalled her. To invade her home and go through her private belongings meant less than nothing to them. It was business as usual. But what did she expect from a bunch of reptiles who killed people in the name of patriotism? Going through a citizen's closets didn't even make the charts.

"Be on that plane, Doctor," said Glinka. "Good-bye."

The connection clicked and she was holding a dead line. There was no use letting him upset her. That was just another form of control. And they liked to think of themselves as masters of control. Exhaling slowly, Isabella replaced the portable phone in its charger and began mentally packing her carry-on luggage. It was better to concentrate on something with little real import than to dwell on the unfairness of it all.

She called Irwin Klingerman and told him of the trip. He was the only friend, other than a few colleagues at the VA who were fettered by the same agreement with the feds, who knew of her obligations to help the CIA with sensitive issues.

An hour later, her hair was dry and combed out. She'd been letting it grow and it was now below her shoulders. Long enough to keep in a clasp all day, allowing her to look neat, but still a little on the bohemian side. When not forced to wear her hospital "uniforms," she liked to affect the funky academic look when she was teaching her graduate school classes. Lots of boots, long flowing skirts, scarves, turtlenecks. A classic style that was never out of fashion, but comfortable and informed. Her Mediterranean heritage imparted a dark, mysterious air to her anyway, and if she wasn't so trapped by her profession, she *knew* she'd have no trouble finding a man who'd be with her the rest of her life.

At least that's what she kept telling herself.

But at thirty-eight, she was getting a little long in the tooth to be called a college girl. And, as many career women her age had been discovering, the pool of eligible men over forty was not all that large or encouraging. The axiom that all the "good ones" were gone by then might or might not be true, but Isabella was not all that anxious to find out. In fact, finding a suitable companion for the rest of her life had never been a big priority for her. It was one of those things she assumed would eventually just *happen*. That it had not bothered her very little.

Besides, it was a small and insignificant matter at this point. The major factors in her life right now had mustered a two-pronged attack on her energy: a death camp figure called "The Little Angel," and a CIA killer who might be so crazy he would have to be exterminated like a rabid dog. How had she allowed her life to become so damned complicated? And what was it going to take to make it simpler?

As she descended the elevator to the lobby, she was fighting an oncoming storm front of anxiety. The last thing she felt like doing was cabbing it to the airport and flying east. By the time they got her briefed, then settled in somewhere, it would be the middle of the night. She hadn't been sleeping very well after her long hospital shifts anyway.

This was definitely *not* the way she had planned her life. The thought lingered mockingly, and she cautioned herself to stop feeling sorry for herself. No room for depression on the schedule.

"Good evening, Doctor Mussina," said Horace, her building's concierge. "Your cab's already here."

Isabella smiled and thanked him as he escorted her to the sidewalk and into the car. She had no idea she had just embarked on a very special journey—to that single moment in her life when everything was going to change.

But she could not know this.

No one ever does.

THIRTEEN

J. MICHAEL KEATING, M.D.
Manhattan, New York

Impossible . . . !

The rational part of his nature screamed out the only possible response to the gathered evidence. He was spiraling downward, into the maelstrom of the paranormal, and there was no escaping its pull. All he'd uncovered in the last few weeks stood like a monument in direct opposition to all he'd learned in a lifetime of experience. It was so . . . so *difficult,* so damned *hard* to accept that, only minutes before, he'd been talking to the "soul" of a person murdered more than half a century past.

And yet, there wasn't much he could validly question any longer. Unless he was the victim of a carefully orchestrated and cunningly connected hoax, he was being forced to accept what should *not* be possible. Not only had Allison Enders and Rodney McGuire described the same place, the same kind of death—details readily available to anyone who sought them out—but they had *both* described the appearance of a single prisoner, a *sonderkommando*, with a gold tooth and sunken eyes. A prisoner who seemed to have special privileges; a lackey of Josef Mengele everyone called *Der Klein Engel.* It was this figure in both dream-sessions that plagued

Michael so mercilessly. A detail that didn't, as far as he knew, appear in any of the history books.

Michael knew, however, he couldn't rest on any assumptions. Already he was unconsciously planning out his methods of research, how he might verify what his subjects had been telling him. But for the moment he had a more pressing matter to deal with: the welfare of his patient.

The session with Rodney McGuire had been a draining emotional experience for both doctor and patient. When Michael awakened Rodney, the man seemed unsettled and suspicious, despite postsuggestions of well-being and serenity—an unusual occurrence. . . .

"So was I right, Doc? There's somethin' weird goin' on, right? I ain't crazy, am I?" The questions jumped out of him rapidly, but Rodney sat rigidly in his chair, staring straight ahead as though facing a firing squad.

"Not at all, Mr. McGuire. You're very healthy."

"So what's goin' on with me? Why am I having the nightmares? And what about that Goldberg guy?"

Michael clasped his hands slowly, tried to assume a pose of authority and control. "The answers to your questions need more than short, simple answers," he said.

"What do you mean by that?" said McGuire, appearing to be more hurt than upset. "You think I'm bein' simple?"

Smiling gently, Michael shook his head. "No, no! Not at all, Rodney. I mean the answers may prove to be more complex than we ever suspected."

McGuire absorbed this for a moment, then: "So that means you can't tell me anything, right?"

"Let's just say I'll need to do more checking around before I can tell you anything meaningful." Michael cleared his throat nervously. He didn't want to sound pompous or unconcerned. "In fact, I have my assistant, Ms. Robbins, working on it right now."

"What about Goldberg?" he said pleadingly. "You've gotta tell me somethin'! Why did I go see him? In the damn snow. In *Pittsburgh*! And why did I dream about him? What's goin' on, Doc?"

Michael exhaled slowly, trying to figure out how and what he should say that would make sense and not upset his patient. "Well, Rodney, I'm not sure yet, but I *think* it goes something like this: you've been dreaming that you're a man named Avram Goldberg, and that you and your brother, Youssef, were at a Nazi death camp, and—"

"Hey, I already know all that," he said with a whisper of desperation on his lips. "I need to know *why*, what the hell it *means*. . . ."

"Okay," said Michael, composing his thoughts again. "Well, it seems that, in your dream, your brother, Youssef, escapes the camp and eventually has a *son* named Avram—which is the name of a man who lives with his family in Pittsburgh. . . ."

Michael let his voice trail away, waiting and hoping that his patient would make the necessary associations. It was always better when the subject worked out the logic on his or her own, and he was quite certain Rodney would make the connections.

The cab driver's expression confirmed this as his jaw dropped in hesitation and surprise. ". . . and he named him after *me*, or, I mean, after the guy I've been dreamin' about."

"I'm pretty sure that's it." Michael nodded.

"Oh, man, that is some heavy-duty business, isn't it?" Rodney rubbed his mouth with the back of his hand. "I went out there in the snow to see this guy's brother's *kid*—that was the guy in the window with the family . . ."

"Apparently," said Michael.

"But *why?*" Rodney smiled in frustration, forced himself to stand, and began pacing back and forth. "What's going on, Doc? It sounds like I'm being *haunted* . . . you know, like a house! We gotta do somethin' about this! If that guy, that *dead* guy, can make me do stuff I don't wanna do . . . man, *that's* some freaky shit, you hear me?"

"Please, please take it easy, Mr. McGuire." Michael stood, joined him, and guided him back to his seat. "We'll find the answers. Don't worry, please. We've already made very good progress, and I'm pretty sure your dreams will not be as much of a problem now that we know why you're having them."

Michael surprised himself with that last sentence and hoped Rodney would not hook him on it. Did they really know *why?* Did they know anything at all?

"I ain't so sure about that," said McGuire, falling silent.

Perhaps he didn't want to face the questions in his own mind just yet. If not, Michael could hardly blame him. If this man, like Allison Enders, had lived before and had died at the hands of the

Nazis, it would indeed be a difficult new truth to accept about themselves and about the nature of the universe.

"Do you want to see me again?" said Michael, moving back to his desk to pick up his scribble-pad.

"You bet your bottom dollar!" said McGuire. "I gotta feelin' this whole thing ain't over yet."

"How about a prescription to help you sleep?"

McGuire shook his head. "Nah, no thanks, Doc. Ever since I quit the hooch, I don't take nothin' to make me sleep."

"That's fine," said Michael. He conferred with McGuire and they agreed on a time for the next appointment, far enough into the month so that Michael and Pamela might have completed some necessary research.

"Listen, Doc," said McGuire, as he walked to the door with Michael escorting him, "I just wanna tell you that I really appreciate you seein' me like this, tryin' to help me like you are."

"Your case is very special," said Michael. "It's my pleasure."

"And you're sure I shouldn't be worryin' about this?"

"Worrying solves nothing. Understanding is the key, Mr. McGuire. You're somehow sympathetic to the memories of someone who suffered very much."

Rodney looked confused. "You mean I'm rememberin' somebody else's memories?"

"That's a very picturesque way of putting it. But I like it," said Michael. "You know, they say that all radio and TV broadcasts are out there, in space, traveling infinitely, and that someone, somewhere very far away, could receive them tonight, even though they might be about things from years in our past. The newscast of JFK's assassination, a World Series game, anything. . . ."

"Huh? I don't get it."

"Maybe our memories are like that—floating infinitely through the ether, and some of us are able to pick them up like radio waves. Someone like you."

McGuire thought about this and nodded. He seemed to like this possible explanation, and Michael smiled, pleased to be so fast on his mental feet.

"Yeah, well, thanks, Doc."

"Call me if you need to tell me anything important," said Michael as he closed the door, entombing himself with his own thoughts.

• • •

. . . and now, as he sat behind his desk, he heard the outer door close softly. Pamela Robbins had joined him. There was a tap on the door and she leaned in to look at him with an expectant little smile.

"Come on in," he said, directing her to the chair beside the desk. "Any luck?"

"I don't know if 'luck' had anything to do with it," she said, lugging a briefcase filled with folders and papers to her lap. "Lots of hard work, I'd say."

"What'd you find?" Michael felt a lump of anxiety growing in his throat.

"Pretty much what you'd expect—if you're not a staunch empiricist," she said with a wry smile. "The first thing I did was get on the Net and establish some connections with people in Germany at the University of Bonn's historical archives. And I tried the same thing at the Institute for Historical Study in Warsaw. From there, I was shunted along from place to place."

"And . . . ?"

"And it was kind of fun, actually. Like being a detective." She smiled again and tilted her head as she looked up at him. She was trying to be coy and coquettish, and it was working.

"Pamela, it's *very* much like being a detective," he said as sternly as possible, knowing he sounded silly. "Now, come on, tell me what you found."

"The village of Chyrnow, in 1938, had twelve thousand people," she said. "More than four thousand of them Jewish. There *is* a river nearby. It's called the Wkra. Allison's details are perfect. It was a small center for trade, getting bigger and getting a reputation among the farm communities as the best small town in the area to do your commerce."

"Incredible," said Michael. "And the family . . . ?"

"There were several prominent Jewish doctors in the town," she said, shuffling through several folders before pulling out the one she wanted. "And here's our man: Doctor Stefan W. Staniciewz."

She pulled out several papers, including a fax-photo from a passport. Depicting a long-faced, bearded man with dark eyes of penetrating intelligence, it also displayed a stamp with the single word "Juden" bleeding across the photo into the text. Michael picked up the piece of paper and stared at the man's face, imagining the faraway moment in time when the young doctor had posed before the lens of fine German-ground glass and waited for the shutter to click. What had Dr. Staniciewz been thinking at that precise moment? Could he have ever imagined the abject terrors that awaited him?

Handing the picture back to Pamela, Michael felt a wave of infinite sadness crest over him.

"The evidence is pretty hard to refute, isn't it?" She looked at him calmly, with just a hint of feminine smugness that usually accompanies a validation of intuitive powers.

"You don't have any problem accepting what all this means, do you?"

"No, of course not," said Pamela. "People are born, they die, and they are born again. Reincarnation. Our souls never really die. They just trade bodies. It's all pretty simple stuff."

Michael grinned, shook his head. "Simple only if you are simple*minded*. And neither of us fall into that category. But you can't deny the admittance of these new factors only gives a whole new set of questions and problems. Of course, that's the way it should be: new discoveries should always bring new questions."

Pamela looked at him. "I think this stuff scares you," she said.

"Don't be ridiculous." But he was thinking: *Could she possibly be right?* "I'm . . . challenged by it, maybe. But I don't know about 'scared.'"

"Well, maybe that's the wrong word," she said. "But I think it definitely bothers you. I think it upsets your applecart."

"Come on, Pamela, you know how much I hate those lame clichés."

"That's why I used it," she said with a grin. "Besides, you know exactly what I mean."

He exhaled slowly, letting it become an exasperated sigh. "What else did you discover? Anything about 'The Little Angel'?"

Shaking her head, Pamela shuffled through some of her folders. "Not yet. But there're several levels of search routines that I haven't been able to get into. The host-servers require validation of our credentials and then we have to go into a priority stack. We should have clearance by tomorrow."

"I can't believe they're so busy," he said.

She nodded. "It's not like the old days. *Everybody*'s on the Net now. Traffic jams everywhere. Ultraspeed lines don't help anymore."

"What about Mengele and the Auschwitz camp?" he said, checking his notes.

"There's *plenty* on all of that. I still have to narrow down my searches."

"We need to establish the existence of Mengele's 'Little Angel.' *Then* I'll be convinced."

Pamela chuckled. "Oh, I'm sure you'll find something else wrong with our data."

"What?" He looked at her curiously. "What do you mean?"

"Some other reason," she said. "You'll find another one—for not completely believing your own findings."

Michael looked at her with a little irritation. Maybe she was right, but he didn't feel like hearing it, or seeing her be so damned smug about it. "I think you've hit on the problem for me," he said. "You said 'believing,' and that's what this is all about. At some point in this investigation, I have to make an *act of faith*—something that's very hard for me."

Pamela pushed her thick auburn hair away from her face. It was almost a calculated gesture, a reminder of her sexual power. A little intimidating, too, and he wasn't sure he liked that in a woman. He wanted women who made him feel comfortable, not always thinking he had to be on his guard. Because of her dynamic personality, her perceptiveness, and her ability to anticipate problems, she was the perfect professional assistant, but he was wondering whether or not she was the kind of woman he'd choose as a wife. But . . . he thought, catching himself . . . what's all this talk about a *wife* anyway? He certainly hadn't been consciously in search of a life-partner. It had been Pamela, he knew, who'd been considering him as a potential husband; the energy she generated must have irradiated his own thoughts as well.

Weird.

Well, just get that stuff out of your head. You're—

"Oh, there's something else," said Pamela in a voice that was half coy, half sincere. She pulled another folder from her stack and handed it to him.

"Really?"

"I decided to see if anyone else had ever reported findings to back up our own cases," said Pamela.

"I thought I told you to check for that," he said, looking directly into her large eyes.

"Oh, did you? I don't remember." She tilted her head and smiled. "At any rate, I found some interesting articles on the Net. I printed them out for you, but the bottom line is that somebody else is onto this phenomenon."

"Really?" he said with genuine surprise.

"Oh yes, more than twenty-five cases."

"What?" This was incredible. Inconceivable. *Twenty-five* cases! "You printed them out? Where?"

Handing him a very thick folder, Pamela smiled. "Happy reading."

"Did you get a chance to look at any of this?" The stack of paper in his hands seemed to be growing heavier by the moment, warmer, as though gathering energy to itself.

She shook her head. "No, I figured you'd want to have the honors."

Michael nodded as he noticed her watching him. "Thank you, Pamela," he said. "You've done a great job. As usual."

"Thank you, Michael," she said. "I'll be out in my office if you need anything."

It was odd to hear her say his first name, but it was inevitable as soon as they had begun to see each other on a social basis. Another aspect of their expanding relationship that made him aware of how complicated it was to be attracted to a woman. No wonder he'd remained single for so long after his disastrous marriage. But he was beginning to believe that it might be different with Pamela. They had been colleagues and friends for years. They *knew* each other well.

Looking up, he noticed that he was alone, and he anxiously carried the stack of papers to his desk like a schoolboy with a pile of old *Playboy* magazines. Just knowing somebody had uncovered similar material electrified him. His own knowledge of his field's literature was extensive, so it was a double-edged surprise. He was glad to know of its existence, but also a little chagrined to not be publishing such findings himself.

But how could he have missed all this? It bothered him more than a little that he'd somehow overlooked any mention of death-camp memories. It was one of those things he'd remember, even though he read reams of professional journals and publications.

As he settled into his chair, adjusted his reading glasses, and began to scan the printouts, Michael began to understand.

None of the articles he read had been written for the professional journals, appearing instead in far more commercial and mundane venues such as *Penthouse, Omni, Psychology Today, American Religion, The Jewish Times, Maturity*, and many other magazines of less dubious credibility. All of the professionally obtained information originated with the work of Isabella Mussina, Ph.D., from the University of Chicago. Some of the material centered on additional research being conducted by a Rabbi Irwin Klingerman in Wisconsin. The information was presented throughout as a wide range of pieces, from papers presented at professional seminars and conventions to clippings from pop-science articles and tabloid newspaper columns.

It was this scattergun range of appearances that disappointed Michael the most. It was as if the authors and the original researchers had been so desperate to get out the word—any word in any form—that they allowed literally *anyone* to report on their findings. As is often the case in the commercial and popular press, the findings of academics were often handled with a less than sympathetic ear.

Still, this didn't deter Michael from working his way through the numerous references and articles. The best material stemmed from Dr. Mussina's own work, and he concentrated on her original sources. What struck him immediately was her clear, almost literary style and her remarkably unbiased conclusions. She was obviously a very bright woman who had been struggling—like himself—to correctly interpret the information offered to her. As he glided through her lyrical, expressive prose, he found himself nodding in silent agreement with Dr. Mussina's observations and cautionary comments. Michael became intrigued with her effort as a researcher trying to retain a high level of professionalism. Tough job, given the highly speculative and volatile nature of her work.

Michael leaned back in his favorite chair and continued to read.

Hours passed quickly, and when he checked his watch, he couldn't believe how fast the time had passed, as though he'd been reading a suspenseful novel. Dr. Mussina's evidence was startlingly similar to his own findings. For five years she had been interviewing subjects who had related similar stories: living in pre–World War Two Europe, then being taken to Nazi death camps where they had been killed. All of them had been having their nightmares or blackouts or hypnogogic episodes since 1991—a fact noted, but not yet fully understood or explained by Dr. Mussina.

And several of them mentioned Mengele's "Little Angel," the prisoner with the skull face and the gold tooth. Time for the act of faith.

In one sense, Michael felt a great sense of relief, of freedom. Seeing his work validated and confirmed in the work of another allowed him to look more confidently in the direction his data pointed. Reading the findings and observations of someone who'd already gained his respect, if for no other reason than her excellent command of language, had given him the courage to not doubt the feelings and thoughts his cases had stirred in him.

Dr. Isabella Mussina said it eloquently when she echoed thoughts Michael himself had grappled with in the lonely dark hours of the night when conversations with his soul could not be avoided: "I feel I have discovered something so important that I currently lack the language to explain it or the intelligence to fully recognize its true nature."

Michael understood perfectly what she was saying. More than once, a thought achingly similar had ghosted through him. Despite his reservations and unwillingness to let go, to surrender to all the cases' implications, he had a nasty feeling—an intuition, perhaps—that some strange mechanism was running, some immense piece of cosmic clockwork had been set into motion, and that he was far too unsophisticated to grasp its full meaning or intent.

At first, the notion simply irritated him, but later, as the disturbing evidence mounted, and the stories of hideous torture and death continued, Michael found himself becoming uncomfortable and finally scared.

Pamela had been correct, although he'd never admit it to her.

But with Dr. Mussina he believed he might have discovered a true kindred spirit, a woman with no agenda other than to eventually solve the mystery. Without coming completely face-to-face with the issue, Michael sensed an awakening within himself, an awakening inspired by the courageous writings of Isabella Mussina.

He continued to digest all her case histories, coming at last to her most recent file on a woman named Anna Smithson from Chicago. Although the style of the monograph seemed less refined, the information and vital facts remained clear—with many of the details mirroring the data of Michael's own files perfectly.

The implications stared him down, and he could no longer deny that something very bizarre was happening, something beyond the normal range of experience. Even in the literature of the paranormal, he had never seen anything similar to such a shared-event phenomenon. The only thing even close was the near-death experience, but those descriptions lacked the details of Mussina and Michael's cases.

Buzzing Pamela, he asked her to make every effort to reach Dr. Mussina at the University of Chicago. He wanted to talk to the psychologist as soon as possible, by phone preferably, but he would settle for an exchange of e-mail.

While he waited, he began to scan through some of the secondary material Pamela had collected, primarily comprised of articles by Irwin Klingerman, an orthodox rabbi from Fond du Lac, who'd self-published a book about reincarnation and past-life regression, and who apparently offered his essays to anyone who would publish them. Klingerman had also interviewed many subjects who claimed to have death-camp "memories." His writing conveyed the information in a journeyman style, but the data was colored by an implied belief in all things paranormal, such as clairvoyance, prescience, and even telekinesis. Rabbi Klingerman's work, while impressive in its quantity and dedication, lacked the discipline of Mussina's efforts.

In fact—

He was interrupted by Pamela's intercom.

"Yes?"

"I've tracked down your doctor," she said. "But—"

"Great! Put her on line one."

There was a pause, dead air full of irritation, then Pamela's voice being silky and sardonic. "I was going to say *but* . . . she's not available."

"What?"

Pamela informed him of Mussina's work with the VA and her inopportune absence.

The news slapped him like an insult. How dare she be unavailable? He *needed* to talk to her right away. "Did they tell you *when* she'll be available?"

"No. They didn't seem to know very much," she said. "Typical government employees. . . ."

Michael made arrangements to leave messages for Dr. Mussina at every conceivable address (real and electronic), requesting her contact as soon as possible.

As he hung up his phone, Michael reflected for a moment on what he was feeling. Deep down, a white-hot core of true excitement burned in him. He hadn't felt so *alive*, so challenged, since he was a headstrong, angry young man, outraged over all the injustice in the world. He sensed something momentous in the near future; he was approaching a crucial point in his life, and he felt himself rushing toward it with an abandon he thought had long ago escaped him.

FOURTEEN

ARNOLD RASSENAULT
Manhattan, New York

The headquarters for the *Journal of Progressive History* were huddled in two cramped rooms above a guitar shop on West Twenty-eighth near the corner of Ninth Avenue. The address, while sounding prestigious to anyone living west of the Hudson River, would, if examined in person, reveal the *Journal* and its "staff" of one to be the shabby operation that it was.

Arnold Rassenault, the founder, editor, and publisher of the *JPH* was also its primary contributor, having written the majority of its strident articles and "studies" under a long catalogue of pseudonyms. As he walked up Twenty-eighth Street, he stopped in Holder's bakery for a blueberry muffin and a coffee—as he did every morning. The clerk, a middle-aged black woman, thanked him, calling him "Professor," just as everyone else did in the neighborhood. No one knew what kind of professor Arnold might be—they only knew he was indeed a professor, because he'd told them so.

Many times.

All the time.

They must respect me, he often told himself. The common man has no respect for himself because he *is* common. The great herds of humanity had a natural *need* for leaders, for men whom they could respect. In the past, during the centuries of Europe's grandeur, respect was attained through the aristocracy's strict system of titles. Arnold often longed for the time when he could have been a duke or a baron, but in his more reflective moments he realized he must settle for whatever was available.

Doctor sounded good, but he preferred *Professor*.

More intelligent-sounding. More hoity-toity. And besides, no one would ever bother to check his credentials. Not this late in the game.

The thought drifted through him and he smiled as he exited the bakery, walking past the guitar shop to unlock the door to the second-floor walk-up. He tried not to look too closely at his reflection in the shop's plate-glass window because he didn't much like the stooped, gray, and wrinkled old bastard he'd become. It seemed like just yesterday he'd been a successful lawyer in Syracuse, but that had been almost forty years ago.

Back before the Jews took over.

Back before the word "lawyer" had become synonymous with *Jewish lawyer*.

Oh sure, Arnold Rassenault knew how it worked. He'd learned the truth a long time ago. Back when he was a young man in his mid-twenties. Those Jews, once they got into something, *never* stopped till they ran it from top to bottom.

Till they ran everybody else out of business.

Because that's what it was always about with the Jews, wasn't it? *Business*. Always business.

Well, Professor Arnold Rassenault had some *business* for them, isn't that right? Rassenault chuckled dryly as he climbed the stairs to "the offices."

Pushing back the frosted pane door, he stepped into the accumulated clutter of more than twenty-five years. Metal shelving packed thick with manuscripts, magazines, photographs, posters, and pamphlets; rusted and dented filing cabinets tilted and leaning against dingy walls; a single window, its sills locked down by years of grime and coats of dirty paint; a desk in each tiny room, covered with stacks of papers, envelopes, folders, notes, and stationery accessories—each guarded by the looming presence of a massive Olympia manual typewriter. And dust and age and other marks of time's passage everywhere. The phone on the corner of the desk was an old black rotary-dial, a Bell Labs model DL-310 from 1938.

A frightful mess, but Rassenault knew the exact nature and location of every scrap of information in the *Journal*'s headquarters. Pushing back some pages scheduled for the next issue, he spread out his muffin on a napkin and sipped his coffee. As he rifled through a stack of mail, ignoring the bills and looking for intriguing correspondence, he heard footsteps on the stairs. Who could be—? Oh, yes. . . .

For a moment, he'd forgotten the appointment with Fritz Hargrove. He was doing that sort of thing more and more often. Maybe it was Alzheimer's on the way . . . just what he needed when he was involved in the most important work of his life! He couldn't—

A short, masculine *rap-rap* on the frosted glass interrupted his woolgathering.

"Yes," he said. "Come in."

The door swung inward, uncovering a large, beefy, red-faced man. He wore a black knit cap and a navy pea coat over a plaid shirt and relaxed-fit Levi jeans. His eyes seemed a little too small for the doughy insistence of his face—which was mostly a big, shapeless nose and puffy cheeks and jowls. Fritz Hargrove was his name, and although still in his thirties, he looked older and fairly high on the list of prospective heart-attack victims. In his left hand, he carried a folder of papers.

Arnold was not sure whether or not he really *liked* Fritz Hargrove, but he had proved, over the years, to be useful. A welder by trade, Fritz fancied himself as a writer of sorts and provided material to the *Journal of Progressive History* in the form of interviews and reportorial coverage of events of interest to the *Journal* and its parent organization, the League of True Americans.

"Fritz, my good man! How are you?" Arnold tried to sound as cheery as possible.

Hargrove removed his cap and coat, hung them on an old standing coatrack in the corner. He placed the folder on Arnold's desk triumphantly. "I got them!" he said. "Those dirty Yids!"

"The pictures?" Arnold couldn't believe it. "In Crown Heights?"

Hargrove pulled up a chair, faced him on the other side of the desk, and began to show him the black-and-white 8x10s one at a time. Mostly crowd scenes of Hassidic Jews standing around the street corners with signs. Arnold thought they all looked so silly in their long black coats, the ugly beards, and the ever-present hats.

"I waited around for days," said Hargrove. "Just hanging around the newsstand off Crescent. And then, it just kind of happened and I was right there. Look at these . . ."

Arnold looked at the next three photos, which showed a gang of Jews beating up two young black boys in front of a kosher bakery.

"Oh, these are perfect," he said.

Hargrove nodded, basked in the praise.

Incredible. But it was exactly the kind of proof he needed to back up his article about how dangerous the urban Jewish ghettos had become. His argument had concluded that it was time to go in and burn them out.

"It was really getting out of hand by the time the cops showed up," said Hargrove. "I was lucky to get out with my camera."

"These will be part of the lead article," said Arnold. "Maybe even break tradition and put a photo on the cover."

"You're kidding." Hargrove was impressed.

"Not at all. The media *never* publishes pictures like this!" Arnold stood up and began to pace and strut behind his desk. It was the way he liked to get air into his chest and pumped up his voice for a proper speech. "And why is that, Fritz?"

"—uh, because the media is run by the Yids!"

"Exactly! And it's only through the valiant efforts of people like me and *you* that the truth will *ever* get out." Arnold paused, drew a breath, and decided to sit back down. He felt a little dizzy from jumping up so fast.

"Thank you, Professor. It's an honor to work for you."

"Your efforts will be rewarded," said Arnold. "Especially when you consider who runs all the avenues for public opinion. Our last issue has gotten us some interesting publicity."

"Publicity? How?"

"Some TV reporter from WCBS wants to talk to me."

"Really? What's going on?"

Arnold ran a hand through his thin, gray hair. "That graduate student from Columbia. Remember he sent us a paper on something about the economics of World War Two?"

"Sure. You were so excited," said Hargrove. "I remember. You published it, right?"

"Of course! Last issue!" Arnold frowned in exasperation. Sometimes, Fritz could come off sounding so absolutely oafish, it was embarrassing. But at least he was somebody to talk to. Somebody who listened.

"Oh, yeah, right." Fritz grinned. "So how come the TV guys want to talk to you?'

Arnold giggled he was so pleased with himself. "Oh, it was so delicious, Fritz! When the student saw his article in my *Journal*, he was extremely upset. He claimed he didn't know we were—as he put it—'a white supremacist, anti-Semitic, hate sheet.' He said his academic career would be 'ruined' by appearing in my magazine!"

"I don't get it," said Fritz. "Why'd he send you the story in the first place?"

"Good question! He claims he believed we were a 'legitimate' publication of academic research." Arnold stood up, laughed dramatically. "That's a good one, isn't it? What kind of an academic does he think he is—if his *own* research is that shoddy, eh?"

"Yeah, I guess you're right." Fritz was getting lost, but Arnold didn't care. He enjoyed listening to himself.

"No matter how you slice it, he comes off looking bad. And we get the publicity!"

Fritz was losing the logical thread of their discussion and remained silent. He had at least learned that if you had nothing of worth to say, it was far better to remain silent. Thankfully, that had never been a problem for Arnold, however.

"When that TV reporter calls me, I will have an earful for him," he promised his minion. "It's time we laid bare the biggest lie the Jews have forced upon the world!"

Arnold knew exactly how to handle the journalist. Make him think he had an eccentric nutcase on his hands. That always made for good, entertaining copy. But Arnold would seize the moment to advance his special agenda—he would read to the reporter from his book in progress, *The Great Holocaust Hoax*. That way, the world would get a taste of the truth. Give them something to think about, all right. . . .

Because that was what was most important, thought Arnold. Get the word out. Get people to hear the truth. At least *consider* the truth. That Germany never exterminated all those millions of Jews; that the only Jews they killed were engaged in espionage against the Third Reich; and the death camps were a complete fiction, and were actually crematoriums for the casualties of Allied bombing raids.

Yes, thought Arnold with a pleasant smile. *I will seize the moment that has been given to me by the reckless and impulsive actions of a foolish student. He has squealed like a stuck pig and the Jews have come running with their microphones and their cameras. Well, fine,* he thought. *I'm ready for them.*

Arnold stood rigidly, smiling to himself as he surveyed the meager expanse of his domain. Soon, he thought, the facts housed in this small bunker of truth would be unleashed upon the world.

FIFTEEN

HARFORD NICHOLS
Langley, Virginia

Good evening," said the woman behind the desk. "I am Doctor Mussina."

Harford had just been escorted by two rookies into the office with no name on the front door. Located ten levels down in the warren that comprised the heart of the agency's op center, the area was designated as super-secure. No one got in or out of this area unless they wanted you to—at least that was their proud claim. As one of the agency's best, Harford had headed up a team assigned to actually test the security of the installation several years back. His men had failed to achieve any serious breaches, much to the happiness of all the division chiefs, but of course Harford's final debriefing did not contain every last detail.

First Law of Survival in the spy wars: Never tell 'em everything you know.

Second Law: Never tell 'em you know about the First Law.

After the rookies conferred with her, she dismissed them. Smiling, Harford took a seat in front of the woman's desk. She was somewhere in her thirties and looked extremely good at her primary function: being a woman. Thick auburn hair, kind of a medium length, fashionably styled. Her face had all the right accentuations, like a painting by Botticelli, and dark brown eyes that looked like they could take in a lot of secrets and never let them escape their depths. He'd always been a sucker for women with intelligently expressive eyes. On this particular level, everybody wore some kind of identifying costume: white for the sci-techs and docs, coveralls for the drones and worker bees, lots of military browns and blues, and suits for the higher-ups. She wore a crisp pale grass green suit beneath her open, white lab coat, which marked her as a civilian who walked around here on a strictly need-to-know basis. Harford felt sorry for those types—they had no clue what was really going on in their midst.

Leaning across the desk, he shook hands with her. "Nice to meet you, Doc," said Harford with a little smile. "I guess I don't really need to tell you who I am. You've probably got the standard two-inch file . . ."

"I *have* been briefed, Mr. Nichols," she said coolly. "You know why I'm here, don't you?"

He chuckled. Why were all these pysch types all the same? He had been hoping for something different in such a striking-looking woman. Perhaps more style, more individualism. "No offense, Doctor Mussina, but they didn't just unhook my drool bucket and wheel me down here from occupational therapy. . . ."

"I'm sorry, I—"

"*I* requested this work-up, if you want the bottom line," he said quickly. "I *know* something's not right, and I want it fixed."

"That's why I'm here, Mr. Nichols." She leaned forward, tapped a few keys on the keyboard in front of her, and checked a monitor, whose screen was hidden from him. "I can't guarantee anything, but with your cooperation, we can give it a very good effort."

He shrugged. "I'll do whatever you want. If I've got a good read on my supers, they think I am *very* dangerous. Out of control. A serious threat to their security and their secrets, right?"

"Probably. Only you can know if you truly are." She remained as neutral and unemotional as possible.

Harford nodded, gave her a little grin and a tilt of the head calculated to be charming. "Yeah, and I also know that if you—or any of the other shrinks they send in after you—gives me a thumbs-down, they're going to trash me. So you can *bet* I'm going to be very cooperative."

She looked at him for moment, as though assessing the level of his sincerity, then: "Very well, shall we begin?"

"Let's do it."

She directed him to the opposite corner of the office to an extremely comfortable, leather-appointed reclining chair, where he folded himself into its palmlike grasp. She sat down across from him at a mobile workstation with keyboard and screen. The lighting was all recessed and deflected, imparting an odd intimacy to the room.

"I'd like to start out with a few general questions," she said.

"Okay . . ."

"I have all the vital stats, but it might be valuable to hear you tell me some of the details in your own words. Can you give me your age, background, training, and anything else about yourself you might think would be helpful in getting to know you?"

Harford looked at her for a moment, then stared off at a point on the wall. She had an interesting look about her. If he kept staring at her, he was going to get distracted too much.

"Okay, I just turned forty-five, but I don't feel any different than when I was twenty-five. I guess it'll start to affect me sooner or later and I'll start slowing down, but right now, everything's still working the way it's supposed to, and I feel good. I've been with the agency since 1984. They wanted me. Chased me around after I'd pulled about two years with a merc force. Run by an ex-colonel—Ross Havlicek. Crazy bastard. Ex-army, 'Nam vet. Never got used to peacetime, so he quit the regulars to start up his own elite unit."

"Tell me," she said, interrupting him with a very soft voice. "Why did you join Havlicek's people?"

"Good question. I think I was bored, and I know I was plenty angry. When boys first turn into men, they discover the world's not a very fair place. And it pisses them off. I guess you've heard that before. Anyway, I'd gotten this piece of paper that said I was an architect, and I realized I couldn't design a garden shed—really, and that nobody was going to hire me anyway. It pissed me off, I guess."

Dr. Mussina nodded. "You were disillusioned and angry. Did you join the mercenaries hoping that maybe you would be killed?"

Harford laughed out loud. "No, no . . . nothing like that. None of that standard 'death wish' stuff. I just wanted to hurt somebody."

"Do you think you're a sadist?"

He chuckled and gave her a look intended to be charming. "You mean do I like hurting people?"

"Well . . ." She looked at him without humor. "That *is* what a sadist likes to do."

This woman was all business. He wasn't sure if he liked her all that much, but if she could figure out what was going on in the Gray Room, who cared?

"No," he said after a pause. "I definitely *don't* like it. What I like is the sense of *justice* I feel being exacted when I finish an assignment. I've always wanted things to be *fair*, ever since I was a little kid. So I usually have a good feeling after I'm finished."

"No politics?"

He shook his head. "I'm my *own* political party—a party of one. I never question the politics because I usually don't agree with *any* of it. If I feel like justice is being served in an ideal sense—beyond any political considerations, then I'm happy."

"You joined the regular army right after high school. Did you like the discipline?"

"Gotta qualify that one. I did it to show my father that I would do *anything* to make him unhappy with me." He laughed as he remembered the last time he'd ever spoken to his father. "I had no idea what I was in for."

"You didn't answer the question." Mussina's face remained passive.

"Oh . . . well, no, I wasn't crazy about the discipline. I hated it. I mean, what'd you expect from somebody who'd been getting orders from his father all his life? I was *sick* of doing what somebody else wanted me to do. But I was stuck—so I decided to make the best of it and took the Special Forces training."

"And what happened?"

"I found that I liked the *personal* discipline—what the training forced me to do. I learned that I was not just a capable person, but actually super-capable." He looked at her with what he knew was a not very attractive arrogance, but he wanted her to realize he believed it. "That I could just about do any fucking thing I wanted to if I really applied the rules I'd learned. So yeah, I hated the discipline, but I liked the results."

"I see . . ." She made some notes, keyed a few things into the computer. "Tell me about college."

"Pitt was great. I even grew to like the city. Between the money from the army program and a part-time job at the local PBS TV station, I worked my way through. Graduated in six years. Took my time. Made sure I learned something. WQED was the home of *Mister Rogers' Neighborhood*—I worked on the show as a production assistant. Did you know that Michael Keaton got his start there?"

"The actor . . . ? No," said Mussina, "I didn't."

He laughed. "Yeah. Mr. McFeely and Batman. I worked with some famous people, huh?"

This time a small grin hinted itself at the corner of her mouth. Finally. Something to reassure him that she was a normal human female.

"Did you really want to be an architect?"

He looked away as visions of endless hours at the drafting tables came rushing back to him. "I liked the *idea* of designing houses and buildings, but I guess I never hooked into the actual amount of effort required. I also—now that I think about—liked the discipline of architecture. There was a real order, a sense of structure that was unchanging."

"You preferred studying more than *doing* it. That makes sense." Mussina keyed something new into her computer.

"Does it?" He wondered what she was writing about him. Maybe later he would compromise the files and do a little recreational reading. . . .

"The time with Colonel Havlicek's unit. Tell me about it in a few sentences."

Exhaling, he leaned into the challenge of summing up two and half years of spiritually demeaning, humanly debasing time: "Some really awful places: Angola, Liberia, Zimbabwe. Sri Lanka. Plenty of money I never had time to spend. Lots of killing."

She looked up from her pad and keyboard. "This is when you first killed someone?"

He nodded.

"Did it bother you?"

"Oh yeah, but not the way you might think."

Mussina said nothing, but continued to look at him expectantly.

". . . I killed someone," he said, nodding in remembrance of that baptismal act. "And then I killed somebody else. And again, and again. And I realized that it didn't bother me. That I felt . . . well, *nothing*, really. I could hose somebody with my Kalashnikov— almost cut 'im in half—and then sit down with a ham sandwich and a Coke. It was the *nothing* that really bothered me."

She nodded, changed her position in her chair as though suddenly uncomfortable. "What did you do about it?"

Harford paused for an instant. He *hated* the textbook questions from this woman. But this was not the time to bitch about it. So: "What I *did* about it was learn to live with it. End of problem."

"End of problem. Do you really believe that?"

"Yeah, I do."

"And you don't think you're cold, or reptilian, or any of the usual terms?" She leaned forward, her body language telling him that this answer was a *really important* one.

So he threw her a little curve: "Yes, I do—but I'm okay with it. It's who I am."

"Have you ever been in love?" She looked at him with only the slightest suggestion of a grin—she could throw curves as well.

"I don't think so. I've always been too selfish, too self-contained."

"Good answer," she said.

"You see, I believe there's a need for people like me. I'm not one of these guys who is trying to shoehorn his behavior into a prefor- mulated moral code. I don't believe I'm doing anything wrong. So I don't have any psychological dilemmas to resolve."

Dr. Mussina looked up, stared at him as she considered his words. "That's a very neat and sanitary package."

Harford shrugged. "If it works, don't knock it. What I do is who I am."

"But maybe it *doesn't* work," she said. "You're suffering from pro- longed blackouts that may very well be pathological—to the point that you might be *killing* people without realizing it. I'm sorry, Mr. Nichols, but I'm not sure I would describe the situation as 'working.'"

Her comments gave him pause. She was right. What was he trying to do with his subtle posturing and bravado? There was no sense trying to sound impervious to psychotherapy. It was either make this exercise work or face termination. End of story.

"All right," he said with a studied weariness. "What're we going to do about it?"

"We're going to stop playing games for starters, okay?"

"Games?"

She smiled a smile designed to be patronizing. "I have to tell you, Mr. Nichols, I have *not* appreciated your performance so far. I am a very busy person, and if I feel like somebody's wasting my time or not taking me seriously, I'm going to dismiss them. Is that what you want?"

"No," he said, really meaning it. He liked her because she demanded his respect. It was time to get serious. "I apologize if I've offended you. This situation is uncomfortable. Difficult. My way of handling it was wrong. I'm sorry."

"Apology accepted. Shall we continue then?" Mussina shifted her position in her chair. Was she relaxing a bit? "What about your dreams? Any nightmares, or recurring themes? Anything you think might give us a clue to what's happening?"

"I never dream. Nothing there I can think of. The blackouts are simply that: holes in my life, chunks of time just *gone*, missing."

She nodded. "In your debriefing sessions, have you undergone any drug or hypnosis sessions? Has anyone tried to open up your subconscious?"

"They still believe in that?" He smiled.

"Most definitely."

"No, they've left that for you and your buddies," he said.

"I would like to try hypnosis," she said.

"Okay." He was still smiling. He'd never been successfully hypnotized, although he'd undergone some very intensive drug sessions during his training to defend against mind control and brainwashing techniques.

"But please remember," she said, "you cannot be hypnotized unless you truly *want* to be. You don't need to believe whether or not it works, but you *must* be willing to submit completely to the process."

Harford nodded again. "I understand. Yes, I am very willing to give it a try."

"You will always be in ultimate control, but for a time, while you are under, you will be . . . in a different state of mind. Some people cannot let go enough to allow themselves to reach that state. You must relax."

"I can do that," he said.

"And you must *trust* me."

She might be tough, but she was *real*—sincere as well as competent. Although not in the habit of delivering himself into the hands of another without protection, he knew he could do exactly that with Dr. Isabella Mussina. He looked at her and for the first time realized he *could* trust her. "Let's get started," he said.

Moving from behind the workstation, Mussina approached his reclining chair, took a small padded stool, and sat close to him. He couldn't help but notice the way she moved with the fluid grace of an athlete or a dancer, the classic lines of her body and legs. Under a different set of circumstances, he would have been inspired to put some moves on her. But another part of him knew she wouldn't be

interested in his type. A professor-type with leather arm patches on
his tweed blazer. No Marlboro men in her life; no way.

After smoothing out her skirt, she issued a series of simple
instructions as she produced a small pendant from her lab coat
pocket: a steel teardrop on a very thin chain—highly polished and
reflective, it was an easy object upon which to fixate . . .

. . . until he heard Mussina speaking to him as though from a
distance, or through the interference of a strong wind.

Straining to hear her, he found himself wanting to surrender to
a very insistent urge to step away from the sound of her voice, to
retreat into a vast shadowy presence that seemed to be looming
over him. Like the blast-sheared cloud of a dark nebula, the presence blotted out all else in his limited sphere of perception. The
sensation was like childhood dreams in which the world is perceived only as a vague, ultradimensional *thing* always threatening
to overwhelm because the young mind lacks the tools yet needed
to comprehend.

"You are very relaxed . . ." she was saying. "Can you hear me?"

"Yes," said Harford, but even his own voice sounded distant,
somehow divorced from the *essence* of his identity. "Keep talking. It
helps keep me . . . connected."

"Connected to what?"

"To *you*, to the rest of the world. I don't feel in control." He heard
himself speaking and couldn't believe he would ever feel so helpless,
much less admit it to someone. What did it mean? What was happening to him?

"We're going to go back now . . ." she said, and gradually
Mussina talked him back through the days, each one falling away
like the discarded shell of a creature molting into its own past. Back
and back until they reached the day of his last blackout. . . .

"Tell me what you see, where you are," said Mussina, her voice
like a line thrown to an overboard sailor.

Grasping for it with desperation, he tried to speak slowly, coher-
ently. "I'm at the bar. F. X. McCrory's. Downtown Seattle near the
Kingdome. It's a huge place. The bar looks longer than a football
field and they have more than a hundred beers and ales and stouts
on tap running the entire length of it. And there's a big wall of bot-
tles behind the bartenders—so tall and long, they've got one of
those ladders that roll along on wheels. The place is full of the

midday business-lunch set, and I can see Faudi ibn Feissel and his buddies. A table right across from me. . . ."

"What are you doing there?"

"My job. Spying on them, recording their conversation. Eating my lunch."

"Do you see anything else?"

He felt a shudder pass through him, but he forced his way past the moment. "Not really seeing . . . but I can kind of tell it's just *there*. . . ."

"What is it? What do you see?"

"I . . . I don't know *what* it is. . . ."

"Please describe it to me."

"I'm sitting there, looking vaguely in the direction of the Arabs' table. Beyond them, a sea of other tables stretching to the plate-glass windows and the sidewalk beyond, but . . ."

He paused, not knowing why.

"But *what?*" Mussina prompted him gently, sotto voce.

"But I can't see what should be there. It's a kind of *blankness*, like there's nothing there. And I am moving toward that *nothingness* like everything is in slow motion."

"Think about it," she said softly. "You know what that blank space really is. . . ."

He *did* know. Just realizing it, but she was right—he knew. "It's my future, I mean the time I've been missing."

"That's right."

"It's the blackout," he said, as though describing the advent of a truly horrible event.

"You are going to let it come to you," she said. "It's only a . . . a veil. You can pass through it and you will see what is on the other side."

"I can't!" The idea pierced him like a blood-guttering bayonet—cold, sharp.

"Yes," she said in a voice almost inaudible. "Let it come to you. *Now . . .*"

And he did.

The nothingness that was filling the space of the Seattle bar moved toward him like a bank of black fog, and he almost ducked his head as he passed through its misty barriers . . .

. . . wherein everything had a slightly *different* appearance, as though the light were not right, as if coming from a sun with an altered spectrum. It was like looking at a film that has been processed with a barely perceivable color shift. Everything else was perfectly normal, but Harford could not shake the impression that something remained out of skew, *wrong*.

As he relived the events to follow, he had a feeling of watching himself as though in a film. An out-of-body experience through the wrong side of the looking glass.

At her urging, he continued. As the nothingness of the lost time devoured him, he told her how he suddenly stood up from the table, abandoning his prey, and paid his bill at the bar's register. Then outside to the street where he flagged a taxi to Sea Tac Airport and purchased from his cash account a United ticket to Mexico with connections via Faucett to Lima and Chiclayo. The name he'd used was Victor Connhauer.

After summarizing the overnight bus trip over the Andes, and his arrival in the village of Jaen, he recounted the details of the next few hours more closely because she stopped him at particular intervals to enlarge the scope of his memory.

He'd left the hotel before sunrise and rented a Volkswagen van that was so rusted and scored that the original color of the paint had long ago faded into a dull beige smear. He drove north on the government highway toward the Ecuadorian border. The roads became progressively worse, threatening to shake the van apart, but he pushed on as the dawn fingerpainted the clouds above the rain forest to the east. Stopping at a village along the Rio Chinchipe, he bought a *cerveza* at the local saloon and asked the proprietor when the local squadrons of the Nacionales would be posting checkpoints on the roads. The closer he pushed toward the border, he knew, the more of a chance he would be stopped by Peruvian troops. And so, after gathering the information he needed (the locals always knew what was going on), he took the van off-road, obscuring it within the seemingly endless tracts of thick-as-a-forest cacti.

He traveled under the heat of the midmorning sun, using the Nav-Sat link built into his notebook computer, plotting a route across the wasted valley that would intersect with a Policía outpost at the junction of several primary irrigation canals. Guard duty at such an outpost was joked about among the troops as less challenging than watching paint dry, and Harford expected no trouble executing both his plan and the solitary man at the post. It was a simple matter to approach the hut from the blind side, facing away from the canal.

The flag of the Nacionales hung limply in the dead air above the decaying roof; all was quiet as Harford moved silently toward the uniformed man's left shoulder. When he was close enough, it was a simple matter to grab him by the hair and break his neck with a single stroke. Taking the man's rifle, he continued along the canal until it joined with the Chinchipe, then east along the riverbank until the bridge was in view. Despite the distance, the air reverberated with the cacophonous sounds of heavy construction. As he slipped through the razor grass along the water's edge, his prey gradually resolved itself into a heavy-shouldered man working in the superstructure of a newly constructed bridge. Harford unslung his stolen rifle, calmly aligned the shirtless, well-muscled man in his sights, and squeezed off a single shot. The report was masked by the ambient sounds of heavy machinery as the target's head snapped back from the impact of the slug. Before the body even hit the water, Harford had jettisoned the gun into the river, already retracing his trek to the hidden van. From that point, he drove back to Jaen.

". . . and from there, you awakened in your hotel," said Dr. Mussina.

"Yes, that's the whole story." Harford could hear himself talking, listening to the reprise of the killing as if from a third party. He remained as separate from the event as if he were a completely different person.

"I want you to tell, Mr. Nichols—as you were remembering the story—did you have any . . . any insight into *why* you wanted to kill those people?"

"The guard," he said slowly. "I needed his gun."

Mussina nodded, checked her notes. "What about the other man—Ortiz?"

"I don't know," he said pausing. "But that's not really true."

"What do you mean?"

"There's a part of me that understands *everything*. Completely."

"How do you know that?" She leaned closer to him

Harford could hear himself talking, but he had no idea what he meant. The words slipped out of him like a lizard's tongue, quickly, automatically.

"I don't know. There's *more* . . ."

"Mr. Nichols," she said in a more assertive voice. "We are going to travel again, are you ready?"

"Where?" He looked at her blankly. It was the weirdest feeling to know he'd been put into a trance, but remained so lucid. The average person's idea of being transformed into some kind of zombie-like thing when under hypnosis was so totally wrong . . . He felt fine; his thoughts as finely stropped as a barber's razor.

"Deeper," she said softly.

"I don't understand."

"Harford, how do you feel—now that we've uncovered the missing time?" She touched his hand with her long, soft fingers. The touch that would normally excite him now afforded him an odd comfort, a needed connection to the warmth of another human.

"I feel . . . good. That I *know*, but the killings . . ."

"It bothers you?"

"Yeah . . . but I don't know *why.*"

Mussina touched his hand again. "It never 'bothered' you in the past—killing people. Why now?"

"It's not what you think. I'm not talking about the *morality* of what I've done . . . it's something else."

"Can you explain it?"

"I don't think I'm the one who killed those people." As he spoke the words, he felt something churn and twist in the deepest center of his thoughts—like a tumor suddenly come to life.

Mussina smiled, stroked his hand. "Let's see if we can find out," she said, and the sound of her voice was like a lifeline being thrown to him, something solid, real, from the familiar world.

"Let's do it," he said languidly.

And so she took him further under, peeling back the onion-skin layers of his awareness, stripping down the memories and the memory blocks, until he felt himself . . . breaking apart.

"Wait!" he heard himself crying out, not knowing why, but knowing something was *wrong.* Very wrong. "Don't! Not yet . . ."

It was like he'd become a jigsaw puzzle with uncountable pieces and the pieces, suddenly unlocked from one another, had begun to slowly drift apart, forever dispersing the essence of his *self.*

"Trust me," said the voice. Feminine. Authoritative. Warm, yet cool. Professional.

"All right," he said. The words oozed out of him. All sense or thought of control had seeped away.

"You are not Harford Nichols," she said. It was not a question.

"How do you know that?" His voice had suddenly sharpened, each word snapped off like shards of twisted, broken metal.

"Because you *can't* be . . ." Again, Mussina's voice projected cool control. Confidence. "What is your name?"

"Dukor . . . Hirsh Dukor." The words were pronounced slowly, flavored with a subtle Slovenian accent.

"Where are you from?"

"An area you would know as 'White Russia,'" he said, making no effort to conceal a distinct condescension.

"Can you tell the year of your birth and the location?"

"I can tell you anything you want. More importantly, I can tell you anything *I* want."

"Answer the question, Hirsh." Her words assumed the cadence of a command.

And he responded: "I was born in 1912, in Eastern Europe."

"Do you know what year it is now?"

"1999."

"That would make you eighty-seven years old," said Mussina. "Is that correct?"

"Your measurements of time have lost all meaning to me."

"Why?" She looked at him sharply. "Because you are . . . dead?"

A dark laugh leaked out of Nichols' body. "No . . . because I am *alive!*"

The doctor paused for a moment, as though considering the meaning of his words. "Yes," she said, finally. "You *are* alive. And for that reason you must tell me about your life. Where you have been, what you have seen."

"My first years were in Kartuska, a small village south of Molczadz. My parents were printers until after the Revolution and the civil war that followed. In 1918, my father was taken into the White Army—he never returned. My mother was killed by Red Army soldiers in the middle of the following winter—after they all took a turn raping her.

"I was only six years old, and I was taken into the house of a man named Bereza. He had been a friend of my father's and there was no one else. No one else to take care of me. Everyone in the village was very poor, and the war of the Red and the White made things very bad. Even worse than when the Cossacks would raid the villages for whatever they wanted."

Mussina touched his hand, but just barely. "I want you to go back, *now*," she said to him. "Back to that time. Tell me about your life . . . with Bereza and onward."

He paused, drew a deep breath, exhaled.

"Bereza is a cripple. One leg twisted up and a club foot. He lives by himself and makes his way by tanning leather. He has a long gray beard that always stinks of his breath and animal fats. He hates me and always tells me I am killing both of us because he cannot afford to feed two people. But he never feeds me much anyway. Each winter, for the next seven years, I spend most of the time locked in his root cellar, waiting for the few times a day when the heavy door opens and Bereza tosses down some suet and soup bones, or a piece of hard bread. For months at a time, I live in almost total darkness.

"But there are other times he opens the door to the cellar. Times when he's been drinking wheat mash vodka. I can smell the yeasty stench of it being distilled in his tanning shed, and eventually I learn to loathe that smell and everything connected to it. Bereza throws back the cellar door and comes down the steps with a leather strap attached to one of his tanning hooks. After tying the opposite end to a metal spike in the dirt floor, he hooks into the back of my shirt just below the collar. Then he stretches me out and rolls me over a thick log, just snug enough to keep tension on the leather strap. If I try to move, the tanning hook digs into my neck and pierces my spine. He trusses me up like some trembling fawn while he unbuckles his trousers and gives me what he calls his 'big greasy.'

"Pain and humiliation become my only companions, other than the darkness. Even though just a child, I grow to hate Bereza, and my fantasy thoughts always involve how I will one day kill him. I burn with hate and loathing. I am small and weak, but as the years pass, my tormentor grows more infirm and contracts a bad case of gout in his good leg. He begins letting me out of the cellar more and more. To do his work. Soon I grow stronger and bigger. When I am thirteen, I am strong enough to earn my freedom. I cleave his head open with a hatchet while he sleeps. From his forehead all the way down to his bottom jaw. Two halves, I hit him so hard. So much blood . . .

"And then I know I cannot stay in the village. I take everything I can carry, and then I torch the miserable hut that had been my prison for so long. I wander through the forests for several days, half crazy with cold and hunger until I am found by a seamstress and her husband traveling to the village of Nieswiez thirty miles to the north. I tell them my parents have been killed by the Red Army (which was not a lie), and they take me to the village where I am taken in by the local rabbi, whose name is Yerechmiel. I work as the temple's janitor, learning a trade from the village carpenter and metalsmith. The rabbi teaches me how to read and speak in three languages, but he does very little for my twisted soul. By that time, you see, I have been having long conversations with the voices in my head. And I have never been able to forget the white hot *joy*, the pure ecstasy, that consumed me the first time I took a life. When I'd stood there watching the unbelievable amount of blood geyser from the cloven skull of the monster Bereza . . . something happened.

"There was a feral resonance in it for me. The slaking of a fine and terrible thirst—but only temporarily. It had been such a totally, overwhelmingly dominant sensation, I knew that nothing I could ever do in life could match it. The hot, wet *pleasure* of it is like sex for me.

"No . . . it *is* sex for me.

"So much so that, as I pass through puberty, I discover my special need. I remain a very frustrated, very warped young man until I devise my own means of release. Killing the small animals of the forest has been more of a curiosity than a life-pattern for me. I cultivate a keen interest in the science of pain and death, and carry out crude but effective experiments with rabbits and mice, the occasional stray cat or sickly dog.

"It is not until I grow into my teens that I develop the techniques and methods that sustain me until I meet my true saviors. Because of my peculiar curiosity, I force myself to become adept at the stealthy arts of tracking and hunting. By the time I am fifteen, I have secured a special place in the heart of the old rabbi because I deliver to him a steady supply of fresh forest kills. I even drag in an old timberwolf one winter—the beast had been old and slow—an easy victory, actually, but I am curious to discover the taste of the predator's flesh.

"As you can imagine, my adaptation to human prey requires very little adjustment to the scheme of my hunting. My sojourns away from the village become longer as I grow older, and I gradually widen the circle of my influence. The roads are often traveled by the solitary stranger, the smaller villages are always producing new young flocks of children, and there seems to be an endless supply of silly young girls intent on testing their powers on dull boys. It is a glorious time. Everything is fresh and new, and it fascinates me that no two people ever seem to die in the same way. I would always try to look them in the eyes at the precise moment of their dying, looking for answers that a small part of me knew would never come.

No matter if I have taken them slowly from their agony with my own hands, or quickly dispatch them with a shot from my revolver, their final moments remain mysterious and unrevealed. But my curiosity never wanes. Indeed, it becomes the driving element of my life, which in all other respects is unremarkable. Most of my time in the village is spent alone, reading from Rabbi Yerechmiel's extensive library, or performing my duties without question or comment. To everyone who knows me, I appear to be a quiet, studious, and seemingly shy young man.

"Only the countless people whose eyes I hood for the final time ever know me as anyone different.

"Years pass, and my explorations down the dark corridors of human suffering continue on a loosely charted lunar cycle. When I first discover the natural rhythms of my mind and body—and how they fall into synch with the world's own clockwork mechanisms— I know I have been taken into the greater chain of being in some kind of divine way. The medieval philosophers had all believed in this kind of perfect natural order, and it becomes a great relief to me that I have been selected for such perfection.

"But it was not until I meet my saviors that I achieve the absolute vindication, the imprimatur, of what has become my life's work. It is only when the wehrmacht-winter sweeps through Eastern Europe that I fully understand the depths of suffering capable of being elicited from the human spirit. Never have I been so overjoyed to be alive as those days with the *Schutzstaffel*.

"In 1942, the Nazi net has begun to close more tightly around Eastern Europe and the Ukraine. I watch as Jews and Gypsies are collected into ghettoes first in the larger cities, and later the towns and villages as well. Having the sensibilities of the predator, I understand the thinking of the Germans, and I am able to remain one step ahead of their troops. I even kill a few of their newer recruits just for the sheer sport of it. There is never a question of my ability to do it. All I need is opportunity, and I am excellent at creating that.

"Although the SS had not reached the more remote areas around Molczadz until the summer of '42, there is no stopping their plans now fully in gear. And then on the 16th of July, while hunting in the woods outside of Horodzei, I see an incredible spectacle. A squad of German regular army, under the command of an SS officer, drive a huge crowd of people into a deep meadow while I watch from a nearby elevation. More than a thousand Jews are herded into the clearing while they nervously finger the tassels of their prayer shawls and reach down to keep their small children at their sides. I remain hidden as I watch, awestruck by the sheer audacity and brilliance of the soldiers' actions. In a sudden eruption of gunfire, the tightly herded crowd of Jews is slaughtered. It is a merciless barrage. I stare wide-eyed as slugs from a machine gun rip a family to pieces, shredding them like wheat chaff. Never have I seen a celebration of death on such a scale! The people are hit with so many bullets, the constant impacts actually hold them up like slumping marionettes, keeping them on their feet, as though dancing a grotesque jig. I am stunned into abject admiration! Reducing my small achievements to something pale and thin, the grand killings cause me to realize how little I have actually done with my life so far.

"As I sit watching the soldiers melt back into the forest, leaving the immense pile of bodies in their wake, I know that I have witnessed a special kind of greatness. That a new force has awakened into the world. And that I long to be a part of it more than anything I have ever imagined.

"The next day, in Nieswiez, the members of the Jewish Council meet in the synagogue, and I listen from an alcove as Rabbi Yerechmiel Szklar urges the others to form a resistance against the approach of the Nazis. I smile secretly at the prospect of these hapless Jews believing they could do anything to stop the Nazi machine. But other village leaders take up the cry—we cannot let them kill us like animals, they say. Jacob Klaczko, one of the most respected elders, holds up his cane like a weapon and challenges the Germans to show their faces in Nieswiez.

"They comply on the twenty-first of July. An *Einsatzkommando* unit bullies into the center of the village where their commanding officer announces through a bullhorn that they will be selecting all of the village's Jewish tradesmen to work in a munitions factory in Szarkowszczyzna, and that all other Jews will be immediately 'relocated.'

"Suddenly, the large crowd that has gathered begins fractionating, selecting parts of itself out of the main body. I watch as the non-Jews of the village begin separating themselves from their Jewish colleagues and friends. As the pronouncement of the Nazis becomes clear, no one wants to be mistaken for a Jew. I stand my ground, confident that these men in their splendid uniforms will never harm me. Labels mean nothing when the great absolutes of the world are at stake. That I live with a rabbi, have been born a Jew and raised as a Jew did not, in my mind, make me a Jew. I have always found the idea of organized religion—all of them—to be quaint, and a rather poor excuse at an explanation for this thing we call the universe.

"Just then, old Klaczko holds up his cane and yells at the soldiers: *No! There will be no selections here! Either we all go free or we fight!* Not giving the Nazis a chance to reply, the crowd suddenly charges the informally assembled group of soldiers, many of whom, in their overconfidence, have not yet bothered to unsling their rifles from their shoulders. The Jews, armed with everything from hunting rifles to pitchforks and axes, stun them with the sudden first strike. Soldiers and village police begin to drop under the attack. I watch from the cover of a statue in the village square as the pitch of the battle shifts in favor of the SS troops as soon as they shoulder their superior weapons. Bodies are strewn about the village center like broken dolls and puppets as the air fills with the smell of cordite and blood. Amazingly, the Jews do not wither under the Nazi gunfire. They seem crazed into action, as though they know they are all going to die, and like rabid dogs, determine to take as many of their tormentors along for the journey. The sound of muzzle-blasts deafen everyone. Machine-gun fire supplies a factory-like rhythm to the slaughter. Everyone is yelling at the top of their voices. Battle cries, shock, and death agonies all blend together in an unholy song of destruction. I can barely contain the excitement that holds me like a fist of iron.

"A sizable section of the crowd has managed to surround a small part of the soldiers' uneven formation. The Jews launch enough hatchets, bricks, and gunfire against the Germans that they are in danger of getting bested. Unseen along the perimeter of the action, I creep closer to the scene, and I see the commanding officer himself fall from an errant stone to the side of his head. As he falls, a tall, broad-shouldered Jew with a pitchfork straddles him to deliver the deathblow. Without thinking, I bound from my cover and grab the Jew by the throat, yanking him away from the Nazi officer. I stand there for an instant, locked against the struggling Jew, and suddenly the Nazi raises his Luger and fires two shots into the Jew's chest. Holding him so close I can feel the concussion of the slugs, the convulsing reaction of the Jew, and the moment of death when all his muscles just *stop* their opposition. In the middle of the screams and the smoke and the blood, it is a glorious sensation, and I burst out laughing as I hold the dead Jew for a moment before throwing him to the ground. The tide of Nazi weaponry finally sweeps over the Jews, and although they never break ranks and run, their numbers are decimated in minutes. Soldiers are swarming everywhere, now with their bayonets mounted, gutting whomever still writhes on the stained earth. A young SS trooper, barely out of his teens, throws himself at me, and I trip on my own boot as I try to sidestep his attack. Looking up I see the soldier raise his weapon and I wonder abstractly what the blade will feel like as it punctures my flesh . . .

"But it does not happen. The young soldier is accosted at that moment by the Nazi officer, who looks down at me with confusion. *Why did you save me back there?* he says.

"I smile at him. *Because I like the work you are doing*, I reply.

"This is not the answer he could have expected and he remains puzzled by me. *You are a Jew?* he says after a pause. I smile again and speak softly: *By your definition, yes.*

"Finally, he tells the young soldier to get me to my feet and into one of the troop carriers where I am watched cautiously. By now the battle is over and most of Nieswiez's Jews lay slaughtered like pigs. The few still alive are thrown into the back of a farm truck where they are kicked and bludgeoned by the outraged troops.

"I am taken by rail with the rest of the selected Jews to Bratislava. They are in boxcars with no place to pee or shit—except in their clothes as they stand against one another. I ride with the soldiers, shunned, but respected because of the orders of their SS officer. He tells me he has not decided what to do with me, but I know it is simpler than that: he does not *know* what to do with me, and he cannot bring himself to kill a man who has saved his life. I smile at this. Sometimes a human heart still beats in the iron chest of the SS. As I ride along in the train, thinking this, I realize that I am different from most people—I truly do not care if I live or die.

"We arrive in a Polish town called Oswiecim. I see the name on the platform we pass as the train slows down, but our cars are shunted off to a siding, which runs for perhaps two miles farther out of the town, stopping finally at a very large compound surrounded by barbed-wire fences and guard towers. The soldiers call it the *Arbeitslager*, the work-camp. Or simply the *Lager*. Beyond these barriers, it looks like some kind of factory—which it is—a factory ultimately for death. Orders are given and the troops stream off the train and begin the practiced routine of offloading the boxcars of the most wretched people I have ever seen. I stand next to the troop car for several minutes, watching the Jews separate themselves into groups, by sex, by age, by family, etc. Subgroup by subgroup. I am amazed at how utterly docile everyone is. How they simply do whatever they are told . . .

"They have no spark, no life in them. They are a beaten race, and I am ashamed to be named among their number. For a people who have accomplished so much in the arts and the sciences, they are an embarrassment to the demands of basic survival. As I stand there, allowing such thoughts to brew like stormclouds, I am roughly grabbed and dragged away from the train. Past the long lines of Jews who are being processed into the camp, I am taken into a small building filled with partitioned-off spaces, each with a desk and an officer of the SS. I recognize the commandant from the Nieswiez incident as I am brought before him.

"*You will be a* 'sonderkommando,' he says, barely looking up at me.

"I say nothing in response, continue to stand there.

"*Do you know what that means?* he asks after a long pause. He is looking at me directly now. There is a coldness behind his eyes and he senses the same lack of warmth behind mine.

"*No,* I say.

"The officer smiles, and it is the smile of a rogue. *It means you will live,* he said.

"Before I can even think about whether I will reply, I am dragged from the small building and taken to a larger one that looks like an abandoned gymnasium. There are many other men already standing, waiting for a further command. There is water on the concrete floor and there are showerheads above us. I am stripped of my clothes, my beard and hair are cut away, and I am hosed down and sprayed with a de-licer. Then other *Häftlinge,* the guards' word for the prisoners, enter wearing striped clothing, and carrying bundles of similar garb. Most of the men in the room with me get shirts with a green triangle on the chest, but on my shirt two red and yellow ones opposed and overlapped to form the star of David. I am the only Jew in this group, and the other men are wondering why I am there.

"I am there, it turns out, to supervise and facilitate the work of the various *kommandos,* which are groups formed for a particular kind of work. I live in one of the barracks called blocks, and the routine is hatefully dreary, the food barely edible, and the chance for inhumanity always rampant. I learn to steal whatever I can—shoes, extra bread, a tin cup or bowl, literally *anything.* I relish every chance to be cruel to my fellow *Häftlinge*, because it becomes the only time I feel *good* about anything.

"In short order, I gain a reputation among the Jews as a monster. They hate me, and I hate them. I become more fearsome to them than the SS themselves, and the most enjoyable part of my day is to feel the *heat* of their stares as they watch me walk past them as they work. Eventually, I am noticed by the SS and they begin to use me at nearby Birkenau, the place called the 'birches' because of the white forest of trees that surrounds the *Lager*. It is the place of the ovens, and I become part of the *kommando* of criminal and political *Häftlinge* who keep the fires hot and the ashes cleared from the grates. The skies above me are always blackened by the greasy soot from the chimneys.

"Until May 24, 1943. That is the greatest day of my life. It is early evening and the columns of Jews are just returning from their sixteen-hour drudge at a rubber plant called the *Buna*. I am herding the last of them into their block, when a middle-aged man collapses ahead of me. I yank him to his feet and slap his face, but I meet nothing but bony angles and a skin as thin and brittle as parchment. He begins crying, saying his feet are so swollen that his shoes are crushing them. He cannot stand, he screams, begging for mercy and understanding. I reach down and pull off one of his shoes, and he screams again in agony. The flesh of his foot is like raw hamburger, a rippling mass of pustulant infection. It does not even look like a human foot, but rather a distended and diseased butt of ham. I signal for a guard, telling him the man can no longer walk. The guard approaches me with an ax, which he hands to me and smiles. I nod, then turn to face the man. With one swing, I chop off the diseased foot at his ankle, and kick it into the drainage ditch by the path. The Jew goes into shock as his blood pumps out of him. He is thrown into the back of a lorry and taken to the ovens.

"I am taking the ax back to the guardhouse when an SS captain approaches me. He is young and handsome, and obviously new to the *Lager*. I do not recognize him and I make it my business to know everyone and everything. He tells me he is a doctor, and wants to know if I would like to be one of his orderlies. There is something about the way this man smiles that is terrifying, even to me, and I am essentially afraid of nothing. I look into the darkness of his eyes and I see a vast *absence* there. Most men have something capering behind their eyes, be it evil or madness or joy, but this young officer—he has

nothing. It repels me and attracts me at the same time. I nod and say
ja automatically. *Splendid*, he says. *I am Doctor Josef Mengele.*

"From that first day, he and I are a perfect match, like a marriage
most only dream of, we become as one person. So much am I in
synch with his methods, his thoughts, I am able to anticipate whatever he wants or needs, or eventually even *fantasizes* about. I help
him create a special lab in the Medical Block, where at first he
works with a Doctor Clauberg—the two of them devising the
method of *selections* both at the train depot and at the *Lager* itself,
deciding who can work and who is be exterminated instantly. I
watch and learn. Soon, I understand the way his mind works and I
am confident I could do his selections and be extremely accurate. In
the lab, he allows me to read medical texts and special papers on the
most current theories regarding biology and race, his most favorite
topics of conversation. Because of my superior intellect and rabid
interest, I absorb the material like a thirsty sponge. I become fluent
in the language and terminology of the medical world.

"Doctor Clauberg begins to resent my knowledge and my close
rapport with Mengele, and makes plans to have me stripped of my
privileges and thrown into a *kommando* mixing quicklime into mass
graves, or digging them up for open-pit burning. When Mengele
discovers this, he employs his rank as an SS officer to have Clauberg
replaced with a doctor named Kremer, who is very much aware of
my position with Mengele and makes certain never to challenge it.
As the months pass, I am entrusted with the execution of many of
the basic experiments Mengele devises. We inject Jews with all
kinds of lethal and toxic substances; we perform operations without
anesthesia; we shock them and burn them with electrodes and ultra-
short wave transmitters. I especially like the experiments in which
we force-pump various viscous or fluid things into the anus or a
woman's uterus. This seems to cause some of the most exquisite fear
and pain in the patients.

"When Mengele begins full-scale experiments with twins, he
becomes quickly obsessive about the need to find ever more sets of
them. We search the entire camp, and try to be very careful during
the train depot selections. Finally, I convince him that we must take
'day-trips' to other *Lagers*, where there are hundreds of sets of twins
being wasted. I do this because I truly want to find more of them
myself, but also because I have grown weary of the world of the
camp and its grim rhythms, the *ausrücken und einrücken* of the pris-

oners, the trains, the guards, the life and the death. I look forward to the trips when we climb into the cars and the trucks and we travel across the landscapes of places become so alien to me they are like other worlds. But the places we visit are very much like Auschwitz-Birkenau, both in design and population. I am convinced the Nazis have rooted out every Jew in Europe; they swell the *Lagers* like harvested wheat bursting the seams of overstocked granaries. When Mengele and I visit the *Häftlinge* blocks, I can feel the desperation emanating from the Jews like a terrible putrefaction. Our missions to find additional sets of twins are spectacularly successful and I am offered special rewards from the doctor in terms of food or privileges. I usually waive them in exchange for the chance to perform some of his experiments on my own."

He paused to gauge Mussina's expression, which had been one of distress and terrible concern, and now changed into something else, something darker. More disgust, more fear. He continued.

"The longer I work with Mengele, the more fascinated I am becoming with pain and death. It is my only source of pleasure or sense of fulfillment. Mengele teaches me that suffering is the culmination of existence, the capstone to all that ever exists. I learn that to exist at all is to experience pain, and that all life is only an elaborate preparation for death. Everything we do is an overture to the final moment, and I am in total synchronization with the cosmic engine, the great mechanism that grinds everything down to the finest atoms. I worship the God Entropy, and I am his agent, his instrument. I exist to deliver His great message of death."

SIXTEEN

ISABELLA MUSSINA, Ph.D.
Langley, Virginia

Something happened to her.

Something that had never happened before.

As she listened to the past-life regression of Harford Nichols, she became so . . . so *consumed* by the story, that she almost became lost in it. Only when the subject lapsed into metaphor did Isabella realize that she must regain control of the session. Forcing herself to stand up and back away from the entranced Nichols, she could almost feel a physical *field* of influence surrounding the man. In all her years of research, she had never sensed such a powerful presence, such an utterly dominating entity as the set of memories filling the psyche of Harford Nichols.

But they might be *more* than memories. . . .

The notion touched her deeply as she backed even farther away from Nichols, who was now weaving back and forth. He looked not *at* her as much as through her. He displayed a small smile, as though in some kind of weird resonance with the idea that he was indeed the instrument of entropy. Isabella could not shake the feeling that she had entered unholy ground. The essence of the story by Hirsh Dukor was easily the most grotesque and loathsome tale she'd ever encountered. It was terrifying—the juxtaposition of

Dukor's utter control and almost mannered language with the catalogue of atrocities and predilections.

Grendel with an intellect to match his ferocity.

And the worst part was this: she felt as if she already knew him. Like any monster of legend, its tales of horror would always precede its possible reality. She knew this creature and need only give it a name.

Dukor truly frightened her, but she could never allow him to know it. She had no choice but to push onward. Despite the fear clawing its way to the surface, she also felt a special excitement, atavistic and urgent. Sensing a unique chance, she dared intrude upon the grim world in which Hirsh Dukor thrived.

"Excuse me," she said quickly, but with a gentle voice. "I must ask you a question."

"Yes." Nichols looked at her dimly, and she had the feeling he saw nothing. Another set of eyes assessed her at that moment.

"When you did these . . . things . . . for Mengele, what did the others, your fellow prisoners, think of you?"

A small grin slashed his face like the path of a straight razor. "They feared me, of course. But more importantly, they *hated* me."

"Why was that more important?"

"Because I *fed* off their hate. It gave me the energy to live!"

Isabella paused, afraid to ask the next question, already knowing the answer, but somehow needing it to be made real, in this world as well as those of nightmare and pain. "They gave you a special name, didn't they?"

He nodded, closing his eyes as though remembering something of particular sweetness. "Oh yes, and it was a beautiful name."

"Can you say it for me?" Her words caught in her throat like the ashes of the dead.

"Der Klein Engel," he said. "What else could you call The Angel of Death's right-hand man?"

Isabella could not hide her shock, her absolute sense of loathing. She actually flinched, leaning away from him.

He nodded, smiling flatly like a skull. "You know me, don't you, Doctor?"

"I know about you through . . . others. Who knew you when . . . when you were alive."

He laughed mockingly, pointed to his chest. "Oh, but I am alive!"

This couldn't be happening, she thought, as she felt suddenly dizzy, losing control. What he had told her could simply not be! It was impossible to be in the center of such a coincidence! No way it could *be* a coincidence. No way that she could have stumbled upon the essence or the memory of such a monster in Nichols. Unless there was something more to the great wheel of karma than she could have ever imagined. A great shuddering pulse of total *emptiness* passed through her, as if she'd opened a door and the wind of eternity had blown in for an instant. It was a moment totally cold and vacant of all feeling, and it terrified her.

It was her destiny to find Dukor.

Could it be possible that her entire life, and all her passionate questing for the truth, had been shaped toward this one, single moment of revelation?

She shook her head, as if to clear it, but she knew she'd pushed herself to the threshold of a place from which there was no escape, no exit, not even death—because the truth of this realm, whatever it might be, transcended such things as mere expiration.

Hold on, she thought desperately. *Get control.* She couldn't lose the thread, or she would be lost in a labyrinth of endless terrors.

"You tell me you are alive," she said, forcing the words out, willing herself into coherency. "But you also alluded to dying."

"The beautiful paradox," he said, and chuckled. "Both true. All true."

"Can you remember your death?"

"Yes. Exquisitely. It was full of the worst kind of irony."

"Can you tell me about it?"

Nichols smiled. "You will be the first."

"All right . . ."

The subject closed his eyes, began to speak in a faraway voice. "As 1944 begins to wind down, Doctor Mengele is smart enough to know that the Third Reich is getting squeezed by the Americans and the Russians. He plans to flee the *Lager* in the middle of a very dark night. He asks me if I want him to put a bullet in my head before he departs, declaring I will be torn to pieces by any surviving *Häftlinge* when the camp is liberated. I smile and thank him for his thoughtfulness, but decline, preferring the adventure of facing the . . . how would you call them? . . . 'do-gooders' who advance upon us. I stay on in the *Lager*, with orders from Mengele to be kept on privileges, which was easy by now because I have become a *komrade* of many of the SS guards. I watch as the last herd of Jews is gassed in late October of that year, All Hallows Eve, I think, which is in some way appropriate. For the next few months, under Himmler's order, everyone works double shifts to dismantle the apparatus for the gassings, and of course the crematoriums themselves. I remain on the job until the end, helping to destroy the huge warehouses full of things like men's and women's coats, suits, watches and eyeglasses, luggage, human hair. Hundreds of thousands of pieces. I smile as I handle the items, thinking that each one represents some hapless Jew.

"In January 1945, the Russian soldiers find us and set us free to roam along the roads with nowhere to go. At first, I imagine my fellow prisoners will try to kill me, but they are such a weak and pathetic lot, I soon realize I have nothing to fear from them. In fact, I am able to resume my age-old games with all the easy prey, being able to kill most of my victims with a single blow—they are such fragile skeletons, it is almost too easy to bring them down. I work my way west into Germany, from village to village, stealing what I need to stay alive as I look for those who match the criterion of my master's vision. With Mengele absent, my work becomes doubly important. I am to send them from this plane of existence, to make them *go away* as efficiently as possible, and so I continue . . .

". . . until I am caught in the act by a soldier from a squad of American Negroes. I am kneeling over the limp body of a young girl, perhaps nine years old. She has a number tattooed on her wrist, six digits from Sobibor. She looks me in the eye with an expression of relief as I strangle her. The Negro soldier has just appeared from behind a hedgerow, and he looks at me with a stunned expression on his face. With my still-shaved head and ragged clothes, I am sure I look frightful. I throw down the girl's body and face him, smiling. This unnerves him, but he raises his M-1 and aligns me in the sight. But he is not sure what to do. I laugh at him, then lunge straight at him. I see him wince, and suddenly I am staring at the heart of the sun. I do not hear the carbine's report, but I am instantly *separated* from my body, the earth, everything. . . ."

Nichols stopped speaking, stared straight ahead.

"No more awareness?" asked Isabella, keeping her distance from the subject. She knew now she had entranced a monster. Always a dangerous thing to do.

"It returns in brief flashes, like tantalizing looks behind a half-closed door. I am a small boy, a young man, an adult. Simple scenes from a life. A kitchen. A classroom. A bedroom. A night sky. A field. These are momentary, elusive, without real meaning. In more recent time, the glimpses have become more solid, with greater duration. I have come to *live* again. Each time I have felt more alive, more powerful."

"Hirsh," she said softly. Not a question. "You have been killing them."

"Who?"

"These victims of Nichols. The ones the CIA is upset about?"

"Yes, of course."

". . . using the body of Harford Nichols."

"It is actually *my* body as well. Or perhaps that is not correct. Maybe I am also Harford Nichols. Maybe Hirsh and Harford are the same person . . . ? Maybe Dukor is gone and I am really Nichols?"

He laughed.

"What?" she said expectantly.

"Does it matter *what* you call me? The only thing you must understand is that I exist! I am here and the person you called Harford Nichols is *gone*."

Isabella felt a coldness pass over her shoulders. The subject was saying things she had already considered. And she knew there was no way she could continue this session. She'd skidded far past the moment when she should've ended it, and she knew she must break in, shatter the fragile shell of containment that had given this soul a palpable presence. Standing, she edged closer to Nichols. She would—

"No," he said gently, almost seductively. "You cannot . . ."

"What—?"

"You cannot stop this," he said, standing, looking *through* her. "You are no longer in control here."

His expression held her like a butterfly pinned to corkboard. His words likewise pierced her, confirming what she had suspected unconsciously, but had been afraid to even consider. Without thinking, she began backing away from him, edging back behind the big desk. It afforded little real protection, but she was frightened, terribly so, and knew she would do anything to get away from him, to feel safe.

"What do you mean by 'control'?" she said. Keep him talking. Keep him occupied. Scanning the desk, she looked for a panic button, but there was nothing. Only the usual phone and intercom. Was there a hidden camera, microphones? This was the goddamned CIA—there *had* to be something!

"Control?" Nichols/Dukor smiled as he regarded her calmly. "I mean *of me*. You were the manipulator, were you not?"

"Of the hypnosis, yes." Isabella sat down, tried to present a cool, reasonable front. If he sensed she was losing it, things might get worse a lot faster. "What else do you mean?"

Tilting his head, the man regarded her with a continuing grin. It was the grin of a village idiot, of an inspired genius. As impossible as she knew it must be, the notion struck her that his appearance had been changing. Nichols no longer looked the same. Subtle alterations in the bones of his face, the shape of the skull.

No, that's crazy. . . .

It was just the way he was using his facial muscles—unfamiliar expressions, contortions.

"Doctor Mussina, I think you know exactly what I mean," he said, as he stood, moved a step toward her desk.

The maneuver sent off alarms in her mind, and she blinked back the wave of terror that jolted through her. She had to get away from him, distract him, keep him talking.

"No, I—" She tried to speak and her words became stuck in her throat.

He exhaled a dramatic sigh and rolled his eyes, as though playing to an unseen audience. "All right, I'll make things painfully clear. Emphasis on the adverb very intentional. You see, before this current episode, something would *jerk* me into awareness for tiny, electric instants. Like thunder and lightning, and then again the dark vacuum of nonbeing. Until the next time, pulled from the emptiness. It was as if something was calling me forth from the grave. Something wanted me. Finally, it succeeded for brief fugues in which I carried out my familiar game of predator. And during these glorious moments I had available to me all the training and experience of my present body and soul."

"Nichols," she added. "You mean *his* knowledge."

"That is correct. But you still make a distinction between us. You do not want to accept that we are the same being."

Isabella didn't really care about that singular point anymore. It was difficult to get excited about metaphysics when you believed someone was going to kill you. All she wanted was to be *out* of that room, away from this maniac-monster-ghoul or whatever he was. Only now did she really understand the hideous and abject terror of her subject's dreams, of their memories of a life better never brought into being.

"I think I could learn to accept that," she said, trying to smile. "I don't see it as a big problem."

"Good." He moved laterally, and the motion was less threatening. He began pacing slowly, but never took his gaze away from her. "Shall I continue?"

She nodded. *Was* anybody listening to their conversation? On the off-chance, should she be trying to signal them? Let them know she was in trouble? But how?

"It was a battle, you see, between my current and former selves. Hence the blackouts, the losses of memory during each state of awareness. Each time, I wanted my original self, the one you call Dukor, to retain control, but it was like rising to the surface of a cold lake, with a heavy anchor chained to your leg. I could only rise so far, and then sink back down again. It happened enough times that I knew it would forever be a stalemate, that total control would never be achieved."

He paused to smile a twisted little smile at her. Then he bowed in mock graciousness. "Until, of course . . . until there was *you*."

She knew he was going to say that, and she hated him for his mordant tone. He was playing with her, teasing her, before he strangled her like the little girl in the hedgerow.

"All right," said Isabella. "What do you want?"

"From you? Nothing." He moved another step closer. "You have already given me the only thing you had of value—the key to my continuing awareness. You, Doctor Mussina, have brought me back to life! With each word of my story, I became stronger, more *real*. Each word like a secret mantra, a spell. A talisman to give me back the existence demanded of me!"

"Demanded by whom?" she said softly. He was getting worked up. Keep him talking.

"By the Fates. By the Cosmos itself! Destiny was denied once in this century, but it will *not* be stopped this time!" He drew in a great breath, exhaled in dark laughter. "I can *feel* it! There is something massive lurching toward us, toward this focal point in time. Something dark and monolithic and hungry. It is something many believed dead, lost in the forever mist. But no, Doctor, it was only sleeping—like a great god stuck in the geologic stone of old myth."

He was right. Isabella could feel the truth of it in the jellied center of her bones. And she'd been the one to throw the latch on it, to push open the door and bring back a thing that was far more than the man once known as Hirsh Dukor. She watched him take another step toward her, and a sudden surge of panic bubbled through her like lava. She heard herself blurt out a question that sounded immediately silly and inappropriate. "Is there anything else you want to tell me?"

He chuckled, shrugged. "Not really. I am finished with you— unless you prove useful in escaping this facility."

"What—?"

Another two steps and he reached the desk. Before she could react, he had leaped over it like a gymnast and grabbed her in some kind of martial arts choke hold. The pressure of his thick forearm across her throat was just enough to cause alarming pain, but not enough to black her out. She tried to talk, to cry out, but no words would come—barely enough air to breathe, much less make a sound. She wanted to plead with him to either let her go, or kill her quickly.

But he did neither, inching her toward the door to the inner office, beyond which was a larger room that connected to other offices and a corridor that eventually led to a security station and elevator bays beyond that. She could feel her blood pumping wildly in her ears and her heart was ratcheting against her rib cage. At any moment she expected him to either snap her neck or crush her throat, and the thought that *this* was how she would ultimately die began to settle over her like a heavy blanket. Oddly, it imparted a calming effect rather than worse panic. She felt—

The phone on her desk suddenly chirped, and the sound startled him as well as her. They both looked at it for a moment before he relaxed his grip on her and pushed her toward the desk.

"Pick it up," he said. "Tell them they don't have a chance of stopping me if they want you to live."

The phone chirped again, crazy, electronic, insistent.

"How do you know what they want?"

He shoved her face down on the blotter and the sheer power in his arms and hands stunned her. "Don't be stupid, you bitch! They've been tuned in on us from the first word! These are my walls! My people! Now *answer* it!"

Weakly, she reached out, lifted the receiver. "Doctor Mus—"

"This is Glinka," said the familiar voice. "Try to stay calm, Doctor. We'll get you out of there."

"He . . . he wants me to tell you something," she said through ragged breaths.

"We know what he said. He's right about being wired up. Just go along with him. Tell him we've guaranteed safe passage—as long as he doesn't hurt you."

"Okay, okay!" she said quickly. "I'll tell him . . . !"

"Just try to stay calm, Doctor. We'll be watching you every step of the way. Good luck."

The line went dead and she replaced the receiver. Then twisting around to look at Dukor, she repeated Glinka's guarantee.

He laughed. "Yeah, we'll see about that. Now let's go."

Locking her up in his choke hold, he moved her along like a dancer. She felt as if her feet barely touched the carpet as they glided to the door. He opened it and danced them through, into a reception and clerking area. If there had been any personnel in this area, they had been cleared, because everything lay eerily deserted. Desks as though suddenly abandoned. PC monitors staring blankly. She hoped they could see her as he directed her toward the outer door with the electronic lock.

"The key card," he said, holding his free hand in front of her face.

For an instant, she blocked on what he was saying, what he wanted, and he clamped down on her throat, bruising the delicate tissues there. "Give it to me!"

And then she was fumbling in the breast pocket of her lab coat, trying to remember where she'd been carrying it. When its sharp, plastic edge cut into her palm, she thought it was just about the best sensation she'd ever felt.

He snatched it up and passed it through the slot. The door's lock clicked open with the heavy sound of a luxury sedan, and he moved her so fast they were almost instantly past its bulk. Entering the vast access corridor, Isabella was shocked by the utter emptiness of the super-long passageway. In both directions—nothing.

Dukor paused for a moment, then yanked her to the left. "Down here."

Scurrying like fiddler crabs locked in combat, they passed under a surveillance camera, which moved subtly to track their movement. Dukor stopped, stared into the lens. "You know I can kill her!" he yelled viciously at the device. "I want Level One access from Bay Seven. *Now!* Anybody tries to fuck with me and the doctor is dead, okay?"

Without waiting for a reply, Dukor started them moving again, staying out in the center of the corridor. Each time they passed a door, his entire body seemed to coil itself up like a snake preparing to strike. And each time she expected somebody to appear from behind one of those doors. If it happened, she knew it would be the last thing she ever saw. She moved along with her captor, offering no resistance, trying to keep her thoughts away from the edge of total panic. Remaining so reflective and calm surprised her, even though she'd always considered herself an extremely rational person. But now, she seemed to be able to view what was happening to her as though through the eyes of an aloof observer. Unsettling, even a little scary. Her complete detachment from what was happening suggested a nihilism, a lack of passion and caring that in itself was disturbing. Better that she'd lapsed into some kind of psychological shock, temporary and with little real import. She willed it to be so—because she never wanted to think she'd stopped caring about life.

Even now.

Especially now.

"Keep moving," said Dukor as they neared the elevators at Bay Seven.

Just at that moment the recessed lighting began pulsing rhythmically to an alarm klaxon, and the PA system echoed down the corridor like the voice of God: *"Attention all personnel . . . E-Con Four . . . Repeat . . . E-Con Four . . . Bay Seven West . . ."*

"What does that mean?" she said with great effort.

He had dragged her to the elevator doors and keyed the access grid with her card. "They're telling everybody they've got a big problem down here," he said with a grin. "The 'Four' means highest priority. And that everybody better keep their asses in the trenches. Out of the line of fire."

The doors opened to display an empty chamber, and he waltzed them inside. Pressing the panel for the top floor, the car lurched upward. Suddenly Dukor released his grip and threw her to the floor in one quick motion. The force of the impact stunned her for an instant. Half dazed, she watched him leap up to grab with both hands a cross-beam bracing the ceiling tiles. Then, pulling himself up as though on a chinning bar, he reached up and removed the tiles to reveal the steel roof of the elevator car.

What . . . ?

Isabella sat up and saw the object of his efforts: a door with a hand latch cut into the roof. Quicker than her eye could follow, Dukor threw the latch and in a single, coordinated gymnast's maneuver swung himself upward so that he went flying through the open hatch feet-first. There was the sound of something banging against the steel roof like a rubber hammer, and several bullet holes blossomed inward from the ravaged ceiling. Then the hatch was filled with Dukor's plummeting bulk. Landing on his feet, he now held a handgun with squared-off edges. It was a dull black and looked very menacing.

"He won't be needing this anymore," said Dukor, glancing upward, then tucking the weapon into his pants. "Don't move." He punched out the control panel to the car with his elbow and grabbed a handful of wiring. With a skillful yank on the yellow and the blue ones, the lights died and a groaning of steel-on-steel filled the air. Plunged into abrupt darkness, she was suddenly aware that they'd stopped moving.

"Okay, let's go . . ."

"Where?"

Without answering, Dukor grabbed her with both hands and heaved her toward the ceiling. The raw strength in his hands and arms terrified her as she realized how *powerful*, how dangerous this man was. In a blurred instant, her head was through the ceiling hatch and he was forcing her legs up and out of the way. On top of the car, crumpled up like a discarded paper bag, lay the body of a man in dark gray coveralls. His head was twisted around badly and there was a thick hemorrhage of blood already clotting at the corner of his mouth. Isbella recoiled from the sight, but said nothing as Dukor pulled himself through the hatch.

She watched him stand up and check the four walls of the shaft that rose above them to a dark and remote vanishing point. The perspective scared her.

Just how deep were they in the facility?

There would be no answer for the moment, because Dukor had located the panel for which he'd been searching and he was caving it in with both arms. A dark aperture revealed itself as the panel fell inward. In the dim illumination of the shaft Isabella could see a crawlspace, like a heating duct, striking off at a perpendicular angle.

"What is it?" she said.

"Shut up!" The words were spat at her as he grabbed her with one hand and literally heaved her headfirst into the duct. "Start crawling forward. Now!"

Hands and knees working furiously, she began moving. Tight, cramped spaces made her uneasy, and she'd always suspected she had a touch of claustrophobia. No suspicions any longer. Pushing ahead into the rectangular darkness confirmed it—the close, smooth walls of the duct seemed to be tapering down, gradually closing in on her. The air, already rank with their sweat and anxiety, was getting thick, heavy with other toxins. If she didn't—

"Move it!" said Dukor, pushing the barrel of the handgun up against her buttocks, subtly probing their cleft in mock violation.

The sick bastard!

Isabella fought the urges to both kick in his face and burst into tears, forcing herself to surge forward on her elbows and knees. Ahead, the light from baffled ventilation feeders seemed to be growing stronger, the passageway slightly larger.

"How far?" she said weakly, trying to keep her breathing even, without panic.

"You will pass two intersections," said Dukor. "When you reach the third, make a left. Then keep going forward."

"Where are we going?" She looked back over her shoulder, but could not see him. The movement reminded her that he was behind her, looking directly up her skirt, and she felt as if she might retch.

"To freedom," he said with a chuckle.

"I . . . I don't know how far I can go on like this." Her elbows were getting raw, her knees burning from the friction of the nylon stockings against the smooth metal.

"If you stop, I'll have to shoot you," he said flatly.

"Then how will you get past me?"

Dukor began to chuckle. "I'll eat my way out."

His words punctured her like a rusty nail. So unexpected a solution had stunned her into silence. Her breath, growing ragged, had escaped her altogether. The claustrophobia returned in a jagged rush, suddenly clawing at her rational thinking. For a single terrifyingly dark moment, complete panic filled her, and she knew she had lost control of her thoughts and her actions. She had no idea if she was moving or not. No senses. No thoughts. Just the sound of an internal, quiet scream.

She was going to pass out.

No! You can't do that! If he has to shoot you . . .

And that single notion, that crystal-hard thought pulled her back from the edge. Without consciously willing it, her arms and legs began churning with renewed energy, and Dukor chuckled again. . . .

An eternity passed before she crossed the first intersection of ducts. She had abraded her elbows and knees until they became slippery with her blood, but she kept moving. Dukor said nothing, but she could hear the mechanical precision of his breathing behind her like the approach of a steam locomotive in low gear.

Slipping into a dull, monotonous rhythm of movement, letting her thoughts become one with the repetitive advance, she almost didn't notice the second intersection. Time had stretched into a sagging, infinite pull of taffy. The stinging sensation in her knees and elbows had been replaced by a dull throb, and her spine felt as if it were cracking like old ice.

"Stop here." Dukor's voice pierced the bubble of her despair and

Isabella was suddenly, sharply, aware of everything in her surroundings. Reaching the turning point, she angled left around the corner and started to push ahead when his hand grabbed her foot. "Stop."

She did. "What's wrong?"

"Back up," he said. "Past me. Into the cross-duct."

At first she didn't know what he wanted, and she was afraid her indecision would be taken the wrong way. "What—?"

"Back up!" he whispered harshly through his teeth. "I'm taking the lead."

"Oh . . . !"

She suddenly understood his intention and slipped backward into the intersecting duct and waited for him to pass her and enter the left passageway. Without being told, she followed him.

They had not gone more than fifty feet when he suddenly flipped over on his back and sat up in the opening to a vertical shaft above them. He wriggled and twisted into a standing position and stepped up, disappearing from view. When she reached the point of his departure, looking up, she saw his shoes above her ascending on a series of ladder rungs running up the shaft. If she was going to get out of here, she would have to follow. Looking up reminded her all over again that they were buried somewhere in the earth, jammed into a warren of passageways that could collapse or suddenly *end* at any moment. Somehow, Dukor had memorized the intricate layout of the duct system, or understood its design in a fashion that allowed him to negotiate its labyrinth.

But if she lost track of him, she would be lost down here forever. The thought hammered her like a brick on the back of the head.

As she maneuvered and twisted into position, she wondered why he had left her on her own. Granted, he had no worry of her escaping him, but if he didn't need her at some point later, why didn't he just kill her?

Of course, she thought, no one had ruled out that option, had they?

As she grabbed the rungs and began pulling herself upward, she felt infinitely weary, but she *knew* she would never quit. It didn't matter what awaited her, she would face it with dignity and as much strength as remained within her. The monster who climbed above her was only that—created through a hideous chain of events that defined the mystery of existence itself. She would triumph over the personified evil of Dukor.

She knew this because she believed she was better than him, and it really was that simple. . . .

• • •

They climbed for what could have been hours, or days. She followed his endless ascent because there was nothing else to do. There was no benefit in thinking about the vast emptiness below them, how far she might plummet if she were to simply *let go*. Her entire world had become the vertical shaft and each succeeding rung. Every joule of energy was dedicated to the goal of raising her foot to climb at least one more rung. And once that was accomplished, she did it all over again.

Until finally, she looked up to see Dukor's bulk pass off to the right as he huddled into a connecting chamber at a right angle. The unexpected movement renewed her. Isabella pulled herself level with the opening and saw a small chamber no larger than the average powder room. Dukor knelt down and began manipulating a panel at the end of the area. He slid back a faceplate, pulled out a nest of multicolored wires, and pinched a few of them back and forth, working them until the metal fatigued and broke apart. Then he assaulted the panel more roughly until it swung inward, forming a hatch.

It opened onto a small platform surrounded by a low railing and accessed by a catwalk across an unexpectedly vast open area with a curved, multivaulted ceiling. The underground excavation was so huge, ten cathedrals could rise up within it and never feel crowded. She looked down on a series of gigantic machines that might be generators or turbines. Bundles of pipelines, thick cable harnesses, and secondary walkways interlaced the entire complex.

"Omigod . . ." she said as she dragged herself to the edge of the railing, where Dukor stood nodding his head and grinning like the lunatic he was. "What is it?"

"Independent power station. Geothermal and fission. Hydroponics and desalinization," said Dukor. "There's enough going on down here to keep them alive for a hundred years."

"Keep *who* alive?"

He laughed. "The government goons who built it. All the fat cats, the power cats."

"Where is everybody?"

"Nobody down here. All automated. Unless there's an emergency." He spat over the railing. "They never found out we compromised this area when we were part of that emergency drill. We never told them."

His words brought her up short and she couldn't resist challenging him. "You said 'we' . . . who did you mean by that?"

"Me and Nichols. Who else?" And then he threw back his head and cackled like a villain in a Republic serial.

Isabella said nothing, deciding she really didn't care that much anymore and that all she wanted was to get out of there. "Where now?" she said with no real feeling behind it.

"This way."

Dukor headed off down the catwalk that bridged out to join another connecting walk. They crossed over the turbines lying side by side like fat sows in a pen. She wondered if anybody could see them as they moved into the center of the open space. If seen, they made simple and obvious targets, but Dukor walked with impunity. He led her down several sets of ladders and through a maze formed by bank after bank of electronics all rack-mounted like books in a vast library. Despite the tension of her own predicament, she could not help but marvel at the immense complexity of the place and how its existence must be highly classified.

And that made her speculate what the government might do to her, even if she did escape Dukor's plans.

"This way," he said, after a half hour weaving a path through the underground warren. Dukor pointed to what looked like a recessed wall case for two large coiled fire hoses and four extinguishers. She watched as he touched a point along the leading edge of the stainless steel sill, and the entire case swung inward on hinges as big as a bank vault's. They entered quickly as the automatic door resealed itself. Beyond the entrance lay six openings in the wall that looked like cylindrical telephone booths.

"What's this?" said Isabella, staring at the booths and noticing that each contained a Plexiglas pod, like a bullet slipped into a firing chamber.

"Emergency escape system," he said, reaching to touch another hidden access point on the closest booth. Its protective casing recessed back to reveal a capsule seven feet tall. "Works like the pneumatic tube systems in old buildings like department stores. Powered by geologic heat and pressure. They've got these things stacked in here like giant Pez dispensers—remember those things?"

"Where does it go?"

"To the surface. Each pod exits at a different location. Supposed to increase survival odds. No matter what kind of catastrophe there might be up there."

"I don't get it."

Dukor looked at her with disdain. "You don't have to. Just get in."

Isabella eyed the pod's interior, which was not much larger than a coffin's. Her claustrophobia would be acute, and she wondered how long the journey lasted. She was about to ask him when his hand vise-gripped her arm and thrust her into the pod. Its foam-padded lining received her gently, and she relaxed. But only for a moment—until Dukor forced himself in with her.

As the Plexiglas canopy slid into place, she tried to twist away from the crush of his hard-muscled body, but there was no place to go. Despite his rugged good looks, she had witnessed the corruption beneath the flesh. He stank of it, and being so close threatened to suffocate her as they lay locked together. Interestingly enough, he seemed to be equally repulsed by her, because she could feel him trying to edge away from as much skin contact as possible. He wriggled his hand low, past their hips, and touched something on the pod's interior.

She felt a vibration on the outer hull and the pod began to move, slowly at first, but gradually accelerating through absolute darkness. She could feel and smell the closeness of him as they were sucked upward through the earth, but these sensations were quickly replaced by an overwhelming wave of motion sickness and claustrophobia. They turned and twisted in total darkness as they shuttled upward. It was like a demented theme-park ride. She heard a high keening scream and for a moment didn't realize it was the sound of her own voice . . .

. . . and she blinked her eyes to see a sky so hard and gray it could have been carved of stone. But it *was* the sky—open and free of the stale clutch of the underground. She felt a surge of joy run through her like an electric current. She lay on her back, still in the pod, as Dukor loomed over her. Reaching down, he clasped her wrist, dragging her from the capsule. Once free of it she could see its emergence had blown the cover from a sod-covered hatch, protected in a small copse of trees. She staggered to her feet, trying to regain a sense of equilibrium, and waited for the nausea to pass.

"So far, so good." Dukor edged closer to the clearing beyond the trees. It sloped down toward a state highway. Beyond the road stretched open Virginia farmland, verdant and full of gently rolling hills. Even against the stone-gray sky, it was beautiful. "If they knew our location, they've already tracked us."

"Meaning?" She chanced interrupting his thoughts to give herself the clearest picture of what was happening. Any scrap of information might prove essential to her survival.

"Meaning they could get here at any time. But I'm already waiting for them."

He cocked his ear into the wind like a dog hearing a pitch a man never will. Everything became so quiet, she thought she might be hearing the sound of a car's engine, far, far away.

"Please," said Isabella, leaning against a young maple. "I can't go on like this. Not much longer."

"You won't have to," he said with a smile, but still watching the road below them. He was listening to the sound—now definitely that of approaching vehicles—waiting for a visual contact as well. She watched him as his whole body seemed to tense up like a spring ready to unleash itself. His eyes turreted in his skull as his hands caressed his weapon.

Another minute passed before she saw movement on a distant hillside—two camouflaged Humvees crested the state highway, then abruptly veered off into the pastureland that gradually sloped upward to their position. One behind the other, the two vehicles rumbled toward them. From their current position, they were less than a half-mile distant.

"Stay there," said Dukor, pointing at her with the automatic pistol, then to the opened pod. "Let them see you, but be quiet. If you don't, I'll have to shoot you."

"What're you going to do?" Isabella backed away from him as he approached one of the larger evergreen trees.

"Arrange my transportation," he said as he jumped up and grabbed the lowermost branch with both hands.

She watched with a mixture of awe and loathing as he swung himself into the first tier of branches. For a succinct moment, she had a chance to collect her thoughts, to reflect on the bizarre episode of total unreality she'd experienced. Even so briefly past, it was hard to believe any of it had actually happened. How long had they been down there? How far had they gone? She had been pushing herself so hard for so long that when the effort was no longer needed, she knew she was near collapse. Just standing there by the ruptured pod was causing her knees to buckle.

Another sound gradually invaded the area. The rhythmic beating of a helicopter. Clearing a distant stand of trees, it hung against the sky like a giant dragonfly, looking for prey. Then slowly, almost lazily, it tilted foward and began to track the progress of the ground vehicles. Even at the great distance, Isabella could feel the earth respond with subtle, echoing vibrations to the *whump! whump!* of the machine's approach.

By then, the first Humvee had gained the top of the long hill and had zeroed in on her location. From the shortened distance she could see its occupants, two young soldiers, looking straight at her. The other vehicle remained out of sight. She had no idea what was going to happen next, but she was afraid to even *move*. Not a wave. Nothing. She wanted to do something to warn them, but she kept imagining the next second being ripped open by a large-caliber bullet, and that image kept her immobile, helpless.

What happened next transpired so quickly, she wasn't really certain what she witnessed. The Humvee rolled to a stop just beyond the low-slung branches of Dukor's position. As the driver slid out from behind the wheel, he was felled by the madman as he dove head-first from the tree. In a choreographed series of movements, Dukor broke the driver's neck, grabbed his sidearm from his holster, and put two quick slugs into the forehead of the other soldier before he could leave his seat.

Stunned, she watched him disappear within the vehicle just as the other Humvee cleared the hill and jammed to a halt close behind it.

Isabella began to shout a warning, but her words were swallowed up in a concussive blast as the second vehicle burst into flames. Dukor leaped from the lead Humvee with a wide-mouthed weapon. He pumped a second shell into the burning hulk and it blossomed into a shower of black and burning fragments. A rippling burst of concussed air slapped her across the face as she turned away, just glimpsing a snapshot of Dukor standing in the cover of the roiling smoke.

Then looking back, she saw him waiting for the helicopter, now angling toward the burning wreckage with all its guns bristling. Dukor waited for it, legs wide apart like a piece of heroic sculpture, and its pilot never noticed him until it broke through the barrier of black fog. Standing directly beneath the bare belly of the aircraft, Dukor launched a shell into its midsection, then dove for cover beneath the intact Humvee.

The fireball strobed from red to blue to white in an instant, a miniature sun, as all the onboard ammo sucked up the oxygen in a series of quick, vaporizing blasts. The ground shook from the concussion, but absorbed it ultimately like a sponge.

And a terrible silence accompanied the waves of smoke and heat that rolled over her, obscuring the wreckage. She couldn't believe it when she saw Dukor emerge from the debris storm and walk toward her with a toothy smile on his face.

"That was fun, don't you think!" he said as he slung the weapon over his shoulder by its webbed strap.

Isabella climbed from the pod and backed away from him. Dukor's eyes had grown large and dark, his gaze darting from her to the landscape and back. The presence behind his eyes leered at her, mocked her, and she knew it was the most purely evil thing she'd ever witnessed. The thing that had been Harford Nichols advanced with a casual swagger and reached for a handgun tucked into his belt.

"I want to thank you for being such a pleasant traveling companion," he said. "For awhile there, I thought you might be a valuable addition to my old kit bag . . ."

He didn't have to finish the sentence.

As Dukor stopped about twenty feet from her and raised the pistol ceremoniously, she knew she was going to die. With unbelievable slowness, the barrel swung upward, pointing at her face. The weapon's black aperture yawned impossibly wide as if she were staring down the depths of a dark well.

"Doctor Mussina," said Dukor. "A final thank-you for giving me life once more, and then I am afraid it is Good Night."

Just as he uttered that last word, she screamed something at him. It was the word "no," but distorted by a combination of terror and anger into a long shriek of outrage. Lunging forward, reaching for her executioner, she never heard the thunderous report of his gun. There was a bright flash, like the smile of an angel, and then . . .

. . . nothing.

PART THREE

TWILIGHT, AND NO GODS

SEVENTEEN

J. MICHAEL KEATING, M.D.
Manhattan, New York

The following day was unseasonably warm and reminded Michael that summer would eventually overtake the city. He preferred warm weather and looked forward to the changing climate. Normally, he'd have been cheered by the omen, but this morning he remained absorbed in his work. He didn't need any outside influence to affect his mood or his outlook.

He was amazed at how much he had learned in the past few days. It made him appreciate how *little* he'd known or understood before discovering Dr. Mussina's work. As he entered his inner office he noticed Italo Calvino's novel on the edge of one of his file cabinets where he'd left it so many, many weeks ago. The unfinished translation reminded Michael of several things instantly: one, how perfectly ordered his life had been, and in turn how *insulated* he'd become from the rest of the world; and now how much more challenging and exciting each day promised to be.

It hadn't been so long ago that he'd been admitting to himself that he was ready to throw in the towel on psychotherapy, unconsciously planning his retirement to what? A quasisolitary life of intellectual exercises and pursuits. . . .

But now he was looking forward to each new hour anxiously; there was simply no telling what awaited him.

Sitting down at his desk, he glanced at the stacks of papers by Isabella Mussina and was immediately reminded of her beautifully crafted prose. It made him wonder what kind of a person she might be.

Maybe he should spend a little time on the Net to uncover some biographical data. It wouldn't be a good idea to assign the task to Pamela Robbins, he knew. She would probably assume his interest in Mussina was more than merely professional, which was untrue. He was just curious about a colleague, nothing more.

But Pamela might think differently.

He smiled when he imagined what Pamela might do or think. It wasn't as if they enjoyed a serious relationship yet. Going to dinner a few times, having a few drinks, didn't necessarily establish anything more than a friendship. But Michael was pretty sure Pamela didn't interpret things so loosely. The woman was definitely interested in developing a deep and intimate understanding between them, and Michael knew she considered it just a matter of time.

Michael smiled to himself as the phrase drifted through his thoughts. Just a matter of time—until Pamela Robbins invited him to a special dinner at her East Side apartment, complete with candlelight and wine and a new dress. Michael was not being smug. He truly believed he knew Pamela well enough to anticipate her plans to accelerate their relationship. The next logical step was the ritual dinner and the "accidental" seduction. He and Pamela both knew a sexual encounter would be necessary to achieve the next level of involvement. He actually looked forward to it, but wasn't certain whether or not such a complication in his life was the best thing right now.

He wouldn't deny Pamela was an attractive woman, that she exuded a sexual energy that made him more than just curious. But he'd reached that point in his life when he felt neither a biological nor a psychological need to bed every sexy woman he met. He'd nothing to prove to any woman about his manliness, and certainly not to himself. He loved sex as much as any man, but it wasn't his only or even primary interest in life. Learning how to live with sexual desire without letting it dominate his thoughts or his activities had allowed him to achieve a comfortable balance. Which meant he wasn't going to jump into bed with Pamela in a moment of weakness or total abandon—he'd do it because he truly *wanted* to. Michael was very much aware of what such a decision would signify.

For his own good, he knew he'd better keep that awareness in focus at all times.

Thinking of Pamela made him check the time. She was scheduled to arrive for work within the hour. If he wanted to do any detective work on Dr. Mussina, he should probably do it now, and so he moused into the Net from the PC on his desk and ran a few preliminary searches. The initial information was unremarkable. Mussina was in her late thirties, unmarried, no ex-husbands or children, educated at the University of Chicago, and recipient of a number of achievement awards and citations.

Photos from various awards programs and symposia, while not studio close-ups, revealed Isabella to be a strikingly arresting woman. Classic Mediterranean features—brown almond eyes, high cheekbones, and full lips. He looked away from the screen as he heard a sound by the door.

"Good morning, Doctor," said a familiar voice as Pamela glided into his office. "Just wanted to let you know I'm here. . . ."

Smiling, he casually but efficiently moused out of the Web site and returned to his homepage. "Good morning, Pamela. Ready to get to work?"

She moved to the side of his desk, glanced at his screen. "Looks like you've already started," she said, raising a single eyebrow, ". . . and on the Net! That's a surprise—I thought you didn't like surfing?"

He shrugged. "Ah, it's kind of tedious, that's true. The graphics usually bore me."

She looked at him with a grin that suggested she knew he was lying, nodded, and turned to leave. Stopping at the door, she looked back. "Oh, I almost forgot: your calls to that doctor in Chicago—Mussina?—haven't been returned. No e-mail either. Should I try to reach anyone else at the VA hospital?"

"Yes," he said, keying up his onscreen infopad to double-check himself. "And you can call that associate of Mussina's—the rabbi. Klingerman. You have the number."

Pamela nodded. "I'll follow up right away."

She turned and exited the office as Michael exited the Net. He felt an excitement that he hadn't experienced for many, many years. And that is why he knew it was important to contact Dr. Mussina.

Even though he had until very recently not believed in the power of intuition, Michael had been overwhelmed by a sense of . . . of *destiny*. He truly felt that he *must* contact Isabella Mussina. The compelling, and in some ways frightening, mystery he had uncovered was deeply connected to Mussina, as well as his own future. He smiled at the way he was thinking. If, several months ago, someone had told him he would be taking the concept of *fate* seriously, he'd have laughed at them, or maybe gotten pissed at them.

The buzz of his intercom interrupted him. "I'm not having any luck reaching Doctor Mussina," said Pamela.

"Who'd you talk to? What're they saying?"

"Her supervisor at Hines Veterans Administration Hospital is Doctor Lansing." Pamela gave him a phone number. "He says she's on a special assignment in Washington, D.C."

"Any way to reach her there?" Michael wrote Lansing's name on his notepad.

"He says no."

"I don't believe that," said Michael. "I think I'll call him personally."

"Okay . . ."

"What about Irwin Klingerman?" Michael tapped his blotter with his fountain pen nervously.

"I left messages at both numbers I've been able to find."

"All right, good. Keep trying him every hour or so—until we hear from him."

Pamela disconnected, and Michael dialed the VA hospital in Chicago. After several minutes of rerouting his calls, he heard the voice of someone young and harried: "This is Doctor Lansing . . ."

Michael introduced himself as politely as possible and stressed the importance of reaching Dr. Mussina.

"You ever worked in a place like this, Doctor Keating?" Lansing's question caught him off-balance.

"What?"

"A veteran's hospital," said Lansing. "It's probably what Dante had in mind when he wrote *Il Purgatorio.*"

"I see . . ." said Michael.

"If I sound like I'm disillusioned, disgusted, and overworked, it's because I *am*." Lansing made no effort to be cordial.

"Sorry to hear that," said Michael. "But I can't tell you how important it is that I contact Doctor Mussina as soon as possible."

Lansing exhaled, and his weariness was transmitted through the phone with great clarity. "Is this a life threatening emergency, Doctor?"

Considering his answer for only a moment, Michael nodded as if to convince himself. "Yes, Doctor, it is."

"Well, that's going to complicate things a bit," said Lansing. "Because it's almost impossible to reach her when she's called to D.C."

"What do you mean? Called by who—? The government?"

Lansing paused. "Ah, let's just say it's just difficult to reach her. Can we let it go at that?"

"Does her work concern classified information?" said Michael. "Is that what you mean? Or am I asking questions that would compromise your own security clearance?"

Lansing chuckled. "Doctor Keating, I don't know you very well, and you could be some government goon checking up on me for all I know, but I haveta tell you: I don't give a shit anymore. I've had it up to my ears with the government and their security and their secrets."

"Does that mean you know where she is?" Michael could feel the honest emotions in this man and he liked him instantly.

Another sigh. "I don't know. Maybe. I'm the one that has to sign off on her travel vouchers and credit card receipts, so I've seen that she goes to Langley, Virginia. That's CIA country."

"Is she a spy?"

Lansing chuckled again. He explained the indentured servitude "program" in which many doctors find themselves trapped. "How else do you think they get good people to work in these shit holes?"

"You make a convincing argument," said Michael. He didn't want to get the man started on a long discourse on federal injustices. "But I really have to find her. It's life or death. . . ." He added the last sentence with less than compelling urgency.

Lansing paused for moment. "The only thing I can tell you is that her 'super' in Washington is some guy named Glinka."

"Thanks, Doctor Lansing," said Michael. "You've been a big help. You wouldn't have this guy's phone number, would you?"

"Listen, Doc, if you could see my desk and the general environment of my workplace, you'd understand what I'm going to tell you, which is: it's around here *someplace*, but I don't have a fucking clue *where* . . . you got me?"

"Yes, yes," said Michael, getting a very clear image of the man's office. "I do, and I'm sorry to have taken up so much of your time."

"Better you than the government, I guess."

"Well, again, thanks."

"See ya, Doc. Good luck in getting in touch with her."

Michael was about to hang up when he spoke impulsively: "Wait! One more thing!"

"Yeah . . . ?" Lansing's tone indicated he'd reached the breaking point and would be lapsing into the territory of the rude at any time now.

"I just wanted to ask you . . . you see, I've never met her in person . . . Doctor Mussina . . ."

"Yeah . . . so?" Lansing was clearly losing his patience now.

"I was just wondering . . . is she . . . is she a good doctor, if you know what I mean?"

Michael could sense a release of tension through the receiver, a sudden warmth coming from Lansing. "She's the best, Doc. If I had twenty more like her this wouldn't be such a bad turn in purgatory after all. She's not only a great doctor, she's just a damn fine human being. That good enough?"

Smiling, Michael thanked him for a final time and hung up. It was not much information to go on, but it was better than nothing. Buzzing Pamela, he passed on the information and asked her to do whatever was possible. Then he scanned his onscreen Rolodex, jogging his memory as myriad names of friends, colleagues, and associates blinked past his view. Judges, lawyers, senators, doctors. The list was as impressive as it was long, and he knew there *had* to be someone who could get him past the bureaucracy of the federal government.

He sighed. There was nothing to do now but start making some calls. Picking up the receiver, he was reminded of how much he loathed talking on the phone. If anything irritated him more than a ringing phone when he was doing something else, he didn't know what it was. He hated being interrupted and likewise did not enjoy interrupting others. But it always seemed more urgent, more legitimate when *he* was the one making the call, didn't it?

He smiled at the irony as he selected the first name and keyed in the number. . . .

Several hours later, after going through normal channels and protocols, Pamela had gotten nowhere. If they believed the answers they'd been getting, no one in *any* government agency had ever heard of Dr. Isabella Mussina or an official named Glinka. Michael hadn't expected her to be successful, and that's why he had enlisted the aid of several well-placed associates. The father of one of his med school colleagues had been seated in the House of Representatives for twenty years. He was probably Michael's best connection, but he also had four other men of influence: a federal judge, another ex-congressman, the assistant to the NYPD commissioner, and a lifetime TV journalist who worked as a Washington correspondent. They all promised him positive results.

But this might all take time, and he was getting impatient. His curiosity was overwhelming other aspects of his life, and the mystery of the Holocaust victims was the only thing that seemed to matter any more.

"Excuse me, Doctor Keating," said Pamela through the intercom, being thoroughly professional.

"Yes . . . ?"

"I have Irwin Klingerman on line three. He says it's urgent."

Michael could feel his pulse jump. Klingerman had worked with Mussina. He had to know how to reach her, he thought as he grabbed for the phone.

"This is Doctor Keating," he said into the receiver, trying to sound calm. "It's good to hear from you, Rabbi."

"Please, please! Call me Irwin," said a loud, slightly accented voice. He sounded like a native New Yorker. "I'm sorry I haven't called you back, Doctor. So busy. I know you've been trying to reach Isabella—Doctor Mussina."

"Yes," said Michael, briefly introducing himself and his credentials. He then added a concise history of the events that led him to contact Mussina. Klingerman was astounded to hear of corroborating research, but his enthusiasm seemed subdued.

"That's certainly good news. I can tell you that Doctor Mussina will be pleased to hear about this."

"I know," said Michael. "Can you help me?"

"That's why I am calling," said Klingerman. "Our research is ongoing, and it . . . well, it's time-consuming. Normally, when she goes to Washington, Isabella checks in with me every few days, but . . ."

"But, you haven't heard from her." Michael knew what the man would say. He also knew exactly how time-consuming their project could be. It was the very nature of obsession.

"Not at *all*! Nothing! And that's not like her, believe me," said Klingerman. "I called the number she leaves for me and they claim to have never *heard* of her! Doctor, I don't mind telling you—I'm more than a little bit concerned."

"Why?" said Michael. "What kind of work is she doing in Washington?"

Klingerman hesitated for an instant. Then: "Everybody thinks she works for Walter Reed or the big Veterans hospital in D.C., but that's not true."

"I know," said Michael. "Doctor Lansing thinks she works for the CIA."

Klingerman exhaled loudly. "Ah! So you know about that . . . ? Good! But like I said, Doctor Keating—this has got me worried. She's been working for them for years, and all of a sudden, they've never *heard* of her!"

"Do you have anyone else you can talk to?" Michael said softly. He could detect true concern in Klingerman's voice, like that of a close friend. A *very* close friend.

"No," said the rabbi. "I'm afraid I'm at the end of my rope. What do you think this means—saying they've never heard of her?"

Michael paused, trying to decide how much to tell Klingerman. "I couldn't tell you. Understanding how the government operates isn't one of my strengths," said Michael. "But I have some friends who might be able to tell us more. Can you give me the phone numbers and contact names you have?"

"Of course." Klingerman gave him the information.

"I'll get these followed up."

"Excellent! I'll call you immediately if I hear anything." Klingerman hung up the phone, leaving Michael to his thoughts. Even though he had no new information, he felt a little more secure to know that he had put some wheels into motion, that people were out there trying to help him.

Actually, Klingerman had added a dire piece of intrigue to what had begun as a simple forwarding of a phone message. The government's refusal to acknowledge Dr. Mussina's existence was a *very* bad sign. He didn't want to tell Klingerman, but it sounded like somebody was trying to hide something. Never a good omen when bureaucrats or federal agents were involved.

Pamela's familiar tap at the door made him look up from his notepad. "Yes?"

"It's almost lunchtime," she said. "We haven't been having much luck . . . so I was wondering if we could take a break. My treat."

Automatically, he looked at his watch. "Well . . . I don't know. I'm expecting calls from so many different people."

"Oh, come on!" Pamela stepped halfway through the door, revealing half of her body like a stripper easing out from behind a curtain. She wore a tailored suit that enhanced her breasts and legs. There was no denying she looked alluring. "There's a new Japanese place that just opened up on Seventy-fourth Street."

"All right," he said. "I feel like we are being stymied right now. I need a break."

She smiled and waited for him to join her.

The food was well-prepared and their conversation was equally satisfying. Making sure they spent most of it talking shop, Michael was able to keep away from any mentions of future plans on a personal level. But it wasn't easy. Pamela's dark good looks had the desired effect on him. He was looking forward to spending a crazy night with her, to satisfy his curiosity, to be sure, but also because he was beginning to really like her.

This was new to him because Pamela had never seemed interested in him, and he'd been okay with that. It was only when she had begun making it obvious they could get to know each other outside the office that he gave his idle fantasies any credence.

As they left the restaurant for the short walk back, a brisk wind was cutting through the streets; he hunched his shoulders against it and she held his offered arm. "You seem distracted, Michael."

"I'm *always* distracted," he said, trying to make light of it. "I'm always thinking about things. You know that."

"I know you're interested in these cases," she said as they reached the corner, waited for the traffic. "But I think I should warn you that it's not a good idea to become so . . . so *involved* in this thing."

He looked at her and smiled. "You think I'm getting obsessed?"

Her expression belied her response. "Of course not. I've just been thinking that we might not ever learn all the answers here, that we might end up in a blind alley . . ."

He shrugged as the light changed and the crowd around them began to move forward as one entity. "I've thought about that."

"But have you accepted it?" said Pamela. "To spend so much energy and time on something that ultimately doesn't pay off . . . it can be very frustrating."

"What're you trying to tell me, Pamela?" He glanced at her as they walked along, smiled to relax her.

"I don't know, really. I guess I just worry about you," she said. There was sincerity in her voice. He could detect an element of self-realization, as if she had just at that moment learned something about herself.

"And . . . ?" Michael had an idea what she was trying to say. There was no harm in urging it from her. Better now than later, actually.

She walked along in the self-contained sphere of their conversation, oblivious to the shrill buzz of the Manhattan hive all around them. Her attention was gathered and focused on him so tightly he could almost feel it. "And . . . I guess I'm trying to say I really *care* about you, Michael."

He stopped and looked at her. "I know that," he said softly.

What she was saying was very difficult for her. They stood in front of an office building as the pedestrian traffic streamed around them. "And what I'm thinking is that I wish you felt the same way, that you were as interested in *me* as you are in these cases . . ."

Pamela couldn't look him in the eye and he could feel her embarrassment. Gone for the moment was her usual air of competence and understanding. What she said took some guts.

"These things take time," he said, taking her hand, kissing it. "But I think I can be."

"I know, but look at us," she said, letting go a bit. "Neither one of us are getting any younger . . ."

"True . . ." He smiled.

"And we respect each other; we like each other, and we like a lot of the same things . . . so I figured why not? Why *shouldn't* we be involved?" She was taking deep breaths, expelling them in dramatic sighs.

The wind was tossing her thick, wavy hair around, and her dark eyes darted nervously from him to passersby. It was a very sexy moment, like a scene from a movie. And this was the point where the script would have called for him to proclaim his love and take her in his arms while the music swelled over them, the camera pulled back, and the credits began to roll.

But there was no script, and Michael wasn't in love with her, and despite her soul-baring exercise, he couldn't make things any better than they were.

He did kiss her, though, and it was a good kiss. "Pamela, I'm a very difficult man," he said in a whisper. "Let's just see where things take us, all right?"

"Sure," she said, kissing him back. "I'm sorry if I embarrassed you, if I acted silly . . ."

"Are you kidding? Of course not. Come on, now. It is getting colder."

They turned into the wind and she held on to his arm as they walked toward the office. It was a comfortable feeling to have a woman holding him like that.

Upon returning to the office, he watched as Pamela resumed her role of employee. Quietly distanced, professional and respectful.

It was an unspoken, unacknowledged transformation, but no less real. For that reason alone, Michael carried a few doubts about the viability of an intense relationship with her—unless she quit her job. And that didn't sound like a great idea because he knew his office would never function as efficiently without her.

"I have to make a few more phone calls," he said, standing by the door to his inner sanctum. "You want to check for messages first?"

Nodding curtly, Pamela had already keyed in the phone service and was adjusting her headphones and mike.

Michael retreated to the security of his large desk. The modern fixtures and furniture of his office were a familiar comfort to him, even more so than his own co-op in Turtle Bay with its spectacular view of the United Nations Building and the East River. Symbolic of the way he'd let his profession define his entire life. Maybe it hadn't been the best idea.

Pamela tapped lightly, then entered, carrying a piece of notepaper, which she laid on his desk.

"Several calls while we were out," she said. "Judge Robert Goald, Representative Sam Hodgkins, and Captain Ellersby."

"Great. Any messages?"

"No, they all want you to call them back. Captain Ellersby said it was urgent."

Michael nodded. "I'll call him first. Thanks."

She smiled perfunctorily and exited his office, but something had changed in her. The warm, subtly flirtatious demeanor had vanished. Their little scene on Seventy-fourth Street was having a negative effect on her. He'd have to have another talk with her, but it would have to wait until he was less preoccupied.

Keying in the deputy commissioner's office, he became anxious about the "urgent" aspect of the return call.

"Captain Ellersby's office," said the receptionist.

Michael identified himself, and was switched through.

"Doctor Keating!" said the familiar voice. "I haven't seen you at any of the card games lately, what happened?"

"Hello, Chester," said Michael. "I guess I've been busy."

"Yeah, I'd say so! That's what I'm calling you about."

"What do you mean?" Michael felt a lump forming in throat. Something was wrong. "What's going on?"

Ellersby chuckled darkly. "That's what I wanna ask you, Doc! Talk about poking a stick in a hornet's nest! When I made a few calls to some buddies at the bureau, they acted like I'd just asked them to kill my wife!"

"What do you mean?" said Michael. "What happened?"

"My buddies told me they'd see what they could find out about this Doctor Mussina, right? Then, Christ, the next thing I know—like a *half hour later*—I got a visit from two feds."

"Who were they?" Something cold had touched the back of Michael's neck.

"Search me—coupla government suits, you know what I mean. They said they wanted to know exactly who I was and *why* I wanted to know the whereabouts of Isabella Mussina, and what my connection to her might be."

"What did you tell them?

"The *truth*, what else!?" Ellersby laughed nervously. "These guys were serious business, Doc. Nobody to fuck around with."

"Do they want to talk to me?"

Another nervous chuckle. "I think you can count on it."

"Did they tell you anything?" Michael was perplexed more than frightened by what he was learning. "Didn't you ask them why they were acting like that?"

"Of course I did! They told me to *forget* I'd talked to them—that usually means we're dealing with something classified. Who *is* this woman you wanted me to check on, anyway? She a criminal?"

"Not that I know of," said Michael, although now he was wondering just what kind of mess he had stumbled into. "As far as I knew, she was an academic working on a study I wanted to read about."

"Well, sorry I couldn't be more help, my friend."

"That's okay, Chester. Thanks for trying."

Ellersby chuckled again. "Hey, you're not gettin' off that easy! You've got to let me know what happens with this one."

"I promise," said Michael. "Thanks again."

"See you in the funny papers, Doc. . . ."

As he disconnected the call and leaned back in his chair, Michael wondered whether or not he had anything to fear from the government. Like Pamela, he believed the federal establishment had grown far too big and out of control. Michael had lost faith in the power of government to govern itself, and its ability to govern fairly. Whenever you give anybody access to that much influence and money, they're going to use it. It was a simple extrapolation.

The next hour passed uneventfully, although it seemed to move at a geological pace. He spent the time scheduling regular patients for the following week. He could no longer justify the disruption of their therapies and knew that he had to return to a more normal routine. As much as he wanted to concentrate on the cases of Rodney McGuire and Allison Enders, he recognized his obligations to the many others who relied on him for assistance.

The scheduling exercise was actually beneficial because it forced him to reevaluate the real priorities in his life. It made him ask the questions that he'd been unconsciously avoiding: did he really want to keep doing this? Why had he become so . . . obsessed . . . with the mysterious Dr. Mussina? Had he really become a True Believer in reincarnation and past-life regression? Or had he allowed himself to be swept away by a storm of strange coincidences and possibly an outright hoax?

His answers, and the introspection they catalyzed, made him feel more at ease and more dedicated to the choices he was making. Despite his prior beliefs about premonitions and intuition, Michael was one hundred percent certain that the experiences of Enders and McGuire were not only real, but represented evidence of a much larger phenomenon. The existence of someone called "The Little Angel" was critical to understanding the real meaning of both Michael's and Mussina's cases. There was no doubt that he would continue to pursue the truth, wherever it might lead him.

He felt better about everything. The just-below-the surface anxiety had begun to leave him, and he believed his relentless search for answers would be rewarded.

And then the phone rang, changing everything—again.

EIGHTEEN

BRADLEY STEVENSON
Manhattan, New York

He decided he would handle Dr. Keating himself.

Things were happening very quickly; the time for quick decisions and don't-look-back actions.

After months of going absolutely nowhere on the Harford Nichols case, the FBI's International Division was suddenly getting more data than it had time to assimilate and follow up. As his bureau chopper prepared to land him on the roof of the World Trade Center, Brad Stevenson leaned forward and closed his notebook computer with its reports and briefings. He'd spent the short flight from D.C. calmly reviewing the history of events.

From his side window, the spectacular clutch of skyscrapers of the Battery loomed ever closer, finally dropping daringly close beneath the fuselage. Looking straight down, Brad lost all sense of size and perspective. The tops of the great buildings looked like the abstract squares of a circuit diagram.

"Get ready to touch down, sir," said the pilot.

Brad nodded absently as he continued to ponder the realities of the case.

When Brunnel from Interpol had inquired back in early spring,

Brad had stonewalled as a matter of policy. Actually, he was surprised that it had taken the Eurocops so long to associate the series of assassinations with a single agent. Several high-profile individuals had become suspects, but Brad had decided to keep a lid on the case, given its volatile nature, potential for international embarrassment, and some unsettling and unexplainable facts reported in each event.

There were a few guys in his division who thought the case was downright spooky, out there in left field with some of the other preternatural phenomena the bureau was sometimes forced to investigate. The one that always came to mind was the guy from the State Department who spontaneously combusted during a transatlantic flight, in full view of the passengers and crew. Intense fireball lasted ten seconds and he'd been reduced to ashes except for his feet (still in his shoes and socks) and skull. No burn damage to the plane, other than the seat cushion. Nobody ever did come up with anything to explain *that* one.

He had a hard time accepting such things, pragmatist that he was, but too many people had sworn to it—just like they had in the Nichols killings. The tattooed numbers on the victims' arms were apparently true. His follow-up talks with Egon Brunnel at Interpol had been very convincing, and Brunnel was a very sincere and trustworthy witness. But what those camp number tattoos might mean remained a mystery to Stevenson and his people. And frankly, he wasn't sure he even *wanted* to know what they meant. . . .

One thing he *had* wanted was to have closed the net on Nichols months ago, before this latest fiasco at Langley. But the guy'd been an excellent operative for so many years, he'd accrued some powerful friends and supporters. Nobody wanted to believe he was over the top, a loony.

But after reviewing the video/audio of the session with Dr. Mussina, there was no doubt the guy was not only a complete lunatic, but also a very scary lunatic.

Christ-on-a-crutch, he thought. Nichols had made them look like idiots—right in their own backyard. Brad wondered how that psycho-session could have been monitored and nobody ever figured that, gee, maybe it was getting a little out of control in there. . . .

And now that Nichols was on the loose, killing like some rabid animal, the Company boys were asking Brad and his people to clean up the mess.

Find Nichols and terminate his ugly, crazy existence.

It wouldn't be easy, Brad knew. Nichols was a tough package. Not only did he have vast knowledge and experience, he was also a very resourceful, creative type. In order to stop him, they would first have to *locate* him, and that would be practically impossible without understanding what was fueling him, motivating him.

That business about having lived before in Ukraine, and the Nazis . . . just what the hell did *that* mean?

The chopper heaved to the right as swirling crosswinds from between the twin towers tried to bat the craft from the sky. Brad's cheek pressed against the glass as the pilot corrected for the aberration.

"Sorry about that," said the pilot. "We'll be down in a minute."

Pulling back from the glass, Brad swallowed slowly, making sure nothing was coming up from his stomach. He hated flying in regular commercial jets—just the sheer size of them made him think it was impossible they could ever get off the ground—but stunting around in the bureau's modified Comanches kept him on the fine edge of panic almost constantly. He'd never been able to figure out the phobia, because he wasn't afraid to do other risky things—he liked skiing down the sheerest of slopes, and loved sailing so much he'd once signed onto a sloop that made an Atlantic crossing with a crew of only seven.

Go figure, right?

The Comanche seemed to hang over the helipad like a lightbulb dangling from its cord for a long time before touching down for good. The pilot jumped down to the deck and ran around to open Brad's door. When he stepped out, he was surprised at the amount of wind snapping across the flat surface of the building's roof. As he took a step toward a shed along the perimeter of the landing area, a bureau employee was running out to meet him.

"Chief Stevenson, hi!" she yelled over the wind and the noise of the rotors as they whipsawed above their heads, slowly shutting down. "I'm Marcie Greenfeld from the Wall Street office. Let's take the elevator down to the lobby. We've got a car waiting for you."

Brad nodded and followed her. She was a petite woman with pointy little features. No ass or hips, almost a boyish figure, and he wondered how the hell she'd ever gotten through basic. Even though he was no grizzled thirty-year vet, he'd been around long enough to see a lot of changes in the policy and procedure of the bureau, remaining far from convinced they were all for the better. Just looking at this little woman made him angry. She couldn't possibly be able to perform as efficiently as men twice her size.

He followed her down a corridor to a service elevator. Once inside, and heading down, he started to relax.

"Do you get into the city much?" Marcie Greenfeld had decided to make a little small talk, but Brad would have preferred silence. He didn't want to talk to her because he didn't want to find out she was a nice person, a likable person, making his anger and resentment of her inappropriate.

"Not much. My wife, Nevah, she likes to come in for Broadway shows. That's about it."

Marcie nodded. "Did you see *Phantom?* That was fantastic! My favorite of all time."

"I like plays, actually. Always thought musicals were kind of dumb." Brad eyed the floor indicator anxiously. For a high-speed car, this was pretty damned slow.

Greenfeld smiled weakly and took the hint that he didn't feel much like talking. They plummeted to the lobby in a web of awkward silence, making him feel lousy with guilt. She seemed like a nice enough kid and here he was being an asshole. But it was too late to save it now, so he kept to his stony silence until the bay doors opened.

"Which way for that car?" he said as warmly as possible.

"This way," she said with a measured coolness. She took him to a set of double glass doors and pointed to an archetypal sedan waiting at the curb.

"Agent Greenfeld," he said as he leaned against the door. "Thanks for the help."

"Sure." She remained cool to him.

"Look, I think I owe you an apology. I shouldn't be taking out my bad day on a fellow agent. . . ."

She didn't have anything to say to that, which was fine with Brad. Constructing what felt like a fairly fatuous smile, he nodded and exited the building. The drab sedan waited at the curb, one agent behind the wheel, another leaning against the rear fender. When he saw Brad, the latter opened the door like a limo driver.

"Good afternoon, sir," he said, shaking hands. "Agent Sid Klepner. Nice to meet you, sir."

Brad nodded, slipped into the backseat. Klepner ran around and jumped into the shotgun seat. The driver, a balding man in his mid-forties, tending toward a weight problem, turned around and smiled. "Agent Andy McShea. How're you doing, Mr. Stevenson?"

"Fine, fine. You guys want to fill me in?"

"Go on, Sid . . ." said McShea.

Klepner reached for a notepad from his jacket pocket. He was a thin guy, almost gaunt looking, his face angular and long, cheeks pockmarked, and small bird-shot eyes. Kind of scary-looking, actually. "It was kinda weird," he said. "We'd just gotten the fax on Nichols' escape from Langley, and then, like fifteen minutes later, we get *another* fax from headquarters—the Police Liaison Division. Seems as if they got a call from . . ." he paused to check the name on his pad, " . . . from Chester Ellersby, the deputy commissioner here in town, and he's checking on the whereabouts of Isabella Mussina."

"Which red-flagged everybody," said Brad, cutting through the fat. "Who is this guy and what does he want with Mussina and how does he even know about her? Right, I know all that . . . so what happened when you went to see this guy, Ellersby?"

McShea chuckled as he maneuvered the sedan down a street lined with double-parked vans and trucks. Klepner glanced at his notes, then continued. "He checked out. Has some old poker buddies at headquarters. They all vouched for him. He was a precinct captain for years on the Lower West Side. A good man, that's what everybody says."

"Go on," said Brad.

"He claimed he didn't know Isabella Mussina. Or Harford Nichols. Had no idea what had happened at Langley."

"You believe him?"

"Oh yeah, he's clear," said McShea. "This guy's just playin' out the slack in his line till he can retire. He doesn't give a shit for anything."

"But he just *happens* to call you the day Nichols shoots her. . . ."

Klepner chuckled. "Yes sir, he was just doing a favor for a doctor friend of his—"

"James Michael Keating," said Brad. "Okay, have you contacted him?"

"He knows we're coming."

"What do we have on him?"

Klepner checked his notes. "Not much. Been in practice as a psychiatrist for twenty years. Upper West Side. Clients are mostly upscale-types. Used to do some forensic work with NYPD, attended some regional seminars, and presented some papers on headshrinking and police work. Has lots of fairly well-connected friends. Belongs to all the right organizations. Divorced once. Single. No criminal record, as you would expect. This guy's a model citizen."

McShea made a right turn, heading north on West End. "We're almost there," he said. "Office is up on Riverside Drive."

"Okay. Let's check it out," said Brad. He looked out the window as they cruised through what were still some of the nicer neighborhoods in Manhattan. Block after block of stately townhouses jammed cheek-to-jowl. It amazed him how people could adjust to living in a space with practically no yard or trees, and everything looking so worn and old and dirty. No matter what they did to make things look classy, they couldn't escape the grime of the city. Having to live in northern Virginia and make a daily commute into bureau headquarters every day had been wearing him down like a grinding wheel, but at least he lived in a place with some landscaping and shade trees. He couldn't imagine living in the center of D.C., but he'd been tolerating the suburbs. Not for much longer, he thought. Pretty soon, his request for transfer should be coming through and he would be working out of either the Albuquerque or the Salt Lake City office, and that meant the chance for some clean, open skies, less traffic, and more chances for hunting and fishing, which, other than his family, were the loves of Stevenson's life. There was little to match sitting on the edge of a lake so clear and clean you could drink out of it, or stalking deer through the mountains with a bow.

"This is it," said McShea as the sedan jerked to a stop by the curb. So much for mountains and lakes.

"Okay," said Brad. "McShea, you can stay with the car. Klepner, you're with me."

They flashed their IDs to the doorman, who smiled and not only let them in but escorted them across the lobby to the elevators. Everything was extremely clean, the interior decorating looking like it was done yesterday, and with about as much warmth as an ice-fishing hut. In other words, it was a typical New York office building.

On the third floor, they made their way to a suite where a receptionist greeted them with a very professional smile. She had thick dark hair and big brown eyes and a pretty face despite being dragged kicking and screaming into her forties. The Ann Taylor suit did nothing to hide her lean, athletic body, and Brad could have figured her for a racquetball player, or maybe a swimmer.

"Good afternoon, gentlemen," she said. "You must be from the FBI."

"Jeez," said Klepner. "Is it that obvious?"

She gave them a mock once-over and sardonic frown. "Yes, I'm afraid it is."

"Is Doctor Keating in?" Brad wanted to skip the bullshit. He was tired and he wanted to get this over with.

"Yes," she said with an overly warm smile, as if to let Brad know she didn't appreciate his hard-ass posture. "He's been expecting you."

After intercomming the doctor, she led them to the door to his inner office and silently disappeared. As Brad entered the room, he was impressed by its Old World feel: lots of books, a standing globe, some pieces of Renaissance sculpture. A glass display case with some old stuff in it. It was a masculine room, but full of reserve and dignity. The fixtures were tastefully functional, not ostentatious, and the decorations were thoughtfully intelligent.

The doctor stood up from behind his desk and moved out to greet them. "Good afternoon, gentleman. Please be seated."

Shaking their hands, he directed them to comfortable chairs to the left of his desk. He wore a charcoal gray suit, nicely tailored and accented by a conservative tie. He was of average height and had light brown hair. His face was angular, nose and jawline prominent, and penetrating eyes dark with intelligence. His complexion was even and healthy. James Michael Keating was a rather handsome guy with a kind of relaxed demeanor.

Brad found himself liking the guy on first impression. In his business, he was always meeting people and almost always getting a quick read on them—one way or the other. People were either thumbs-ups or thumbs-down. Nice guys or dickheads. It was pretty simple, really. . . .

"We need to ask you a few questions, Doctor Keating."

"Of course," he said evenly, with great courtesy.

"You asked your friend Chester Ellersby to help you locate Doctor Isabella Mussina."

"That's right. I didn't know I would be putting so many people to so much trouble."

"How long have you known Doctor Mussina?" asked Klepner.

"Actually, I don't know her at *all*, I only know *of* her through her work."

When Brad pursued this statement, Dr. Keating provided them with a brief summary of his work with two patients in hypnosis and a possible connection with some of the experiences of Mussina.

"What connection might that be?"

Keating hesitated, not because he seemed to hiding anything, but more out of a desire to be precise. When he explained the common thread of death-camp experiences and the mention of the figure called *"Der Klein Engel,"* something churned deep in Brad's gut. It was a feeling reserved for those times when everything he knew to be true and good was going to be ripped inside out—just to remind him that he really didn't know much about *any* damned thing.

Less than twenty-four hours ago, he'd been briefed on the Nichols case—watching videos of the psycho-session with Dr. Mussina. He remembered sitting there, and feeling the hair on the back of his neck stiffen up three or four times, and being afraid to admit it to any of the others in the room. There had been something just downright *scary* about Nichols, that's all.

During his years in the bureau, Brad had listened to plenty of nut cases and *none* of them had sounded as convincing as Nichols. The guy was *beyond* crazy, whatever that meant, and Brad still hadn't decided he could handle the guy face-to-face.

". . . are you all, right, Mr. Stevenson?" Dr. Keating was looking at him with concern.

"I . . . uh, was just thinking of something."

"Something I said, no doubt," said Keating. "You know about this *'Klein Engel'* fellow? Did Doctor Mussina tell you anything about him?"

Brad looked the doctor in the eyes, but reading people was this guy's business. There had been no hiding Brad's reaction to that German name reference. "I'm afraid I can't say anything about it at this time," said Brad.

"Mr. Stevenson, I can't tell you any simpler than this—I am only trying to reach Doctor Mussina so that we can compare our findings," said Keating. "I have no idea what it all means at this point."

Either do I, pal, thought Brad. "That's not going to be possible, Doctor Keating."

Keating smiled, opened his hands in an ameliorative gesture. "Mr. Stevenson, it is very possible that we are all involved in the same phenomenon. If we are allowed to work together, to pool our knowledge, we may be able to figure out what is happening, what it all means."

"That's a great idea, Doctor, but right now I'm in the middle of a preliminary investigation. Maybe a little later on, I might want to talk to you again. That okay with you?"

"Of course," said the psychiatrist. "But could you do me a favor in the meantime?"

"What's that?"

"Could you at least give Doctor Mussina my message—that I would very much like to speak to her as soon as possible?"

"Sure," said Brad. "I can do that."

Keating thanked him, and Brad wrapped up the interrogation, brief as it was, with a promise to stay in touch if necessary. He led Klepner out of the office, pausing only long enough to smile at the receptionist.

Once in the elevator, Klepner tapped his arm. "None of my business, really, sir, but why didn't you tell him about Mussina?"

Brad closed his eyes, massaged his temples. "I don't know," he said, honestly. "He seemed like a nice guy. I didn't want to get him upset."

Klepner considered this, shrugged. "Can you tell me something else?"

"What's that?"

"What was that business about 'the little angel'?"

Brad looked at him in surprise. "How'd you know what he was saying?"

Klepner smiled sheepishly, waved it off. "Ah, my grandmother used to speak a lot of Yiddish around the house when I was a kid. Guess I picked up more than I realized. What's all this got to do with the concentration camps?"

Brad looked at Klepner, aware at that moment of the man's inherent interest in anything to do with the Holocaust. "I don't know, Klepner. Honest, I don't. But I'll tell you, I have a feeling that whatever it is, it's pretty fucking weird."

"You going to do some follow-up on this guy, Keating?"

Brad looked at him and grinned. He liked Klepner—he was always paying attention and he seemed to like thinking ahead, planning. "Yes, I think so. You want the job?"

The doorman waved at them as they exited the building. Klepner opened the back door to the sedan. "Sure," he said. "It sounds like it might be interesting. You want a full dossier?"

Brad shook his head. "Nah, don't waste your time. He's one of those squeaky clean people, I got a feeling. If you're lucky, you *might* find out he cheated on a spelling test when he was in the fifth grade, and then again you might *not*."

They both climbed into the car as McShea looked at each of them expectantly, but they ignored him as they continued the conversation.

Klepner leaned back in his seat, nodded, took out his little notepad, and scribbled for a second. "Okay, so just concentrate on his current 'work,' whatever that is?"

"You got it," said Brad. "Just get me all the connections between him and what Mussina was doing, between him and Nichols."

"So how'd it go up there?" said McShea.

"So far, nothing," said Klepner.

"Okay, what now, boss?" McShea had turned around to regard him, like a talkative cab driver.

Brad leaned back in his seat, shook his head. God, he hated it when he started spinning his wheels like this. He needed a minute to sort things out. He need McShea to just shut up. Even though this Dr. Keating was clean and knew nothing, there was something about the connection with Mussina that might help them find Nichols. No reason to think so—Brad just had a sense for this kind of stuff. A feeling. A hunch. Whatever. Experience had taught him to play out the hunches because they'd paid off more than they hadn't.

Finally, he looked up at his driver. "You guys have an office?"

"Sure. There's a Greek diner, down off Second Avenue," said McShea. "Great burgers."

"Let's go," said Brad. "We need to make a plan."

NINETEEN

DER KLEIN ENGEL
Baltimore, Maryland

Dukor drove the Jeep Grand Cherokee north along I-95, and the traffic at 3:00 A.M. was very light. He had taken the Jeep from a young black man in his twenties who had been waiting for a light to change on C Street N.E. in downtown D.C. The Negro had been surprised to see him when Dukor had opened the driver's door, put a single bullet in his torso, and literally ripped him from behind the wheel. Before the man had even hit the pavement, Dukor had slipped behind the wheel and drove straight to the nearest access ramp to I-295, heading north. From there, he intersected I-495 and merged with I-95, again heading north. If any police noticed the stolen vehicle and had thoughts of interference, he was prepared to dispatch them.

He had been driving for almost an hour when his headlights illuminated a sign that read BALTIMORE 10 MILES, and he found himself reflecting on the city forty miles north of Washington.

It was a funny town, hard to describe even if you were very familiar with it. The city and its surrounding metro area comprised about two and a half million people, all fragmented into little neighborhoods with harshly drawn boundaries of economics, race, religion, and nationality—or combinations of them. The downtown area had been developed around the city's natural harbor and served as the cultural and economic center, but it remained surrounded by pockets of blight, worn-out industrialism, moral corruption.

Into one of these pockets, Dukor now drove.

Sitting so high off the ground in the Jeep, he was reminded of the Daimler troop-carriers in which he rode with Mengele. Hard to imagine the memory was more than a half-century old. . . .

He could not help but notice (and be continually fascinated by) the dual tracks of knowledge and experience that fueled his every action. Just now, for example: to have an understanding of both the contemporary urban profile of Baltimore and a sixty-year-old Nazi military vehicle both amused and pleased him.

And yet, he realized, there seemed to be a *third* track of—if not knowledge, then some other force or directive that motivated him and provided him with information he could not have obtained as either Harford Nichols or Hirsh Dukor.

How utterly provocative. . . .

He could sense it and respond to it, but he could not feel intimate with it, as though it were some overriding sphere of total influence in which he operated—self-contained and irresistible in its special momentum.

But he had no idea what it might be, nor did he care.

It was like a constantly humming, low-frequency beacon in the core of his being. Something that guided him in some atavistic, yet totally accessible, manner. The directive spoke to him in an unknown, never-spoken language, but remained lucid and intelligible on a completely unconscious level. He knew he understood its message, because he'd witnessed the proof of it firsthand.

Neither Dukor nor Nichols could have known the identity or location of Carnofl in Greece, Littlejohn in England, Ortiz in Peru, or any of the others. And yet he knew where they worked, their schedules, where they lived. Whatever presence or power lurked within him, he rejoiced in its choice of him—he felt as though he'd tapped into a trunkline to the universe's own generator.

Not just alive . . .

. . . but literally *seething* with power and the life force.

And the most intriguing, intoxicating thing about it was the effortlessness of it all. As simple as leaning into the wind, and he was in the complete *thrall* of it. There was something exciting about surrendering to such a totality, a consummate power, and to feel it take over like a pilot sliding into a cockpit, a driver behind the wheel. As natural and perfectly fitting as that.

And it was happening now.

He had felt it much earlier, from the very opening moments of the hypnosis session, but it had been far more subtle. Now it had broken the surface, in total control. The sensation would be difficult to describe: because he knew where he was going and why he was going there, but he did not know *how* he was doing it—the information he needed such as names, directions, addresses, and street locations was simply *there* in his mind as he needed it.

Such as right now.

The green highway sign in his headlights indicated ramps intersecting with I-695, a beltway loop around the Baltimore metro area. He took the north ramp toward Towson and pushed the four-liter engine past eighty mph. He passed the national headquarters for the Social Security Administration, leaving I-695 at the next exit, heading southeast toward Northern Parkway and the neighborhoods bordering Pimlico Racetrack.

As the digital dash clock blinked past 4:00 A.M., he approached an intersection at Park Heights Avenue. Somehow, he knew that this particular road was called by locals "the longest road in the world" because it stretched from "Africa to Israel." It was a pejorative reference to the ethnicity of the neighborhoods comprising the opposite ends of the metropolitan street. It was into the "Israel" section of the avenue that Dukor now drove. And that made him smile. It was his fate, his destiny, to be ever connected with that strange little tribe—the Jews. Even in the dim yellow light of the streetlamps, he could see a preponderance of synagogues, counting one on almost every street corner for block after block.

During the days, the sidewalks would be filled with orthodox Jews—the men in their long black coats, beards, and fedoras, the women in demurely long dresses and long, plain hairstyles and kerchiefs. But now, everything lay desolate and quiet. The only other vehicles to pass Dukor were several delivery vans from the *Baltimore Sun* and Faulstich's Bakery. As he slowed to make a right turn on Glendale, he noticed a young man heaving a large cloth bag over his shoulder and entering an apartment building. The morning paper folded and bagged in plastic, as if sanitized for everyone's consumption, would be waiting for the eager hands of all the Jews in this neighborhood, but Dukor was bringing them a bit of news breaking a little too late for their morning editions.

He smiled again at his cleverness and eased off on the accelerator. As he looked absently at the rows of old homes on the residential street, he looked for a side street that would intersect with the alley running parallel behind the houses. Finding it, he turned left, then left again into the narrow passage. He avoided the trashcans and discarded appliances scattered in his headlighted path like debris from a V-1 bombing, and stopped the Jeep next to the backyard gate of a particularly dilapidated house. Even in the pale glow of a streetlamp, it was obvious the house had seen no paint or nails for generations.

Dukor jumped out of the car and smelled the air, tainted by the smell of humid, rotting garbage. He slipped through the gate and carefully picked his way through a patch of overgrown weeds and crabgrass, littered with broken yard tools, the rusted hulk of a LawnBoy, and the skeletons of forgotten patio furniture. Reaching the back door, he inspected the rotting jamb and threshold, the thin, plate-glass pane, and the lack of even a deadbolt above the tarnished knob.

Laughable.

Balling his fist, Dukor punched out the pane with a sharp jab. It shattered into so many pieces, they made very little noise as they dusted to the black-and-white tile of the kitchen floor. He reached through, turned the knob to unlock the door, and let himself in.

Instantly, his nostrils began to sting, burning with a pungent acidity. His first thought was some kind of alarm, somehow triggering a tear-gas deterrent, but he calmed himself, using his training, and stood rigid for a moment, letting the fouled atmosphere seep into him. The lancing, acrid odor was ammonia. He recognized it just as his shoe tapped against a plastic tub on the floor. It slid grittily across the tile and he looked down at it in the ambient light from the alley.

A cat-litter box, heaped full with turds, surrounded by huge hydrated clumps of accreted urine. Like obscene pieces of sculpture, they mocked him, assaulted his senses. Moving deeper into the room, the overwhelming stench of cat piss filled the room like a thick yellow fog. Dukor felt as though he might puke from the violent attack on his nose and throat, and he had to use his training to calm and control his body's automatic responses.

No time for weak stomachs now.

Moving deeper into the house, as his eyes adjusted to the darkness, he could see the phantom shapes of furniture and other oddments in each room of the first floor. Most of the space had been filled by cardboard boxes, stacks of old magazines and newspapers, empty cat food bags, and other junk. Something brushed the cuff of his pants and he knew it was a cat, and soon he was surrounded by its brothers and sisters. As he reached the stairs to the second floor, he could see a vast sea of fur around his feet—twenty, thirty cats.

Disgusting.

Looking up the staircase, he saw a stained-glass window, through which leaked light from the street. More than enough to guide him to his target.

Now, so close, he could finally allow himself to begin to get excited. He *loved* the thrill and the passion of the hunt! The act of stalking a victim had always been far more electric than the actual kill.

The anticipation.

The imagination.

Always better than the real pay-off.

Dukor smiled, began his ascent to the second floor. With each step, he became more aware of his penis, growing as it flapped against his left leg. Part of him trembled with the promise of what would come, while another part reflected on the commingling of sexual fire and bloodlust.

When he reached the top of the stairs, he noticed the stench of cat piss was stronger in the upper reaches of the house, and he could smell the labored, sinusoidal breathing of labored sleep. Following the sound into the nearest room, he paused to assess the layout of the room and the lump of body and blankets on the sagging bed in front of him.

Before he could take another step, however, the sleeping figure bolted upright to a sitting position and stared at him blankly. Martha Pasek was gray-haired, overweight, homely, looking far older than her years. Over a flannel nightgown, she wore a sweat-shirt that said *Syracuse University*.

"Omigod!" said the woman.

"Hello, Martha," said Dukor softly.

"I . . . I was just dreaming about you." Her voice was shallow, thin, and quavering with confusion and fear.

"Yes, I know."

"But you didn't look like you do now," said Martha.

"That's right."

"But it's *you*! Jesus Christ, it's still *you*!!"

"Oh, yes," said Dukor. "You knew I'd be coming sooner or later, didn't you?"

"I don't know! I didn't know anything!" She gathered up the blankets around her, squinched away from him toward a scratched and scarred headboard.

"I think you did, Martha. Or should I call you Isaac? Isn't that the name of the person you dream you are?"

"No!" shouted Martha, but she nodded vigorously, as if unable to deny what he had said to her.

"And you know why I am here, don't you?" Dukor stepped fractionally closer to her, clenching and unclenching his fist, feeling his blood pumping high and hard behind his ears.

Martha opened her mouth to scream, but only a dry rattle emerged. He chuckled as he reached for her, and was surprised by her sudden movement.

Jumping up from the mattress like an uncoiled spring, she slammed into his shoulder with all her weight. She caught him off balance, in midstride, and with the leverage of a perfect jujitsu maneuver, her bulk spun him around, twisting his feet together so that he fell hard to the floor.

And then she was by him, bounding toward the staircase, still trying to make a sound louder than a raspy whisper.

Reaching out, he grabbed her ankle for an instant, and she tripped, falling out of the room into the hallway. Scrambling to her knees, she pitched forward off the top step and head-rolled down to the bottom. He could hear her whimpering as she tried to drag herself away from the landing, working her way through the narrow canyon formed by the stacks of boxes and old magazines.

Slowly, Dukor descended the stairs, letting each footfall resound through the night-dead house, letting her hear each advancing step.

"Please . . . leave me alone . . ." she said hoarsely. Her voice sounded plaintively beautiful in the semidarkness. "I . . . don't get it, I don't get any of this."

He chuckled softly, letting it echo down to her.

"What do you want with me . . . ?"

As he reached the bottom landing, he felt the swarm of cats at his shoes and ankles, and an idea touched him with the light force-fulness of a cat's brush. Hunkering down, he scooped up a kitten and instantly felt a subtle vibration as it began to purr. He ignored this as he stepped forward to pursue his target.

Martha had reached the litter-grainy floor of the kitchen and was vainly trying to pull herself up by the edge of a small table. When she saw him, she redoubled her effort, but fell back in greater pain. She propped herself up on a single elbow and tried to drag herself to the back door, a move that earned his respect. She was a tough woman and would not go gently into that good night.

He'd always liked that in a victim.

"It's time to say good-bye, Martha," he said, holding the small cat in his hands.

"What're you doing with Popsy?" she said with surprising indig-nation.

"You'll see . . ."

"Leave 'im alone, you bastard!" She tried to push herself up to her knees, grimaced from the effort. "You'll hurt 'im!"

Dukor smiled. "You mean like this?" And holding the kitten out toward her with both hands, so she could see it clearly, he wrenched its head so viciously he almost separated it from its body. He could feel its soft bones snap, the flesh go immediately limp, and imagined he could feel its life force escape the suddenly useless carcass like air from a ruptured balloon.

Martha tried to scream, and the sound lapsed from her in a series of pitiable squeaks. He smiled as he bent low, looking her in the eyes. Her jaw remained slack as she trembled from loathing and despair, but there was no fear in her eyes. Reaching out, he grabbed her face in his powerful hand, forcing her lower mandible open even wider. She tried to writhe away from him, and he had to flat-hand her skull just hard enough to stun her for an instant.

Just long enough to stuff the kitten's body into her mouth. Her eyes bugged wide as he jammed the furry clot deeper and deeper until its tiny head sealed off her throat and esophagus. Martha fell back against the kitchen floor, and still he shoved the dead animal deeper into her mouth, splitting the flesh of her cheeks, crushing her tongue, and *filling* her with the pliant carcass.

With her eyes swelling from her skull like hard-boiled eggs, she began to flutter-kick violently, convulsing and clawing at his hands upon her face, but he recognized the flailing, panic-powered motions for the futile gestures they were.

One final, savage thrust, and he watched the light fade from her eyes. It lasted for only an instant, and it was that single moment he always anticipated and tried to savor beyond its briefest manifestation. And he always felt an infinite sadness when it evaporated like ectoplasm—the exquisite instant of death teasing him yet again.

Standing up, he washed his hands at Martha Pasek's sink and turned to slip out the back door. As he did this, he sensed movement behind him and spun to see a swarming feline mass flowing across the kitchen floor to get as close as possible to their stilled mistress.

Such warmth and attraction made Dukor smile. Closing the door behind him, he sealed the cats within their fetid prison. *Don't worry, little ones . . . at least you'll have a good food supply.*

TWENTY

J. MICHAEL KEATING, M.D.
Manhattan, New York

As he knew she would, Pamela glided into his inner office as soon as the FBI agents had left. She wore an impish smile like a new dress, and he had to smile himself.

"Wow, looks like you poked a sharp stick in *somebody's* eye, didn't you?"

"I'm guessing you had the intercom turned on?"

She shrugged. "Sure, I heard everything."

"Which wasn't really much," said Michael. "All they wanted was to know what I knew about their 'case'—and my relationship to Doctor Mussina."

Pamela was walking slowly around the room, looking at his furniture and wall art. "You don't think they planted a bug in here, do you?"

"I don't think so. . . ." He laughed lightly. "I didn't know you were so paranoid."

"You want me to look around just to be sure?" Pamela walked to the chairs in front of his desk. "They sat here?"

Michael nodded. She gingerly overturned the chairs, looked carefully along their bottoms. After righting them, she checked the edges of his desk, behind all the picture frames. When she started on his desktop, he gestured for her to stop.

"They never left their seats," he said. "I really think this place is clean."

Pamela smiled cynically. "I read somewhere that if they *really* want to know what's going on, they can get the phone company to turn any telephone receiver into a microphone, *even when it's on the hook*, so they can hear anything said in the room, *at any time*."

Michael held up his hands in mock surrender. "Well, if that's true, you're *really* wasting your time."

Pamela sat down in one of the chairs in front of this desk. "Seriously, what do you think is going on? Why would the government be interested in anything you or Doctor Mussina might tell each other?"

"I have no idea," he said, "but I think it's a good bet her obligations to work in Washington—to keep her federal grant—are to blame. It's certainly nothing I've done."

She tilted her head coyly, pointed a finger at him. "How can you be so sure?"

Michael considered the question. Interesting possibility—could he have uncovered some government secret unwittingly?

"Well, I *can't* be, can I?"

"In the meantime, what? Do we continue to do our own checking around?" Pamela made an adjustment to her hair that was completely unnecessary.

"Certainly," he said. "We have nothing to fear."

Pamela grinned, stood up to leave the room. "Not yet, anyway."

He was about to comment, telling her she was getting too melodramatic for her own good, when the phone rang.

She picked up the receiver on his desk, recited the usual salutation, then looked at him. "Judge Goald . . ."

Michael accepted the receiver. He'd intended to call him back before the FBI had interrupted his schedule. "Hello, Bob. Sorry, I couldn't call you right back. It's been a little hectic here."

"I'll bet it has, Mike. You're nosing around into places certain people don't want you, I can tell you that."

"You know about the FBI being here?" Michael felt a lump forming in his throat, his pulse quickening. *What had he gotten into?*

Judge Goald chuckled. "No, but I figured they'd get around to talking to you. Already shook you down, eh?"

"Listen, Bob, the feds are suddenly very interested in me." Michael applied a slightly weary tone to his voice. "I'd like to know *why*. What do you know about Isabella Mussina?"

"Not much, except that she was shot and killed yesterday."

"Shot?" The words stung him. "Are you sure we're talking about the same person?"

"What I have here is she was a Ph.D. from the University of Chicago. Assigned to the Hines VA hospital there. Also part of a field agent debriefing unit for the CIA."

"That's her . . . " said Michael, fighting off the shock, the disbelief. "And they told you she was killed?"

"That's what it says here," Goald said softly.

"I . . . I just can't believe this."

"Was she a friend of yours?"

"No, not really. But I . . . I was very familiar with her work. I guess I felt like I knew her. It's hard to explain."

"Christ, Michael, I'm sorry to be the one to tell you this. Anything else I can do to help?"

"Did you find out where it happened? How?" Michael's voice came out sounding detached, dulled.

Judge Goald cleared his throat. "I couldn't get any details. And I have to tell you, it was like pulling teeth to get *this*. I have a son-in-law working at the State Department. He has access to all the classified communications between agencies."

"Classified?" said Michael, shaking his head, still trying to accept it.

"Search me. I can try to find out, but Keith tells me they have a pretty solid lid on this thing."

"Thanks, Bob. I would appreciate anything you can do."

"Sure, but I just want you to understand—I have to go about this with a little, ah . . . decorum, if you know what I mean. I don't want to raise too many eyebrows."

"I understand," said Michael. "Whatever you can do would be great. And I owe you one."

"Who says we ever kept score?" Goald tried to make a small pleasantry, and having failed, he simply said good-bye.

As he replaced the receiver, Michael felt as if he'd lost a friend.

Even though he'd never met her, he felt like he had somehow *known* the woman.

He shook his head. More quasimystical nonsense.

What was happening to him? A grown man ascribing reasons to things better relegated to the realm of the tooth fairy and the boogeyman.

Dr. Mussina dead.

The thought kept repeating itself. Shot? Who would want to shoot her? And what could she have she done to deserve it?

The more he thought about it, the more convinced he became that he'd stumbled into some hideous government operation. He couldn't let it go until he understood everything more fully. And this did not even consider his initial need to see her studies and her findings.

Pausing to take an inventory of things he needed to do, he scribbled a few items on his ever-present notepad: call Hodgkins, call Klingerman, stay in touch with Judge Goald, and resume scheduling sessions with Enders and McGuire.

He asked Pamela to return Sam Hodgkins' call, and she kept him on the line while she put it through.

"Congressman Hodgkins' office . . . "

"Doctor J. Michael Keating returning his call," said Pamela.

"Oh, yes! Mr. Hodgkins is expecting him. Hold the line, please."

He slipped into phone limbo for an instant; Pamela disconnected her line. Suddenly, the congressman's distinctive Georgia accent was booming at him. "Mike Keating! How the hell are ya, Doc?"

"Good afternoon, Sam. I'm sorry to have to bother you, but—"

"Bother me? What's an old fart like me have to look forward to except another round of golf? Nah, you made my day a little more interesting. Besides, if it wasn't for you, Teddy would've never made it through med school."

"Thank you, Sam. How *is* Ted doing at Dartmouth, by the way?" Michael did not really care about the welfare of his old classmate, but he understood the need for following protocol.

"Well, you know my son! He's figured out all the angles by now. Turns out he likes professoring a lot more than he liked doctoring. His students love him and he's finally getting used to all the snow."

"That's great," said Michael with as little enthusiasm as possible. "But, listen, Sam, I don't want to take up too much of your time . . . "

"Bullstuff, Doc! You just want to grill me and get me off the phone!" Hodgkins laughed heartily. "Hell, boy, I don't blame you! I'd want to do the same thing."

"Well, to tell you the truth, I am kind of pressed for time." Michael didn't want to be rude, but he wasn't in the mood for a lot of small talk right now. "Were you able to find out anything about Doctor Mussina?"

There was an obvious hesitation, an embarrassed pause on the line as Hodgkins struggled to find the right words. ". . . Listen, Mike, was this doctor a friend of yours?"

"She was a . . . colleague. I already know she's been shot," said Michael. "I was hoping you could get me some details."

The old congressman exhaled dramatically. "I'm not going to ask you how you knew *that*. God knows *I* had a hell of a time digging it out of anybody."

"Do you have anything else?"

"Not really. Nobody feels much of a need to tell retired congressmen a damned thing these days. I'm just calling in old favors, if you know what I mean."

"Sure, Sam, I understand. I appreciate anything you can do."

They exchanged good-byes, and as he hung up the phone he wondered if Sam Hodgkins had a phone safe from wire-tapping. . . .

The hell with it, he decided. They already knew where they could find him. There was still more work to be done. He had Pamela ring up Irwin Klingerman, and he gave the rabbi the bad news about his friend.

Klingerman turned out to be an effusively emotional and dramatic mourner, and Michael was forced to endure long minutes of what the Jews called *gesherying* and wailing. He listened patiently as the rabbi went on about Mussina's character and life, composing her eulogy on the fly. Understandable, but difficult to endure. He asked many questions—ranging from arrangements for the disposition of the body to the philosophical exigencies of a universe that would allow a young woman such as Mussina to be killed—for which Michael had no answers.

Eventually, Klingerman gathered himself together enough to attempt a rational conversation, which began with him apologizing for going on at such dramatic lengths.

"That's okay," said Michael. "She was obviously a good friend. But I think we need to talk about what all this means, and what we should be doing about it."

"I . . . I don't think I follow you, Doctor." Klingerman spoke softly, holding back sobs.

"It's occurred to me that maybe something about your work with Isabella is what got her killed." The words spilled from Michael so quickly they were a surprise even to him. Did he really feel that way? How had his unconscious suppressed such a dangerous notion.

"What?!" said Klingerman. "Why?"

"I don't have any real reason," said Michael, redressing his own thoughts, trying to find some logic there. "It's just a hunch, really."

"Well, what should we do now?"

"Did she ever say anything to you about her work in Washington?"

"No. Practically never. Only that she hated it and the people she worked for."

"Hated it—why?"

"Because it kept her from her real research interest. Even more so than the VA hospital."

Michael paused to consider this, then offered: "So that would suggest that her CIA job was not connected with her past-life regression studies. . . . "

"Yes, so it would seem."

"Rabbi, you worked with her, probably closer than anybody. I want you to think about this very carefully—is it possible she would have lied to you about anything?"

Klingerman paused. "I . . . I don't think so. And please, by the way, please call me Irwin."

"Sure, sure. But listen to me: other than saying the work was classified, do you think it had anything to do with what we've discovered?"

A longer pause, then: "No, I honestly don't think so. Her studies were the most important thing in her life. If the government was involved in them in *any* way, I think she would have told me."

"Okay," said Michael. "That's good. I was hoping you would say that."

"Why? What do you mean?"

Michael paused for a moment, trying to get the sense of what he'd been thinking. "I mean that as long as our work isn't connected to the CIA, we're probably safe to continue it."

"Safe?" Klingerman's voice lilted upward. "What 'safe'?"

"Otherwise, it's very possible we could end up like Doctor Mussina." As he spoke, Michael wondered just how safe they actually were. Until talking to Klingerman, he hadn't really thought about being in danger. But it was definitely a possibility—not allayed much by the rabbi's assurances.

"You mean we could get ourselves shot?"

"Do you always have such a talent for stating the obvious?" Michael smiled grimly.

"That's funny," said Klingerman. "Isabella used to say the same thing."

Michael did not respond immediately. Klingerman was his only connection to Mussina's work. He would have to cultivate it. "Let me ask you something, Irwin."

"Of course. Anything."

"Do you have access to Isabella's files?"

"Files?"

"You know—her records and papers. On all the cases."

"Most of it is on her computers and videodiscs. . . . "

"Where are they located?"

"At her apartment, and also at the hospital."

"Can you get into her apartment?"

Klingerman coughed nervously at the suggestion of any impropriety. "We didn't have that kind of relationship, Doctor. But that won't be necessary."

"Why not?"

"Because she gave me copies of everything—'just to be safe,' she'd said—and I've taken good care of them."

"Excellent," said Michael, carefully choosing his next words. "And so, Irwin, I guess my next question is whether or not you would think Isabella would like you to be carrying on her work?"

"Oh my, yes! Of course she would!" His answer was sincere and heartfelt. "It would have destroyed her if she'd ever thought all her efforts would ever die with her."

"Okay, then I must ask you one more thing—would you willing to share her files with me, and . . . continue her work with *me*?"

There was a long pause, and Michael wondered if he'd over-stepped his bounds. Then, finally: "Doctor Keating, I have never met you. And neither did Isabella. In talking to you, I believe you are sincere and professional. But in light of what has happened, I hope you will not take this the wrong way . . ."

Here it comes, thought Michael. *He's going to crush the whole thing.*

". . . but I would like to . . . how do I say this? . . . have you checked out first. Before I give you a definitive answer."

Michael released a breath he didn't realize he'd been holding. He grinned as he spoke to Klingerman. "Oh no, that would be fine! In fact, I was going to suggest you do something like that. Believe me, I would consider it an honor to carry on her work."

Klingerman seemed relieved that he hadn't offended him and promised to contact him as soon as possible.

Michael hung up the phone and leaned back in his chair. God, he was feeling anxious, even confused.

But not scared.

And that was interesting, because even though Klingerman didn't believe Mussina's death had anything to do with her work, the idea that it might be central to it kept snagging at the base of all of his other thoughts. He couldn't shake it loose, and therefore, had to pay attention to it.

Later that afternoon, after fending off Pamela's attempts to join him, he departed the Riverside office building and headed for a favorite bar of his near Columbus Circle called Farley's Place. It was dark and quiet and didn't offer any of the trendy drinks or entrees; a burger and beer joint with a good assortment of bourbons, which was just what he needed right about now. He didn't plan on getting wasted or anything like that. He just wanted a little solitude, and a few drinks seemed like the only company he would need.

As he was working through his second Maker's Mark on the rocks, someone approached his right shoulder and stood silently behind him for a few seconds. Sensing the presence, Michael felt intimidated to turn and face the guy, and then it suddenly struck him to look in the mirror behind the bar.

Tall, thin to point of being gaunt, dark eyes staring at him. The guy looked very familiar, thought Michael as he turned slowly on his stool.

"Doctor Keating, I need to talk to you," said a voice, also vaguely familiar.

Looking him in the eye, Michael recognized the sidekick of the FBI honcho Stevenson.

"I'm sorry," said Michael. "I don't remember your name . . ."

"Special Agent Klepner. Sid Klepner."

"Right . . . well, sorry, Sid, but I gave at the office. . . ."

Klepner looked kind of tired, embarrassed. "I know. This isn't official business. Far from it, actually."

That made Michael smile. "Yeah, sure. Like you guys are *ever* off duty."

"We're not all creeps," said Klepner. "Some of us just need a job. We've got families and bills like everybody else."

Interesting reply. Michael hadn't expected anything like that. He eyed the man carefully. After many years of evaluating patients, he had become pretty adept at judging abstract traits like loyalty and sincerity and even deceitfulness. Looking at Sid Klepner was like staring at a sheet of glass. The guy's face was a portrait canvas where everything lay revealed in the colors of pain and compassion.

"You know, I have to admit," said Michael, "you look like you're telling the truth."

"Mind if I sit down?"

Michael gestured at an open stool, then took another sip from his glass.

Klepner climbed aboard, ordered a Rusty Nail from the practically invisible bartender, and waited in silence until it was delivered.

Michael waited for him to take a long pull off the glass, then: "So what do you want to see me about?"

Klepner turned and looked at him squarely. "Listen, Doc, I could get in some very deep shit for telling you this . . . but contrary to *whatever* else you might hear, *Isabella Mussina is alive.*"

TWENTY-ONE

BRADLEY STEVENSON
Baltimore, Maryland

This guy was one sick fuck.

He stood in Martha Pasek's kitchen watching the ME's people wrapping up the body. Like everybody else at the scene, he'd been forced to wear an oxy-osmotic mask. Besides the rank stench from all the cats, Pasek's son hadn't discovered the body for almost a week, and some of the little bastards had started to get hungry.

As they slipped the poor woman's remains into the zipper-bag, Brad caught one last look at the series of numbers on her inner forearm. Just like the others.

He followed the med techs outside as they carried the bag to their van. Brad yanked off the mask, sucked in some humid but fresh air, and walked back to his car in the alley. After getting in, he picked up his notebook and glanced at some of the recent jottings.

With his prints all over the place, there was no question this was Nichols' work, but the big question was *why*? Just exactly what was going on? How could he explain this whole mess to himself in terms that didn't sound like a lot of goddamned voodoo? After watching the video of the Mussina interview over and over, the connection of Nichols to the Nazi death camps was undeniable, and the numbers on the arms of his victims did correspond to those used by the Germans (he'd already checked that out, discovering that each camp had its own set of numbers).

But what did this *really* mean?

It meant, for starters, accepting some pretty weird stuff that wouldn't look all that great on his reports to his superiors.

He thumbed through the pages of notes at his list of "facts."

1. If Nichols' story under hypnosis to Mussina is accepted as the truth, then Brad would be forced to conclude that Nichols was being "controlled" by the reincarnated "soul" of some Ukrainian psycho-killer named Hirsh Dukor.

2. If Dukor survived the Nazi death camps by helping Josef Mengele kill Jews, then

3. the appearance of the camp serial numbers on all of Nichols' victims could mean they were like him—they had all "lived before" during World War II and died in the death camps.

4. Therefore, Nichols was systematically killing people who had been "reincarnated."

Brad looked at the notes and shook his head. Not much concrete to go on.

And the biggest question remained unanswered: *Why* was he killing these people?

If he could come up with the answer to that one, he might be able to anticipate Nichols' next move.

But the trail was very cold, and the only thing he had to go on was a look into Martha Pasek's past. Maybe there was a clue to what was going on?

Brad keyed the ignition to his government sedan and slipped it into gear for a drive downtown to the Federal Building. Time to do a little research.

TWENTY-TWO

ARNOLD RASSENAULT
Manhattan, New York

There was something very scary about this man.

Arnold sat in a booth at Thelma's on West Twenty-ninth looking across the table at the man who called himself Harford Nichols. The man was well-dressed in a white oxford button-down shirt, pressed khaki pants, and a fashionable tie. He looked to be in his early forties and had the angular good looks of an ex-athlete. He could have been a broker on Wall Street, or an editor at one of the city's many publishing houses, but he had just told Arnold he was a *soldier*.

And that's what scared him. It was in the guy's eyes. They focused on you, but it was like they were really looking *through* you.

And what was this "soldier" stuff . . . ?

"What kind of soldier, Mr. Nichols?" Arnold figured there was no sense playing games. "I'm afraid I don't follow you."

"Aren't we all soldiers in the same war, Professor?" Nichols leaned forward and smiled.

"Ah, what war is that?" Arnold knitted his fingers nervously in front of him.

"The war against the mongrels and the Jews."

The mention of Arnold's sworn enemies snatched his attention, disarming him, and making him immediately more receptive to whatever Nichols might have to say to him.

"Oh, of course, *that* war. Of course."

"I have come to help you," said Nichols. "And to also ask for your help in return."

"How did you find me?" said Arnold, feeling slightly more at ease.

Nichols paused before answering as Thelma, a large-boned woman of obvious Aryan ancestry, descended on their table with two plates of fries and greasy burgers. She smiled at them, then disappeared back behind her busy counter. Nichols grabbed his hamburger, took a large bite from it, and chewed slowly. He gestured for Arnold to eat as well.

"I knew about you because of your publication and the lawsuit from the Columbia student," said Nichols.

Arnold smiled. "Yes, that was good for me. I was in the news quite a bit, wasn't I?"

"Which is surprising when you consider who's running the entertainment and news media," said Nichols.

He was right about that, thought Arnold. "Yes, but the kikes can't help themselves," he said eagerly, warming to his favorite subject. "They never pass up a chance to put *themselves* in the public eye."

"Especially any of that nonsense about the Holocaust, right?" Nichols grinned knowingly. Arnold was beginning to like this fellow.

"The worst hoax of the twentieth century!" said Arnold. "You know I'm writing a book about that whole pack of lies and distortions."

"I'm not at all surprised," said Nichols as he finished off his hamburger in three manly bites. "The Jews lie about everything. Look at the world today—I think the prospect of a world depression is very likely, don't you?"

Arnold paused to consider this. He wasn't much on economics, but he did remember the horrible, inflationary economy that threatened to destroy Germany before the National Socialists saved them. "I think you could be right," he said carefully.

Nichols nodded. "Look today at the banking systems of Germany and Switzerland!" he said as he pounded the Formica tabletop. "They are both close to collapse, and if those two granite-hard structures go down, they will take all of Europe with them!"

"Most certainly," said Arnold, wondering where this was all going.

"And who do you think is running the world's money? Our friends with the hooked noses, of course!" Nichols smiled. "The fucking Jews are running the world's money, all right. They're running it right down a rat hole!"

Arnold Rassenault could feel the glow as his own eyes lit up. *Of course!* It's happening all over again, and Mr. Nichols had very keenly perceived the process at its very beginnings. "You are so right, sir," said Arnold.

Nichols nodded, then continued. "Do you realize what that kind of bank collapse would do? Not only Europe would be devastated, but there would be ripple effects all over the world! Japan and the United States would go like dominoes.

"And if you think it's bad now—with some terrorists setting off a goddamned bomb somewhere in the world almost every day—just *think* of what it will be like if global depression strikes."

"People will get desperate," said Arnold.

"That's right," said Nichols. "And they will look desperately for new leaders who can give them hope as well as promises."

Arnold leaned forward, listening intently. There was much he could learn from this man. "What can we look forward to? How can we make it work toward our own goals? Is that what you're getting at?"

"Well, just look at places like Africa—where almost every one of those miserable nigger republics is sliding into civil war, where the only successful leaders there are the fascists and the dictators." Nichols gestured wildly with his hands, sweeping the air grandly. "And it's spreading to other places: South America, India, and Eastern Europe, maybe even China."

"And look at the crime right here in America," said Arnold. "It used to be just the drugged out jungle-bunnies, but now it's spreading to the regular people, too!"

"Don't you know why?" said Nichols. "Because the good, hardworking white people are getting fucked too! People who aren't used to economic hardship are getting slammed by a group of Jews who want to systematically wipe out the middle class."

"And people aren't stupid, you know," said Arnold. "Sooner or later they're going to wise up and see what's happening to them."

Nichols laughed broadly. "They already are! Look how many Third World countries have embraced fundamentalist, religious-backed governments. Look at all those half-nigger Arabs getting their own nukes so they can wipe out Israel once and for all!"

"Israel!" said Arnold, as if he'd just been reminded of that pustulant sore in the Mideast. "Yes, they're to blame for everything, aren't they?!"

"Why do you think the skinheads are so powerful in the Slavic states?" Nichols smiled. "And the Neo-Nazi party has established an electoral voice in Germany!"

"Our time is coming round again," said Arnold, feeling his blood pounding at his temples. He liked this Harford Nichols very much. This man had obviously kept his fingers on the world's pulse, and he was so much smarter, more articulate, than poor Fritz Hargrove.

"Yes, it is," said Nichols. "And I want to help you. But I will need your support as well."

"What do you need, my friend?" said Arnold. "Just name it."

"I will need some of your workers, your supporters, to help me do my own work."

Arnold hesitated. He didn't want to tell him he only had one man he could count on, and he was afraid he would laugh when he met Fritz. "My . . . ah, my supporters are widespread. That is, they are not all here or readily available. And of course many of them wish to remain anonymous for the time being."

"I can understand that," said Nichols. "But I will need some of them. For my work."

Arnold cleared his throat. "Ah, I've been meaning to ask you about that—just exactly what *is* your work?"

Nichols looked straight at him, and it was like staring into the flat, dead dinner-plate eye of a shark, and suddenly Arnold did not feel any warmth toward this man. "My work is to get rid of the Jews," he said coldly.

Something icy twisted in Arnold's gut. "'Get rid'? Do you mean *kill* them?"

Nichols nodded, grinned like an old-time movie villain. "Yes, of course, that's what I mean."

Arnold leaned back from the greasy tabletop. Nichols' eyebrows arched. "What's the matter, old man, too strong for you? Too *real?*"

A cascade of conflicting thoughts and emotions tumbled across his mind as Arnold tried to make some order of them, to say something sensible. This Nichols character had jammed a spike into the center of his world, his raison d'être, as it were, and now he was forced to accept in that instant the terminus of all his hate-mongering. Where else could he logically expect all his Nazi rhetoric to take him if not to the place where Nichols already so comfortably resided?

"Hey, Professor!" said Nichols, slapping him playfully on the arm. "You still with me?"

"Yes," said Arnold. "I was just thinking, that's all."

"So, have I come to the right place? Can you help me kill some Jews?"

Arnold wanted to speak, but there was something terrible stuck in his throat like a spicular sea urchin. His old, sclerotic heart had begun hammering in his chest, and his hands would have been trembling if he had not been keeping them firmly locked together on the tabletop. But he knew he had been called, perhaps by some higher power, as had those who heeded the call of their Führer more than half a century past, and he knew he must comply.

If he did not, he would in this single instant render the bulk of his life and his life's work impotent and meaningless.

And so, he drew in a great breath, unlocked his hands, and held up his right in a small, but proper salute. *"Heil Hitler,"* he said, tasting bile in the back of his throat.

Nichols chuckled. "Well, I haven't heard that in quite a while," he said. "But that's good. I like it."

Arnold could speak no more, but he managed to nod his agreement.

"Can we go to your offices so we may talk more privately?" said Nichols.

"They are kind of messy," said Arnold.

Nichols grinned again. That scary, out-of-kilter grin. "The whole *world* is kind of messy, Professor. That's why we're here—to straighten things up."

TWENTY-THREE

J. MICHAEL KEATING, M.D.
Manhattan, New York

Several days had passed since Agent Klepner had stunned him with the news about Mussina being alive.

It was hard to describe how it had affected him because he had been so completely overwhelmed at first. A very similar reaction to learning of her death: disbelief, and the unanswerable question of *why*. But now he felt like his life had been suddenly put back on track again. Abruptly, there was renewed purpose in everything he did.

He was standing outside Gate 27, waiting for Klingerman's flight to deplane at LaGuardia, calmly going over the facts the FBI man had volunteered to him in the comfortable shadows of Farley's Place. Dr. Isabella Mussina had indeed been shot, but she had survived, although she was currently in a coma at the Bethesda Naval Hospital in suburban Maryland. She had been shot by a man named Harford Nichols, who worked for the CIA as a Level One Operative, and who was now being hunted by the FBI for a variety of assassination-type murders. Mussina's condition had been kept secret for two reasons: to keep her safe from Nichols, and secondarily to keep her available for any helpful information she might be able to provide in the event she recovered.

Klepner had also hinted that he had more to reveal about Harford Nichols, but he wanted Michael to see it in its original form—a videodisc—rather than through a secondary source. That had piqued his curiosity to a great level, especially when Klepner said it would be very "controversial" data.

When Michael called Klingerman with the startling news, the rabbi abandoned any caution or reservations he may have had. He gathered up all the records and files and scheduled the next available flight to New York. Michael had no concrete idea how he would get along with Klingerman. That man seemed effusive, excitable, and more than a little mystical—all characteristics almost totally opposite to Michael's. There was another important factor that would be of interest as it played out. Michael had always worked pretty much alone, and the prospect of having a research "partner" unsettled him.

Such were his thoughts as the PA system announced the arrival of Klingerman's flight. Michael scanned the faces and physiques of everyone filing past him until he saw a very large man walking toward him with an exaggerated, rocking gait. Wearing a fedora and sporting a thick, black beard and horn-rimmed glasses, he carried a dark suitcoat over his shoulder. A thin, black tie divided his billowy, sweat-stained white shirt. In his other hand he lugged a carry-on bag that was obviously quite heavy.

If this wasn't Irwin Klingerman, Michael would be very surprised. He approached the man and introduced himself.

"Doctor Keating!" said the man in a stentorian voice. "So glad to finally meet you!"

Before Michael could say a word, Klingerman had dropped his luggage and thrown both huge arms around him, pressing the air from his lungs like a set of bellows. He could not speak or move until the rollicking greeting was finally over.

"You can just call me Michael," he said, smiling and shaking hands.

"And me Irwin," said Klingerman, pausing to wipe his sweat-sheened brow before picking up his luggage. "I can't tell you how excited I am to be here, Doctor. Do you think they will let us see her anytime soon?"

"Not too likely. They don't know we officially *know* about Doctor Mussina."

"Oh, that's right! What am I thinking?" Klingerman laughed at his silly mistake and shook his head. "Which way do we go?"

Michael led him along the corridors to the lobby and the cab-stands beyond. A turbaned cabbie rushed to help them into his old yellow Checker, and Klingerman gave him an address on East Eighty-fifth Street.

"I am still shocked by the news," said Irwin as they settled into the backseat. "Did this FBI man tell you *why* he decided to tell you the truth?"

The cab slipped into the arterial flow of Manhattan's traffic. Michael looked from the window to the rabbi. "It's funny, I asked him the same thing: 'Why are you telling me this?'"

"Did he tell you?"

"Yes, he did," said Michael. "He said he was Jewish, and his father's brother had been killed at the camp in Majdanek. When he heard about what Doctor Mussina had been studying, and after he had listened to my own discoveries, he said . . . he said something happened to him."

"Something *what?*" said Irwin.

"He said he had never been a religious man, and certainly not a very good Jew, but something touched him about the possibility of . . . let me see, what were his exact words for it . . . ?"

"*Atoning* for it?" said Irwin. "For forgetting his heritage."

"Right, that's the word he used."

Irwin smiled. "Yes, yes! That's a popular term among us," he said. "We believe we have all committed many sins, and we have much guilt about that, and therefore much to atone for."

Michael nodded. "Okay, I can understand that."

"Do you think he was telling you the truth?" Irwin asked the question as he stared out his window, idly watching the Manhattan cityscape slip past.

The question was like a cold dash of water in Michael's face. He'd never even *considered* that Klepner might be lying, and he confessed that to the rabbi. "What reason would he have to lie?"

Irwin shrugged. "To set you up maybe? I don't know. Maybe he would think you would volunteer more of what you know if you knew Isabella were alive to substantiate it, or reveal it anyway."

"But that means Klepner might think I'm *hiding* something from him." Again, a concept that had never occurred to him.

Irwin chuckled "He's a cop! Of course he's going to think like that—it's part of the way they're trained."

"I didn't know that," said Michael in a very low voice, feeling so naïve, so foolish.

"I used to do volunteer work for Cook County Juvenile Services," said Irwin. "I learned a lot about how kids *and* cops operate."

"That puts a new spin on everything," said Michael. "I think we should call Klepner on this one."

"What do you mean?"

"Maybe we should *demand* to see her?"

Irwin grinned. "'Demand' is an interesting choice of words when dealing with the FBI."

Again, Michael felt naïve. "Well, you know what I mean. I can't help it—your question made me rethink everything."

Irwin Klingerman patted him on the shoulder fraternally. "That's okay, I understand what you're feeling. Sorry my natural paranoia sprang loose without me even thinking about it. It's just that whenever law enforcement types get involved, my antennae go up."

"Well, I hope she *is* still alive," said Michael. "I'd like to meet her and talk to her. I think she's the kind of person I'd want to know."

"Yes," said Irwin, smiling softly, wistfully. "She is indeed."

They rode in silence for a few moments; Michael had suddenly run out of things to say. The prospect of working with Klingerman seemed less daunting now that they'd talked for a bit. He seemed like a decent enough guy and the initial feelings of awkwardness had dissipated.

When the rabbi broke the silence, he suggested they use the remainder of the ride to firm up their plans.

Irwin had arranged to stay with a colleague working at a synagogue on the Upper East Side, but he promised to come to Michael's office the following morning. They would spend the day examining Mussina's records and slowly assembling a larger picture of the puzzle. Agent Klepner had also arranged to meet with them late in the day.

As the cab pulled to the curb at the corner of Second and Eighty-fifth, Klingerman thanked Michael for meeting him at the airport and began to urge his bulk from the backseat of the car. "Oh, one more thing," he said, as he worked himself free. "I've got a suggestion that you may find radical as well as interesting. We can talk about it in the morning."

"All right," said Michael. "I'll look forward to it."

The door closed and he directed the driver to his co-op at Turtle Bay forty blocks to the south. As the car slipped back into traffic, Michael reflected on the roller-coaster ride he had given his hopes and expectations over the last twenty-four hours. So much had happened, he couldn't recall if he'd told Pamela about Dr. Mussina being shot. It would disturb her, he knew, and perhaps unconsciously he'd withheld telling her for that reason.

He was starting to really care about her.

From years of listening to the romantic and emotional problems of his clients, he knew that most people didn't often pause to evaluate their love lives with much rational thinking. Likewise, Michael realized how much the exception he was. But having crawled out from the wreckage of his first marriage with deep, long-healing scars, he had always promised himself he would not ever fall so totally in love with any woman ever again. Most certainly, he'd become over-sensitized to the possibility and had spent many years alone as compensation. But there is balance in most things, and he had no real regrets. Choices were never helped by looking *back* at them.

Maybe it was best to stop analyzing everything so much. . . .

The thought lingered as he stared out the cab window at the towering presence of the office buildings. It was as if he were noticing them for the first time, forced to stare like a gawking tourist. His driver checker-boarded out of the traffic flow and reached the curb at 41st Street. After paying the fare, Michael stepped out onto a sidewalk thick with pedestrians and began walking toward his building. Harry, the doorman, smiled and winked as he let him in. Michael missed the point of the gesture until he entered the lobby and saw Pamela sitting on the tapestried lobby couch. He wasn't used to seeing her in anything other than her perfectly tailored suits, but she looked equally stylish in jeans and an L. L. Bean shirt. She had several brown paper grocery bags on the floor beside her.

Talk about synchronicity. . . .

"Hello, Doctor," she said cheerily, unleashing a blazing smile. "I thought I might try surprising you."

"You already have," said Michael. "Funny, I was just thinking about you."

Pamela ran her hand through her thick, dark mane of hair, tilted her head. "Oh really . . . ?"

"Honestly," he said, pausing for a moment to look around the lobby. "Have you been waiting long?"

"Not at all. Just got here." Pamela bent down to pick up the grocery bags, and he helped her. "I had some shopping to do— thought maybe I would make you a good home-cooked meal for a change."

The idea made him smile. "Sounds like a plan," he said, pointing toward the elevators. "This way . . ."

As they ascended to the top floor of the building, Pamela talked more rapidly than he'd ever heard her. She was a little anxious as she carried out her plans, and he found it charming. It was refreshing to see her *not* in such total control of everything. He led her down the hall to his top-floor apartment, unlocked the door, and allowed her to go in first.

Pamela had been to his place many times over the years for Christmas or New Year's parties, but she had never visited alone. As she walked slowly through the bookcase-lined living room, she nodded with approval at his decorating choices as if seeing them for the first time. He had filled the space with large chairs and tables, display cases for interesting artifacts, gargoyles, and even an Old World globe.

"Very nice," she said. "Your furnishings are very eclectic."

"I guess I've picked up a lot of stuff over the years. 'Baronial clutter' instead of any particular style. That's how an interior designer once described my place. He said he wouldn't change a thing." Michael snickered. "Right—like I'd wanted him to . . ."

"Is it always this neat?" Pamela entered the short hall leading past the kitchen and dining room.

"Better out here than in the den and bedroom." He smiled as he followed her into the kitchen. "And all bets are off when it comes to the bathroom."

"And you men all seem so *proud* of that."

"I think we just don't see things the same way," said Michael. "Would you like me to give you a hand?"

Pamela shook her head as she turned on the light and began to unpack the groceries, looking in the various cabinets and drawers for the accessories and utensils she'd need. "This place looks like you never set foot in here."

"Well, I do tend to eat out a lot." He shrugged, backed out of her way. "I have breakfast in here. A little toast and juice. Coffee, cereal. That sort of thing."

Pamela rolled her eyes and turned back to her task, laying out a cutting board, an assortment of knives, a colander, and several bowls.

"So," he said. "You don't want any help, eh?"

"Don't need any. But if you have any white zinfandel, I'll have some. And a little Bach on the stereo would be nice."

Michael nodded and opened the refrigerator. How did she know he had wine in there? He poured her a glass, then keyed up the Brandenberg Concertos on the stereo. As the opening strains of the first movement filled the apartment, he felt himself unwinding like a spent mainspring, and it felt damned good. An evening like this was exactly what he needed after all the stress, both real and imagined. Pamela had already started her special magic in the kitchen—incredible aromas blended with the sound of a harpsi-chord—and Michael poured himself a Maker's Mark on ice.

But the phone rang before he could take the first sip.

"Doctor Keating . . ." he said, making an effort to not sound irri-tated.

"Michael!" boomed the caller's voice. It was Irwin Klingerman. "I'm not bothering you am I?"

"Well, I was getting ready for dinner . . ."

"So I won't keep you!" said Irwin. "I just wanted to tell you something—something you might want to mull over until we get together tomorrow."

"Really?" Michael tried to sound interested as he stole a long sip from his glass. "What is it?"

"I've been putting together all Isabella's notes and files. Categorizing them according to her list of variables, and I noticed something that might be important." Irwin paused to clear his throat, then continued. "All of her subjects' episodes have occurred within the last eight years. Nothing before 1991."

Michael had been listening only halfheartedly. Anything he had could surely wait till tomorrow, but there *was* something definitely odd about that 1991 date.

"You're sure about that?" he said. "That's unusual at the very least."

"Oh, yes! I've checked it a few times. I don't know . . . for some reason, it just kind of jumped out at me. Any ideas?"

Just then Pamela called from the kitchen, needing the location of a blender, if he owned one.

Irwin chuckled. "Oh, I am so sorry, my friend! I had no idea how much and what kind of a dinner I was interrupting! Good night, Michael. We can tackle this little mystery in the morning."

"That sounds good," said Michael, but the flamboyant rabbi had already hung up.

He went into the kitchen to ferret out the blender from his pile of never-used appliances under the sink. "Wait till you meet Rabbi Klingerman," he said as he started moving around pots and pans. "He's a real character."

"Was that him?"

Michael nodded and told her about no subjects reporting episodes prior to 1991.

"Interesting," said Pamela, obviously filing the information away for further use.

He located the blender and gave it to her as she returned to her careful and artistic preparation.

"What're we having?" he said as he stood by the entrance to the kitchen.

"It'll be better if I surprise you," she said.

And she was right about that.

Lamb chops with a light mushroom and marsala sauce. Yogurt and curry sauce over risotto, and a Caesar salad. He never would have expected anything so good could originate from his kitchen. Combining the repast with several more cocktails, candlelight, and an attractive dining companion was enough to make him feel more relaxed, more free, than he had in years. If a dinner date could be this pleasant, why had he been avoiding it so completely for so long?

They dined slowly and kept their conversation away from the concerns of the office. He wasn't sure if it was Pamela or himself who was responsible, but he decided he didn't care—he was enjoying the evening far too much to care.

Afterward, they sat out on his roof patio to enjoy a late spring night's view of the East River and the familiar architecture of the United Nations Building. She'd brought two snifters of sambuca, each garnished with three coffee beans, and they shared a few moments of romantic silence.

"This was a great idea," he said, finally breaking it.

"Glad you thought of it, are you?" Pamela had pressed herself close to him on the chaise lounge. Despite the hours in the kitchen, she still smelled perfumed and rich in pheromones.

"Oh, yeah," he said smiling, then turned to kiss her. All the drinking had damped down his inhibitions and second thoughts about how appropriate it might or might not be. He didn't care if she was his assistant; she was a good-looking woman and he found himself wanting her.

She kissed him with the aggressive energy he'd unconsciously expected and did not take too long to begin the timeless ritual of undressing each other. That they were doing so under the sparkling stare of the Manhattan night only made it more exciting.

And then they were naked. Hands everywhere. Kissing with a crazy urgency. Touching and slipping and caressing from every possible angle and attitude, they carried each other aloft on wings of desire, soaring above the feelings of vulnerability. They pushed deeper and farther into the delicate realm of passion, taking the time to share and instruct, never ignoring any chance for intimacy.

It had been so long since Michael had let himself go like this that he was operating half on autopilot and half on fiery inspiration. Because Pamela was a good lover, full of activity and energy, she had given him the push and the motivation to respond in kind. And he felt as if he'd been awakened from a long, debilitating sleep.

She sensed something fragile in him and that only made everything better. Making it last, stretching out the time like a piece of hot, pliant taffy, they embraced the hot night to themselves and made it a part of their joining.

When he could last no longer, she urged him into a gently explosive release, then held him in her arms. For a brief moment, like the starry path of a meteor's dying, he felt as safe and warm and happy as any child ever could. And he was reminded why all men are doomed to be forever also little boys. He felt so damned *good* that he almost laughed out loud and could barely contain the grin that widened within him. Is *this* what he'd been so afraid of? Had it been so long that he had so totally forgotten the primal beauty of two humans huddled against the void, even if only for an instant?

If for no other reason, he would always be grateful to Pamela for having the persistence necessary to complete his reawakening.

Unable to contain his feelings, he told her haltingly what miracle she had performed upon him. But before he could finish, she put a long, thin finger to his lips.

"Shhhh . . ." she whispered. "Before you say something you'll regret tomorrow."

"I'm not going to profess my undying love or anything like that," he said. "I just wanted you to know that I realize I've been fighting this . . . attraction we've both felt . . ."

"Okay . . ." She lay back in the chaise, hands behind her head, breasts full and pointing proudly at him. She had taken care of herself and he admired the results of all the time she spent at the Manhattan Athletic Club.

"And I just wanted to thank you for not giving up." He grinned, took her hand, and held it close against his cheek.

"Well, let's just say I had a feeling you were worth it." She tousled his hair playfully and he felt very young again.

They lay against one another for a long time, saying nothing. Occasionally, the hint of a breeze passed over them as the city cooled down for the night like a volcano heaving into reluctant remission. It had been so long since he'd felt the long languid press of a woman's flesh against his own that he was in no hurry to retreat into the shelter of the apartment.

Suddenly he felt Pamela's long manicured nails dig into his back like the talons of a hawk.

"Oh, my God!" she said in a burst.

"What's wrong?" His first thought was that he'd done something wrong, something stupid, and was afraid to ask what it could be.

"Oh, nothing, really," she said, pushing her hair from her face. "I was just thinking about what you said before—"

"That's kind of scary. I said lots of things."

"No," said Pamela. "I mean about none of the patients having any episodes until 1991 . . ."

"Right. What about it?" Michael looked at her as she pulled her knees up to her chest, held them in her arms as though suddenly chilled.

"I don't know why it came to me, but I was just thinking—wasn't that the year that Germany was reunited?"

TWENTY-FOUR

ARNOLD RASSENAULT
Manhattan, New York

". . . and that is why I am here," said Harford Nichols, pausing to sip from his mug of coffee.

He sat across from Arnold at the little table in the second room of the *Journal* offices, seemingly unaffected by the squalid disarray and obvious poverty of the offices. Nichols possessed the dashing good looks of an Errol Flynn or Douglas Fairbanks, but he had the eyes of Rasputin, the twisted smile of de Sade. Arnold was not yet sure what to make of him—other than that he was most likely a very dangerous man.

And what was he to make of the story!?

The story Nichols had confessed to him—the life of Hirsh Dukor, the death camps with Mengele, the reincarnation into the body of a CIA agent named Nichols, and the recent assassinations—had to be the most fanciful ideations of a textbook schizophrenic.

But Arnold believed every word of it.

Because he was terrified to do anything else.

They had been sitting there, staring at one another for several minutes as Arnold struggled to free himself from the spin of his own thoughts. Finally, Nichols leaned forward, grabbed Arnold's wrist in a bone-twisting grip.

"You've been silent long enough, Professor. What do you think? Will you help me?"

"I . . . I don't know *what* to think," said Arnold, trying to make sense of this man who would invade his lonely territory of Aryan supremacy. "I'm an old man. Why would you need my help?"

Nichols smiled. "Do you believe in destiny, Professor Rassenault?"

Arnold shrugged. "I don't know . . . perhaps I do. Why? What are you getting at?"

"Because I not only believe in it," said Nichols, "I have no choice. I'm *forced* to do so!"

"What do you mean?"

Nichols jumped up from the table, began pacing slowly within the crowded confines of the junk and cardboard boxes. "Destiny is real! Destiny is the engine that runs the universe. I can feel it humming in my ears all the time! I am *driven* by my destiny, Professor, and so, I fear, are you."

"What—?" Arnold leaned back in his chair as Nichols held a fist in the air, then pointed at him like a mad accuser. How had he let this man into his life? He wished that Fritz were here, if only to witness the seriousness of the problem.

"Something is happening in the world, Professor, can't you feel it?"

"Yes, I can," said Arnold, lying automatically. He could feel nothing but the hollow pit opening beneath his stomach, threatening to unloose his bowels into his baggy underwear.

"The Old Gods are awakening!" said Nichols, looking off as though seeing them as he spoke. "The mongrels are everywhere! All over the world! And the rest of us are rushing to bow at their feet, full of silly talk of guilt and reparation and retribution! But that kind of talk has awakened the spirit of the old times. There is a new *Zeitgeist* ready to stride amongst us, can't you feel it!?"

Arnold was about to nod his head and lie again, when he realized that *maybe* the madman was right. In years past, when Arnold allowed himself a rare moment of honest introspection, he could admit the smallness of his life, of the pitiful notions to which he'd allied his energy. There were times when he knew he was wrong about some things—it was good policy to deprecate the Holocaust, but in his heart he knew it happened. Sometimes, in the middle of the night, when the merciful release of sleep would not come, he would sit up in the darkness and question his beliefs, wondering if there was much of a future in the hate business.

But lately, he *had* felt something different, like an electrical charge in the air, and he had seen evidence in the burgeoning new Eastern European countries of the old Soviet bloc—the old ways, the old enemies, had never really died, they'd just been hibernating and waiting for the time to come round again. Nationalism was again thriving in places from Azerbaijan to Poland, and even in France where the National Front Party's xenophobia had become the rule.

Maybe this Nichols character was right? Even if he *did* believe he was reincarnated from a death camp . . .

"Professor, are you listening to me?" Nichols had leaned down to peer into his eyes.

"Oh, yes," said Arnold. "Very much, and too well."

"Then you must know . . . when you reach down into that primal mud of your deepest thoughts . . . that I am right. That there is some really bad shit working its way through the pipe and it'll be here pretty fast."

"I . . . I, yes, I think you're probably correct, Mr. Nichols."

Nichols stood up, looked over Arnold's head as if he could see something far beyond the cramped walls of the tiny room. "And by that I'll assume you see your own destiny as well?"

"You mean to help you?" Arnold took a wild guess. It was hard to follow Nichols' thoughts as they skittered from place to place like a waterbug.

"Yes, precisely. You *do* see it! That's good."

"But . . ." Arnold paused, trying to be very careful how he phrased his next question. He didn't want to piss off this man, who might be a maniac, or who might actually be telling the truth. Arnold's biggest problem was himself—he'd believed his own rhetoric for so long that what Nichols was saying to him was so damnably appealing, so ineluctably *right* in its very sound, that Arnold *wanted* to believe him. Racial superiority, he realized long ago, was like the existence of UFOs: if you wanted to believe in it, that made it that much easier to do so.

Nichols was looking down at him again. The man adjusted his tie and rolled down his oxford shirtsleeves. So deceptive; he looked like a half-million other office-dwellers in Manhattan. He wore the camouflage so perfectly, even his dark hair had been trimmed in the proper, modern fashion. "But *what,* Professor?" he said evenly.

"As I said before, I am an old man. How can I possibly help you?"

Nichols drew in a deep breath, exhaled slowly.

"Very well, let me tell you a few more . . . shall we say . . . *feelings* I've had about my destiny."

Arnold picked up his coffee cup absently. It had been long empty and he wasn't thirsty anyway. "I'm listening," he said.

Nichols sat down, stared at him intently. "I believe I am here for a distinct purpose," he said. "I believe I have been yanked back to almost total sentience by a cosmic force of some kind. One of those primal, basic, elemental things all the philosophers and the mystical religions talk about. Do you follow me?"

Arnold nodded. He did, in fact, understand, having read some of the work by writers such as Teilhard de Chardin, Alan Watts, and others. It was perhaps possible the universe turned upon the energy generated by the pairing of great forces in eternal opposition. Perhaps our concepts of Good and Evil are merely primitive perceptions of these equal, and necessary, opposites.

"Okay, then, I believe I am here as a counterbalance to *others* being called back on the *opposite* side of the Great Wheel, or whatever you want to call it. The ones I've been killing are only a few of them."

"Called back? The others?"

"There are *many* of them!" said Nichols. "Others who were killed in the camps. They've been reincarnated, too—I already told you that! Aren't you listening to me?"

"Oh yes, of course I am."

"Then what's the problem? I am obviously here to do a job—to kill them *again*! Don't you see that?"

"Well, yes, I do. Yes . . ."

"They need to be killed. Over and over again. If necessary!" Nichols leaned down, close to him again. He was so handsome, he was scary. "Don't you agree?"

Arnold swallowed with great effort. His mouth was dry, his tongue sticky. "Yes. Yes, I do," he said with awful difficulty.

Nichols smiled. "Then it's very simple. I want you and your organization to help me get rid of them."

My organization. Arnold would have laughed if he thought he could get away with it. It occurred to him he'd be better off just agreeing with this guy than trying to discuss any of it. There *was* a simple logic to what he was saying: kill all the Jews. Isn't that what he'd been preaching for so many years? Of course it was.

"I will do anything I can," said Arnold with as much conviction and enthusiasm as possible.

"Good. I will need to set up a base of operations here. You have a cot or a foldaway bed?"

Arnold shrugged, shook his head. "No, I—"

"No matter, I'll buy one," said Nichols. "Set it up in that corner. Do you really need all these fucking boxes in here?"

"No, I don't suppose I do." Oddly, Arnold was not as disturbed by the idea of Nichols laying up in the offices as he might have first imagined. There was something exciting, something *dangerous*, in this man. And infectious. Arnold felt infused with new purpose, and he liked it, even though it scared him.

"Good, I'll get myself dug in tonight."

"Is there anything else I can do?" Arnold spoke with renewed sincerity and energy. He'd suddenly realized what good fortune looked down on him with the arrival of Nichols.

The strange man with the movie-star good looks turned to face him. "Yes, there is one more thing we should discuss."

"What's that?" Arnold could see the resolve driven deep into the man's eyes. It was both frightening and intoxicating.

"You remember what I was telling you earlier—about a new *Zeitgeist*, about the Old Gods being awakened?"

Something very cold slithered through him for an instant as Arnold nodded. "Yes. Yes, I do."

"I have been doing a lot of thinking about it," said Nichols. "And if someone like myself has been called back, then surely others more . . . more *worthy* than me—"

"Are also here?" Arnold finished the question that was really more of a statement. It was at that moment he realized that he truly *believed* everything Nichols had been telling him. No proof. No reason to do so. He simply did.

"That's right," said Nichols. "Mengele. Hoess. Himmler. All of them. Even Hitler. *Especially* Hitler!"

"Yes . . ." whispered Arnold. Good Christ! To imagine such a thing! That someone, somewhere in the world, carried within them, like a sacred scroll in a clay vessel, the essence of the most powerful man in all of history—*der Führer*.

Arnold tried to stand up, but a sudden paralysis held him. He felt no fear, however. Its grip came not from panic or malaise, but anticipation.

"Don't you see it?" said Nichols in a voice as soft as the flutter of a bat's wing. "It has to be true. It follows logically. If I am here? If my victims are here . . . then somewhere . . . we're *all* here."

The words drifted through the office as evening lapped upon the windowsills. But Arnold could still hear them, coiling about the room in ever widening spirals. Echoes across the vast gulf of time: *We're all here.*

TWENTY-FIVE

BRADLEY STEVENSON
Baltimore, Maryland

Exiting the Federal Building at Hopkins Plaza, Brad walked down the steps to an open courtyard. Fountains punched at the late summer humidity and thousands of office workers tried to stretch their lunch hours in the plaza on benches and under shade trees. It was the same in every city's downtown area—despite the feminists' claims to the contrary, he saw lots of young businesswomen dressed to kill, looking for mates among the middle management crowd.

But that wasn't what concerned him today. Somewhere, in a big crowd like this, a killer could be sliding and slipping. Harford Nichols had come to Baltimore to kill a lonely old woman, and Brad needed to understand what was going on as thoroughly as possible. It was the only way he could ever hope to anticipate the killer's next move. The only chance of catching him.

Finding an empty bench at the edge of a line of shade trees, Brad sat down to look at his notes. An hour of keystroking at one of the bureau's computers upstairs and some phone calls had established a few items that tied in, disturbingly, with the overall pattern. One, Martha Pasek's attack on the skinheads, and two, her visit, a month later, to the Northwest District Police's shrink, a guy named Harold Schlossenberg.

She saved some Jewish kids from the skinheads, and the police reports said she'd called the arresting officers back about a month later complaining about nightmares. Brad exhaled slowly. It was time to find out if he was still a good detective. Thumbing through a few pages on his notepad, he found the number he was looking for.

Keying in Dr. Schlossenberg's number on his PCS phone, Brad waited for a reply. After passing through the doctor's receptionist, he waited for him to pick up the line.

"Harold Schlossenberg, can I help you?"

Brad introduced himself, then asked a few questions about Martha Pasek.

"I'm not sure I can tell you much," said the shrink. "I only saw her once and there's the confidentiality business . . ."

"Not anymore," said Brad.

"Why not?"

"Martha Pasek was killed last night."

"Oh Christ, you're kidding!"

"No, I wish I was."

"How did it happen?" said Schlossenberg.

Brad filled him in quickly with the details. "Whatever you know might help me find the bastard."

The doctor cleared his throat. "I'll be waiting for you, Mr. Stevenson."

Harold Schlossenberg was a small-framed, well-dressed guy in his forties. He liked the thick-framed black glasses look of accountants, computer programmers, and NASA scientists, and he carried it off well. His office at Northwest District Headquarters was arbitrarily dreary, full of constant reminders of his indentured service to the city government: the obligatory plaques, certificates, and commendations from flummeried public officials. Only a family portrait on the corner of the desk proved the humanity of the police psychiatrist.

"I only saw her once. One of the officers asked me to do her the favor. I referred her to a private shrink, but I knew she wouldn't go—she couldn't afford it."

Brad nodded. "What was her problem? Note I have here says nightmares."

Schlossenberg smiled. "Yeah, I guess they *were*! Every night, she told me, she was dreaming of being in a concentration camp. Every night, they would kill her."

Brad nodded. "The gas chambers?"

"Well, kind of . . ." said Schlossenberg. "This particular day at the camp, the day she kept dreaming about, there was some kind of problem in the shower room. The gas wouldn't come through the nozzles. Some kind of foul-up. So the soldiers, they had to herd this big crowd of naked women and kids across an open pasture, through a small woods full of white birch trees. She remembers the trees being so pretty, she told me. And then, they lined them up in front of a huge open pit where they just started shooting and shooting. Martha felt herself get shot, but it didn't kill her. But the soldiers thought she was dead and they threw her into a huge pile of corpses that they were burning in the open pits . . ."

". . . and they burned her?" Brad shook his head in disgust.

"Alive. Yes," said Schlossenberg. "And she kept having the same dream every night."

"Was she Jewish?"

"No, she wasn't."

"Were you able to help her?" Brad made a note on his little pad.

"Nah, she was a sad old lady. I felt sorry for her, but I couldn't prescribe any drugs that might help her." Schlossenberg removed his glasses for a moment to rub his temples, then replaced them. "Violation of my employment contract."

Brad didn't say anything for a moment. He was trying to put it all together, to look at what he'd gathered without bias and just accept what he had and get on with it. It was just so damned hard for a pragmatist like himself to make much sense out of the "facts."

Facts.

The term made him grin. He'd worked an awful lot of cases and he'd never had such flimsy crap to go on as this one. He'd never been one of those people who paid much attention to any of that occult business, and he was having a lot of trouble taking the information he tracked very seriously. But it looked like he didn't have much choice.

After a long silence, Schlossenberg cleared his throat. "I guess you can't tell me what's going on?"

"Not a chance," said Brad, closing the little notebook. "I can't tell you until I know myself."

He thanked the shrink and left. As he reached his car in the back parking lot, Brad knew he would need to talk to Dr. Keating again.

TWENTY-SIX

J. MICHAEL KEATING, M.D.
Manhattan, New York

Pamela had been correct.

1991 was indeed the year of the reunification of Germany. Michael was sitting in his office, staring at his desktop monitor, which displayed archived pages from *Time* magazine detailing the official end of the two Germanies. The significance of the date and the predominance of death-camp memories surfacing was not lost on him or Pamela.

They had come into the office together, earlier than usual because both of them had awakened in what he could only describe as a sweet panic and full of *oh-what-have-I-done?* kind of thoughts. As fantastic as their evening had been, neither one of them seemed to be comfortable with the newest aspect of their relationship.

Michael smiled. He'd known it would be an awkward situation, and that's why he'd been avoiding it for this long. But now it was done, and they had no choice but to face it and get past it. Especially since there were new factors to be evaluated in their . . . reincarnation case study. Michael mentally stumbled on the word *reincarnation* because he remained uncomfortable with the concept, but the term was how Pamela had been referring to both their own files on

McGuire and Enders, and the bulk of Dr. Mussina's files. Since he had not come up with a more appropriate name for their current research, he had begun thinking of the study the same way.

A light tap on the door and Pamela appeared. She was dressed casually in her jeans outfit because they had not stopped at her apartment on their way across town to the Riverside Drive offices. Not that it mattered—they had no patients scheduled today, and Michael wondered if their lives would ever return to the staid routine they once had been. So much had happened in the last few months. . . .

"You don't have to knock," he said softly.

"Klingerman called," she said, approaching the desk with an uncharacteristic shyness. He knew he was going to have a difficult adjustment too, because he could not look at her without imagining her naked and kneeling above him. "He's on his way. He should be here any minute."

"That's good. We should have an interesting meeting."

She nodded. "There was also a message from Agent Klepner of the FBI. He wants to see you today, too, but I haven't called him back yet. What do you want to do with him?"

"See if he can stop in late in the day. As late as possible. I want to talk to him, but I want to give Klingerman as much time as possible."

"Okay," she said, turning away without ever having looked him in the eye.

He let her go a few steps before speaking up. "Hey, girl, wait a second."

Turning, she couldn't conceal an incipient grin at the corners of her mouth. "Did you say *girl* . . . ? That's a new one."

"Look," he said with a small smile. "We both know we're feeling funny about this thing. We need to get past it."

"What do you mean?" He sensed an undercurrent of alarm in her voice. "Get past it *how*?"

"I mean this *awkwardness* we're both feeling. I don't know about you, but I don't think I was prepared for anything like last night."

The tightness in her shoulders seemed to untense a bit as she looked at him. "Really?"

"Believe me, Pamela, it knocked me crazy. I can't stop thinking about it."

"Really, well, I kind of liked it myself," said Pamela, smiling her usual, natural smile for the first time that morning.

"I guess that means we can relax and stop worrying about what the other person is thinking, right?"

Pamela grinned. "That's right."

"Okay, great," he said. "So while we're *here*, working, we can keep our minds on our work—"

"—and when we're *not* working, we can keep our minds on playing . . ." she said stretching out the last word.

"Yeah, something like that." He returned to the stack of papers on his desk, feeling better about everything. That schoolboy anxiety he'd been feeling would have kept him from getting anything done today.

Pamela was about to say something else when the office doorbell sounded. "That's our rabbi," she said. "I'll send him in, then I'll call back Klepner."

Michael nodded. "Then I want you to sit in on this one, okay?"

"Sure, if you want . . ."

"We need all the insights we can get," he said. "And besides, you're *good*."

"Hey, Doctor, tell me something I *don't* know."

Pamela winked at him then walked from the office in long strides, emphasizing the cut and fit of her jeans. He could hear Klingerman's boisterous and approving salutations as she greeted him at the door. She escorted him to the back office and slipped away to her desk.

"Ah, Doctor Keating! What traffic!" said Klingerman as he kind of exploded into the room carrying two large shopping bags and a valise. Just as at the airport, his black suit was disheveled and his tie was crooked. "And I always thought they had it bad in Chicago . . . Oy!"

"Good morning, Rabbi," said Michael, getting up from his desk to shake hands. "Let's put all that stuff over here on the conference table where we can spread out."

Michael helped him unload some of the file folders, binders, and cases of CD-ROMs and discs. They spent the next half hour rough-sorting and organizing the material, chronologically and by patient. It was slower than expected because they were not Klingerman's records, and Michael knew everybody had their own little quirks when it came to filing and compiling information. It wasn't until Pamela joined them, contributing her innate sense of organization, that they solved the system of Dr. Mussina's records and began to make real progress. Soon, the huge conference table resembled an architect's model city, with tall stacks of papers, folders, and bound documents neatly blocking and mapping out the entire polished cherrywood surface. It was interesting to watch Pamela take charge of the operation, and to see how Klingerman became ever more charmed by her with each passing minute.

But there wasn't much time for small talk. Seven years of intense case study research by Isabella Mussina had yielded an enormous amount of information. She had personally sessioned twenty-four patients and had amassed medical records and personal correspondence with another forty-one people. Rabbi Irwin Klingerman, working in a less clinically targeted environment had, on several occasions, encountered Jews who were experiencing "past-life Holocaust trauma"—the term Mussina had coined to describe the phenomenon she had discovered and had written about in several ground-breaking monographs that employed the phrase in her subtitles.

With Pamela's help, they began the time-consuming task of reading abstracts, articles, and patient logs. On the cases in which Klingerman had personal experience or involvement, they were able to move a little faster, but the hours fell away like melting candlewax.

The deeper they excavated into Mussina's records, the more impressed Michael became with the woman's thorough methods, her unfailing dedication, and her almost lyrical prose. Each subject, each *person*, she interviewed or sessioned had been chronicled with obvious compassion and insight. Each case study crackled with the personality and pathos of the individual. Mussina wrote about her patients with such care that no one could read her files without coming to feel that they knew the patient personally. The imprint of Dr. Mussina's talent and intelligence marked every file and document they inspected, standing out like a distinctive and stylish watermark on fine parchment. Michael found himself wondering if she would ever escape the coma.

They sent out for a deli lunch and worked into the afternoon, reading, taking notes, fine-tuning their evaluations and organizing techniques. Gradually, a larger picture of Mussina's work came into focus, enabling Michael to more fully appreciate the scope and depth of Mussina's massive study. Just from a single day's brief analysis of the evidence, Michael had become convinced they were onto something significant and perhaps even frightening. A more intense and careful analysis of Mussina's work would take weeks and maybe even months—time that would be unnecessary if she had been able to join them and guide them.

After seeing the staggering amount of corroborating evidence, Michael was certain that some kind of important mechanism was at work. Something happening on the metaphysical level that bowed to forces and influences greater than those of nations or their politics.

Later, when the trio had retired from the conference table, sitting in the comfortable chairs in the reception foyer and sipping hot coffee, they began to exchange impressions and ideas.

"I had no idea there was so much material," said Michael. "And a good percentage of the subjects reporting shared experiences."

"That's right," said Pamela. "The same camps, or memories of the same personnel, like Mengele or The Little Angel . . ."

"Or Brechtstadt in Majdanek, Rossbach in Treblinka," said Irwin Klingerman. "If anyone ever wanted to dismiss these stories as fanciful dreams or nightmares, they cannot if they do their homework. These officers and *kommandos* were *real*!"

Pamela nodded. "I know, I've been looking at her documentation. The rosters from the Polish and German camps—how long did it take for her to get those lists, and how long to check them?"

Irwin Klingerman shrugged. "Isabella has friends and colleagues all over the world. If she wants to find something, she could usually figure out a way to find it."

"But what does it all mean?" asked Michael. "We cannot doubt that something very significant and very singular has been taking place . . . but *why*?"

"You've read Isabella's notes," said Irwin. "What do you think of her hypothesis?"

Michael frowned. "You know, there was a time when I would have laughed at you and her work. Laughed you right out of my office," he said. "I would've called you a bunch of charlatans, or at least gullible fools . . ."

"But now . . . ?" said Irwin.

"But now, I have to agree with Doctor Mussina's notion that camp victims have been reincarnated."

"Is that *all*?" said Pamela, tilting her head at an angle that said she could see through his cautious, defensive positioning.

"Well, no, not really," he said, realizing where she was leading him and deciding she was correct in doing it. "That the incidence of the past-life evidence—you know, the nightmares and the dreams and the blackouts and whatever else these poor people have reported, all of it—began immediately after the reunification of Germany . . . well, that's got to mean something."

"Go on, what else?" said Pamela. She wasn't going to let him get away without spelling out everything.

Michael cleared his throat. "Doctor Mussina believed the victims were being marshaled back to somehow keep the Nazis from ever coming to power again."

"But how would they accomplish that?" said Irwin. "It's something I've thought about long into more than one lonely night."

"By telling their stories, by not letting us forget what happened to them?" Michael shook his head. "That sounds kind of ineffectual to me, doesn't it?"

"There's got to be more to it than that," said Pamela.

"Exactly," said Klingerman. "The shared memories of monsters like *Der Klein Engel* and Mengele and Rossbach . . ."

Michael pushed back his chair from the big table, walked to the window, and looked up the Hudson. "It's funny. I feel like we're just dancing around the edge of this thing. That we're onto something and it just won't come clear."

"Well, there's plenty of material here," said Irwin. "We've barely examined more than ten percent of it."

"That's true," said Michael. "But it would be nice to have Doctor Mussina on board. She could save us a lot of time."

Pamela grinned. "Are we in a hurry?"

Her question, although intended to be light and casual, seemed to get hung up in the serious atmosphere of the room. Everyone looked at each other as if, having been touched by a deep and philosophical argument, they were now pondering its implications.

"I don't know . . ." said Irwin, after a long stretch of silence. "Maybe we *are*."

"That sounds kind of ominous," said Michael. "Which reminds me—you said you had an idea. When you got out of the cab yesterday, remember?"

Irwin nodded vigorously. "What? And you think I forgot about it already?"

"Well, no, not really." Michael had to smile at him. Even when he wasn't trying to be animated, Klingerman had an irrepressible verve about him.

"Okay, listen, it's not really *my* idea, it's Isabella's. But I think she'd like to see us get it off the ground."

"Let me guess," said Pamela. "We try to arrange a seminar, or conference, or whatever you want to call it. We bring as many of the subjects together as possible . . ."

Klingerman looked at her as if she'd fired a hot slug into his expansive middle. "How did you *know*?" he half-bellowed. "How could you possibly have known?"

Michael shared his surprise, but tried to be nonchalant as he looked admiringly at Pamela.

She just shrugged. "I don't know—it seems pretty obvious to me. Get the patients together. For starters, it would be good for them to have first-hand proof that they weren't alone in their suffering, and secondly, the odds of somebody coming up with real answers would have to go way up if there were more people sharing experiences and ideas."

"Well, I guess that pretty well sums it up," said Michael.

"So the idea—" said Klingerman. "What do you think?"

Michael sat on the edge of the table, looking at the rabbi in his rumpled clothes. He was one of those men who could buy his suits at Barney's or Kmart, and it simply would never matter; he would look the same regardless. He was not really a funny man, but he definitely projected a Falstaffian image. You wanted to like Irwin Klingerman. But his suggestion to convene a seminar of the trauma subjects didn't make much sense logistically or economically. It would require—

"So, Doctor, you are listening to me, or perhaps you are daydreaming, *nu*?"

"I'm sorry, Irwin, I was just thinking over the whole idea."

"And . . . ?"

"And while I think it's a great idea, it would be hard to bring it off. There's the initial difficulty in just contacting all the subjects, and then the cost of transportation would be tough. Even if we tried to narrow our range to people in the States, it would still cost plenty."

"And we couldn't expect the patients to pay their own way," said Pamela.

"But you know," said Irwin, "I'd bet some of them would do it gladly!"

"You're probably right," said Michael. "But we couldn't count on it. I think the best way to get it to happen is to get some company or organization to sponsor us."

"That sounds like a lot of work," said Pamela, with an expression of mock suspicion. "I wonder who gets to make all the phone calls?"

"I think you already have the answer to that one." Michael smiled as he turned to Klingerman. "But before we get too far ahead of ourselves, I think we should contact as many of the subjects as possible—at least the ones in the U.S. and Canada. We need to find out how many of them would be willing to spend a weekend or maybe a whole week working on this thing."

"You're right," said Irwin. "Pamela and I could get the list together and start right away . . . if you think this is what we want to be doing?"

Good question, thought Michael. Ten minutes ago they were still shuffling papers around the table, and now, suddenly, they were getting ready to throw themselves into an organizational maelstrom. For what? Was it worth it?

Whenever he began to think like that, the acid-sharp memories of his patients surged up inside him. He could see the gray skies and the frigid breaths of the Jews being herded into trucks and boxcars. He could feel their jagged panic and desperation as they were led into the dark mouth of the gas chambers.

There was no real question of *worth* here. They had uncovered something that *demanded* their attention. Isabella Mussina had felt the importance and the urgency; so did he. They must do whatever they could.

"Yes," he said after a pause in which they had respected his silence. "I think it's a very good idea, Irwin. I think we owe it to ourselves . . . and all these people in these files. I think we have to at least try to make it happen."

"Okay!" said Klingerman, pushing back his rolled-up sleeves. "Let's get started."

Moving to a stack of folders, Irwin began winnowing out the prospective subjects and handing them to Pamela, who copied down contact information. Michael returned to his desk to compose a carefully worded letter to the subjects.

But they were interrupted by the arrival of FBI agent Sid Klepner.

The thin, Semitic-looking Klepner appeared anxious but in control as he stood there looking at each of them fleetingly. He had thick eyebrows and thinning hair, and the kind of vulpine, pointy face you didn't easily forget. He had a general appearance that communicated caution . . . maybe even danger. After introductions were made, he opened a briefcase he was carrying and produced a videodisc.

"This is an unofficial visit, Doctor Keating," he said. "And this disc doesn't actually exist . . . and even though you're not actually seeing it, I'm not the one who showed it to you, understand?"

As he moved to slip it into the disc player and monitor in the corner of the room, Michael held up his hand. "Hey, wait a second. After all that, do you mind telling us what we're, ah . . . *not* going to see right now?"

Klepner paused as the deck accepted his disc, but he didn't push the On button. "It's a video record of the session Isabella Mussina had with Harford Nichols."

"Who's Harford Nichols?" said Irwin.

"I told Doctor Keating about him. He didn't tell you?" Klepner looked at Michael, to see if he was saying something he shouldn't.

Michael waved it off with a casual gesture. "It's okay," he said quickly. "With everything else going, I haven't had time to remember everything. Can you get everybody up to speed?"

Klepner nodded, spoke succinctly. "Nichols was a CIA agent who went psycho. Started killing innocent people—assassination style. Doctor Mussina was interviewing him. They wanted her to find out whether or not he was, ah . . . salvageable."

"And if *not*," said Pamela, "they were going to kill him?"

"Yeah, that's the way it works," said the government man.

"And you think we should see this?" said Michael.

"Oh, yeah," said Klepner, poising his finger over the button.

"Excuse me, but I have one more question, Mr. Klepner . . ." said Pamela.

"Sure, what?"

"Why are you doing this? Can't you get in trouble for this?" She moved her chair closer to the TV monitor.

Klepner shrugged. "Maybe, I don't know. I don't really care. I told Doctor Keating about this video, and I think you should see it. I think it might give you some information that you're going to need."

Irwin Klingerman leaned forward and looked into the FBI man's eyes, sensing there was something else lurking behind them. "No offense, sir," said Irwin, "but that sounds very altruistic. A little too good-hearted from somebody who works for the government, if you know what I mean."

Klepner chuckled. "Yeah, you're right, it does sound like a setup, or at least something fishy, doesn't it?"

"Can we take your word that it's not?" said Michael.

Klepner looked at each of them with a humorless expression. "You have my word. But my reason for wanting to help might mean more to you."

"What do you mean?" said Irwin.

"My father and his two brothers were born in Germany. They had a dry goods business in Berlin, but it was burned to the ground in November 1938 . . ."

"Kristallnacht?" said Irwin Klingerman.

"Yeah," said Klepner.

"The infamous *Night of Broken Glass*," said the rabbi, looking from one to the other as though he were lecturing to a class. He spoke as if he were a village shaman reciting an ancestral tale. "The evening when the mobs swarmed all over Germany and Austria destroying anything they could find that had any connection to the Jews. Offices, shops, synagogues, libraries . . . a lot of it went up in flames."

"That's right," said Klepner. He looked off toward a blank wall at the end of the room and began reciting a litany of his own. He spoke in a half-whisper—a story that would be passed down from one generation to another. "My father and my uncles lost every-thing. Then they were rounded up and taken to the Belsen concen-tration camp. After almost two years of forced labor, it almost killed them. They were put on a train to Treblinka, but the engine broke down and the cattlecars they were in had to be towed to a siding until repairs could be made. My father and his two brothers tried to escape. Uncle Sid was caught by the soldiers, but my father and my other uncle, Julius, got away. They eventually made it to France, then England. Finally the United States, but my Uncle Sid was sent to Treblinka, where they killed him."

"And you are named after that man, aren't you?" said the rabbi.

Klepner nodded. "That's right. Sidney Klepner. And when I came here with Agent Stevenson, when we first talked to Doctor Keating, he told us about Doctor Mussina's work, and his own patients . . ."

Klepner paused, collected himself, exhaled.

". . . and everything about the death camps and the Nazis, it just really . . . affected me, you know? I couldn't stop thinking about it, and about my uncle and everything that happened. And then, after I saw this video with Nichols and Mussina, I knew I had to do whatever I could to help."

Irwin Klingerman walked over to the FBI man and put a fatherly hand on his shoulder. "That's good enough for me, Sidney. A blessing on your house."

Klepner could only nod, choking back his emotions. Michael believed him implicitly. "Let's watch that disc," he said.

Klepner keyed it up and the monitor rezzed into a fairly good picture of Isabella Mussina dressed in a white lab coat sitting across from a ruggedly handsome man in casual clothing. They began talking and everyone in the room became transfixed by what followed.

An hour later, after listening to the story of Hirsh Dukor, The Little Angel of Death, and witnessing the daring abduction of Isabella, no one could speak as the screen went dark. The silence extended for several minutes as everyone tried to assimilate what they had seen, what they had heard. Looking around the room, Michael noticed that everyone was looking at him, waiting for his response.

"It's all connected, isn't it?" he said softly, as he gestured toward the mountains of paper on the table. "A lot of these people have been dreaming about Nichols . . . or Dukor . . . whatever we want to call him."

"Incredible," said Irwin. "Absolutely incredible. And yet very sensible when you think about it."

"What do you mean?" said Pamela, her complexion ashen as she recovered from the horrors of the video.

"Well," said Irwin, "think about it: it would be unwise to assume that *everyone* gathered up in the Nazi net was good and pure and virtuous."

"Good point," said Klepner. "There're rotten apples everywhere . . ."

"Yes," said Irwin. "And we have certainly found ourselves a monster, haven't we?"

"We need to decide if this new information changes our thinking about the seminar," said Michael.

"What seminar?" said Klepner.

Pamela and Klingerman gave the agent a summary of their plans.

He shook his head, looked around the table. "I don't know if that's such a hot idea. If Nichols is hunting down your subjects—and it sure looks like he *is*—then gathering them together might be really risky. Crazy, even."

"I've been thinking about that myself," said Michael. "We're going to have to weigh all the variables and give the whole plan more thought."

"I think my agency's been dropping the ball, by the way," said Klepner.

"In what way?" said Michael.

"I think we should have been sharing information on this case from the beginning." Klepner ejected the disc from the deck, replaced it in its case.

"Well, let's not forget," said Michael, "none of us have been dealing with information or real evidence that could be considered 'normal.' I mean, a lot of what we've discovered is *very* hard to believe."

"Maybe, but it's all we've got," said Klepner.

"That's not true," said a slightly familiar voice coming from behind them, at the door to the office. "I'd say you've *also* got yourselves a lot of trouble."

Turning to face the speaker, Michael was shocked to see Agent Bradley Stevenson, resplendent in his obligatory dark suit and plain tie. He was holding a gun in his hand.

TWENTY-SEVEN

BRADLEY STEVENSON
Manhattan, New York

The expressions of surprise and shock on all their faces amused him. Not that there was anything funny about what was going on, but he knew they wouldn't be expecting him, especially Agent Klepner. Brad looked quickly around the room and, convinced the area was secure, hosltered his sidearm.

"Do you always walk onto private property, uninvited, with your gun out?" said Dr. Keating. "Or is this an arrest?"

"Not exactly," said Brad, looking at Klepner. "But it *could* be if I wanted to ring up my agent on charges of stealing government property, sedition against the United States, and a slew of bureau policy violations . . . and all of you as accessories to the fact."

"But you don't want to do that?" said Pamela.

"Not really," said Brad, moving toward an empty chair at the conference table. "Mind if I sit down?"

Michael nodded, pointed at the chair.

"I'm sorry, sir," said Klepner. "I can explain—"

"I know you can," said Brad. "Relax, and listen to me . . . everybody."

Brad summarized Nichols' murder of Martha Pasek, including

the appearance of a death-camp tattoo on her arm. Everyone listened with a stunned expression. "That's why I came in here with my gun drawn, by the way. If Nichols knows about your research and your own patients, this might be one of the first places he'll come to look for more victims."

"So what do you propose?" asked Irwin.

"I'm not sure," said Brad, looking at the overweight rabbi. With the beard and the cheap suit, he looked like every other orthodox Jew he'd ever seen. Not that he was prejudiced or anything, it was just that, man, they all really *did* look the same. "But I think it's time we had a long talk, shared all the information we have, and try to come up with a unified plan. That's why it was ultimately a good thing that Klepner let you see the videodisc. I was going to do it anyway."

"Thank you, sir," said Klepner.

Brad waved an index finger at him. "Don't think you're not still twisting in the wind with me, Sid. You went off the chart, and we need to talk about it privately. But it'll wait for now."

"Yessir."

Brad invited everyone's participation, and while it took a few minutes for them to feel comfortable, the rational ideas and the emotional responses started to break loose fairly quickly. After about an hour with the group, Brad was convinced he'd made the right decision to bring them into the loop. They were intelligent, dedicated, and well disciplined. Their files and organization were impressive. Dr. Keating was obviously well-spoken and refined, as was his assistant, Ms. Robbins. He liked both of them almost from the start, and as he observed their continued interaction and body language, Brad suspected the two of them were a sexual item. He was usually pretty good at spotting that kind of thing. Klingerman was also likeable in spite of his less-than-fastidious appearance and mildly irritating mannerisms. He talked too loudly, tended to spray his words with minidroplets of spittle when he became excited (which was most of the time), and waved his arms around a lot. Brad had a feeling he was not exactly enjoyable to watch at the dinner table. But Klingerman had a good heart, you could tell right away, and he believed fervently in the importance of his work.

The only thing about the group that bothered him, and not in a negative way, was the suggestion of mysticism at work. Bradley had already admitted the existence of supernatural elements in the case, and definite paranormal manifestations, and he could live with them because he had to—plus, he'd worked with psychics on cases in the past, and he'd known bureau guys who'd liaisoned with the CIA's "far-seeing" operations. But some of Dr. Mussina's notes, and some of the references made by Klingerman, and even Ms. Robbins, implied some kind of cosmic forces at work . . . and that's where Brad was having trouble staying connected. He was basically an uncomplicated guy—his detective work balanced out by a little fishing and hunting on the Eastern Shore and he was happy.

Not much room for karma and ying/yang stuff in that kind of world.

When Klepner volunteered Klingerman's idea to convene a "seminar" of death-camp trauma patients, Brad found the idea an intriguing one and filed it away for later use. It was a card he might play when things got more dicey.

And he was counting on them getting that way.

His main objective was to catch this guy Nichols, or Dukor, or whoever the fuck he was, and Brad had decided he would do whatever was needed to take Nichols out of the game. There was no sense impressing on these people how desperate the bureau and the CIA were feeling, or how resolute they were to rid themselves of the embarassment Nichols represented.

With the arrival of a delivery boy, they took a break for some coffee and pastries from a shop near Columbus Circle, and while they were spreading out their cups and napkins at the table, Dr. Keating hit Brad up with several unexpected questions:

"You never told us Doctor Mussina's condition—how is she?"

Brad nodded. "I had a feeling Sid might have told you she's still alive."

Klepner flushed a few shades redder, but said nothing.

Brad shrugged. "Hard to say. She's recovering from a pretty severe gunshot wound. Still in a coma last I heard."

"What are her chances?"

"Of surviving like she is? —or coming out of it?"

"Coming out of it."

"Better than fifty-fifty, they told me," said Brad. "But not a lot better than that."

"I think I'd . . . I'd like to see her," said Keating in a very soft voice. The others were gathered at the opposite end of the large table chatting and not paying attention.

"Really?" Brad was genuinely surprised by the request. "What for?"

"I'm not sure," said Keating. "I've spent so much time immersed in her work, I guess I feel like I know her."

"Hmmm," said Brad. "Well, I don't know . . . that's not really my bailiwick, as they say. Clearance would have to come from somebody else, some other agency."

"Is there anything you can do?"

Brad grinned, shook his head. "Officially, you're not even supposed to know she's alive. Even your friends in Justice and Congress couldn't get that info."

Keating nodded. "I was wondering if you guys knew that was me. You know, getting them to poke around."

"Oh yeah."

"Well, what can you do?"

"I'll see. But you've given me another idea."

"Really? What?"

"You'll see," said Brad.

He called for everybody's attention, then started talking.

"I've got something . . ." he said slowly, drawing them in, "and I'd like to know what you think about it."

"Okay," said Klingerman.

Klepner looked at him with open suspicion, but said nothing.

"I think you should go forward with the seminar idea. I think I can get the bureau to cover the expenses."

Everyone exchanged glances, and he could read the tacit approval in their faces. Yeah, thought Brad, it was real fashionable to knock government spending, but as soon as people thought that endless money machine was going to kick some cash *their* way, they changed their attitudes in a hurry.

"I thought you said it could be dangerous?" said Pamela, who was standing at the end of the table, hands on hips. She looked good in the jeans, and Brad was thinking that if the doc was tapping her, he was having a good time of it.

"Normally it would, but if my people are involved from the start, we can pretty much guarantee everyone's safety."

"No offense, Mr. Stevenson," said Ms. Robbins, "but in the wake of your bureau's recent history, from the Butte Riot all the way back to Ruby Ridge and Waco, I'm not sure that many people would feel very good about their safety being guaranteed by the FBI. . . ."

The past few years had taught Brad to ignore statements like that. He looked at her, but said nothing.

"You want to use the seminar to—how would you say it?—bait the trap?" said Keating. His tone of voice didn't betray how he felt about it, so Brad had to play this one out carefully.

"Not really. But I think if we leak the story to a few key media points where we have friendly correspondents, we could be pretty damned sure to get Nichols' attention."

"I don't think that's the main reason we want to bring these people together," said Keating.

"I agree," said Klingerman.

Brad nodded as though he were thoughtfully considering their opinions. What none of them realized was that his people would set up a seminar whether they approved or not. If the bureau believed it was the best way to catch Nichols, then they'd make it happen. End of story.

"Yes, I understand," said Brad, "but it would give you the perfect opportunity to completely understand what this whole phenomenon *means*, what it portends . . ."

"That's true," said Keating. "I don't know . . . maybe we should talk about it."

"Why don't you take a few days," said Brad. "I'm sure it's going to take my people at least that much time to analyze all the data you've provided."

Keating nodded. "Yes, I think we definitely need to talk about it. I think we should contact some of the subjects and see how they feel about coming to New York."

"That brings up an interesting ethical question," said Klingerman. "Do we tell these poor people their lives may be in danger?"

"I would advise against it," said Brad. "We have no way of verifying that. I don't see any reason why you would want to scare people."

"Scare them or save their lives?" said Robbins.

Brad shrugged. "I think it all depends on how you look at it, don't you, Agent Klepner?"

Klepner said nothing, but continued to regard Brad with a cold eye. Not surprising. Klepner knew how the bureau operated, knew what was being implied here.

Brad wrapped things up with a few platitudes and requested Klepner to accompany him back to the Manhattan offices at Federal Plaza. He didn't plan to do anything to the field agent other than a wrist-slap in his personnel jacket, but letting Klepner sweat a little longer would never hurt him.

When they'd exited the offices and had entered the elevator, Klepner faced him down.

"You're going to use them," he said.

Brad smiled. "I *have* to. The situation is perfect, and I think everything points to Nichols targeting these patients—and anybody else like them. Do you know I did some follow-ups on Nichols' hits in Europe and South America—and guess what? *Every one* of his victims had reported Holocaust nightmares, visions, and that kind of crap."

"It's not crap," said Klepner, his voice edged with what could only be described as a newfound dignity.

"You know what I mean," said Brad. "It's obvious we've found the key. We've got the way to get him."

"You've got to tell them what you're going to do."

The elevator exited into the lobby, and they continued talking as they walked to the street where Brad's sedan waited with a parking ticket under its wiper blade.

"Maybe I won't have to," said Brad. "If we're lucky, we can convince them to get those people together anyway."

"And if we're not so lucky?" Klepner stood by the shotgun door, waiting for his superior to unlock it.

"Then we make a few adjustments," said Brad. He slipped in behind the wheel, keyed the ignition, let Klepner in, then looked him in the eye. "But I'm telling you right now, Mr. Klepner—"

"I know," said the field agent, putting up his hands in mock surrender. "I've heard this one before: 'remember who writes your paycheck,' right?"

Brad chuckled as he pulled the car away from the curb with a sharp acceleration. "Actually I was thinking of something more like: If you try to fuck this up, I'll have to kill you. . . ."

TWENTY-EIGHT

J. MICHAEL KEATING, M.D.
Bethesda, Maryland

Doctor Keating?" said the woman in the white navy uniform. She had suddenly appeared in front of him as he sat in the physician's lounge on the fifth floor of the naval hospital.

"Yes," he said, looking up from a magazine he'd been browsing absently.

"I'm Ensign Vandermeer," said the woman. She had severely cut short hair, broad shoulders, and a tight, thin-lipped mouth. "You're here to see one of our patients—Doctor Mussina."

"That's right," he said. "It was by special arrangement with—"

"This way, Doctor," said the ensign, who turned crisply to exit the lounge and began striding down an antiseptically polished corridor. It was quite clear she didn't care how or why he was here, and that was just fine with Michael. Having missed an "opportunity" to serve in the military, he'd always exercised a healthy caution around its members. While acknowledging the need for excessively trained soldiers and sailors, Michael understood the human psyche well enough to know that military people were never really happy unless they were fulfilling the purpose of their training, their raison d'être, which was, of course, to wage war.

And when they couldn't do it, they tended to get a little cranky.

As he followed her down the hall to a private room, he realized he'd been anticipating this moment.

Isabella Mussina had been such a complete and total *victim* in all the events vortexing around her, Michael felt terribly sorry for her. The dedication and the poetry of her work had shone through every page of her meticulous documentation, and the imprint of her compassion for her patients was an undeniable presence in everything she did.

Ensign Vandermeer stopped at the last door on the right, pushed it open, and held it for him until he passed, then silently removed herself to the corridor. Upon entering the room, the first thing he noticed was the way the light slipped through half-opened blinds in autumn-orange shafts. The room felt warm, inviting, despite the presence of the bone-white walls and bedclothing, the stark plinths of the vital signs monitors. With each step closer to the bed, Michael grew more unsettled. The form beneath the sheets looked small and frail, and the woman's face was so pale. With folded hands on her chest, she looked like the ubiquitous Catholic saint in stately repose, and he had a fleeting memory from his childhood of Mass cards the nuns had given him with pictures of the first candidate for sainthood in the United States—a woman they called Mother Seaton.

But this was surely no scene from Sleeping Beauty. Tubes were running in and out of her. While her monitored life-signs appeared sound and strong, she had not yet regained consciousness, and he knew that each passing day reduced ever further the chances of that happening. Michael edged to the bedside and looked at her.

She had stared into the face of the monster, had fallen under the cold aspect of a beast calling itself an angel. What had it been like for her? he wondered. How had she kept from withering under that terrible breath of corruption and evil? She had seemed so strong, so assured and in control during most of the video session he'd watched, it was tough for him to imagine her being scared or helpless.

Maybe she wasn't.

It was possible Mussina held the key to everything, the single unknowable fact or proof or aspect of Dukor that could bring him down. It was an idea Michael wanted to believe, needed to believe.

She might know his weakness.

She *had* to . . .

"Hello, Isabella," said Michael. "If you can hear me . . . I'm a friend of Irwin Klingerman."

He stood watching her eyelids, long-lashed and unmoving, as though some abrupt movement might indicate a sign of understanding. Where did we go in the coma state? The question burst through him, and he imagined her knifing through a dark and timeless sea, leaning forward like the figurehead on a frigate. In that single moment, he felt an overwhelming need to be with her, wherever she was, if for no better reason than to tell her he *was* with her and everything would eventually be okay.

It was a silly notion, but it made him feel good as he found himself smiling at her.

"You don't know me," he said softly, "but I need your help. I need your strength and your insight."

He paused, watching her for any sign of recognition. Seeing nothing, he continued, compelled to do so. "I need to know about Nichols. I need to know everything you know about him. So I can stop him. So *you* can stop him."

Reaching out, he took one of her hands, relieved to feel her body's warmth radiating there. Squeezing it, he spoke in a loud clear voice. "Come back, Isabella. Come back and help us. My name is Michael. And I need your help. Squeeze my hand if you can hear me."

He stood, unmoving, holding her hand in a firm grip, waiting for a reaction.

Even the slightest pressure would have sent his heart soaring, but there was nothing. No sign. He was still standing there, holding her hand, when a young nurse entered the room with a refill bag for Isabella's IV.

"Hello, Doctor," she said. "I'll only be a minute."

Michael smiled at her as she quickly disengaged the almost empty plastic bag, slipped the new one into place. "Have you been taking care of this patient since she got here?"

"Yes," said the young woman. She had red hair and lots of freckles.

"You've been taking good care of her," he said.

"Oh, yes, Doctor. Thank you."

"I want you to do me a favor," said Michael, reaching into his pocket for his wallet. He gave her a business card. "I want you to promise to call me immediately if she ever gives you any sign. Any movement, a blink, a hand squeeze, whatever. Will you do that?"

"I promise," she said.

"You can call me at any of those numbers. *Any* time, day or night, okay?"

Michael watched the nurse nod, then return to her task.

He felt very helpless standing there. It was time to leave.

PART FOUR

NIGHT OF
BROKEN SOULS

TWENTY-NINE

TAMARA KEURAJIAN
Brooklyn, New York

One month later.

Her intercom buzzed while she was in the kitchen, fixing a Stouffers vegetarian lasagna. Somebody wanting to bug her. . . .

God, she *hated* to have her privacy invaded once she reached the supposedly safe shores of her own home. Reluctantly, she keyed the speaker switch.

"Yes?"

"Sorry to bother you, Ms. Keurajian, it's Billy—I've got a Federal Express delivery down here for you."

"Thanks," Tamara said to her faithful doorman. "Can you just sign for it? And I'll pick it up the next time I'm down there."

"I tried to do that, but the driver said he ain't got no waiver. Sez *you* gotta sign in person."

Tamara exhaled in exasperation. "All right, tell him I'll be right down."

What now? It was always *something* with her job, and even though she usually thrived on the pressure of deadlines and grand expectations, some days left her totally exhausted, disgusted, and just completely used up. Today had been a day like that, and all she wanted was a chance to retreat into the cocoon of her Brooklyn Heights apartment. A microwave dinner, a couple of glasses of Sutter Home, a movie from Blockbuster. And the hell with everybody.

But not yet, apparently. She entered the elevator to the lobby, signed for the FedEx letter pack, and opened it on the way up. It was from Brad Stevenson—a name she knew very well, and had to respect, in spite of his sometimes abrasive personality. He was one of those inside-the-beltway, career Washingtonians who'd been drunk on the power so long, he had no idea what the rest of the country did for kicks.

But . . .

His well-timed leaks of upcoming events in the national arena *had* provided her with great stories. Newsbreaking stuff that had vaulted her over more seasoned writers at *Time*, placing her in the first rank of respected journalists, and landing her a salary so comfortable she'd been able to put a lot of money in the bank *despite* living and working in New York.

All because she'd happened to date Stevenson's younger brother when they were both in graduate school at Boston College . . . which gave some credence to that old aphorism about "who you know or who you blow."

And so, yeah, even though she was dog-tired, and never really liked Stevenson, she was excited to see something he'd thought was so important he sent it by overnight delivery. She knew it would be very sensitive material for Stevenson to avoid using phone, fax, or e-mail. These days, using electronic encryption only served to call attention to yourself, Stevenson had warned. Anybody using the PGP was assumed to be a criminal. End, as they say, of story.

Exiting the elevator and reaching the privacy of her apartment, Tamara opened the letter pack and read a fascinating summary of what Stevenson called "past-life Holocaust trauma." She read abstracts of the work and discoveries of Dr. Isabella Mussina, Rabbi Irwin Klingerman, and Dr. J. Michael Keating; she read a bureau briefing that detailed a seminar to be held in Manhattan, in which thirty-two trauma subjects would share their experiences in an effort to determine the significance and meaning of the suddenly appearing phenomenon. Publicity on the event, it was hoped, might encourage other people who had experienced the phenomenon to come forward. This last point was very important to the researchers, who wanted to confirm their suspicion that most Holocaust trauma cases occurred *after* the 1991 reunification of Germany.

Interesting stuff, she thought as she shuffled through the remainder of the package, which included bio and biblio information on the seminar organizers, times, dates, locations, and a contact sheet on how to reach everyone for interviews. As was usually the case, she had no way of connecting the story she was "encouraged" to promote to whatever secret agenda the government enforcement agencies might be following.

But sometimes, when she lay awake at night, unable to sleep, and not knowing why, those thorny, ethical considerations and nagging questions of social responsibility would gnaw at the edges of her thoughts. Most of the time, she tried not to think about what her story splashes might be doing behind the scenes, about what takeovers, coups, assassinations, or *worse* might be gathering momentum because of her tweaks and tinkerings with the information machine.

At least this latest data package exhibited some unique elements.

Stevenson had no way of knowing it, but Tamara had always had an interest in the paranormal, ever since she'd been around fifteen and picked up a book called *The Sleeping Prophet*, about a guy named Edgar Cayce. So this business about hypnosis and past-life regression and reincarnation was all a refreshing change of pace from the endless grind of the national political machinery where facts and ideas remained true only until the results of the next poll.

The nations of the world were being dragged kicking and screaming into the next millennium because they wanted to cling to social and economic strategies and policies that had been long ago outstripped by a technology that changed ever and ever faster. As a journalist, Tamara had grasped this principle early on in the game, and the truth of it had helped her deal with the dynamic, always mutable aspect of national and international relations on a technology-driven globe. There were so many hot spots, so many places where catastrophe could occur, it was hard for writers and their editor-bosses to project the source of next week's interest point.

And that was the name of the game in the media arena: get your story on the pages and covers and screens of the world *before* everybody else; get your story in everybody's face the *exact moment* they've become fascinated or interested in it. Impossible? Maybe, but her media empire bosses prided themselves on attempting and usually achieving the impossible every week.

Right, she thought. At the expense of a lot of migraines and ulcers and coronaries.

But Tamara had no valid basis for complaint, and she knew it. Being a journalist was what she'd wanted to do since entering college. She placed that priority in the number one slot, ahead of family, relationships, or any of the other traditional goals of ambitious people. There was plenty of time to find a suitable husband and have the baby that was starting to become a more important consideration with each passing month. Still, she had no regrets. To have sailed to the top of her profession in less than ten years had been a feat few could equal. She knew she was good, even if she *did* have a private pipeline to a lot of inside information.

Carefully replacing all the printouts in the FedEx envelope and leaving it on the table, Tamara returned to the kitchen and her microwave lasagna. So forget about Blockbuster. And easy on the wine. It was going to be a long night at the keyboard.

THIRTY

ARNOLD RASSENAULT
Manhattan, New York

The next issue of the *Journal of Progressive History* lay spread across his worktable in hard-copy pages. Arnold was supposed to be proofing it one last time before fine-tuning it on the screen of an old Power Mac, but his heart wasn't really in it. For the last six weeks, ever since he'd been "adopted" by Harford Nichols, Arnold had been forced to look at the world through the lenses he'd been so carefully grinding for the last forty-five years.

And he wasn't so sure he liked what he saw.

Arnold felt so tired, so overwhelmed by everything that was happening around him. He had nothing left. No drive. No energy. Only a terrible uncertainty that seemed to be sapping him. Checking his watch, he saw how late the afternoon had become and decided to quit for the day . . .

. . . and do *what*?

The idea struck him that he had no life other than this miserable little rag of a magazine that nobody ever read anyhow. And now, the arrival of Nichols had begun to even render the importance of his *Journal* null and void. Nichols had informed them that the time of talking and writing had ended; it was time for action. And to that end Nichols had conscripted Fritz Hargrove into a conditioning and training regimen. Fritz had responded with enthusiasm and had already started to lose some of the flabby bulk that had defined him for so many years.

And that wild, improbable story of Hirsh Dukor reborn in Nichols had begun to sound believable to Fritz—especially when he thought of the possibility of *other* Reich figures being reincarnated as well.

All we have to do is find *them.* That's what Nichols had said. Find them entombed in the uninspired husks of ordinary humans.

And when Arnold had first imagined the scenario of finding the trapped spirits of those great men, waiting for their glorious rebirths, he saw himself as an anointed angel, touched with a special mission.

But now he was not so certain it was a good thing.

Because Harford Nichols *scared* him.

And what he was doing to Fritz scared him even more. Poor Hargrove. The big guy had always been a kind of malleable, hapless kind of fellow who never seemed to have much luck in his life. One of those people who met defeat, no matter what he attempted. And so, he had kind of slogged through life like a man walking through thick mud.

His shining moment had been a brief stint in the public eye as a Holocaust denial "expert" when Arnold's *Journal* had sponsored his "inspection tour" of the Auschwitz death-camp machinery. The trip had been an attempt to explain away the ovens by a "thermal engineer" who theorized the installation was a prototype German energy experiment. When the media unmasked Fritz as a steam-fitter with no engineering experience, degrees, or job titles, his fifteen minutes of fame had become a nightmare of derision and embarrassment.

The incident left a mark on Fritz as if from a branding iron. His hatred of the Zionist-controlled media seethed, and he'd vowed his revenge.

And now he was learning how he might exact it.

The downstairs door opened and, as if on cue, Arnold heard the heavy footfalls of Fritz Hargrove ascending toward the offices. It was a familiar sound, one that Arnold had grown to recognize auto-matically, but now he noticed something new, something different in it. The usual leaden drop of each shoe had been replaced by a hard, lively cadence, as though Fritz were leaning forward, attacking each step.

And then he was there, bursting into the room wearing a black sweatshirt stenciled with the letters B.U.M. across the front and a pair of matching sweatpants. A nylon backpack, looking small, stretched across his broad shoulders. He stood tall and rigid as he extended a salute.

"*Heil Hitler*, Professor!"

"Hello, Fritz," said Arnold with a studied weariness. "What brings you here so early? I thought you were going to be with Nichols all day?"

"Change of plans," said Fritz. "Haven't you seen the news?"

"No, what're you talking about?"

Unshouldering his pack, Fritz unzipped it to pull out a *Time* magazine. "Look at this!" he said excitedly. "It just hit the stands this morning, and look at this!"

"What . . . ?" said Arnold, adjusting his glasses as Fritz flipped through the pages with his sausage-thick fingers. He stopped as he came to a two-page spread entitled *Reliving the Horror of the Holocaust*. There were individual pictures of people identified as a psychiatrist, a psychologist, and a rabbi, plus a group shot of perhaps twelve to fourteen other people. The article detailed a seminar being held at Koch Conference Center on Park Avenue South, bringing in subjects who claimed to be reincarnated victims of Nazi death camps. The article went on in great detail, but Arnold had seen all he needed for the moment.

For a second or two he felt dizzy, his bowels twisting, knotting.

"Oh my God . . ." said Arnold. "This is incredible."

"It's a sign!" said Fritz in a booming voice. "Can you believe it?"

"This is exactly what Nichols was talking about. It's really happening, isn't it?" Arnold let the magazine drift downward to his lap. All that talk about having lived before. All the things he said . . . could they really be true?

"Could *what* be true?" said Fritz.

Arnold realized he'd been speaking his thoughts aloud. A habit growing more pronounced as he grew ever older. How much had he said?

"Oh, what . . . ?" said Arnold. "I was just thinking out loud."

Then, holding up the magazine, he looked into the eyes of Fritz Hargrove, where something dark lurched with every blink. "What did Nichols say about this?"

Fritz smiled. "He said they were making it too easy for him."

"What does that mean?"

Fritz shrugged. "Search me. But I'm sure he'll come up with something."

I'm sure he will, thought Arnold. "Where is he now?"

"He rented a U-Haul van so he could go over to Jersey."

"Jersey? What for, did he tell you?"

Fritz nodded and smiled that silly schoolboy grin. "Yeah, he said he had to buy some fertilizer."

THIRTY-ONE

J. MICHAEL KEATING, M.D.
Manhattan, New York

The Koch Conference Center on Park Avenue had been a recent addition to the high-rent architectural neighborhood of midtown. Michael would have never chosen it for the site of their conference, but Brad Stevenson liked it because of its distinctive design: lots of open spaces, skylights, clerestory windows, and window-walls. Even the seminar rooms had been designed with as few partitions, closets, or other dividers as possible.

"No nooks and crannies," Sid Klepner had told him. That meant it would be very difficult for Nichols to surprise them. No places to hide when the building closed, no places to plant monitoring or explosive devices. No laundry chutes, ventilation shafts, catwalks, or any other oddities from which a clandestine operation could be launched. It also had five floors of hotel space so that participants would never have to leave the premises—which was exactly what the FBI agents preferred.

The idea, Stevenson had explained to everyone, was to present a target for Nichols that would be too desirable to pass up, but also present him with a series of very difficult attack options—all equally challenging. Given the parameters they'd established, Nichols would be hard-pressed to create a successful plan.

Or so they said.

Michael and Pamela had never been convinced of the inherent safety of the operation, despite lengthy meetings and brain-storming sessions where they attempted to cover all the possibilities. In fact, the only reason Michael agreed to the seminar operation was the hopelessness of keeping it from happening. Klepner secretly confided to him that his boss was going to make the seminar happen—with their consent and assistance or *without* it. Realizing this had made Michael's decision to participate all that much easier.

He hadn't said any of this to Stevenson, of course, and had allowed the FBI chief to go through the charade of offering Michael a chance to see Isabella Mussina in exchange for his imprimatur and participation in the seminar. Her condition remained unchanged, but Michael continued to be committed to her recovery. He still believed there was a special significance to her coming out of that coma.

But that was for a time in the future. There was a more pressing issue at hand. And it was time to put all the theorizing and suppo-sitions on the line. Time to put up or shut up, as Stevenson had said at their final briefing. At that last meeting the FBI man warned Michael and Klingerman: they were not to let their subjects know *anything* about any possible danger. Klingerman had reacted pretty strongly to that one, and even called the policy something right out of an old Nazi handbook.

What the rabbi had never really grasped was that the FBI did not give a damn about the whole past-life trauma phenomenon. Stevenson and his people were plainly not interested in what the death-camp memories might actually mean or portend. The agents could only concern themselves with the stark reality of Harford Nichols as a very dangerous enemy. They had dedicated themselves to finding their rogue colleague and destroying him. It was also interesting that they continued to call their target *Nichols,* even though it was quite clear that the person known as Harford Nichols had been supplanted by a separate entity calling itself Hirsh Dukor.

A thorny issue the pragmatic FBI agents chose to ignore—or at least not talk about.

Michael had been discussing this and some of the possibilities with Pamela as they had dinner at an Italian restaurant called Nanni's.

"Irwin is very nervous about all this," said Pamela. "He called the office just as I was leaving. He said he'll meet us at the Koch Center by 8:15, but he kept saying he has a 'very bad feeling' about this weekend."

"I think we all do," said Michael. "There's no turning back now. But that's not the only thing Klingerman's right about. . . ."

"What?" she said.

"We've gotten so hung up in Stevenson's mania to catch Nichols, we've almost been convinced that's the *only* reason we assembled this seminar." Michael looked at his linguine *fra diablo* with little real interest. Anxiety had curbed his appetite. "We can't forget about the people who traveled all the way here—because they believe we can help them."

Pamela chuckled softly. "*Can* we help them?"

"I don't know. But we have to keep focused this weekend. We have to block out this whole spy-versus-spy routine and pay attention to our patients."

Pamela leaned forward and touched his hand briefly, a small signal of intimacy that spoke of understanding and commitment. Then she settled back in her chair and stared off into the distance for a moment. "You know," she said finally, "maybe we should redefine the object of this seminar. . . ."

"In what way?"

Leaning forward, Pamela focused her gaze on him. "Maybe we should not try to think of 'curing' the subjects, or 'helping' them, as much as trying to figure out *why* this phenomenon is happening."

"Even though we implied we were going to help them?"

"Yes," she said emphatically.

He'd been thinking similar thoughts, and he paused as he considered his answer. "You're right. It's just too weird. I mean, it took me awhile to face it, to accept it was really happening, but now that I do, I feel *worse*, not better."

"I know the feeling."

"And consider this," he said. "With the appearance of Dukor, Mengele's 'Little Angel,' we have evidence of something nobody seems very willing to talk about—that it's not just the 'good guys' being reincarnated since Germany reunited."

Pamela's expression did not change, and her lack of reaction confirmed his feeling that she'd been thinking about this other facet, too. "I know what you mean," she said. "I guess the idea's been floating around in my mind for awhile now, but I didn't want to be the one to suggest that maybe we've got, well, you know, maybe—"

"Maybe there's plenty of other people out there walking around with the reincarnated spirits of the whole Nazi gang," said Michael in a half-whisper. "All of them. Himmler. Goebbels, even *Hitler*. . . ."

"It's hard to imagine," said Pamela.

"But we *did*, didn't we?" Michael took a sip of his wine. "So that means it could be happening. Jesus, how would we ever discover such a thing?"

"Maybe we're jumping to conclusions," said Pamela. "Wouldn't there be evidence of the Nazis being reborn—in the psychiatric files—just like with their victims?"

Michael thought about this. "Logic suggests it, doesn't it? But maybe that's not the way it works. God knows, there hasn't much been happening so far that could really be called *logical*."

"You mean maybe it's only happening to the 'good guys'?"

"Well," said Michael. "We know that's not true. We've got Hirsh Dukor, remember?"

"Right, so why haven't we found more like him in the literature?"

Michael thought about this. Good question, but he didn't like the answers that suggested themselves. "Well, let's see . . . I can think of two possibilities: either the subjects are all like Nichols— they're getting 'taken over' by the reincarnated spirit—or they are all too scared to admit what's happening to them."

Pamela nodded slowly as she thought about it. "So what are the chances of everybody remaining silent? Nobody cracking, nobody telling anybody *anything*?"

Michael shrugged. "I don't know, but I'd say the chances are somewhere between slim and none."

"Meaning what?"

"Meaning that maybe we've got a secondary phenomenon, a potentially dangerous one, and *absolutely no way* of discovering it." The very idea of such a thing sent a chill through him. Michael could not begin to try to explain the gist of their conversation to the authorities such as Stevenson and his people, but even worse was that they wouldn't give a damn anyway.

"You know," said Pamela, after a lull in their exchange of ideas, "there's something else that ties in with all this. . . ."

"What's that?"

She tried to smile, and failed. "It's complicated."

"As most things worth anything usually are. Go on. I'm listening."

She looked at her watch. "It's getting late. We have to meet Klingerman at the center. And you have to address the subjects again at nine."

"I know, I know. We have a few minutes, just give me the highlights."

She shook her head. "More like *low*lights . . . but okay, listen. I think that . . . *something* . . . I'm not sure what to call it—karma, the fates, the earth itself . . . I don't know—is responding to what's going on in the world."

"In what way?"

Pamela paused, then continued: "Well, you how they say nature abhors a vacuum? How it will send in anything to fill it?"

Michael nodded. He had an idea where she might be going with this, but he kept silent.

"Okay," said Pamela. "I think things might be a lot worse than we think in the world. Maybe the economic disasters, the recessions, and market crashes of the last few years—you know, in Japan, Germany, England, here—maybe they *are* what some of the doomsayers are saying: just temblors before the Big One, the worldwide collapse of money, trade, investments, everything. I mean think about it: everybody and every country has spent into the red for so long that the bubbles are starting to burst. Maybe this is an orchestrated thing?"

"How so?" said Michael. He loved listening to her when she slipped into pure analytical mode. Her observational skills were keenly focused in financial matters, and she'd made studying the economic arena a passionate hobby, but filtering it through the politics of a classical libertarian. He loved listening to her theories, although he knew it was tough to stop her once she got wound up.

"Well," she said, "look at what's been happening. Mergers and takeovers and nationalizations of things like pension funds, health insurance, savings banks. An avalanche of new federal regulations. Always new attempts to control what is euphemistically still called 'free enterprise.' It's starting to look like it's all part of some big plan to create the Super Global Village."

"Where everybody's part of the same machinery," said Michael.

"Oh, yeah," said Pamela. "More specifically, a time and a place where *everybody* works for the government. And not their own national governments, but some kind of monolithic, One World scenario. A kind of UN gone wild, where central control starts steamrollering pesky ideas like personal freedom or individual achievement."

"You're starting to sound very scary," he said.

"I hope so. This is scary stuff."

"It's hard to believe something like this is even possible—in the 'land of the free.'"

"And that's the key," said Pamela. "The personal freedom thing. Sooner or later, we get a movement or a rebel group that's had enough, Michael. And what are we looking at?"

"Revolution," he said.

"Of course," said Pamela. "That's precisely why the government doesn't like private militias—people who are free and have a means to protect their freedom."

Michael nodded. "They're considered dangerous."

"That's why the power-elite goes out of their way to brand them as kooks or racists or white supremacists. Labels that make the average citizen see red, that keep him from investigating any further."

"*Argumentum ad hominem,*" said Michael, bringing to mind the most effective totalitarian smear and propaganda tactic. "From the folks who brought you Dachau . . ."

"But the one problem the world bosses can never get around is that there's *always* going to be more of the common rabble around than them."

"And sooner or later," said Michael, having heard this idea from her previously, "the corruption gets too pervasive and the bosses too arrogant, and the commoners, the workers, get too pissed off, right?"

"And if things get completely intolerable—like they could real soon—then we have a situation that screams, Michael, *screams* for a savior, somebody who can give them back what's been stolen from them. Their money. Their dignity. And everything in between."

Michael smiled sardonically. "Sound familiar?"

"Sure," she said. "Europe in the thirties. Germany under oppressive European controls and murderous inflation. Or America today."

"You're good," said Michael. "You should teach college."

"Really?" Pamela grinned. "I admit I've thought about it."

"Students need to get passionate about something, and you could get them jump-started."

"Thanks," she said. "But I already have a job. Something a lot of people *don't* have, or are scared of losing."

"Good jobs are hard to find, sure," he said. "But hasn't it always been that way?"

"I don't think it's been this bad in a long time," said Pamela. "Regular working people are taxed to death—more than sixty percent of their earnings are paid out as some kind of tax."

"Christ, is it *that* much?" Michael shook his head.

"Maybe more. I haven't done the math lately."

"I'm sorry," he said, only trying to be half serious. "But where is this conversation going? I think I lost the thread."

"C'mon, Michael, you purposely got me talking about this stuff. You *know* it's one of those things I feel very strongly about," she said. "Are you trying to upset me?"

"Of course not! I was just trying to lighten things up a little. You're making things sound pretty damned grim."

"That's because they are!" she said a little too loudly. Other patrons turned at their tables to look at her, but she ignored them. "Listen Michael, people are getting pushed to the wall. They've had it."

"I know what you mean," he said sincerely. "You've said it before: they're sick of seeing money they've earned by being productive taken from them by the government and given to people who are completely unproductive."

"Well, *thank* you!" she said. "You *have* been listening to me."

"I always listen to you," he assured her, then sipped from his wineglass.

"So do you believe me when I tell you the world's ripe for a radical new hero?"

"Unfortunately, yes, I do."

"Why do you qualify your 'yes'? Your belief isn't going to make it any less possible."

He shrugged. "Force of habit. But what does this mean? What can we really do about it?"

"I think we should use the chance we have this weekend to see what our subjects might know about it."

Michael nodded. "Good idea. If there *are* bad guys out there, our subjects might be 'keying' on them—like they did with Dukor."

"That's right," said Pamela. "I think what all this points out is that we have to be vigilant and be prepared to warn the world what might be coming."

"That's going to be a tall order. I don't think people care that much anymore."

Pamela frowned. "Then we'll have to *make* them care."

Michael said nothing as he signaled for their check. It was time to go meet some people who'd been dead for more than half a century.

THIRTY-TWO

DER KLEIN ENGEL
Manhattan, New York

The clock is ticking, Mr. Hargrove," said Dukor. "You will drive to the corner of Forty-fourth and Park and start the mission."

"Yessir," said Fritz, who had been driving the Voyager minivan south on Fifth Avenue. It was 7:00 P.M. on a Friday evening, and while the traffic was thick, it remained navigable.

Dukor sat huddled in the cargo bay of the van, checking his array of rack-mounted instruments and consoles. He and Fritz had spent a complete day and half the ensuing night installing everything needed for the Koch Center assault; now all that was required was a little fine-tuning. Dukor smiled as he checked connections, relays, and sensors. The equipment seemed to be working perfectly.

The equipment.

He smiled as he recalled Fritz Hargrove's oafish query when he first saw Dukor pull into his Bensonhurst garage with a brand new van filled with cartons of ultra-high-tech equipment. "Jeez, Mr. Nichols, where'd you get the money for the car and all this stuff . . . ?"

"I stole it," Dukor had informed him.

And Fritz had merely smiled. "That's great," he'd said after a long pause. "From who?"

Dukor had briefly filled him in.

After spending several days in recon at some of the most high-density drug dealing and distribution street corners in Brooklyn's notorious Brownsville neighborhood, Dukor had been ready to finance his operation. His target was a twenty-eight-year-old Negro named Kwa-Shon Jackson—loud-mouthed, arrogant, and stupid as a rock. Jackson demonstrated several bad habits as he strutted and marauded around his neighborhood; he brandished automatic firearms wildly, which belied his ability to use them effectively, and he flashed large amounts of money, which he carried in his crack-fueled Lamborghini.

Two evenings before pulling into Fritz's garage, Dukor waited for Kwa-Shon in the parking garage of the InterContinental Hotel, where the druglord kept a suite. After scouting his prey for a week, Dukor had learned Jackson's habits well enough to select the best time to isolate him. And so when the Negro turned off the ignition key of his low-slung, Italian coupe and unfolded himself from its interior, Dukor rose up from the shadows of the garage to greet him. It would have been so easy to merely slit the dealer's throat and take his money, but Dukor always liked to feed on the pain and desperation in his victims' eyes—it always provided a special sustenance for him.

The Negro reached awkwardly for one of his automatic pistols, but he hadn't been prepared for Dukor's body to be so quick or so highly trained in the killing arts. Springing forward like an uncoiling snake, Dukor cleared the hood of the car with his legs outstretched. In midflight, he executed a spin-move, with the first foot-blow disarming Jackson and the second stunning him across the jaw. As the dealer tottered against the side of his vehicle, Dukor drew close to him, smelling the man's panic as it ran wet and rank, stronger than his expensive cologne.

"Give me all your money and maybe you won't die," Dukor had whispered into his ear like a lover.

"You gotta be fuckin' crazy, white boy!" Jackson said, his voice full of bravado, but his knees beginning to tremble.

"Yes, that is very true," said Dukor as he subdued his target with a hammerlock across his larynx—any attempt at movement would effectively crush it, choking him to death. Jackson had no choice but to drop to his knees as Dukor quickly searched him with his free hand. The effort produced two knives, and two other pistols—one a Sig-Sauer with a silenced muzzle—a wad of folded cash, and a wallet filled with additional hundreds. He dropped the weapons to the cement floor and pocketed the money.

"How much here?" asked Dukor.

Jackson said nothing, so Dukor increased his forearm pressure by an inch or so, and the dealer's eyes bugged in terror from the incipient pain. "Hey, wait!" He forced out the words. "Shit! About ten *large*, man! Jesus!"

"I'll need more than that. Is there more cash in the car?"

No hesitation this time. "Oh yeah! Box under my seat. . . . Take it, man. Take the *whole* motherfucker! Just leave me alone."

Still retaining his death-grip on Jackson, Dukor reached into the car and removed a small metal hinged box, just large enough to contain a brick-sized stack of 100-dollar bills.

He placed the box carefully on the cement floor, picked up the silenced Sig-Sauer auto. Jackson's eyes bulged a little more.

"Now, what am I going to do with you and all this shit?" he asked the dealer.

"Just let me go, man. You got what you was after. . . ."

"Not really . . ." Dukor mugged in mock sadness, like a bad clown.

"Huh?"

Dukor held the gun up to the Negro's face. "Have you ever used this? Ever shot somebody?"

"Shit—yeah!"

"Did you look in their eyes when you killed them?"

Jackson's expression flashed confusion for an instant. "Huh?"

"Did you ever wonder what it was like for them? To know you were going to kill them?"

"Nah, I don't think so."

Dukor let the pistol drop from the Negro's face, and just as his expression started to relax, Jackson heard a sudden *pffftt!* He screamed as the bullet savaged his left kneecap and tears exploded from his eyes. Dukor put another slug in the right kneecap, released his grip on the target's throat, and let him sink to the floor, screaming like a baby.

"Why don't you *think* about it for a moment," said Dukor as he pumped additional caps into Jackson's elbows and shoulders.

"Jesus . . . why'd you . . . you *do* this, man?!" Jackson's blood stained the concrete floor, throbbing from all the wounds. His face revealed the agony that twisted beneath his flesh.

"Why?" Dukor smiled as he leaned close, placing the now-hot muzzle of the Sig-Sauer's silencer against the dealer's throat. "Because I really don't like you," he said. "And now, it's time to say good night. . . ."

He squeezed the trigger, blowing away the man's lower jaw and throat. He would writhe and squirm a little longer before finally sliding into the darkness.

The next day, he purchased the minivan from a classified ad in the Sunday Post; its Staten Island owner was more than happy to receive cash, and as a favor he agreed to leave the plates on it for a week. Several hours later, Dukor had located a supplier of false driver's licenses and purchased twelve new identities. Then he took a leisurely drive through New England, where he spent the next twenty-four hours buying the most sophisticated surveillance equipment from a variety of laboratories, vendors, and government surplus outlets. He purchased only pieces of each component at each source, in each city from Bridgeport and New Haven through Boston, Providence, Nashua, Concord, back down through Springfield, Hartford, and finally New York. He knew the FBI would be watching out for any suspicious purchases of spy gear or sophisticated weaponry, but his multistate, multi-ID strategy would give him enough time and enough cover to complete his mission long before anybody at the bureau would put all the pieces together.

The next day, he and Fritz stripped down the minivan's interior and rack-mounted his equipment. They also tinted the windows for extra security. It had been tedious and sometimes exasperating because his slow-witted disciple often had trouble grasping elementary concepts, but the end result was formidable indeed.

And now they were ready to begin.

As Fritz set the parking brake and slipped from the driver's side, he opened the hood and began poking around the engine. Three blocks south of their present position, across the double lanes of traffic, lay their objective, the Koch Center. Through the tinted glass, Dukor aimed a device that looked like a deep-dish mini-parabola toward the target building's glass facade, then watched a small screen display. The dish was a signal source locator that worked by beaming its probe radiation against any glass surface, which acted as a resonator and collector for a variety of electromagnetic field signatures.

Dukor smiled as he read the preliminary data on a small monitor. The probe had found and listed an incredible 112 devices emanating different EM fields. Dukor browsed the list, eliminating most of the obvious stuff—elevator controls, electric-eye doors, lamps, microwaves, and coffee-makers—to concentrate on the alarm systems, security cameras, computer screens, and other communications and data storage systems. Then, by a process of elimination, he was able to key up all the information he would need. He had snooping/infiltration equipment gaining access through paths as innocuous as the building's electrical wiring, its phone lines, and cable TV wiring. One instrument actually employed the steel skeleton of the building as a collecting antenna for EM from selected computer monitors stealing and relaying whatever images appeared on the target monitor. The average citizen had no idea how sophisticated and efficient their government had become in gathering information.

Within the hour, Dukor had acquired a complete set of architectural detail floorplans for the Koch Center; a set of disarming codes for all the alarms on all doors, elevators, the shipping dock, and emergency exits; a list of all hotel guests' names and room locations; a complete schedule of events for the entire weekend; numbers and extensions for every telephone, intercom, modem, and faxlink; plus total access to all bureau communications links in the target building and all the adjoining scout locations in the buildings surrounding the Koch Center. In minutes, he was listening to the remote conversations among the scouts and marksmen.

The FBI was playing this one by the book (or so it seemed) and Dukor was able to plan several steps ahead of them. Unless the entire operation was a complete ruse, and the bureau boys had filled *every* system with false data (which was highly unlikely), there was no way they could keep him away from the target.

The next thing he did was steal a signal from each security camera capturing an empty hallway or area. From these images, he created digitized "loops," which he then fed to each security camera. The loop images intercepted and replaced whatever the cameras might actually see and transmit, so that whoever was watching their security monitors would only see what Dukor wanted them to see.

Finally, he signaled Fritz, who had been tinkering with the minivan's engine, to get back behind the wheel and begin phase two. Hargrove complied by heading north several blocks before cruising slowly for a parking space. As they drove, Dukor monitored the outgoing calls of all the seminar guests. Not long after finding a curbside harbor on Forty-eighth Street, Dukor intercepted the kind of call he was looking for—Ms. Anna Smithson, in Room 723, had forgotten to bring her asthma medication. After calling the front desk and getting the number of the nearest all-night pharmacy (Ryker's on Second Avenue), she called her doctor in Chicago and had him fax a new prescription for albutenol sulfate inhalant to the Manhattan chemist.

Dukor smiled. "That's all I need," he said to no one in particular.

THIRTY-THREE

THE SEMINAR
Manhattan, New York

Earlier, during the day, Dr. J. Michael Keating had greeted the assembly of thirty-two subjects in an airy conference room with a vaulted ceiling. His plan had been to be as casual and nonthreatening as possible, and it seemed to be working. After introducing his colleagues, Irwin and Pamela, he shared the fascinating story of Isabella Mussina's research and interest in the group's experiences. And as he looked over the small gathering, he could almost feel them growing more comfortable with each passing moment. Each one of them had felt so alone, so terrified, he could not actually imagine the joy and relief they must have felt when discovering there were others *exactly* like them, others with whom they could share their pain and their renewed hopes for understanding, and perhaps control.

As he summed up his welcoming remarks, Michael looked over the small group, trying to take a few seconds to study each face, to imprint it upon his memory. They comprised a wide cross-section of the generation called the Baby Boomers, all born since the close of World War II. From various parts of North and South America and Europe, men and women of all races, they were as diverse a group as possible. The only common point necessary was that everyone speak English. He recognized some of them from their medical records: a surgeon from Providence, Rhode Island; a widower from Chicago; a machinist from Buenos Aires; a writer from Pittsburgh; a director from Hollywood; a British officer in the Royal Navy but stationed in New London, Connecticut; a civil servant from Toronto; a Lutheran minister from Iowa City; a producer for the local news at ABC in New Orleans; in addition to his own patients, Allison Enders and Rodney McGuire.

They were all smiling softly at him as he stepped down from the podium, and he could feel the warmth of their applause caress him like summer sunlight. With tears in their eyes, they were thanking him for finally bringing them together. As Irwin Klingerman faced them, he was visibly moved by the simple emotional outpouring from the small but already intimate group.

"Thank you," he said, after wiping away his own tears. "I will be very brief, but I must tell you that I believe we are doing something very, very important here tonight. And I think you know it, too. I think you *feel* it—which is far better than just knowing it. You are all very special people to me. I am a Jew, and I know that very few of *you* are Jewish—at least in this present life.

"And that tells me something. It tells me that it doesn't matter what race or religion we are. Because we have been asked to come together as human beings. To testify on behalf of humankind against those of us who would be monsters."

The group broke into spontaneous applause at this point and Michael could feel their strength, their resolve, bursting from them like escaping radiation. It would not be contained.

As he sat next to Pamela, facing the group, he leaned close, whispered to her: "Is it me, or do you feel it, too?"

Reaching out, she squeezed his hand. "It isn't you," she said.

And he felt reassured. Something special was truly happening this day, he thought, as Klingerman continued:

"And so, we will try to come together this weekend and become a family. Because we *are* a family. And we will do as families do— we will listen to each other's stories and help each other to heal.

"But we will also ask ourselves some important questions about who we really are and *why* this has happened to us. If there is some greater reason, we must attempt to find it, do you agree?"

The group voiced their assent quickly and forcibly. Every one of them spoke out in positive exclamations. Michael was impressed with their energy and their strength.

"Thank you," said Irwin, pausing to look at them and smile. "Very well, then we must begin. In this first session, Dr. Keating, Ms. Robbins, and myself invite you to come up here, one at a time, in any order you choose, and share with us your own past-life experience. And while we engage in this sharing, we should all be listening and searching for the answers we seek."

Irwin paused for a moment, drew a breath, and exhaled. "Who would like to begin?"

As if the entire program had been rehearsed, everyone turned to look at a man in the second row. He appeared to be in his mid-forties, balding, with a round face. He wore baggy jeans and a forest-green sweater. Raising his hand only for an instant, he stood up and approached the podium.

John D. Fortune:

I live in Pittsburgh, and I'm a writer. I do paperback novelizations based on computer games, and I write reviews of fantasy role-playing games for Dragon's Den *magazine. But I have the same nightmare almost every night of my life: I am a teenaged girl living in a Polish village called Frysztak. I have two younger sisters and I'm teaching them how to make simple clothes for their dolls when the German soldiers come to our town. They are wearing long coats and carrying big guns with knives on the ends of the barrels. They give my parents patches to be sewn onto all of our clothes: yellow stars of David with the word* Jude *printed in the center. I remember my little sisters asking me if their dolls would have to wear the yellow stars, too. I tell them only if they are Jewish dolls to make them laugh. But it is not very funny. All of us, all the Jews in the village, are not allowed to use the sidewalks anymore. My father is told to remove his hat if he ever passes a German on the street. My mother can only buy her groceries in one store isolated for Jews. I cannot play with any of my friends who are not Jewish, and when the SS comes to finally take us in trucks to the train depot, I am happy to be away from all the embarrassment. I am riding in a truck carrying young girls like myself. On the road to Wloclawek, our truck suddenly is directed off into a field by a troop carrier full of* Schutzstaffel *soldiers. They pull some of the girls down and drag us into the fields, where they rip our clothes from us until we are kneeling naked in the pastures. Then we are raped by the soldiers. One of the girls tries to get up and run, and a soldier pins her to the ground by jamming his bayonet through her shoulder. He rapes her and then shoots her in the face with his Luger. I do not move when I see this, and one man after another takes his turn with me. I feel nothing; I see nothing except for the gray sky, which has turned to stone above me. When all of the SS are finally spent, one of them kneels down and looks me in the face as if he will kiss me. Then he unsheathes his knife and cuts my throat. As I feel my life froth and bubble away, the sky turns from gray to black. . . .*

Victor Accardi:

I live in Buenos Aires, Argentina, where I work for the Vizcarraldo Iron Works. I make bearings and shafts for oil freighters. I am not Jewish, but all my life I have had an . . . understanding, an attraction for the culture of the Jews. Seven years ago, I injured my hand on my lathe and was taken to the hospital. When the doctors put me to sleep, they said I talked to them the whole time they operated on my hand. I told them a story that I now remember every day: I am a tailor and I live in the Polish village of Radom with my wife, Moesha, and our daughter, Pauline. My name is Karl Frenkel. The Nazis have a district civil service office in our village and there are soldiers everywhere, and all the rules are strictly obeyed. One rule prohibits any Jews from owning or playing a radio, and I remember the day all my friends line up with me at a "collection depot," where we had to turn in our radios and sign a sheet that promised a safe return of our property at the "end of the occupation." About two months later, I am sitting at dinner with my family. We finish the meal and my daughter is cleaning up and washing the dinner plates; she is singing absently as she works. My Pauline has a beautiful voice, and we have enjoyed her singing since she was a small girl. Suddenly the door to our home is splintered by rifle stocks, and several SS men barge into the living room. "Who is hiding a radio in here?" demands one of the soldiers. I am shocked and I almost smile, but say only, "There is no radio here, sir." The soldier smacks me and calls me a liar. "I heard Erna Sack's voice in here!" says the soldier. "You have a radio." Ms. Sack was the most popular soprano in Europe and had a most distinctive voice. I assured the soldiers that it was only my Pauline and instructed her to sing for them. When she did so, they were stunned by the beauty of her song. But one of the soldiers drew his pistol, grabbed my daughter by her long hair, and twisted her head down to the barrel of his gun. And he shot her. In the head. Right in front of her mother and me. My wife screamed, asking why over and over. And the soldier shook his head. "No Jew should be able to sing as well as Erna Sack. This way," he told me, "no one will ever know." I told them that my wife and I would always know, and he thought about this for a moment and nodded in agreement. Then he shot my wife through the forehead and had his men take me outside where they hanged me from the branch of one of my own persimmon trees. The last thing I remember is the soldier's voice: "Now no one will know," he says with a smile. . . .

Maya Lafayette:
I live in New Orleans in a neighborhood called the Crescent. I work for the ABC affiliate, WVUE-TV, as a producer on the local evening news. For eight years, I have been having "blackouts." They always happen when I am sitting reading or sometimes writing at my desk. They usually last for several minutes, and people who have seen it happen to me say I look like I am in a trance or have fallen asleep. For a long time, I never knew what was happening while I was blacked out. I couldn't remember, but I would always wake up feeling utterly terrified and so cold my skin would be crawling. It would take days for the feeling to go away. I've been to so many doctors, I can't remember how many anymore. They checked me for epilepsy, narcolepsy, brain tumors, and a whole list of other neurological disorders. None of them could find what was wrong, what was causing the blackouts . . . until I was referred to Doctor Mussina. And then, like the rest of you, I discovered the details of my previous life: in it, I am a man named Hyram Alutsky, and before being taken to a camp in Belsen, I had been a melamed, *a teacher of the Torah, for the young Jewish boys in my village outside Bergen. But the* einsatzgruppen *had taken all the Jews into the camps, and we are forbidden to teach or hold ceremonies on any of the religious holidays. Many of the men defy this rule by having small secret meetings on such days. It is 1942, on the holiday called* Purim, *and I am leading a prayer in the barracks when the guards catch me. When they ask me what I am doing, I tell them the prayer is a small celebration of a new harvest, and we thank God for food to eat. They laugh at me and tell me if I am hungry, I don't need to ask God, I can ask the guards. They drag me outside, in front of everyone, and bring me raw pork flesh to eat. They stuff it into my mouth and I keep spitting it out. It is against kosher law to eat* traif, *the flesh of the unclean animals. The guards laugh at me as I keep spitting out the raw meat, until finally they get bored, and one of them tells me that if I don't eat the meat, he will kill me. Still I shake my head. He*

pushes me down, onto my back, and has another guard kneel on my chest and pry open my jaws. The soldier stuffs a large piece of pig fat down my throat, pushing it deeper with the barrel of his pistol. I begin to suffocate and spots blink before my eyes. I feel myself convulsing, but the soldier's weight keeps me from moving very much. Finally, the guard laughs and tells his comrades, "The Jew is having trouble swallowing. I'd better give him a little help," and with that he jams the pistol deep down my throat and squeezes the trigger. I feel an instant of intense heat and pressure before a white light fills me. . . .

Ira Miller, M.D.

My name is Ira Miller. I am Jewish, and I am a surgeon. I live in Providence, Rhode Island. About once a week, I, too, dream about my past life: I am living in the Auschwitz Lager, and I work as a schreiber, one of the sonderkommandos who tattoos numbers on the arms of my fellow prisoners. One day, when leaving the barracks for the morning feeding, I catch my ragged shoe on the step and fall. Some of the prisoners behind me fall on top of me, and my lower leg is broken. I'm taken to the medical building where Doctor Mengele and his assistant, Der Klein Engel, receive me with inviting smiles. The doctor looks at my leg and says it is broken in two places, that it will take much too long to heal, and that a new schreiber could be taught to take my place in much less time. His Little Angel smiles at me and I see he has one gold tooth. He tells me that I am no better than a draft horse. I know what this means, and I expect to be taken outside and shot, or sent to the showers. But the doctor and his smiling friend don't do this. Instead I'm kept in their lab for several days, until they aren't so busy. When that day comes, I am strapped to an operating table, and Mengele lets his assistant "experiment" on me. With no anesthetic, the Little Angel dissects me with a scalpel and a handsaw. I pass out from the pain and the shock, but he keeps reviving me by throwing ice water in my face. But finally, with my chest opened like a picnic basket, I lose too much blood to remain conscious no matter what my tormentors do. The last thing I remember is a circle of lightbulbs hanging over my table. The circle begins to spin, faster and faster, like a shining carrousel carrying me off to oblivion. . . .

One by one, the people told their stories. Although they spoke each with their own unique voice, everyone delivered the same testament to a suffering that spanned the gulf of time, to a pain so acute it would never abate, to memories that would never grow dim. Michael listened to every detail as if hearing them all for the first time, even those of his own patients, Rodney and Allison. At the end of the session, a profound silence permeated the room. Everyone sensed the depth of the communion that had taken place.

Michael could feel it. It was as if everyone had suddenly begun to breathe at the same rate, at the same time. As though all their senses had been abruptly focused, locked together and functioning as one great, single entity.

"What's happening here?" he whispered to Irwin and Pamela. "Do you feel it?"

"A bonding," said Irwin. "We have created something very special today."

Pamela leaned close to him. "We'll make a fine mystic out of you yet, Doctor."

Michael smiled as he turned to ascend the podium again.

The next phase of the seminar was about to begin—an open forum in which everyone was invited to offer their own ideas about the phenomenon itself. He wanted the group to contribute to the knowledge pool not only their experiences but also their feelings, intuitions, and thoughts or insights into the central meaning of the entire event.

And so he asked them: "Why do you think this has happened to us? What does it mean to you personally and to the world in general?"

At first the assembled group remained silent, as though everyone needed time to consider his questions, to gather up their own feelings and thoughts.

Then a man stood in the back of the room. Automatically, everyone turned to regard him intently.

"I have been feeling like this is a very important event," he said. "Until Doctor Keating posed his questions, I hadn't been able to focus on what anything might really mean. But I know I was feeling scared, uncertain, and now I feel better. I feel like . . . just being in this group has made me safer, made us *all* safer. Does anyone understand what I'm trying to say?"

The room suddenly burst into conversation as everyone voiced their assent, their own variations on the same theme. The man had struck a resonant chord in them and had focused in on a basic anxiety they had all felt. Michael was impressed and encouraged by this initial response, making him feel that he and his colleagues had done the right thing by bringing them together.

Another man stood up and volunteered his speculations. "For a long time, I wondered what could be the cause of my own nightmares and fears. I must confess that I had allowed my own beliefs, my religious beliefs, to slide away, and if someone had asked me if I believed in God, I would always tell them 'probably not. . . .' But now, I'm beginning to think that maybe there *is* a God, and that He's taken quite an interest in what's happening to his world. Or maybe he has something special in mind for his 'Chosen People'?"

"What took him so long?" said a woman in the second row.

A scattering of chuckles peppered the room as she continued. "I *am* a Jew," she said. "But I stopped believing in our God for precisely the same reason you are mentioning."

"What do you mean?" asked Michael. He would attempt to moderate the open discussion as little as possible, but felt that the occasional question was necessary to keep the forum in focus.

The woman looked very distressed, infinitely sad. "I began thinking that any God who would allow such a thing as the Holocaust to happen was not much of a God. Which meant that He probably didn't exist at all. And if He *did*, He wasn't worth believing in," she said with an ironic sneer. "'Chosen People'! Chosen for what? Genocide?"

Others in the group nodded their heads, and Michael wondered if he should explore that notion or let the first man finish his position, but the man solved the problem by pushing on.

"I've thought about that, too," he said in a loud voice. "And it seems to me that maybe we're dealing with the Old Testament God, a god of vengeance and cruelty. Didn't that God wipe out whole nations, whole tribes, when He proclaimed He'd been offended?"

Choruses of cautious agreement cantoed through the room.

"So what's happening *now*?" asked the Jewish woman in the second row. "Did the God of Israelites change his mind? Have a change of heart?"

The man looked at her and then at Michael. He executed a small bow and smiled. "I don't know what He might be thinking, but we can't deny the influence of a Higher Power at work here."

"I agree," said another man. "It doesn't really matter what name we give the power or the cause of all this. By having all of us here, admitting the existence of this . . . force or influence . . . well, I think that is sufficient."

"But what does it mean?" asked Michael. "Why have we been called together? Why are you all reliving what is probably your past lives under the Nazis?"

The physician from Rhode Island, Dr. Miller, stood up and faced the group. "I've been listening to everyone and thinking very hard about all this," he said softly. "And I think we're missing the point."

"What do you mean?" said Michael.

"Has anyone considered the possibility that maybe others—from the enemy side—are also being reborn?" Dr. Miller paused as audible reaction to his question grew and filled the room with answers.

"They're coming back!"

"The Nazis! They never went away!"

"We're going to stop them this time!"

"How do we find them?"

"Maybe they're going to find us?" said Michael, thinking to plant a seed in their minds, to prepare them in even a small way for any danger they might be in.

"There is no way to know these things," said Dr. Miller. "But I think it is wise for us to at least be aware of the possibilities. I, for one, however, will continue to believe that we have been called forth for a purpose, a grand and necessary purpose—to never again let the world, or ourselves, forget the horror that once was. And to destroy it utterly if it appears ever again."

"Well said," said Rabbi Klingerman. "I believe in signs of portent from God, and this thing that has happened to all of us is indeed a sign. I believe we must be ready for anything."

There was general assent from the crowd, and Michael felt pleased with not only the variety of responses he received, but also the high levels of both intelligence and sensitivity expressed by everyone.

The moderated discussion continued, carrying on for several hours, with almost everyone contributing to the speculations. Michael was especially impressed with the growing feeling of solidarity among them. Irwin had called it a *bonding*, but it was actually more than that. More like a *merging* of their experiences into a greater gestalt, a merging of their collective wills toward a solemn resolution of power against perceived evil.

The sessions lasted all day and into the evening, resisting his efforts to interrupt the discussions and the "sharings," as Irwin called their exchanges of ideas and experiences. Michael wanted everyone to get a good night's rest because tomorrow had been planned to be a very intense day.

He had no way of knowing it would be a very long time before anyone got their chance to rest—especially himself.

THIRTY-FOUR

ARNOLD RASSENAULT
Manhattan, New York

He sat in the corner booth at the Greek diner on West Thirty-first Street, sipping coffee from a scarred porcelain mug. The regular dinner crowd had thinned out, leaving only the people like Arnold, the ones with no place better to go.

But that wasn't quite true, was it?

Arnold had several places he could go: the local precinct house, the FBI, or the Koch Conference Center.

Earlier that day, he'd been sitting in the offices of the *Journal of Progressive History* listening to Fritz detail an evening of mayhem. He described the encounter with Nichols and the drug dealer with loving accuracy, then he told him how Nichols had mixed up an "Oklahoma cocktail" just like the one those other guys had used to take out the Federal Building, and how they were going to serve it up for a bunch of Park Avenue kikes later that night.

Arnold held the mug tightly, sipped automatically, ignoring the dull taste of cold coffee. How had this happened to him? How did he get thrown into the middle of this damnable mess? Nichols had told him a story that could only come from a maniac. Dead Jews, from the death camps (camps Arnold had always known in his heart had been real, despite two decades of attempts to "prove" them away), had been reborn to stop the Nazis who were also being reborn.

Told like that, it was clearly the tale of a madman.

But Arnold had listened and let himself be carried along by the tethers of his own twisted philosophy. He looked at his watch. Almost 9:30. Nichols had planned to strike at midnight. Not much longer. A few more cups of coffee, maybe some pie.

But there was another part of Arnold that knew it wasn't going to be that easy. Goddamn Nichols! Before he'd shown up, Arnold had been so comfortable in his beliefs, his way of life. He'd always thought he really *believed* all the things he said, wrote, told Fritz and the few other followers he'd had over the years. In fact he'd pronounced them so many times that the major assertions of his Holocaust-as-myth position underlay all his thoughts.

Arnold knew he had reached the crossroads of his life—the place where his thinking and his actions had finally coincided. He needed strength to go on from this point. A forceful resolution of the "facts" would help both fortify his decision to support Nichols and pass the final hours.

Germany had never planned to annihilate the Jews, only emigrate them. (If so, why did they build camps inside Germany?)

No Jews were ever gassed at the camps. (What about the testimony of guards at Nuremberg who admitted dumping Zyklon-B into the shower chambers, claiming they were "following orders"?)

Any Jews who disappeared during World War II did so in territory controlled by the Soviets, not the Germans. (What about Poland and Germany itself?)

If any Jews died by Nazi hands, they were subversives, partisans, saboteurs, spies, or plain criminals. Their deaths were all legitimate reprisals of war. (But how could he explain the newsreel footage of children and old women being shot in the streets of Polish villages?)

The famous "six million" killed figure has never been proven by the Jews, especially since Israel refuses to open its archives on the subject. They do this in fear of being exposed, belying the money they have received from Germany in "reparation." (What about Eichman's own testimony that proudly indicates the figure is "quite accurate"?)

Why can't Jewish scholars produce the names and personal histories of *all* the victims? (Is it possible the Germans were more effective in *totally* erasing any trace of millions of people than even they thought possible?)

Arnold wrestled with his doubts as he tried to recite his beliefs like a hollow litany in which the words have been reduced to mere sounds without true meaning.

He thought about the real reason he was sitting in the diner, going over all the history and the statistics and the numbers. And he knew he wasn't very successful in trying to convince himself of any position—one way or the other.

Because that's not what this was all about.

Arnold had been trying fitfully to enact some kind of magical conversion—to talk himself out of his convictions and the basis for what had comprised the majority of his life. But in the end, he knew it didn't matter *what* he believed because that was not his primary motivation.

Be honest with yourself, he thought pitifully.

10:15 P.M.

The hours moved past him like a glacier. He knew that sitting here like some shivering, little toad was completely unacceptable. He should be out there with his soldiers, if not leading them, then at least helping them achieve their objective.

To kill people.

That's what it's all about, Arnold, he thought bitterly. The world's always been about killing *somebody*, and the one he was most worried about getting killed was Arnold Rassenault.

Because he had looked into the eyes of a monster named Hirsh Dukor, and a terrible feeling had washed over him—a hideous premonition that the monster would kill him.

And that's what it all came down to. . . .

It didn't matter whether he believed his own lies anymore. In the final analysis, Arnold discovered he had no great affection for any group or *anyone* other than his own sorry ass.

Arnold Rassenault released his arthritic grip on the coffee mug, stood up stiffly.

It was time to *do something.*

THIRTY–FIVE

DER KLEIN ENGEL
Manhattan, New York

He continued to monitor his inputs into the Koch Center. His training within the world's most sophisticated spy-network machine had been such a perfectly appropriate skill, Dukor was convinced of the existence of pure fate. He could not be any better qualified to rid the world of this pack of inferiors.

Fritz had driven across Forty-eighth Street to Second Avenue, parking in front of the target pharmacy. They waited patiently, not speaking, until the delivery boy emerged with a plastic handbasket full of small, white, paper bags stapled across the tops and a clipboard. Dukor watched the tall, wiry Negro, assessing the potential problems such a long-limbed opponent might present—if things did not go to plan. The boy was thin, but he moved with agility and grace. It was possible he was a student of the martial arts himself. The boy climbed into a white Ford Escort with an illuminated, removable sign on the roof which read: RYKER'S PHARMACY—WE DELIVER—24 HOURS.

"Follow him," said Dukor.

Fritz nodded, keyed the ignition, and pushed lightly on the accelerator as they eased into medium traffic. They followed the Escort south on Second Avenue, where the boy made two deliveries in the East Twenties, then across to Third, where he turned right and headed north. Fritz kept the Voyager minivan close to the Escort's rear bumper, matching the little car move for move. When the Escort turned onto Thirty-first Street, Dukor leaned forward, scanned the surroundings, and nodded quickly. It was a dark residential street. There was no one visible and there were no parking spaces in sight. The boy in the Escort was moving slowly up the block, looking for a place to double park, his emergency flashers blinking wanly.

"It's going to be here. When he stops, do it like I taught you."

"Okay, captain," said Fritz, knuckling the steering wheel more tightly.

The Escort stopped, and while the boy leaned down to pick out the correct prescription bag, Fritz drifted the Voyager forward giving the Escort a slight bumper-tapping jolt. At the same time, Dukor opened his passenger side door, dropped down to the street. The delivery boy jumped up, sprang from the car full of indignation.

"What the fuck's with you, man? I got my fuckin' blinkers on!" He stormed directly toward Fritz, who was leaning out the driver's side window with a silly grin on his face. Dukor fell into step behind him silent and gracile as a cat.

"Sorry . . ." said Fritz.

"I gotta job to do, man. I ain't got time for shit like this!"

Before Fritz could reply, Dukor stepped close to the boy, slipping his arms around his long neck and along the side of his head. Tilting him off balance on his hip, Dukor snapped the vertebrae just beneath the skull, severing his spinal cord. As everything short-circuited, the boy's feet did an involuntary tap dance for an instant before he went limp and very dead. Dukor regretted attacking from behind; he couldn't see his victim's face, but surprise had been the essential ingredient this time.

Dragging the boy to the back door of the minivan, Dukor opened it and folded his body into the dark space.

"All right, good. You will take the delivery vehicle. Get the addresses off the clipboard. Be courteous and efficient. Don't do any-thing to arouse suspicion," he told Fritz. "I will follow you until we reach the target."

Fritz nodded, exited the van. Dukor watched him climb into the little car, consult the clipboard, and drive off slowly. They still had plenty of deliveries to make.

But they were saving the best for last.

THIRTY-SIX

J. MICHAEL KEATING, M.D.
Manhattan, New York

Would you like another drink?" Michael asked Pamela.

He was sitting with her in the lounge of the Koch Center. It was 11:15 P.M. and he had just knocked back the remainder of his Maker's Mark. He'd needed something strong after listening to so many stories of terror and desperation. No one could be exposed to such tales and not be changed forever.

"One more," she said, "but that's going to do it for me. I'm exhausted."

"So am I, but I'm also pretty anxious. I feel like I need to get some sleep, but I'm too wired up to let it happen." Michael signaled the waiter, who appeared almost instantly to acknowledge their reorder.

Pamela leaned forward. "Michael, please tell me something—and hold the testosterone, please: are you scared?"

"Are you?"

"Uh-uh," she said. "You first."

He grinned sardonically. "Sure I am. I keep seeing that creep, Nichols, in the video, and I just *know* he's going to try something."

Pamela just stared at him, then: "And I feel awful that we're not

telling these poor people they might be in danger. I have to tell you—
I've been toying with the idea of just telling them anyway. . . ."

Michael looked at her. Yes, that sounded exactly like Pamela.
She'd analyzed her feelings and the situation, and had decided the
best way—for her—to handle things. "I can't disagree with you," he
said. "But if you're trying to convince me to go along with you, I
don't think it'll be necessary."

"Why not? What do you mean? Did you already tell them?"

"No, nothing like that." Michael leaned closer to her and spoke
very softly. "I don't want to be the one sounding like the occultist
here, but I'm serious—I think this group *already* knows the situation."

"How could they?"

He shrugged, sipped his bourbon. "I don't know. I just have a
feeling that they *do*. I could sense a . . . a power in that room. You
said you felt something, too. I know it sounds over the top, and I
know I was always laughing at the paranormal stuff, but I can't
deny it anymore. There's something to it, I'm pretty damned sure."

She looked at him, taking a long studious sip from her glass.
"You know, there was a time when I would have ribbed you about
this. But it's too tense right now. Too serious."

"You mean, if we all get out of this okay, I'm going to be hearing
it from you?"

"Oh, yeah . . . for a long time, Doctor."

He smiled but didn't speak right away. He imagined both of
them were feeling contemplative, and both realized the need to
speak all the time was becoming less necessary. Michael knew very
well that as two people became more intimate, and more comfortable with their intimacy, the things you sometimes *didn't* say
become just as important as the things you did. It was certainly true
for him and Pamela.

The last woman to speak during the introductory session had
been one of the last patients seen by Isabella Mussina. Her name had
been Lillian Karnow, and she said something so insightful, so trenchantly perceptive, that Michael couldn't stop thinking about it.
He couldn't stop replaying her words, weaving them endlessly
among the strands of his own thoughts:

I will never be the same person now that I have experienced what another
soul suffered. I lived through the humiliation and the pain of having your

humanity peeled away layer by torturous layer. And as I try to answer the single most asked question about the Nazi terror—the one that demands to know how it could have happened?—*I am led back to a quiet evening in Germany when all the dreams and hopes and plans of generations were shattered during a dark mob-driven assault on an unassuming group of people. Something horrible was born into the world that night.* Kristallnacht. *That is what they called it. The night the upstanding citizens of a country turned upon their fellow countrymen like rabid beasts, intent on destruction of not only their temples and their homes and businesses, but their spirits as well.* Kristallnacht. *Night of broken glass. That is the night I believe the monster was finally loose, the night it became real instead of just an ugly idea thrown from a speaker's podium. And the most interesting thing for me is that I sense this quiet evening is very much like that one sixty years now dead.*

Something new is being born as we sit and speak and listen.

But I believe it is a good thing, a necessary thing. The world turns like a great wheel toward the beginning of a new millennium, and I believe we have been called back from the gray limbo of pain never to be suffered again, to not just remind the turning world we can never be forgotten, but to never let the terror happen again. This is our night. This night of broken souls. And I believe we have been called together for a divine purpose—to stop the monster, who I fear has been awakened, and may live in others like ourselves.

THIRTY-SEVEN

DER KLEIN ENGEL
Manhattan, New York

Fritz Hargrove drove through the streets of Manhattan's East Side like the dutiful servant he was. Large-shouldered, ham-handed, the man had the florid, doughy face of a peasant. A man fit for the bull-work of a mill or a shovel. And the best part, thought Dukor, as he sat in the van watching Hargrove walk toward an apartment building in Gramercy Park, was there would be no worry of any freelance thinking, no ad-libbing during an assignment. Fritz went about his work with the single-minded trudge of a plow horse wearing blinders.

When he told Fritz to do something, it would be carried out according to plan, and tonight had been no exception. Fritz had been instructed to be a delivery boy, and for the last hour or two, he'd been the best delivery boy anyone could ever hope for. Ryker Pharmacy would be very proud. Dukor smiled as he checklisted himself and his plans until Fritz reemerged from the building. The big man was smiling, walking with his shoulder-swaying, half-lurching gait as he approached the driver's side of the van.

"That's the last of 'em," he said, chuckling as he reached into his pocket and pulled out a handful of cash. "I forgot they were all going to *pay* me! And a lot of this is tips!"

"See that," said Dukor. "I knew you could do a good job. I'm proud of you, Fritz."

"Thank you!" Fritz smiled. "Can I keep the money?"

Dukor smiled as though looking at a child. "Yes, of course, you can. Now, listen: we enter phase three. You know what to do?"

"Oh, sure."

"You have the floorplans?"

Fritz tapped his shirt pocket. "Right here."

"Just to put me at ease," said Dukor, "why don't we go through your assignment step by step . . . right up to where you've let me into the building."

"Sure," said Fritz as he launched into a series of movements and contingencies, reciting them as a fifth-grader might parrot back a Longfellow poem, but getting it just right.

Satisfied, Dukor nodded. "All right," he said. "Get in the car. Let's go."

As midnight approached, the traffic through midtown was intermittent and easy to negotiate. Dukor trailed the little Escort as it homed in on the Koch Center like a cruise missile, programmed for a single, final mission. Parking the minivan across the center island on Park, just up from the Waldorf-Astoria, Dukor watched Fritz drive his delivery vehicle right to the front doors of the Koch Center, under the porte-cochere by the huge plate-glass doors. A doorman, wearing pseudomilitary parade livery, approached the car as Fritz climbed from the Escort.

Holding a pair of night-vision binoculars to his eyes, Dukor dialed the resolution up high enough to read the eyes of the doorman as he regarded Fritz and his little white bag that held asthma medicine.

This was the single moment upon which the entire mission would hinge. He knew that if the simple doorman believed him, approved him, then everything else would be easy.

Through the tinted lenses, Dukor watched the dull Fritz deliver his lie to an even duller doorman. The dupe nodded, turned from Fritz, and held open one of the thick, brass-handled glass doors for him.

Smiling, Dukor put down the binoculars and crawled from behind the wheel into the shadowed interior of the van. Beyond the rack-mounted equipment, and before the stiffening corpse of the delivery boy, lay three industrial drums clustered like the engines of a NASA booster. Dukor's Oklahoma cocktail had been mixed and poured and was about to be stirred.

THIRTY-EIGHT

FRITZ HARGROVE
Manhattan, New York

When the doorman gave him that quick little nod of the head, Fritz felt his stomach suddenly sag down into his bowels. The tension kind of eased out of him like a lazy fart, and his knees felt weak for a second or two. Till then, he hadn't realized just how damn nervous he'd been.

Just act natural. Don't let them think there's anything funny with you. Nothin's funny.

And so, he let his arms swing and his shoulders rock as he entered a pink marble lobby that looked like you were walking into some kind of castle. And right up in the middle was this big desk that looked like a kid's fort where these three guys in guard's uniforms were sitting. All three of them were watching Fritz as he walked up to them, like he was naked or something. There was also a fourth guy standing behind them. He was wearing a dark suit and he had government written all over him. Mr. Nichols said there'd be one like him.

One he could see. There might be more watching from somewhere else. Course, if they were watching him on the cameras, Mr. Nichols would a have a little trick for them.

"Gotta delivery for a Ms. Anna Smithson," said Fritz, before any of the guards could open their mouths.

"Delivery from where?" said the guard sitting in the middle seat. He was wearing headphones and watching a set of three computer screens in front of him.

Fritz identified the pharmacy, showed them the bag and his clipboard with his delivery log.

"Check it out," said the guy on the left. He opened the bag, read the name of the medicine, and handed it to his colleague.

The guard at the central console keyed in a few numbers, waited, then spoke quickly to Ms. Smithson. "Just verifying your call for a prescription, ma'am. We have a driver here who says you're expecting a delivery of an allergy inhaler. Do you have a prescription for albutenol sulfate?"

The guard listened to the woman's reply, nodding his head, and Fritz knew what she was telling him. Everything was aces.

"Okay," said the guard. "She's expecting you, but I'm going to need some ID."

"Sure thing," said Fritz, giving them his best smile. Flipping open his wallet, he handed the guy his New York driver's license.

"Thanks," said the guard. "It'll just be another minute."

"What's the matter?" said Fritz, still smiling, but stopped, thinking that maybe he'd done that enough.

"Nothing," said the man at the console. He punched in a phone number and Fritz figured it was just like what Mr. Nichols had said would happen—the guard was calling the pharmacy. Fritz knew that his boss was sitting out in the minivan picking up the numbers as the guard keyed them in. And even if Fritz had no freaking clue how Mr. Nichols could do it with all that electrical stuff in his face, he believed it would happen just like he'd once believed Santa Claus was gonna bring him presents at Christmas. Mr. Nichols would answer that call to the pharmacy and tell these fuzz-nuts that yessiree, that's Fritz Hargrove and he delivers for my pharmacy and he's just about the best delivery man I've ever had.

So he stood there and nodded to himself as the guard checked him out. Finally the guy hung up the phone, handed him back his license. "Okay, the elevator's off to the right."

"Wait a sec," said the government guy in the dark suit. He had a gray mustache and looked kinda like Kirk Douglas. Fritz had been wondering when he was gonna say something.

Everybody stopped, including Fritz, who leaned against the counter. *Act like you couldn't give a shit whether you deliver this stuff or not.* That's what Mr. Nichols had said. So Fritz leaned against the counter and tried to look as bored as possible.

"Howie," said Dark Suit, pointing to the third guard at the end of the desk. "Why don't you go with him, just to be sure."

The guard nodded, slipped out from behind the desk, and moved silently next to Fritz.

"For your own safety," said Dark Suit.

"Right this way," said the other guy.

Fritz followed him through a metal detector, something that had become as normal in most public places as wall clocks, and headed for the elevator. Only he wasn't anywhere near as relaxed as he was just a minute ago. Damn, he thought quickly, feeling a sudden jolt of adrenaline that made his heartbeat spike.

The guard pushed the button for the elevator and they both stood silently waiting for the doors to open.

Fritz drew in a long breath, tried to stay calm enough to use his training.

This was one of those "con-tin-ja-cees" Mr. Nichols had prepared him for. If they decided to send a man with him to make the delivery, Fritz had been trained to take care of it.

And he would.

The doors opened and he strolled in with the guard. "How about them Yankees?" said the guy.

"Yeah, they're sumthin', ain't they?"

Time kinda stretched out and sagged in the middle and he stood there waiting for the car to stop and the doors to open for what seemed like way too damn long a time.

Maybe they found out the call to the pharmacy was bullshit? Maybe they'd been playing along with him all along? The doors were gonna open and there'd be ten guys waiting for him with automatic rifles.

Hey, take it easy! Get control. Remember all the training. Mr. Nichols had worked real hard on this kind of stuff.

So he used the passing seconds to do like he'd been trained. He sized up his prey and made his decisions. The guy was about Fritz's height, but maybe twenty or thirty pounds lighter. He looked wiry and like maybe one of those workout types who was a lot stronger than he looked. That eliminated several techniques and highlighted others. Fritz mentally prepared himself.

There was a soft *ping!* and Fritz inhaled, watching the polished metal doors part, revealing . . .

. . . an empty corridor that looked like any one of a hundred hotel hallways. Dumb paintings broke up the wallpaper along with the occasional house phone or fire extinguisher.

"Seven twenty-three's down here," said the guard, pointing along to the left wall.

Fritz followed him to the door, waited for him to knock. This was going to be a little tricky.

"Who is it?" came a muffled female voice.

"Howard Stillman, Ms. Smithson. I'm from security and I've got your delivery."

She *had* to let them in. If they stayed out in the hall, the camera watching them was going to have to go haywire at the wrong time, and that was going to cause the security guys to come running. Which would screw up the timetable.

Clicks. Clacks. The door unlocked and swung inward to reveal a pleasant-looking woman in her mid-forties. She was dressed in a pair of jeans and a baggy sweater and looked like one of the women on TV advertising makeup that would always keep you looking young.

So far so good, thought Fritz. *Now, just let us in your room.*

"I'm sorry to bother you men like this," she said with a really nice smile, "but I left my medicine back in Chicago. I can't sleep without it."

Yeah, yeah, lady. Let us in, okay?

"Here you are, ma'am," said Fritz, giving her the little white bag. He quoted her the cost and she nodded. "Come in, please. I'll have to get my purse."

Bingo! Fritz exhaled, smiled, and walked in past Howie-the-guard, who followed quickly. If the lady hadn't invited them in, Fritz would have tried several "scripts" Mr. Nichols had made him memorize—stuff that might get them inside and out of the hallway.

If the script didn't work, well, then it would have been free-for-all time . . .

But it *did* work, and Fritz knew that Mr. Nichols would be real busy right about now, reprogramming the cameras and the alarms and all that stuff. They'd find out what he'd done, sure. But by the time the security guys were wise to anything, Fritz would be done with his job.

"Here you are," said Ms. Smithson, bending down to pull something from her purse at the little vanity desk in the far corner of the room. "And here's something for you, too."

Fritz smiled as he took a step forward and extended his hand.

A very measured, carefully planned step. Him and Nichols had practiced what was coming from a hundred different angles and positions. Every which damn way but loose. For days and days, that's all he'd been doing: nothing but practicing how to take out this guard. The only thing he hadn't known was that his name was Howie. . . .

And with his hand out, making like he was taking the money, Fritz suddenly spun on his left foot, faster than any man his size ought be able to move, and wheeled quickly inside the punching/striking radius of the guard. He stomped heavily on the guy's foot to give him that single instant of distraction—all he would need. Screaming, Howie-the-guard's eyes bugged as he reached, way too late, for his weapon. When his fingers groped for the pistol's handle, they met the resistance of Fritz's hand, already locked down and pulling the standard police-issue Glock from its holster.

Howie tried to grab Fritz's wrist or arm, but Fritz was way ahead of him. Still turning into him, going *with* the attack, instead of against it, was the perfect move. *This was great, just like Mr. Nichols said it would work.* Howie's own weight threw him forward, off balance, as Fritz rolled him with one guiding hand across his hip. Bringing down his elbow, like the point of a lance, he delivered a stunning blow to Howie's neck, and the guy was staggering down and away from him as Fritz brought up his knee to connect with his temple.

Just like they'd practiced it a million times—and Fritz was still shocked to see how *easy* it had been, how *perfectly* the guy went down.

The best part was that all this had happened in like, one second, maybe two, and it hadn't been enough time for the lady to do *anything*. Not even scream.

So, easy as pie, Fritz spun around and cold-cocked her with an old-fashioned barroom swing, catching her almost straight on in the jaw and putting them tweety-birds in her eyes. He watched them kinda roll back into her in that second before she collapsed.

Then, moving real fast, he did what he really wasn't sure he could do until the time actually came. Fritz ran into the bathroom, threw two big bath towels under the tub faucet, and soaked them real good. Then he doubled them over, covered up the Glock and put it up against the guard's head. And then he had to think through the idea that if those government guys caught him now, they'd kill him anyway, that he'd already gone over the wall.

And it worked.

Pulling the trigger was like an afterthought. *Whummmpht!* The heavy wet towels absorbed almost all of the sound of the muzzle-blast and the 9mm slug took out enough of Howie's brains to fill a cereal bowl. Scratch one guard.

Doing it to the lady wasn't as easy because she was kinda nice looking and she'd given Fritz a nice tip. But when he put that thick wet towel around the barrel and laid it across her temple, the damn gun kinda coughed without him even thinking about it.

Man, that was fast!

Mr. Nichols was right again. Once you killed the first one . . . everybody else is easy.

Fritz smiled, tried not to look at his work. There wasn't any time for it anyway. His watch said 11:46. Right on schedule. This was the time when he had to trust Mr. Nichols. That he was doing his job as good as Fritz had done. Nothing left to do but run out into the hallway, right past the cameras, and *believe* they were "looped" into showing the desk guys a blank hallway. Nichols told him he'd have about another sixty to ninety seconds before the security guys would start wondering what happened to him and Howie, and they might either call the room or send somebody up.

Moving to the door, Fritz paused to take a deep breath, hold it for a moment, then exhale slowly. Full of oxygen, his head was clear and sharp. First thing to do was stash the guard's gun in his jacket pocket. Shouldn't be needing it, but just in case. . . . Then he reached in his shoe, pulled out the floorplan to refresh his memory, then stuffed it into his other pocket.

Okay, let's do it.

Out into the hallway, Fritz ran as fast as his heavy legs would propel him, past the elevator bay and through the stairwell doors. He bounded downward, aided by gravity, and swung himself around the pipe railings through the core of the building. Counting the floors was easy because they'd painted big numbers on the doors. When he cleared the mezzanine and the lobby levels, he started to feel good. No alarms had gone off, nobody yelling or chasing him yet.

No sweat, baby. . . .

The next door read PHYSICAL PLANT, and that's where he had to get off. There was a number keypad next to the door and a sign read EXIT ONLY, but that was bullshit. Fritz drew a breath, exhaled, and imagined himself keying in the code Mr. Nichols had picked up with his machines. Then he pushed his kielbasa-thick index finger against the pad, keying in an eight-digit code. There was an almost inaudible click, and Fritz turned the knob.

Like magic, the door drifted inward and Fritz slipped onto the level of the Koch Center where you could make things happen. Remembering the floorplans, Fritz stood for a moment to look around and orient himself. Directly ahead lay a huge heating and air-conditioning array. Pipes, ducts, and wire harnesses ran in and out of a monolithic block of machines. To the right ran a walkway flanked by breaker boxes, switches, and meters. Overhead industrial lighting cut deep shadows and crevices into every open space. Visibility was just okay, and Fritz was glad he'd been drilled on the layout by Mr. Nichols. Slowly, but with confidence, he pushed ahead.

Down there. That's the way.

Breaking into a trot, Fritz ran to a junction corridor, turned left, and saw his objective: a triple set of garage doors leading to the loading docks. They were painted a bright safety orange. He glided to a stop, scanned the wall panels till he found the big red and green buttons to run the doors, then looked for the keypad to disarm the alarms. Mr. Nichols had promised him the two sets of controls wouldn't be far apart.

And they weren't.

Standing there, looking at the keypad, his mind suddenly went totally *blank*. The codes, the little sets of numbers he'd spent two days memorizing, had just flown out of his head like a canary with its ass on fire. Dammit! As a backup, Mr. Nichols had him keep the numbers on a business card in his wallet, made up to look like people's phone numbers, but he didn't want to have to look there. That would mean he fucked up, and that would mean *he* was a fuck-up.

No way, bub. You just stand there and get those numbers back in your head.

And so he forced himself to calm down, take a breath and let it out, then used that trick Mr. Nichols taught him: imagining himself standing there punching in the code. He did this, and watched himself hit the numbers and damn if he didn't see the code right there in his head.

Repeating the task for real, Fritz smiled as the panel blinked and winked and finally went green. With the flat of his big hand, he slapped the green button on the door control and listened to the sturdy hum of the electric motors beginning to lift the doors.

As the panel slid upward, Fritz stood there grinning, feeling pretty good about himself. It was like watching the curtain going up on one of those fancy Las Vegas shows. But instead of some guy like Wayne Newton standing there, it was Mr. Nichols, dressed in black coveralls and baseball cap. He had a very big gun in his hand.

And it was pointed at Fritz.

THIRTY-NINE

J. MICHAEL KEATING, M.D.
Manhattan, New York

He and Pamela had just entered his fifth-floor suite at the Koch Center when the phone started ringing.

"Who's *that*?" said Pamela wearily. "What time is it?"

"Quarter to twelve," said Michael, moving quickly to the small writing desk and grabbing the receiver. "Hello?"

"Hello, Doctor Keating . . . this is Allison Enders." Her voice was soft, weak. "I hope I'm not bothering you . . ."

"Hello, Allison! No, course not!" he said brightly. He'd been especially happy with the way she'd presented her story during the introductions, but hadn't gotten a chance to tell her in person afterward. "It's always a pleasure to talk to you. What can I do for you?"

"I . . . I don't know. Something just happened and it scared me."

Michael didn't like the sound of that. He pantomimed at Pamela to pick up the extension phone in the bedroom, and she rushed to comply. "Allison, what's wrong? Can you tell me?"

"I'm not sure. I was just getting ready to go to bed and I turned out the lights, and was reaching for the sheets when I . . . saw this flash . . . it was like a bomb going off . . . like a flashbulb on a camera . . . but it wasn't really there, you know what I mean?"

"No, not really," he said. "But go on . . . what else?"

"I mean the light, the flash, it was inside my head. But it was this blinding explosion. And there was this terrible pain. A thousand times worse than the worst headache. Like a big needle in my head. . . ."

"Allison, when did this happen? Are you all right now?"

"It just happened! Now. Right before I called you. I got so scared I called you right away."

"And you're okay now?"

"Yes, I think so."

"Do you want me to check you out? Are you feeling faint? Queasy? How's your balance, your equilibrium?"

"I'm okay, Doctor Keating. I'm just scared. I have this feeling that something really terrible just happened. And that . . . whatever it was, I somehow was able to feel it happening."

She paused to breathe deeply, to calm herself.

"I just don't want to be alone right now."

"I understand," said Michael, giving her his suite number and instructing her to come down right away.

Hanging up the phone, he noticed Pamela coming toward him from the bedroom, an expression of concern tightened her features.

"What do you make of it?" he said.

"I don't know, but as she was describing what happened, I felt my skin start to crawl."

"Yeah, I felt pretty weird myself. I'm not sure what she was talking about, though."

Pamela shook her head. "I don't think she did, either."

"When she gets here we'll—"

The phone rang again. Pamela moved to answer it. "Doctor Keating's suite . . ."

"Is Doctor Keating there?" The voice was male, crimped by anxiety, but loud enough for Michael to hear it through the tiny earpiece that Pamela projected slightly outward from her.

"Yes he is. May I tell him who's calling?"

"Ira Miller. I was just at the seminar, and . . . something's happened . . ."

Pamela's expression tightened as she handed him the receiver.

"Yes, this is Doctor Keating. It's *Doctor* Miller, isn't it?"

"That's right, and I'm sorry for bothering you like this, but I just had some kind of . . . well, it was like a vision, I guess."

"You *saw* something?"

"Not really. More like I imagined seeing it. It was like an explosion. A terrible burst of energy or something like that. And I felt a pain, but a physical pain. But, you know, like the pain of loss. Sorry, but that's the best way I can describe it."

"You did a fine job," said Michael. "I'm not sure what this means, but somebody else in the group described the same thing. Why don't you come down to my suite on the fourth floor . . ."

"I'll be right there."

Michael hung up the phone, and it rang immediately. Looking at Pamela, he grinned ironically. "Why do I think I know what this one's about?"

"I'll take care of it," she said, picking up the receiver.

She stood there listening, and Michael walked to the bar unit at the far end of the room and poured himself a bourbon, neat. Pamela spoke almost nothing as she listened to the caller. Finally she held her hand over the phone and looked at him. "It's Rodney McGuire . . . same thing. What do we do?"

"I don't know, but I think we should all be together . . ." Michael knew something important was happening, and he was having trouble thinking clearly. The day had been so long, so exhausting. *Think!* "All right, tell him to meet us back at the conference room immediately. Call the desk and tell them to call *all* the subjects with instructions to meet right away in the conference room. I'll head down there now."

"What about Allison and Miller?"

"Oh, yeah, can you wait for them here? Then meet us down there?"

"Sure."

Michael knocked back the remainder of his glass, headed for the door, and stopped. "And you'd better call Klepner or Stevenson, or whoever's on the bureau phone—tell them something weird is happening and that they might want to be here."

The phone started ringing again, but she ignored it. Walking to him instead, she kissed him. "You're very sexy under pressure, did anybody ever tell you that?"

"Actually, no. But thanks." He kissed her once, then held her for an instant. In that quick span, he could feel himself spinning down the well of his memories to a time when he was very young and he'd held on to his mother. Scared at night. Not knowing why.

"You'd better get going," she said finally. "I'll make those calls."

FORTY

AZZIZ IBN MAHMOUD
Manhattan, New York

One half hour and his shift would be over. Azziz could take the old Checker back to the garage on Tenth Avenue, turn in his log and his cash box, and go home. Friday nights in the city were always insane, but this night had been especially frustrating. Everybody who'd climbed into his cab this night had the look of a crazy person in their eyes. Since the sun made its retreat, not one normal fare.

Azziz popped a wintergreen Lifesaver into his mouth as he pulled up to the traffic light at Twenty-eighth Street. Maybe he'd go up to Penn Station. See if maybe there was one more train. One more fare to a midtown hotel. End of a most wearying evening.

But just as the light turned green and he dropped his foot off the brake, someone sprang from the darkness and slapped both hands on his left rear window.

"Wait!" cried the voice.

"Where do you wish to go?" said Azziz, winding the window down a crack and turning to the see the identity of the shadow-man.

"Koch Conference Center," said the man. His voice sounded old, but edged with tension. "S'on Park Avenue, but I don't know the cross-street."

"I am familiar with it," said Azziz. "Okay, come on. Get in."

The door opened and a gangly old man wearing a long shabby coat slipped in. He had longish gray hair and a carefully trimmed little mustache. He looked to Azziz like a man of culture who was down on his luck.

"Thank you so much," he said to Azziz. "This is very important to me."

Azziz looked at him for an instant, nodding his head. "Yes, sir. I am most certain it is."

He pulled away from the curb and joined the traffic flow. The old man appeared to be very agitated and nervous. He kept rubbing his hands together and looking out the window as if he expected to see something quite horrible.

"Can you go any faster?" he said as Azziz slowed down for a red signal at Thirty-fourth Street.

"Not unless you want me to ride on the roofs of the cars in front of us," said Azziz. It was one of the favorite standard answers he kept at the ready for his customers. Others were: *I am from a place you have probably never heard of called South Yemen; No, I don't own this cab, but this is America, and therefore I will someday expect to do so;* and *Yes, it is a lot colder here than in my home country.*

"Please," said the old man. "It's an emergency."

"Do you want I should call the police?" said Azziz. This was another good question. Usually calmed down the fare. But this old man was thinking about it. Maybe he was serious instead of just crazy.

"No, I think they wouldn't believe me," said the old man.

Azziz shrugged, turned right on Forty-second Street.

"Something bad is going to happen tonight."

"Okay," said Azziz.

"Don't you even want to know what I'm talking about?"

"This is your business," said Azziz. "Not mine."

Actually, he was finding himself very interested. But he knew much about this city. New York was a great machine of great complexity. Stand too close to it, you get caught up in its gears. Better to not wonder how it works. Just know that it does.

The traffic along Forty-second was thinning out and he reached Park Avenue very quickly. As he headed toward the Koch Center, Azziz knew something was going on. A stream of black sedans were converging on the building, jamming the entrance drive and portico. Men in dark suits were stationed along the sidewalks and outside the building. As he guided the cab closer to the activity, two men wearing topcoats signaled him curbside. The one closest moved to his window and held up an ID that read *FBI.*

"The Koch Center is closed, sir. For the rest of the evening."

"Tell him I have important information!" said the old man.

Azziz did not want to get involved. He said nothing as he put the cab into reverse.

"Tell them!" the old man yelled, then he wound down his window and started screaming at the dark-suited men. "Wait! It's about Harford Nichols! You've got to help me! You've got to save me from him! Nichols! It's fucking Nichols!"

The cab had begun drifting backward, away from the sedan-blocked driveway, when suddenly the two FBI agents were trotting alongside, banging on the hood.

"Hold it!" said the closest man. "What did he say?"

Azziz shrugged. Better to play very dumb on this one.

The old man was frantically winding down his window. "Harford Nichols!" he yelled the words again.

One of the agents spoke into a small radio transmitter, while the other pulled out a large handgun. Brandishing it at Azziz and his passenger, he spoke in a very firm voice. "Okay, both of you—out of the car. Now!"

FORTY-ONE

DER KLEIN ENGEL
Manhattan, New York

11:50 P.M.

Fritz Hargrove was standing there on the loading dock with a silly grin on his face. Insipid. Unvigilant. Stupid. If he didn't think he might still need him, Dukor would shoot him now.

No, not yet.

Quickly, Dukor scanned the area behind him. Actually, Hargrove's face put him at immediate ease. The big oaf was incapable of any ruse. Had there been an ambush waiting for him, it would have been announced in the man's doughy features.

"What's wrong?" he said flatly, although his eyes had zeroed in on Dukor's automatic pistol.

"You were thirty seconds behind schedule," he said. "I had to take out two units guarding this entrance! We have *maybe* sixty seconds before they realize what's happened. . . . *Every* second is critical. Get moving!"

Fritz nodded and ran to the rear door of the van, where the three-drum cluster on an orange handcart awaited him. Fritz grabbed the handle, tilted the load forward, and muled it across the loading dock.

"This way," said Dukor, running down a corridor just wide

enough to allow the drums of explosives. Moving at a brisk jog, he reached the outer bay of service elevators and waited for Fritz to catch up. "Keep moving! Hurry!"

They passed the bay, following the corridor deeper, toward the central core of the building. Dukor knew that to completely consume the building, to ensure maximum carnage, he would have to detonate the device as close to the exact center of the structure as possible.

Any minute now, the security force would realize they'd been breached and duped. The building would be locked tight. By that time, Dukor would have to be clear of the target. Another thirty seconds was all he would need to get the device into place. Two minutes to clear the area.

It would be tight. But he'd worked close to the bone before.

The second set of service elevators lay just ahead, thirty yards up the corridor, which was flanked by ductwork and pipe railings. Running hard, he reached the bay in several seconds. He pushed the button to summon one of the cars, then stood off the line of sight of the doors with his weapon extended. Behind him echoed the sound of Fritz's labored breathing and the creak of the dolly rolling forward.

With a soft, metallic sigh, the elevator doors parted. Dukor checked the parabolic mirror inside the car, leaping past the opening while sweeping it with the barrel of the gun.

No need. The interior lay empty.

A dull *clunk!* sounded behind him, and he spun quickly to see Fritz leaning forward, pulling on the dolly handle like a plowhorse in deep mud.

"Oh shit . . . !" whispered Fritz.

"What are you doing, idiot!" Dukor pushed him out of the way. "You'll wedge it tighter! Push it back!"

His copies of the blueprints of the building had provided him with everything he'd needed to calculate his plan—right down to the maximum width he could make the bomb cluster, the size of the drums, dolly, everything. Along the catwalks and access corridors, he'd allowed a three-inch clearance on each side when he designed the bomb.

Getting stuck like this was impossible.

Or so he assumed until he bent down to examine the problem: at some point, there must have been a wiring or plumbing problem along this walkway. To fix it, to provide access to a vertical shaft intersecting the corridor, a technician or a workman had installed a metal casement with a hinged faceplate, like an oversized breaker box. The addition extended into the walkway just far enough to wedge the bomb and dolly.

"Here!" he yelled to Fritz. "Push *with* me! Back!"

They did, but the cluster and the dolly did not budge.

"Again!"

This time their combined effort forced the dolly backward, freeing it from the occlusion.

But not solving the problem. There were only two choices: either leave the device here, detonate and hope for the best, or dismantle the cluster and feed it piece by piece into the elevator. Physics demanded he get the device into the center of the building for maximum effect. He could not risk an explosion like the one at the World Trade Center, where it became contained within the foundation.

"Hold this!" he said as he produced a Navy Seal serrated-edge assault blade from his belt. The titanium-steel blade could cut through just about anything and it made quick work of the cables he'd used to lash the drums together into a triad cluster. Fritz eased one of the drums off the dolly, then pushed it past the barrier.

The rig cleared it with plenty of room to spare.

"Into the elevator! Hurry! Then back for this one."

Hargrove hustled the dolly into the elevator, then returned to help Dukor lift the single drum so that it could rejoin its mates.

They had lost precious seconds because of the fuck-up. He had to assume that security was onto them by now. Reaching into his coveralls, he pulled out a device that resembled a hand calculator with a small LCD screen. Turning it on, he watched a grid appear, displaying a rectangle surrounded by ten or twelve red dots. They were waiting for him outside.

"No time to relash this thing. I'm setting the detonator for four minutes. Even if they find it, they won't be able to defuse it in time."

"Does that give us enough time?" Hargrove's voice sounded hoarse, strained. "To get out . . . ?"

"We've lost valuable minutes. We have to adjust," said Dukor. "We'll get out."

Dukor leaned close to the digital face of the detonator. Keying in his security code, he locked down the time at

$$00{:}04{:}00$$

then activated the panel. Stepping outside the door, he pushed the elevator button for the fourth floor and smiled at Hargrove.

"All right. Move your ass!"

FORTY-TWO

BRADLEY STEVENSON
Manhattan, New York

His PCS phone buzzed the exact moment he'd dropped his pants and started to let go.

Why did everything happen at the worst possible time?

The eternal question jetted through his mind as he struggled to pull up his pants and get everything tucked in. Banging his elbows on the walls of the toilet stall, he cursed the tight parameters of the rest room and the events of the last five minutes.

Bursting from the stall, Brad almost collided with Sid Klepner and Andy McShea, who'd rushed to meet him in the bathroom. "All right, brief me! Quick!"

Andy McShea wiped his brow with a rumpled handkerchief. Brad noticed the man was sweating heavily and observed that he must be one of the last guys on earth still carrying around linen hankies—even if it was for a very good reason.

"Okay," said McShea. "We've got two dead on seven—security guard and a guest. Perp's still loose in here somewhere. Building electronics have been breached and pretty well fucked over. Doctor Keating has a possible mass-panic situation up on four. And the perimeter team just apprehended a guy out on the street—says Harford Nichols is bringing a bomb in here."

"I think he's a little late on that one," said Brad. "Anybody sweat him yet?"

"No, he's still at the front desk," said Klepner. "I figured you wanted to see him first."

"Good figuring. We got ID on him?"

Klepner's features tightened. "Yeah, it's Rassenault!"

"*That* old kook?"

"So what're we doing?" said McShea. "If there's supposed to be a bomb in here—"

"I'm sure there is," said Brad. "But why're you getting excited?" he said with a shrug. "Isn't this what we planned on?"

"I didn't plan on getting blown up," said McShea.

"Nichols is still in the building. Relax."

"Yeah, but *where*?" said Klepner. "The delivery boy was definitely *not* him."

"Probably one of Rassenault's goons . . ." said Brad. "What're we doing to catch him, by the way?" Brad walked to the rest room exit door and pushed through without waiting for his men to follow.

"A-Fours just landed on the roof," said Klepner as he held his earphone in place and listened to an update. "They blew their way in and the assault team's on its way down, floor by floor. Hang on . . . there's more . . ."

"What about from below?" Brad continued to head back to the lobby security station commandeered as the HQ. He felt as though somebody had hooked him up to a high-voltage cable. *All* jacked up, pal! He loved it! Everybody looking up to him for all the answers. The ultimate power trip. Some guys thrived on it; some guys choked.

Klepner continued to hold his miniearphone in place as he looked up and shook his head. "We've got two more units terminated. They'd been assigned to the loading dock entrance."

"That's probably how Nichols breached us. Any sign of forced entry?"

Klepner shook his head. "No go . . . All the door codes have been scrambled. But there's a Voyager minivan at the loading dock full of high-tech gear."

Brad nodded. "Tell everybody to hold their positions. No forced entry at this time. We've got him bottled up. If he does have a bomb, he's trying to send it up the central elevator shaft. But unless he's on a suicide mission, he's going to try to break out somewhere."

Brad paused to take in a deep breath. Jesus, this was what it was all about, wasn't it? This is why they paid him so well. If he thought about it too much, he knew it could start pulling away. He had to kind of play it out by instinct, as quickly as possible. There just wasn't any time to weigh decisions. You just made them and hoped they were right later.

McShea brightened, as if just remembering something. "Sir, we figured—"

Ignoring him, Brad jogged the rest of the way down the plushly carpeted hall to the security station. He grabbed the closest building guard still seated at one of the consoles. "Any way to kill power to the entire building from here?"

"Sure, but nothing's working right now!" said the man in a panic. "Everything's locked up."

"Manual override?"

"You gotta do it from the physical plant—downstairs!"

Brad nodded, turned to Klepner. "Take some A-Fours, and this security guy. Get down to the physical plant and shut this building down. All I want is auxiliary power—some lights in the halls and the security consoles in this area. Can you do it?"

"Sure," said the security man. "If we can get down there . . ."

"Mr. Stevenson," said the other security officer, who was seated at the main console, checking screens, "we've got a service elevator lifting from the physical plant level . . ."

```
00:03:59
```

"Looks like we're a little late," said Brad. "Klepner, we have the bomb wagon here yet?"

"On their way. Any second—the chopper's touching down in the street right now."

"Send them up to four right away."

"Got it," said McShea, barking the order into his PCS phone.

Brad paused, coordinating everything, keeping his thoughts together. *Don't lose it now.* He was juggling a lot of balls in the air. "Okay, take some A-Fours. Get down there anyway. Try to flush Nichols back toward his van. We've got a team outside the loading dock doors."

Klepner nodded silently as he produced an automatic pistol from inside his jacket. He signaled to the security officer and the commander of the A-4 team to follow him to the emergency stairwell.

McShea stood by, pressing on his earpiece. "A-Fours just reached Keating's people!"

"Everybody okay?" said Brad.

McShea gave him a thumbs-up. "Want to start E-Vac?"

Brad shook his head. "No, that many people will get in our way."

McShea wiped his shiny face again. That hankie was soaked and looking kind of nasty. He edged closer to Brad, arched an eyebrow. "Listen, if we've really got a bomb in here, don't you think maybe—"

"Forget it," said Brad. "If it's going to go off, we've got to take our chances. We didn't all come rushing in here just to run away. Now, give me a minute to talk to our pigeon. Get him over here."

McShea spun off to a far corner of the security station, through a door to a small office, then returned almost immediately with a spindly, gray-haired man in a long, ratty-looking topcoat. Rassenault looked beaten and scared, but Brad didn't have much sympathy for him.

"So, Arnold, how's the hate business these days?"

"You've got to get everybody out!" he said in a painfully weak voice. "He's crazy!"

"We know that. When'd you hook up with him?"

"Weeks ago. He found me, hounded me."

Brad grinned. "See, you're a famous guy."

"A terrible mistake," said Rassenault. "My whole life's been a mistake. I just want to help—any way I can."

Brad chuckled. "Yeah, sure. What's the angle—misdirection? Disinformation?"

"Nothing like that, really! You've got to believe me . . ."

"Yeah, we've heard that line before," said Brad. He looked at the old guy; he looked like he hadn't slept in days—like holy hell, really. If he was here to put on an acting job, Rassenault was doing it *too* damned well. But he had to push him. "You expect me to believe that you had this sudden conversion, eh? Forty years of being a Nazi wannabe—that's over, huh?"

The old man hung his head, shook it slowly. "I don't know about that anymore. All I know is this bastard scares the living hell out of me! He's like the Devil himself! He thinks I'm his friend—and you've got to stop him, you've got to keep him away from me!"

"What did he tell you about this whole thing?" said Brad, starting to understand what was going on with the old guy.

Rassenault shook his head. "Not much. But he's so smart. You have no idea how smart he is!"

"Did he say anything at all?"

"He said he mixed up an 'Oklahoma cocktail for all the kikes.' Some kind of bomb, right?"

"Yeah, you could say that," said Brad.

"Can you stop him?"

"Sure," said Brad, with a sardonic smile. "We're the government, remember? We're here to help you."

"Please . . ." said Rassenault. "Nichols is a monster."

Brad said nothing, but inwardly he acknowledged the hideous truth of that. Nichols was probably the scariest foe he'd faced in a long, long time. And if he thought about it too much, it could intimidate and influence his thinking. Better to just forget about it.

He looked at McShea, who was holding on to Rassenault's arm. "Go put him back in his cage," said Brad. "He's got nothing else we don't already know."

He checked his watch. It was almost midnight. If that was when their friend scheduled the blast, they were all very deep in the brown stuff.

00:03:50

FORTY-THREE

DER KLEIN ENGEL
Manhattan, New York

> **00:03:43**

Fritz did indeed move his ass.

Faster than Dukor'd ever seen him move, the big, slow-witted man lumbered down the physical plant corridor toward the loading dock. Dukor followed him with the stride of the natural athlete. He reveled in the excellent tone and condition of his body. Gifted with power and grace, Dukor felt as if he could do anything.

Keeping his gaze on Hargrove, he watched him reach and pass the outer bay of elevators. Almost done. Another minute and they would be out of the building. The lost thirty seconds were inconsequential now.

When he was within ten yards of the elevator bay, the maroon door to the emergency stairwell suddenly opened.

Instinctively, Dukor pulled up, flattened himself against the padded ductwork of the access corridor. Hargrove had already cleared the area and could not see the movement; he would be an easy target if he didn't turn around. Unslinging his Heckler & Koch

MP5, Dukor dropped to one knee, watched a squad of eight commandos stream from the open door with the precision of army ants, carapaced in distinctive black Kevlar armor. These guys were slick and tough. A-4s were some of the best assault squads FBI money could produce. They weren't as fearsome as Navy Seals because there weren't enough thoroughly lunatic agents available to fit that mold. Regardless, they would have to be handled almost instantly if he was going to clear the building in time. If he didn't surprise them successfully the first time, they might get him. Very quietly, he arranged his LCD remote in his outer coverall pocket and unhooked a concussion grenade from his belt.

But he had to be very careful.

Patient.

Even though they knew he was down here, even though they were looking for him, the element of surprise remained with Dukor. *Wait till everybody clears the cover of the door. Wait till they're all exposed. Plan your moves, anticipate their counters.*

Remember—those men were running on fear energy. They didn't know what they were walking into. But one of them was going to spot Hargrove any moment now.

The last guy out the door always wore the black suit and tie, and this operation didn't disappoint. As soon as the bureau man appeared, Dukor activated the grenade, heaved it with the classic straight-arm toss right into the middle of the assault team.

It arced gracefully downward, clattering dully at the feet of one of them, and he reacted the way most men in the same situation did—the man stood rigidly looking at the thing that was going to blow him to pieces, unable to move or even cry out. Somebody did, and the rest of them started diving to the floor when the grenade hammered them with its fiery blast.

White heat and light blinded him for an instant and the sonic concussion grabbed him like a barroom bouncer and threw him up against the wall. Roiling smoke choked through the contained area and he couldn't see how effective the attack had been.

But it didn't matter. Dukor had no alternative now, other than running past the carnage toward Hargrove and the loading dock doors. Breaking into a sprint, he shot past the edge of the blast area, where smoldering debris and pieces of what had been people lay scattered like burnt trash.

Ahead, Hargrove had been stunned by the explosion and had been thrown forward on his face. The big man was still scrambling to his feet when Dukor reached him.

"Get up!" Dukor said as he wheeled and sprayed a clip into the chaos behind them. "Get up and start shooting."

Hargrove's face numbly reflected the terror that churned in him. Dukor had seen the look before in men who'd never taken their own words seriously enough, who'd never realized they might die for the cause they claimed to love so much.

Incredibly, three commandos and the guy in the dark suit staggered forward from the dissipating smoke. Dukor knew they had to be still shaking off the effects of the blast, but that wouldn't stop them from shooting wildly in their general direction. Hargrove opened up on them with his own HK-MP5, which he picked up from the dolly, but his hand trembled so badly, the slugs stitched a path across some PVC plumbing over the commandos' heads. In turn, they raised their own automatic weapons.

Absorbed by the action, Dukor had lost all sense of time. He had no idea when the nitrate would go off and couldn't think about it now anyway.

Unleashing a second clip, Dukor put enough slugs through the lead man's body armor to drop him. The other three broke into a run, heedless of Hargrove's defensive fire. They both turned and ran for the automatic doors on the loading dock, taking cover behind several pallets of unloaded cartons.

"Fritz, you've got to hit that door button."

"No way!" shouted Hargrove, his eyes brimming over with stinging fear. "No fucking way!"

Dukor smiled as he moved inside his guard like a cat. Before the big man could blink, the barrel of Dukor's HK was stuck under his jaw. "I think there *is* a way, my large friend. You keep yourself lined up so these boxes stay between you and them. You do that . . . or I'm going to spray paint the ceiling with your brains."

Hargrove didn't say a single word and managed only the slightest of nods. Turning away from Dukor and his weapon, Fritz bolted for the red and green slap-buttons on the near wall. As he did this, Dukor reached into his outer pocket and grabbed the remote keypad. With his other hand, he unloaded the rest of his clip into what was left of the A-4 commandos.

Behind him, Hargrove stumbled and rumbled to the corner of the building and whacked the big green button with his palm. Instantly, the electric motors began grinding and the steel security doors began to rise on the final act. From where he was standing Fritz had a clear view of the Voyager minivan, and as Dukor took a read on his expression, he knew what was coming.

Hargrove opened his mouth in warning, but a volley of bullets ripped him across the stomach and neck too quickly for words. Hargrove's body slammed back against the wall, hung there for an instant like a marionette on tangled strings, then collapsed.

The attack had been the sign Dukor was waiting for; he smiled as he touched the keypad in his pocket.

Time for a little surprise. . . .

FORTY-FOUR

J. MICHAEL KEATING, M.D.
Manhattan, New York

00:02:38

Until now, Michael did not believe in miracles.

But as he stood in the midst of these very special people, he knew he would be witness to one.

"Something special is going to happen," Allison had just told him. She was standing at the entrance to the conference room where everyone had assembled.

"What do you mean?" said Pamela.

"Ms. Karnow says we've been brought together to stop the Devil," said Allison. "She might be right."

"There's something else," said Ira Miller, stepping close to Allison.

"What's that?" said Michael, feeling a vague sense of unease.

"I was thinking about this when I went back to my room," said Miller. "It's almost the millennium. Lots of cults and religious groups think it's going to be the end of the world."

"The same thing happened in the year one thousand," said Michael. "I don't follow what you're getting at."

Miller shrugged. "So maybe the end of the millennium *is* a milepost, not signaling the end of something—but the *beginning*. . . ."

"Beginning of what?" said Pamela.

"I'm not sure, but if the Nazis are also being reborn in people like us, the way we've been reborn, then maybe it's like that Yeats poem . . . you know the one—something evil 'slouching toward Bethlehem' ready to be born."

"So what are we talking about?" said Michael. "Some kind of spiritual Armageddon?"

Miller and Allison and all the others slowly nodded as they looked at him. It was a moment of chilling certitude. Although Michael had no evidence to support what they were telling him, he believed it might be true, and just the idea of it unsettled him. He didn't like the idea of being tangled up in such metaphysics. Perhaps—

His last thought was interrupted by the arrival of the FBI's black-clad A-4 assault force. They reached the conference room silently, en masse. They carried automatic rifles, utility belts strung with arcane devices, and ebon-visored helmets that made them look very much like menacing insects. Everyone stood silently looking at them as they soldiered into the room

"Which one of you is Doctor Keating?" said their leader as he approached Michael and the others.

"I am," said Michael.

Flipping up his visor, he revealed himself as a handsome young man in his twenties. "I'm Commander Tasker," he said. "We've got a very serious situation here." The commander summarized Anna Smithson's killing and the bomb on the elevator.

As though expecting panic, Tasker scanned the room, but everyone remained calm, perfectly silent; they'd already sensed what he now told them. In fact, the utter serenity on their faces was disturbing in itself. Michael could feel it, so could the FBI agents who stood among them.

"It's going to be all right," said Allison Enders. She had approached Michael, touched his cheek, then went to join the others as they assembled into three concentric circles in the center of the room, holding hands, closing their eyes in unison. Michael, Pamela, and the FBI team stood closer to the room's entrance, watching them.

"What's going on?" said the commander.

"I don't know exactly," said Michael. "But it's nothing to fear, I can tell you that."

The space seemed consumed by a wondrous silence, but Michael could feel more than hear a very low humming sound, like the subtle vibration of a gigantic piece of machinery slowly whirring up to speed. A turbine gathering revolutions until its keening wail of sheer power left the register of audible sound. The air began to crackle, and some of the FBI men tried to reach under their helmets to protect their ears.

Irwin Klingerman had fallen to his knees, reciting a Hebrew prayer that began, *"Sh'ma Y'Israel . . ."*

"Michael . . . !" Pamela held him ever tighter, but could say nothing more.

Michael felt as if he was standing at the edge of an endless beach, where the star-filled sky stretched to infinity, and a summer storm flirted with the earth. It was both scary and comforting.

"What's going on?" said the commander, trying to remain stolid, in control.

Allison Enders stepped from the outer circle, her long strawberry-blond hair tossing in an unfelt wind. She had a detached look in her eyes, but something strong and hard and bright lurked behind them. Michael could sense a force in her, coming from the others. They were radiating it like a uranium pile with the control rods being slowly extracted.

```
00:01:47
```

At the same time, two new FBI men appeared in the doorway, wearing dark metal or plastic gear and looking like something from a medieval armory. "Bomb wagon, sir!" said one of them to the A-4 commander. "We've got big trouble—"

"How big?" said the commander.

"Okie Cocktail. Three drums of nitrate. Digital scrambler on the timer! No way to stop it!"

"You talking E-Vac? *Now?*" The commander did nothing to conceal the panic in his voice.

Michael could deduce enough to realize there was nothing they could do to stop the device. Nichols or Dukor, or whatever ominous force had been controlling him like a puppet, had beaten them. He'd listened to the FBI and their swaggering confidence, their prideful arrogance, and played into the hands of the beast.

The bomb specialist shook his head. "No time for that! Either we start cutting wires and hope for the best, or we just sit back and wait for the fireworks."

> **00:00:53**

"Okay, take your best guess," said Commander Tasker. "We'll get these people down the corridor and as far away from the blast as possible."

The bomb guy's expression said it all: a facial portrait of words never spoken, or of kids he'd never see again, of the soft curve of his wife's hip touched no more. He swallowed hard, saluted, and turned to leave.

Allison Enders had been listening and now moved in between them. "Wait . . ." she said. "It's okay. Don't touch anything."

"Lady, we've got to try!"

"No, you don't—"

"Chucky," said Tasker to one of his assault team, "get these people outta here! Double time!"

"No!" screamed Allison, grabbing the bomb specialist by the breastplate of his armor. "*We've* got it!"

Michael, who'd been standing there with Pamela, mute witnesses to what should have been the final minute of their lives, had remained calm. As if waiting for something beautiful, something special. The way Allison had looked at everyone, with the graceful gaze of an archangel, he'd simply known they were all right.

All around them, the subtle vibration and the crackle in the air grew stronger, like a rising wind. Like a ghostly chorus, an atonal resonance filled the room.

"C'mon, lady, you've got—"

"No!" yelled Michael, grabbing the commander's arm. "Stop! Can't you feel it?"

The FBI man's eyes gave it away. He could feel it, all right. Everybody could. It was like standing on the deck of a ship that had suddenly started to vibrate. It was like placing a just-struck tuning-fork to the side of your skull. Michael knew he could feel it all the way down to his toes.

The bomb specialist stood unmoving, staring past Allison at the concentric rings of people.

Holding hands, closing an arcane circuit, like the mystical pattern of a crop circle, everyone became filled with light, radiating a burst of holy fire that shot through them. Painless. Cool. Eternally bright.

Michael felt his back arching as he was practically lifted off his feet by the sudden ebullience. Something had been generated among them. Something that had literally burst from the group, passed right through the rest of them—the FBI men, Pamela, Irwin, and himself.

Something that now rushed to snuff out the bomb like a tired candle.

00:00:17

As the energy passed through him, Michael's knees buckled just enough to make him stagger. He felt as if he might black out, but he didn't care. He felt something inside him—only for an instant—so sweetly pure, so all-consumingly just and righteous and *good* that nothing would ever harm or corrupt him again.

The final seconds devoured them.

FORTY-FIVE

BRADLEY STEVENSON
Manhattan, New York

00:00:12

Even if he wanted to play hero, protocol and his superiors wouldn't allow it. As soon as he'd been given word there were several major snafus in progress, and no time for the bomb wagon to get their fat out of the fire, Brad had been E-Vacked from the building and into a black chopper on whisper jet. He was hung out to dry above the Koch Center listening to the final frantic seconds of the botched operation. The only reason the bureau chiefs wanted him alive, he knew, was so they could toast him themselves.

Brad had the bomb wagon channel in his headset as the chopper hovered over the building like a hungry dragonfly.

"What's happening out there?" said one of the poor bastards near ground zero.

"Can't see it! The light! What's that light?"

Suddenly the ambient noise of the city was sucked up in a fireball that blossomed behind the Koch Center, unfolding its deadly petals and throwing off waves of heat and sound that bounced off the tall faces of the surrounding buildings, battering the chopper in the backwash of the blast.

FORTY-SIX

DER KLEIN ENGEL
Manhattan, New York

00:00:08

The explosion was a lot bigger and a lot louder than he'd imagined. Where the minivan had rested, a small sun novaed, sending deadly shrapnel that had only a moment before been wheels and sheet metal, steel beams and rack-mounted consoles. Now hot flaming slabs of junk took out everybody within fifty yards of the plastique he'd applied to the Voyager's gas tank.

He laughed as he ran off the edge of the loading dock, straight through the flames and out to what his colleagues liked to call the perimeter. As he cleared the bank of snarling, curling smoke, he almost ran into the ATAV—all-terrain armored assault vehicle. But his quick reactions allowed him to throw himself into a tuck and roll, sending him under the vehicle's balloon tires and up on the other side before the turret man ever saw him.

No sense worrying if anybody else was watching. In one quick motion, he pulled himself up to the deck of the ATAV and emptied half a clip into the man on the .50-caliber gun.

"Hey, Eddie!" said a voice from inside the vehicle. "What was that?"

Dukor dropped through the dead man's open hatch, shot the driver in the back of the head, and yanked him from the control seat. Punching the ignition, he jammed home the throttle. The ATAV leaped out into the street like an angry armadillo.

He smiled as the powerful machine surged under his touch.

He was going to make it.

FORTY-SEVEN

J. MICHAEL KEATING, M.D.
Manhattan, New York

00:00:07

Something has passed right *through* him.

Like the others, it had paralyzed them with its icy touch, but he could *see* it now as it encircled the cluster of explosives in the elevator. Like a vortex, a whirlwind of light, fueled by the fires of six million ovens, it surrounded the device and held it within the crucible of its righteousness.

And it was gone.

No sound.

Not even the whimper promised in that Eliot poem.

Nothing to tell him . . .

. . . but Michael knew it was over.

FORTY-EIGHT

BRADLEY STEVENSON
Manhattan, New York

00:00:06

Somehow, they were still airborne, though foundering in the superheated air of the shockwave. Brad's pilot wrestled expertly with the chopper's controls, keeping them aloft.

"Hang on, sir! We're okay!" he said in a voice that belied his surprise. "What the hell was that?"

"Not the target," said Brad, pointing down at the Koch Center, bathed in the play of temporary searchlights.

"Christamighty!" squawked somebody's voice in the headset. "We just lost the van!"

"Control, this is Stevenson . . . what's the situation?"

"No contact, sir," said a flat, radio voice. "Looks bad from here. . . ."

Directly below them, the square of asphalt behind the building, where Nichols' van had been surrounded, had been transformed into an open barbecue pit. Littered with a thousand pieces of flaming debris, it looked very bad indeed.

"Hey, what's that?" said his pilot, pointing to the roof of the Koch Center.

Following the pilot's lead, Brad saw a pure white dome of light coalesce on the flat roof. A perfect hemisphere, maybe twenty yards in diameter, it glowed with a mother-of-pearl intensity of color and swirling energy.

". . . it's . . . beautiful . . . it's so goddamned *beautiful!*" said the pilot as he angled his craft back to the right, swooping down for a closer look.

"My God . . ." said Brad in a half-whisper, as he watched the dome of light begin to transform.

Slowly at first, and then with stunning quickness, the dome distended skyward, extruding itself into a narrowing shaft of the purest, whitest light Brad had ever seen. Like a laser beacon, the column of energy reached for the edge of the night itself. And as it grew ever stronger, brighter, Brad could see it transform itself into a double-edged sword. Churning across its mercurial surface spun a million ever-changing patterns of helical complexity. The narrowing gyre sharpened to a fine edge, forming a pointed column that pierced the blue isle of the night. If there was such a place as heaven, thought Brad, then it most surely reached it.

FORTY-NINE

DER KLEIN ENGEL
Manhattan, New York

Driving the ATAV was like riding a wild boar. Its oversized tires bounced severely as Dukor vaulted over obstacles. Despite the chaos spinning all around him, several NYPDs fired their handguns at him to no effect. Straight ahead, blocking access to Park Avenue, stretched an ambulance and several emergency light stanchions. Dukor rammed the throttle forward and the vehicle's huge Chrysler engines whined like turbines.

The ATAV cleaved the thin sheet metal of the ambulance like a Ginsu knife, scattering equipment and debris out into the traffic lanes. Sparks ignited the emergency oxygen tanks and Dukor had created yet another explosion to liven up the drab colors of the city.

The thought reminded him that something had gone wrong with his nitrate bomb. And his failure truly wounded him, igniting a seething fury deep within him, down in that core where a dark engine drove him.

Fuck it.

They live only at my pleasure. They're together because my destiny demands it. I destroyed them all before; I'll do it again.

He allowed himself a small smile as he cleared the wreckage and angled across the divided lanes of Park Avenue. He knew none of his opponents could have anticipated his next move—one of several escape options he'd carefully structured—and just the thought of it amused and sustained him.

And so, with the throttle still red-lined, Dukor sent the ATAV hurtling and balloon-bouncing over the concrete dividers on Park. He entered the lanes of northbound traffic, facing the oncoming cars and trucks head-on. With no running lights, his vehicle became a shadowy dreadnought. As he angled the vehicle across the lanes, homing on his target, several cabs braked and swerved, but couldn't avoid slamming him broadside like dud torpedoes. The sharply beveled armor of the ATAV sliced through the cars, ripping them open like rotten fruit, and Dukor lumbered on, leaving more destruction in his wake. He literally jounced and rolled *over* a row of parked cars and commandeered the entire sidewalk at interstate speed, taking out streetlamps and telephone poles along the way. The few pedestrians in his path scattered, passing beyond the scope of his periscoped view. Whether or not they escaped the steamroller advance of his giant tires was of no concern to him.

Several blocks down, his target lay bathed in a majestic play of lights and landscaping and elegant banners. From the quickly closing distance, he could see guests and staff under the marquee of the Waldorf-Astoria scrambling for the shelter of the grand old building's lobby.

Wrong move, folks. . . .

Seconds compressed as Dukor reached the entrance to the hotel and wrenched the vehicle into a careening powerslide to the left as its great tires wailed in spinning defiance. Then, gaining purchase, the ATAV lurched forward through the array of glass and revolving doors of the Waldorf. In a brilliant eruption of masonry and glass and steel, the entire entry facade to the building imploded into the grand lobby, lacing the patrons with a variety of deadly missiles. Like a giant, charging rhino, the ATAV surged forward, its driving wheels ripping up the plush carpeting and spewing it out behind in a great roostertail of fabric.

The panic in the lobby was total and irreversible. People swarmed in any direction, as long as it was away from the berserker machine that crushed through the expertly paneled mahogany front desk, taking out partitions that supported ceilings and crystal chandeliers.

Dukor didn't stop the mad onrush of the ATAV until it rammed against the steel supports of the old elevator shafts and cages. Calmly, he threw back the hatch, climbed out, and headed for the stairwell down. Of course, no one tried to stop him. He chuckled as he watched the few remaining citizens running away from him, their eyes wide and their jaws slack.

What a bunch of terrified sheep. . . .

He raised his HK, wishing he had time to take out a few of them for being so stupid and gutless.

No, not now.

He had the advantage of surprise and total shock, and he would only succeed if he held the advantage. And so, with a wry grin, he saluted a uniformed bellhop who'd been half-crawling, half-staggering away from the splintered nightmare of the front desk, then disappeared through the doors leading into the bowels of the building.

FIFTY

J. MICHAEL KEATING, M.D.
Manhattan, New York

Until tonight, the phrase "religious experience" had just been another piece of clinical terminology for Michael. Something from the days of William James and his profound ruminations. Intriguing, certainly, but abstract and without passion.

But no longer. . . .

With his arms held tightly around Pamela, Michael allowed himself and the others to be escorted from the fourth floor. They passed the elevator, where its doors had been pried open, and saw the dolly that had carried its deadly cargo now strangely empty. The air in the corridor had a clean, almost antiseptic odor to it. Michael recognized the smell of ozone and wondered what kind of bizarre and wonderful transformation had happened here.

No one spoke as they were led down to the first-floor reception area. And Michael understood perfectly—there was no need, when all the people in their group had communicated in some deeper, and perhaps far older, manner.

It was not until they reached the security desk and were forced to interact with the FBI agents and other uniformed people that the spell was broken.

"I feel like I've been in church," said Pamela, "and God actually came down to have a talk with me."

Michael nodded. "I think that's how we *all* feel."

Irwin Klingerman moved through the crowd, embraced both of them to his wide chest. "Sorry if I'm too familiar," he said excitedly. "But I don't think I could go through something like that without hugging *somebody*."

"It's a very human thing to want to do," said Pamela. "Count me in."

"I don't want anybody asking me what happened up there," said Michael. "I don't want to know . . . I don't ever *need* to know."

"I know exactly what you mean," said Pamela. "I just feel . . . *blessed* to have been allowed to witness it."

"To *feel* it is more like it," said Michael.

"Yes," said Irwin. "But even though we didn't really see anything, I still feel like we saw everything—am I making any sense?"

"Oh, yes," said Michael.

Paramedics and support staff had begun filtering through the crowd, checking everyone for any kind of trauma and making every effort to ensure that all were safe and comfortable. Michael scanned the FBI types, looking for Klepner or another familiar face, but there was still too much confusion among them and the uniformed police now streaming through the vast reception foyer.

From the ambient sound and energy in the big room, it sounded as if there was still something serious going on. Michael maneuvered his way to the security desk, now aswarm with people on radios and telephones. In their midst, Michael finally spotted a familiar face: Andy McShea, Klepner's partner.

Waving to get his attention, Michael walked over to him. "Mr. McShea?"

The man glared at him. "Yeah, what do you want?"

"What's wrong?" said Michael. "What happened?"

"Sid . . . goddammit . . . he didn't make it," McShea said, taking a deep breath.

"Oh, no . . . I'm sorry, I—"

McShea read his shocked expression, shook his head sadly. "Hey listen, Doc . . . sorry about that. I was outta line."

Michael nodded, said nothing. He hadn't known Klepner very well, but he'd liked him a lot just the same. The agent had probably instilled that feeling in most people he knew.

"I'm sorry," said McShea, adjusting the knot on his tie. "We still have work to do here. What can I do for you?"

"We just came down from upstairs . . ."

"Yeah, I heard it was some show." McShea arched his eyebrows.

". . . and we wanted to know what happened down here. Did they stop Dukor?"

"Who?" McShea tilted his head just slightly.

"Nichols," said Michael. "I mean *Nichols*, did they get him?"

"Oh, Jeez, you didn't hear, did you?" McShea summarized the shoot-out that killed Klepner, the bomb in the van, and the hijacked ATAV. He was going into a few details when he was interrupted by the appearance of Brad Stevenson and a small squad of underlings.

"Doctor Keating," said Stevenson, who looked rakish and formidable dressed in a dark blue jumpsuit and carrying a flight helmet. "Glad to see you made it through this mess. Everybody okay in your group?"

"Pretty much," said Michael. "What's going on? You didn't get him?"

Stevenson shook his head. "Outside, you mean? No, we couldn't chance any rounds from the chopper—too many civilians around."

"McShea says he crashed it into the *Waldorf*?"

Stevenson looked embarrassed as he rubbed a hand over his face, as if to remove the expression. "Yeah, that's where we lost him. . . ."

"In the hotel?"

"Well, not exactly. Witnesses say he escaped down the stairs into the building's basement, or *below*," said Stevenson. "Some of my people followed him and they found a door to a subbasement blown off its hinges. The stairs leading down had either rotted away or had been damaged in the blast. They went down anyway and found the damnedest thing—"

"I *know* what they found," said Michael, his heart hitching up a few extra beats.

"You *do*? How—?"

"They found the tunnel, didn't they?" said Michael slowly.

Stevenson nodded. "Huge thing, yeah. Heading north. No lights. Two lines of narrow gauge railroad running down the middle."

Michael nodded.

"How do *you* know about that place?"

"We toured it about five years ago, my museum group," said

Michael. "Park Avenue's like a thin pie crust from Grand Central Station all the way up past the nineties. Last century, the wealthiest people in New York got together and had a little railroad built for themselves and their families *underneath the city*."

"You're kidding!" said Stevenson. "What the hell for?"

Michael shrugged. "Privacy, mostly, and also just because they *could*. They used to have a private handcar pick them up at their houses uptown and take them down to their offices at the Grand Central building. And whenever bigwigs or a president came into the city, they could be secreted off into the suites at the Waldorf without ever poking their heads above the ground. Straight from their train just in from Washington."

"How come nobody knows about this place?" Stevenson shook his head in mock disbelief.

"Nobody's used it in a long, long time. Some people still do—the museums and the archeological society, and apparently our friend Nichols." As Michael talked, several ideas occurred to him. He decided to save the best for last.

"Incredible," said Stevenson. "Fucking incredible."

"Listen," said Michael. "You wouldn't believe what's under this city . . ."

"Tell me some other time," said Stevenson. "We've got to get after him before the trail's cold. Any place we can get some maps of that area?"

Michael shook his head. "No place quick and dirty. But *I* have one."

Stevenson grinned. "In your head, right?"

"Yeah," said Michael. "But better than that—I think I know where he's going."

That last sentence seized everybody's attention, especially Stevenson's.

The FBI chief looked at him with a look of tired exasperation. "Where? When? Do we have time to head him off?"

"Probably . . . but if we do, I have a big favor I'm going to need."

"Name it," said Stevenson. "Just get me to where that crazy fucker is."

"If we catch him," said Michael, "I have a feeling my people are going to want a piece of him—a big piece."

Stevenson chuckled, wagged a black-gloved hand at him. "No way, Doc. He's ours. We have our own plans for him. Just tell—"

Michael smiled. "Uh-uh. I can tell you right now. They won't go for it."

Stevenson's voice notched a little higher. "They're not in charge around here."

"Sorry," said Michael, "but I think they are. You used them as *bait*, remember? And they didn't care, even though I'm pretty sure they knew what was going on. They didn't care because they sensed that this was their only chance to get this bastard—this monster they've been waiting two lifetimes to get."

"You don't know that for sure!" Stevenson's face was flushed and his eyebrows were pinched down. Tension and anger knotted him up. "You can't expect me to base my decision on some religious mumbo jum—"

Michael edged closer to him and spoke purposefully lower. "Look, Stevenson, *you* saw what happened here tonight. From what I heard, you had a better seat than most of us. So we all know that these people, these victims, are the ones who stopped that bomb."

"I can't say for—"

"Well, *I* can," said Michael. "And we can't exclude them now. Not after what they've been through."

"Listen, Keating," said Stevenson. "If you don't help me now, I'll have you arrested for obstruction of justice. I can—"

Michael grinned. "Stop the bullshit. You're running out of time. You want this guy or not?"

"Jesus Christ . . ." said Stevenson, shaking his head in frustration. "How am I going move that many people that fast?"

"If you were sending troops," said Michael, "could you get them in there?"

"Hell, yeah. You know that." Stevenson nodded his head, threw up his arms. He knew where the argument was leading him.

"Well, let me tell you something," said Michael in almost a whisper. "These people *are* your troops! You aren't going to need anybody else."

"All right, all right!" said Stevenson. "Goddamn it. Let's get moving."

Michael reasoned that the most obvious place to come up from the Park Avenue tunnel was an underground station just south of Eighty-fifth Street, located below what used to be the immense townhouse of one of New York's biggest railroad families—the Vanlandinghams.

During the thirties, the building had been transformed into an embassy for New Zealand, and after World War II it was renovated for offices by Harry Reuter and Sons, the international currency exchange broker. Other than a single night watchman and a state-of-the-art security system, the building was deserted at this hour.

Stevenson agreed. If Nichols was coming up to the surface, the Reuter Building was the perfect exit point. Even at a stiff jog, along a decaying roadbed, in hyperborean darkness, Michael calculated Nichols' transit of the almost forty blocks to take no less than twenty minutes, and Stevenson thought that was a pretty good estimate.

Operating on this premise, the FBI chief mobilized three transport choppers to get everybody up to Eighty-fifth Street with a five-minute "window." McShea suggested bringing along Arnold Rassenault as a negotiator, and even though Michael sensed Stevenson wasn't in the mood for any gunpoint rhetoric, the FBI chief assented to the move—for public relations, if nothing else. He also sent in a squad of commandos with the promise that they would only be employed as a last recourse. Michael had exacted an oath from Stevenson, in front of witnesses, that his group would be given their chance first.

What they did with that chance, or *how* they did it, was left completely up to them.

Leading them down into the subbasement turned out to be a major expedition. The stairwell was far narrower than Michael had remembered it, and progress was slow as forty people descended through a dank stone foundation to a platform made of wood ripe with mildew and rot. Stevenson had ruled against flashlights or torches of any kind, and the only thing keeping the operation from being next to impossible were night-vision goggles that everyone wore.

Flanking Michael were two commandos, assigned to recon the area with infrared body-heatseekers, just in case Nichols had in some way beaten them to the station. Michael smiled at the nod toward technology, but he felt very comfortable with the idea that his group could sense the monster's presence a lot more effectively than a piece of electronics.

Once satisfied that Nichols hadn't been there yet, Stevenson allowed Michael's entire group to funnel out across the platform. They'd been briefed by Stevenson, who was more than a little shocked when he'd received a briefing of his own—from the group's spokesman, Rodney McGuire:

"There's no need to tell us about how dangerous this man is," Rodney told him. "We've lived and died and lived again with the horror that's in him, that can come out of him. He's already given us his best shot, and we took it, we rolled with it. Now it's our turn. He's finished hurting us."

Short and to the point. But perfectly stated, and with just the right amount of conviction and truth to make Stevenson respect what was happening on the quiet side of midnight. That's why Michael stepped aside to let them fan out across the sunken rails and cross-ties. Stepping back to the far end of the platform, Michael joined Pamela and Klingerman, who'd been the last to enter the underground station.

The view from under Park Avenue was bizarre, indeed. Like a vast plain, painted by some twisted surrealist, it stretched off into endless darkness. Featureless, foreboding. A low ceiling hovered over them, a repressive presence that Michael could feel as much as see. The place was so empty and cold, it could have been a thousand miles into the earth; it was hard to imagine traffic pounding the asphalt just above their heads.

As they stood there waiting, after long minutes dragged by, Pamela whispered in his ear, asking him if he thought he might have misanticipated Nichols' plan.

"No way," he said sotto voce. "This is the only logical way out." Additionally, he trusted the instincts of the group above his own hunches. If they didn't feel they would intersect with their nemesis, they wouldn't be here.

And so he waited, like Beowulf and the villagers for the inevitable approach of the monster, Grendel.

Bringing them together, Michael knew now, had been a magical but necessary event. It was just another element in the fantastic sequence of things leading to this moment. He only wished Isabella Mussina could see the fruit of her passionate labor.

"What's taking him so long?" said Pamela, shivering. "It's cold down here."

"The tunnel is a mess," said Michael. "I've never walked the whole thing, but I hear it's pretty rough in spots."

"What about the—"

"*He's coming!*" someone whispered, and the words passed among them like notes from a trumpet.

Others echoed the feeling, and once again, just like on the fourth floor of the Koch Center, Michael had the impression of being exposed as a bad storm approached. The group surrounding him was unconsciously bonding again, allowing their natural chemistry to create a force far greater than the sum of all their energies. They were ready for him all right; Michael could feel their rightful anger resonating deep into his bones.

They could sense the approach of the beast.

"I've got a body-heat blip," said one of the commandos behind them, who was hunched over a portable console.

"Affirmative," whispered Stevenson. "Let's keep the noise down!"

"What're they going to do to him?" said Pamela.

Michael shrugged. "I have no idea, but I have a feeling that whatever happens tonight, it will end it for them."

She nodded. "The nightmares will be over."

"Without question," he said. "This is going to be *it*."

Looking out beyond the line of his people, who'd spread themselves across the wide tunnel, he lifted his goggles for a moment just to remind himself how consummately *dark* it was beneath the streets. Had Nichols been prepared for such abject blackness?

That's when he saw the approaching light. With goggles off, a bobbing splash of light danced far off in the distance. Like the glow of a cigarette, it marked the forward progress of their prey. Michael smiled at that thought and found it extremely gratifying to think of such a hunter and killer as the prey himself.

But he was. And it was a very good thing.

"Look," he said in his softest whisper as he nudged Pamela and pointed in the direction of the weaving light. "That's *him*. . . ."

Yanking his goggles back on, he was amazed at how much they enhanced the small penlight in Nichols' hand. The point of light, when seen through the green lenses, had been transformed into an outrageous beacon, broadcasting his presence and approach. Even though still far away, Michael could see the vague trace of his features in the faint backwash of illumination.

Suddenly, the bobbing light stopped.

And was extinguished.

But they could still see him, approaching the line of people in a crouching, stalking posture, as though he sensed everyone out there in front of him, but continued to believe he had the upper hand on them. It reminded Michael of the briefing they'd had with Stevenson, who had insisted on bringing the commandos in case of gunfire. Rodney McGuire had smiled at that remark, reminding the

FBI man that since the group had protected itself from a bomb, it certainly had no fear of a man with a gun.

The logic was unassailable, but Michael still felt nervous about bullets from assault weapons flying wildly through the darkness. He was thinking about how vulnerable he and Pamela might be, standing on the handcar platform, and was considering a safer vantage point when the darkness was pierced by the sound of a single peal of chilling laughter.

What a way to announce himself, thought Michael. *You're a bold son of a bitch, I'll give you that.*

"So we meet again, my friends!" said Dukor, his voice loud and deep, rattling around the vast interior.

Michael could feel and hear everyone take a breath together, as if to demonstrate their unity, but not one of them spoke.

"Oh, come on, you fucking bunch of sheep!" yelled Dukor. "I know you're out there! Even us villains have feelings, too!"

And he laughed again, either at his own humor or perhaps to intimidate them.

He wasn't funny and they weren't scared.

"Let me talk to him!" said Arnold Rassenault, his voice surprisingly strong, confident.

"Shut him up!" said Stevenson harshly.

Michael, the image of gunfire lighting up the tunnel still fresh in his mind, touched Stevenson's sleeve. "Wait a second," he said.

"What?" Stevenson's voice had a rough edge from either anger or fear.

"Let him talk. Rassenault might be able to save everybody a lot of trouble."

Stevenson sneered. "You don't really believe that, do you?"

"Not really," said Michael. "But I think it's worth a chance. What do we have to lose?"

Stevenson considered the proposition, then signaled to McShea. "Okay, let the old guy through."

Michael watched Rassenault work his way through the crowd of FBI men and step off the platform. Pausing only to adjust his IR goggles, the old man walked with no hesitation, no fear. It was as if he knew the danger of confronting a madman like Dukor and didn't care. Michael could understand this. If Rassenault really was seeking forgiveness, then how better to receive it than to martyr himself at the altar of the false god he'd worshiped?

Everyone watched the old man approach Dukor.

"Nichols, wait! Nichols, it's Arnold Rassenault, wait!"

Dukor flicked on his flashlight for an instant to pin the old man's face, then slipped back into the darkness. He chuckled madly.

"Fuck you," said Dukor.

"It's over," said Rassenault. "We were very, very wrong."

"You disgust me, you old bastard! I took away your typewriter and offered you a gun . . . and look at you!"

"Nichols, please . . . we are all ghosts. We should be at rest! *You're* the aberration here. You gave my twisted thoughts life and made me see how sick I've been."

Dukor snickered. "You haven't seen *shit*! You're just scared of me."

"Do I look like I'm scared?" said Rassenault.

"Get out of my way, old man. . . ."

"Enough. End it, now, Nichols. . . ."

Dukor's voice coiled through the darkness, soft, almost seductive. "No, that's what you'll never understand—it can *never* end! You and I, and even these pitiful sheep, we're *all* proof of that."

"Please . . ." said Rassenault.

"Why don't you tell me what you really want, old man."

"I think you already know," said Rassenault.

Michael had been watching the interchange play out under the fuzzy resolution of his IR goggles, which imparted a gauzy, other-worldly feel to an already surreal scene. He was shocked to see the old man suddenly leap forward and wrap his hands around Dukor's neck. For an instant, the madman must have been equally stunned because he stood there, reeling briefly under the feeble attack. And then, jaguar-quick, Dukor grabbed him by the hair, holding him in one hand at arm's length. A serrated blade suddenly appeared in his free hand, and Dukor raked it across Rassenault's neck with a single flick of his wrist. So fast, Michael was not sure he'd actually seen it, but the hideous death dance tapped out by the old man as Dukor continued to suspend him off the ground confirmed the result.

Then, tossing the body to the trackbed, he rushed forward, raising his automatic weapon from his hip. Suddenly the gun muzzle erupted in a series of hollow, rapid *pops* and Fourth-of-July sparklerlike flashes. In the thick air the sounds were swallowed up almost instantly, and what should have sounded threatening seemed empty and ineffectual, instead. The slugs themselves never reached them or appeared to have touched anything. It was as if they too had been absorbed into the air like Dukor's laughter.

The commandos unshouldered their own assault rifles, and the machinelike clicks of clips being checked and reseated announced their readiness to respond. Only a negative command from Stevenson kept them on their leash.

Responding to the attack, the group adjusted their goggles in a weirdly choreographed move, surged together, forming a larger entity. They moved forward, gliding over the old trackbed toward Dukor. Having exhausted his ammo, he let his weapon drop to his feet. Eerily, he smiled at their encircling advance and laughed again as they drew ever closer to him.

"What's happening?" said Pamela, straining to see anything beyond the group's move to surround him.

"They're going to tear him to pieces," said one of the commandos.

"No," said Irwin Klingerman. "I don't think so."

Michael said nothing, but he imagined the rabbi's hunch might be right. They were standing at the edge of a dark stage, where the players had been selected and cast more than a half-century past, where all the lines had been spoken once long before, and which awaited only a final curtain.

Watching the group, Michael could see that they had completely surrounded Dukor, and now the group closed in. His laughter had trailed off, echoing away across the vast, dark plain of the underground until it sounded more like a pathetic whimper. And a new sound was rising like an unstoppable wave, softly at first, but gathering power like an engine wanting to redline. Michael had heard it once before, when they stopped the bomb. It was a chorus of millions of voices, scored by suffering and anger and pain and innocence and evil.

The sound of retribution, of cosmic reparation. The signature of a force summoned into existence by divine imperative and driven by the simple prayer of *never again*.

Dukor's laughter had been transformed into a twisted chain of agony and despair. Totally enveloped by the group, Dukor screamed, a sound of abject torture radiating from beyond the circle only to be drowned in the ever-rising chorus of souls.

Suddenly, Michael and the others were pushed back by a shock wave of heat that rippled out from the center of the group. A perfect sphere of light and fire rose above them, lighting up the wide tunnel like a miniature sun. And in the center of that burning sphere, for an instant, he thought he saw something twisting and blackening and curling against the all-consuming fire.

In that single moment, it became a pure act of revenge.

Anticlimactic in its simplicity, but perfect in its symmetry.

Then, abruptly, the sphere of light collapsed in upon itself, shrinking into a tiny white speck that winked out like a single spark in cold air. At the same time, the entire group of people who'd been crushed into a circle collapsed.

"Something's wrong!" yelled Pamela, breaking free of the platform and rushing toward the group of bodies, which had fallen in an awkward heap all over themselves. Stevenson unleashed his men, and suddenly the area was bathed in emergency floods and the commandos were bending to attend to the stricken group.

With Irwin Klingerman, Michael rushed to join them, and upon reaching the first fallen member, he used his med-school skills to determine that the man was okay, the victim of a fainting spell. A quick check of some of the others confirmed this—the entire group had been rendered unconscious en masse. Now they were all beginning to revive simultaneously.

Michael found Pamela with Allison Enders, who was shaking her head and looking very confused.

"What happened?" said the woman.

"Don't you remember?" said Michael.

Allison shook her head, pushed her hair from her face. "I'm not sure. I feel like I've been dreaming, but I can't remember the dream. There was a bright light and I had this terrible headache—God, is it starting all over again?"

Michael smiled. "No, I think it's finally over, actually."

"Why did they pass out?" said Pamela. "Are they really all right?"

Michael shrugged. "Hard to say what happened. They were obviously undergoing some kind of intense experience. Emotional and physical. It just tapped them out for a moment, I think. Like the sudden and total exhaustion that overtakes a runner after a marathon."

"Where's Dukor?" said Klingerman as he huddled down beside them. "He's gone! Stevenson's crazy upset."

"I think we know," said Michael. "Didn't we all see the same thing?"

"We all saw *something*, but I don't know what it was . . ." Pamela said as she helped Allison to her feet.

All around them, the FBI team and paramedic support gathered to aid the confused and shaken group. Slowly, they began escorting everyone from the oppressive atmosphere of the tunnel.

"We are very fortunate," said Klingerman as he walked along with them. "Most people can go a whole lifetime and never see a miracle. . . . I think we've seen *two* tonight."

"I *know* I have," said Michael, who had been reflecting on the profound changes in his life since the day Allison Enders entered his office. "But where do we go from here?"

"I've been thinking about that, too," said the Rabbi. "Is this the end of something . . . or only the beginning?"

"There were a lot more monsters than Hirsh Dukor," said Michael. "And a lot worse."

"Right, but are we supposed to keep looking for them?" said Pamela.

"Maybe not," said Klingerman, gesturing toward a group of seminar people being ushered ahead of them to the stairwell. "But I think *they* are."

Michael nodded, put his arm around Pamela, and continued walking. It felt so good to feel her closeness, her support. He couldn't wait to get out of the tunnel and up into the cool, clear air. As they teetered on the edge of a new millennium, the world churned and twisted under new pressures that were also old and familiar. If everything did turn on some great, dark and cyclic wheel, he knew now that he and Pamela and the others had been summoned to witness what might be coming round once more.

If this had been a night of broken souls, Michael prayed it would be the last.

EPILOGUE

Two hundred and thirty-nine miles away from the underground tunnel, where Hirsh Dukor had been consumed in a crematorium of tortured memories, Isabella Mussina woke up.

The coma in which she lay dreaming had abruptly ceased at the moment of Dukor's end, and as she looked up, blinking at the ceiling of the naval hospital room, she somehow *knew* this. The monster was dead.

She knew and understood so much more now. The coma had been necessary. She had been given the chance to rest, to grow strong once again. She felt as if she'd been revived from the hibernation needed for a long journey, as if she'd somehow been stretched across the light-year gulfs of time as well as space.

Her mind brimmed over with a thousand dream-images, still warm and fresh in her memory, and each one a key to unlock another door, another mystery. The coma had been a gift of images, but of all of them, she embraced a single dominating scene where she stood upon a great platform, flanked by grandiose banners of red and white and black, by stanchions topped by eagles carrying the twisted cross. She stood there, as if *drunk* on the sound of a hundred thousand cheers, while *der Führer* whispered in her ear and called her Heinrich.

Heinrich . . . *Himmler.*

No.

She rejected the idea, but the memory of the scene would not leave her. Too vivid. Too real.

Isabella knew now what had happened, what had been happening all along. The *other* within her, lurking in the dark well of her soul, had been sleeping, waiting, until the time when he could return. She could sense a turning of the great wheel, and her time had come round.

No. Not her turn . . . *his.*

Isabella closed her eyes as if to make the terror go away; but of course it could not—it dwelled *within* her. Now she felt what it had been like for Harford Nichols, who'd carried the evil presence of Dukor in his own soul. Isabella had watched it take control, completely *obliterating* the self that had been Harford Nichols.

And she knew it could happen to her just as easily.

She was the reincarnation of Himmler.

Impossible.

Yet true. Hence the reason she'd been driven so passionately and heroically to locate all those wretched souls . . .

The final solution had not been final enough. Still a job to be done.

The thoughts, clearly not her own, stunned her; and Isabella prepared for the most important conflict of her life—the battle for her very existence.

Dark thoughts pressed against the door of her soul like invading barbarians. It would be so easy to slip the latch and surrender.

But she would not. She would never give in to the seductive and poisonous logic of evil.

Never again.